"Alo's adept ability to intertwine multiple threads of tension keeps the intensity impressively high throughout, weaving a thick tapestry of terror."
—Kirkus Reviews

*

"The blend of psychological and social insights are thought-provoking, compelling, and often entirely, delightfully unexpected."
—The Midwest Book Review

*

"This book is a brilliant yet unsettling exploration of trauma, nightmares, and the thin line between reality and the surreal."
—The Book Commentary

*

"This novel will scratch readers' horror itch like the writing of H.P. Lovecraft or modern-day master Stephen King. A non-stop, spine-tingling thriller."
—Chanticleer Book Reviews

*

"A gripping horror novel."
—Readers' Choice Book Awards

THE STREET BETWEEN THE PINES

J.J. ALO

Copyright © 2021/2023 by SNE Horror LLC
All rights reserved.
No portion of this book may be reproduced in any form without written permission from
the publisher or author, except as permitted by U.S. copyright law.

"Rang Tang Ding Dong" by The Cellos
Written by Alvin Williams, Copyright © 1957
Licensed use courtesy of
Couch And Madison Partners dba Bess Music Company

Cover Creature Design – David Romero
https://www.deviantart.com/cinemamind

Cover Designers: Najdan Mancic & Crystal Denise
Editor: Nicole Arch
First Draft Editor: Nic Goodall
https://www.archeditorial.com/

Photography of J.J. Alo courtesy of Erin Stark
https://www.erinofboston.com/

This is a work of fiction. Names, characters, places, and incidents either are a product of the
author's imagination or are used fictitiously, and any resemblance to actual persons living
or dead, businesses, companies, events, or locales is entirely coincidental.

*For Wesley and Sandy.
My two feline rescues. The former for the inspiration and the latter—my muse—for getting me through it.*

*And for writer/director Kevin Smith who said,
"In the face of such hopelessness as our eventual, unavoidable death,
there is little sense in not at least trying to accomplish all of your wildest
dreams in life."*

And, "To make a thing."

PROLOGUE

Frank Cavanaugh jolted awake on his olive recliner, blinking at the big-box television that blared before him. For the briefest instant, he'd thought he'd felt a mild tremor. A commercial truck reaching the end of Forest Street must have turned around in front of his house without him noticing. His hearing wasn't quite what it used to be, after all. Over the New York Giants in the background, even a ringing phone would likely go unnoticed. His wife, Estelle, would attest to that.

Since the game still appeared to be at half-time, he knew he had only dozed a few minutes. Sports, exciting as they were, did very little to warrant his attention despite the nail-biting, score-tying play against the Monsters of Midway (*Da Bears*). And he knew it was only a matter of time; his eyelids would eventually shut him out.

This Monday evening began the same as any other—with Frank, lounging, putting back can after can of light beer, eating marshmallows, watching whatever relevant sporting event happened to be airing that night. The marshmallow binging was something he'd developed as a replacement for cigarettes, which he successfully quit fifteen years earlier—triple bypass surgery made sure of that. Empty cans, junk food bags, and finished crossword puzzles cluttered the side table and floor around him—a natural occurrence when Estelle was out for the evening.

Frank stood and headed through the kitchen to get another drink, the sliding glass door catching his eye as he made his way across the chilled tile floor. Tonight was the first unconditionally clear evening in weeks, following a streak of unfavorable weather. And although the moon shone full and bright, its reflection shimmering across the undulating surface of the river that stretched behind Frank's house, the neighborhood sounded anything but peaceful. The crickets screeched especially loud, their deafening chirps rivaled only by the critters rustling through the foliage and a great horned owl hooting in the distance.

After a long, concerning hunt through leftovers and an endless supply of condiments—mostly expired—Frank unearthed a solitary can in the fridge. Slipping on thick, round prescription specs, he walked out to the back deck while turning off the light to "admire the view," or, more accurately, to satiate his curiosity as to what was happening on the island across the water. The *usually* quiet area of town was becoming increasingly inhabited in recent weeks, bustling with activity. Frank identified it as some development underway but had a hard time delineating further with his poor vision, further hindered by a desperate need for a prescription update.

A cool breeze off the current whisked through the grayish hair around the side of his shiny, bald scalp. Frank savored it as he sampled his newly cracked beer. Though the bustle of activity on the island intrigued him, the night grew late, and he thought he might have to call in a favor with a few old friends to file a complaint if it continued. The racket across the way ruined the otherwise beautiful, picturesque view of the Yantic and Thames confluence, which he had often marveled over since purchasing the property more than fifty years ago.

Sighing, he turned back toward the house but stopped short, his heart almost leaping from his chest. Something flashed across his face, and he gasped out loud, dropping the can and spilling it over the deck. It took him a few seconds to refocus—to evaluate what just happened and why his last beer drained down a crack of sun-damaged cedar. A gray cat had leaped from the roof, landing in front of him. Its large, piercing yellow eyes and dilated pupils caught Frank's gaze; it let out a long, penetrating hiss.

Confused and a bit startled, he took a step back, not breaking eye contact with the fierce creature. The cat kept its ears flat back, baring teeth, and carefully watched Frank's every move while puffing up the spiked fur along its raised spine, crouching low on high defense. After a brief standoff, Frank slowly sidestepped left, the cat mimicking the move, as two anxious gunslingers would, studying one another, anticipating who'll draw first.

The wind gently picked up, setting off Estelle's Corinthian windchimes, which hung from a metal hook on the edge of the house; the soft ping of each aluminum tube struck a multitude of long, mellow bells resonating amid the tension. A low grumble reverberated from the animal with each step he took across the chafing floorboard. As he neared the door and finally regained some confidence, he became immediately irritated by the situation, ignoring the cat as he pulled open the slider. An orange tabby trotted along from around the corner and up the steps as Frank squeezed through, closed, and locked the door.

The cat skipped over and stood up on hind legs, tapping vehemently on the glass with its golden, fur-tufted paws. A third made an appearance, followed by a fourth, then a fifth. Frank backed up slowly, bewildered, watching as the strange phenomena commenced.

What in the name of good Christ is going on? For years, he had been accustomed to an occasional feral in the area, and from time to time, he would see a few pass through his yard. A couple of times, he had even caught one or two stretched out along the deck railing taking in the riverfront view before jumping away, as he would turn on the light to do the same. This particular event, however, seemed most bizarre. The cats had never before come close enough to make actual contact—not that he had any interest. He flicked on the outside light and gazed beyond the deck, where he noticed the garbage bin tipped on its side with bags ripped open, trash scattered, dissipating into the night.

Little scavengers...

Frank closed the curtain over the door and went back to the recliner. Though annoyed, he knew the trash cleanup would have to wait 'til morning. The excitement exhausted him. And as the Giants' Amani Toomer went forty yards for a touchdown, Frank put the cats out of his mind and reached for a marshmallow. Since he still expected Estelle, currently visiting a friend's house across town, he decided to stay up to wait and watch more of the game.

Not long into the fourth quarter—mere minutes in fact—the Giants were down—again—and Frank started to have a hard time keeping his eyelids open. Moderately interested as he was, his expectations remained quite low, and not without reason; he was used to the disheartenment that being a fan of New York football would bring.

Hell, there's always next weekend, right?

Finally, he surrendered, figuring Estelle would just wake him for bed when she returned—whenever that was. Tonight was bingo night. All bets were off.

With one last slow blink, he glanced over at the dated pictures of his wife on the mantle. Their wedding photo in particular caught his eye—she in her white dress, and he in his Navy Service Dress Blue. They had married as soon as he returned from Korea, though, knowing his wife had fallen for a man in uniform, he'd then joined the police force, continuing to wear his badge for all their family portraits. He smiled, eyelids sagging as he finally dozed off.

POP!

Abruptly and extremely disoriented, Frank woke, jumping out of the chair. Everything went black. He stumbled into the coffee table, knocking over a lamp while he yelled the Lord's name in vain. A noise that sounded like a gunshot had brought him to consciousness, though now, blinking through the shadowy room, he struggled to process whether it had been real or dreamt.

Unaware of how long he'd slept this time, he called for Estelle, but her returned silence assured him he'd passed out only briefly. The moonlight beamed through the windows, guiding him around the dark house while he rustled through drawers in search of any source of light. Eventually, he decided to check the garage. The automatic door didn't function, so he opened it manually, letting the moon pour in, hitting the workbench against the back wall. He located a heavily scraped Maglite in one of the drawers—a relic from his time on the force that at one time shone light through the darkest of alleyways—and tested it, surprised yet thankful it actually turned on.

Faint meows and the pitter-patter of feet sounded in the driveway as he quickly made way across to close the garage, but he was too late; those outlaws began to invade, tails waving in the air as they made their advance. Frank panicked and paced toward the house door, barely entering before they neared. Without a second thought, he carried on. The power outage took precedence, overruling any other thought process in his mind.

A transformer had probably blown, but Frank at least wanted to check the fuse box in the basement first. He took each creaking step, slowly, one at a time, down to the bottom, holding firmly to the railing. Though he usually only went downstairs during the day, navigating in the dark wasn't out of the norm for either Estelle or himself due to the inoperability of the basement light switch—one of many home improvement projects he had *underway*, put off for another time.

Soon, rows of tall, narrow cubed shelving came into view, brimming with muddled collectibles from generations past: porcelain china—dinnerware, cups, saucers—odd trinkets of crystal art, glass vases, copper jewelry boxes, animal figurines. They lived untouched for decades on crowded shelves. Much like the attic and every spare room in the house, the basement had become storage for decades worth of junk and unused appliances, along with the washer and dryer unit. Cardboard boxes dispersed throughout, some stacked high against each wall, filled with effects from every decade they lived on Forest Street. Somewhere, long-buried away, the Cavanaugh's still kept their four children's baby clothing and first pair of shoes.

An old, plastic-covered, tufted leather sofa sat in one corner, also holding boxes. Lying next to it stood a Westport billiards table—feet removed—and a 1960s wooden console television. Frank had a workbench of southern yellow pine near the foot of the stairs, much like the one in the garage, but it hadn't surfaced from the depths of boxes in years. Grime coated the waning aggregate walls, and a well-aged Tabriz Persian animal rug partially carpeted the floor. The smell of must emanated from growing dry rot shrouded by the quarter-inch of dust that adorned most surfaces in the space. Anyone familiar with the Cavanaughs would kindly consider them amateur antique collectors, while anyone else would probably just call them hoarders.

As Frank reached the bottom of the stairs, the flashlight started to flicker, the ancient batteries battling their way out of stagnation. He stepped over a dirty laundry pile and made his way to a utility closet, where he retrieved a heavily dusted oil lantern. He specifically recalled, for reasons unknown, picking it up in Old Saybrook at a yard sale right before his deployment. After wiping some grime off the glass cover with a sleeve, he lit it with a wooden match taken from a stockpile of odd matchboxes collected over time.

Even with the soft glow of the oil lantern, pitch black cloaked the room, and Frank, already having difficulty seeing, walked face-first through hanging cobwebs, trying to locate the fuse panel. After moving a few mildew-covered boxes to create a narrow path, he came across familiar territory. He saw the panel next to the dryer and opened the rusted hatch, nicking a finger on a serrated edge as he checked the circuits. Everything looked fine. Scratching his head, he figured at this point, a transformer *must* have blown, which would account for the noise heard earlier. With all the activity happening across the water, his assumption seemed a safe bet. Frank turned, held up the lamp, and proceeded toward the exit.

A succession of shrill rings next to Frank caused him to nearly jump out of his skin; the flashlight dropped from his hand, rolling out of sight. Several hardwired telephone landlines hung throughout the house, with the basement having one installed in the 1970s—a time when the family utilized the room more for hobbies, gaming, and of course, laundry.

Frank picked up the receiver, which hung from a square pillar in the center of the room. "Frank, did I wake you?" Estelle asked with a hint of guilt.

The sound of her voice flooded Frank with relief. He pictured her standing in the kitchen, holding the end of a green wall phone in Florence's house, on the other end of town. Behind her, Florence and three other elderly ladies sat around a rectangle table littered with paper bingo sheets and various colored ink dotters used to mark the sheets. The image of her made him smile.

"Estelle? No," Frank said, as if her assumption was preposterous. "The power is out at the house—you have power by you?"

"Huh, that's strange. Everything is fine over here. Did you check the fuse box?"

"Yeah, looks fine to me. I heard a bang—I think a transformer went or something."

"Well, I'm all *bingo-ed* out—just going to say goodbye to everyone and head home. Do you need anything while I'm out? I can swing over to the gas station and get some candles or batteries. I'm assuming you've found flashlights?"

"Yup. I found ole reliable in the garage. We also have the oil lamp, and wouldn't you believe it, it actually works!" Frank snickered. "I don't think I've lit this thing in over thirty years or so. What a great find this was. I ever tell you that story, dear?"

"Only about a hundred times, hun. It was at the house with all the old stuff that got you into your antique hobby," Estelle said in a storied tone. "All right, I'm leaving shortly. See you in a bit, Frank. Be careful, will ya? You don't want to hurt yourself down there in the dark."

Frank smiled. "Heh, I make no promises, dear."

Hanging up the phone, he grabbed a nearby rag for his finger, which had begun bleeding significantly now, then held up the lantern to see where the flashlight had rolled. He started toward the back, then stopped abruptly. To his astonishment and disbelief, a tear in the foundation corner protruded outward from the floor and wall. Chunks of slate and dirt lay scattered around the edges of the gap. Frank pinched himself, wondering if he'd nodded off to sleep again. Then, squinting his eyes in an attempt to focus, he took off his glasses, inspecting the lenses. His eyes didn't deceive him. Frank cautiously stepped toward the corner to examine the damage. His vision began to adjust as he grew close, revealing much more than he had anticipated.

The *tear* became an oblong hole three to four feet in diameter. Frank picked up a chunk of rock, and on further inspection, noticed deep corrosion. Some degeneration of concrete, he figured—not uncommon, especially in older houses so close to saltwater. He dropped the rock and reached over to touch the edge of the orifice, where he felt a thick, viscous substance, tacky to the touch as he rubbed it between his thumb and index finger.

Frank leaned in to smell it when a curious *thud* prompted him to look up. The sound came from the adjacent side of the room. Now wondering if a squirrel or other small woodland creature could have made its way inside, he walked over to take a look. For an instant, he recalled three years earlier, when he found a raccoon that had snuck in an open window and had given birth to a small litter under the workbench.

The sound of something large clattering to the solid floor resonated through the damp room, and Frank stopped in his tracks. Slightly unnerved, he decided to end his exploration, snatching up the flashlight and heading straight toward the stairs with a much brisker pace. He rounded the corner and caught a glimpse—a double-take—of bright, glowing eyes in the reflection of a six-foot-high and profoundly tarnished, mid-century Gilt mirror situated diagonally from him. The sight provoked an immediate response laterally, causing him to trip over a milk crate filled with various gardening tools and knocking over several leaning billiard cue sticks.

Frank came crashing to his knees, dropping the flashlight to better secure the lantern in his other hand. The glasses flew off his face and slid out of reach. His vision now blurred; all he could see in the darkness were two round, bright auras from each light source. Frantically, he began to crawl and feel his surroundings. Adrenalin started pumping through his veins, elevating his heart rate rapidly. The first item he discovered, to his instant relief, was his glasses; quickly shoving them to his face, he proceeded.

Next, he spotted the flashlight, but it appeared oddly distorted. The lenses had cracked, and everything he saw began to have a stained-glass effect. He picked himself up as fast as his aging body would allow, panting, out of breath, and scanned for the exit, disregarding either light source in his frantic attempt to escape his unknown aggressor. At that moment, nothing mattered more than leaving the basement.

A low, gurgling growl shattered the stale air. His hair stood on end, and he froze.

ONE

Curtis took one last pull from a half-finished cigarette before dropping it into the turbulent pool of a flushing commercial toilet. Quite impressive, he thought, considering he lit it at the start of strained piss. He supposed walking across the department store and taking a proper break outside would've been much more satisfying. Ten minutes of tranquility in the crisp autumn air was nothing short of refreshing.

As if he had that kind of time. He huffed at the idea with a sardonic smirk, finishing a swift and sloppy hand washing before returning to the stock room of the Mondo-Mart Superstore shit show telecom renovation job. Miguel, his coworker, smiling obliviously—shaking his hips to techno music blaring from a small radio nearby—continued to lift screws from metal shelving with an electric screwdriver. Behind it, another wall they'd have to get inside. Curtis sighed before jumping back into a removed wall where Miguel *had been* feeding him cable.

Miguel snickered. "Man, I don't know how the fuck you do it, yo."

Curtis grunted as he pulled a handful of cable, led in from an exposed ceiling, down through a dense maze of metal framing, sheetrock, and masonry blocks. "Yeah, what's that?"

"*You*, man." Miguel finished lifting the screws, tossing the expensive equipment haphazardly into a tool bag. He walked into the doorway of the nearby employee lounge where twelve boxes of spooled cable sat, leads tied, feeding to Curtis.

"You don't know how I do me?" Curtis continued to pull, sweat already dripping from his head, and looked back to the large, round analog clock above the stock room door. Although they arrived early this particular evening, now only quarter after eleven, still relatively early in the shift, they remained days behind schedule—nowhere close to finishing the room as anticipated. He sighed deeply, wondering if the red needle of the seconds hand was working double speed.

"Yeah, *this* fucking job. Away from your family for weeks at a time, bro. I miss my girlie and my three beautiful little princesses back home; this shit is just too far away. I did a job in Vermont, like four months ago, somethin' like that, and I never thought I was gonna see them again, man." Miguel went on from the other side of the wall.

Curtis continued to pull wire.

"I really don't live that far away. A couple hours' drive."

"Oh yeah, you' in Connecticut, over by them big ass Indian casinos, right?" Miguel finished by imitating the infamous jingle from the casino commercial. *"Meet—me—at—Foxwoods!"*

"Yeah, near there—Norwich. And home is not exactly a good time right now anyway. Me and the wife are kinda—" Reluctant to finish, he dribbled out, "Separated."

"I've been there once."

He blinked, not knowing he'd been married. "Wife?"

"Casino. Me and my three cousins took, you know, one of those 'weekend getaways,' right? It was New Year's Eve when we got there, and you know, we were *all* kinds of fucked up. We split a twelve-pack of Heiny on the way down, smoked a couple joints, and did a few bumps—cuz my cousins can't go *nowhere* without a brick of *llello*—and that's even before we entered the place..."

Ugh, Christ, here we go.

"My cousins are crazy gamblers, too, yo. They will bet on *anything*—like, who can finish shotgunning a beer first—who's got the bigger dick... they're into some weird shit, too—they *looove* them some Ferret Bingo..."

"Ferret—Bingo?"

"Yeah, man. You stick a ferret in, like, a giant box with this built-in maze, right, and a bunch'a numbered exits, and you *bet* on which tunnel it'll take to get out. It's crazy—I once won a hundred and fifty bucks on that shit. Roulette is my thing, yo—you know, I like a game of chance—reminds me of life. Which also reminds me, I fuckin' lost every bet I made. The goddamn ball kept landing on GREEN—I didn't even know that was a real option! So much for fifty/fifty, am I right?"

Curtis rolled his eyes. All he wanted to do was tell Miguel to shut the fuck up, as they really needed to hustle; however, the man provided the only human interaction he would have in a given day. The solitude of his hotel room had begun to wear on him. *Two weeks, two weeks, two weeks, two weeks, uggh...*

"So anyway, this fucking place is packed, right, like INSANE busy. Every club was sold out, which was fine anyway, cuz tickets were like, fifty bucks just to get in, and we lost everything on the floor. So, we walked around sulkin' like couple *putas*, 'til we came across this wide-open club, called *Mist*, right in the middle of the gaming room floor! It was crazy; there was the gaming tables, you know—Blackjack and Roulette—and then a huge oval bar, and then a fucking *lit-up* dance floor. Free admission and everything!" Miguel said with the enthusiasm of an eighteen-year-old after his first legal night out. "Yo, you know why they call that place Mist?"

Curtis shrugged, indifferent. "I don't."

"Cuz randomly, *mist* will *shoot* down from the ceiling *onto* the dance floor all around you! It's crazy, right? You can get nasty on the dance floor, and they can't see you through the dense fog! So many honeys, bro—so many."

After unspooling the remainder of fiber optic cable, he began to run the length of it over his stocky shoulders. Though only 5'8," and noticeably out of shape with his potbelly poking through his way-too-tight blue flannel button-down, he lifted surprisingly well for his size.

An entire minute of awkward silence ensued.

"Damn, man, I feel bad for you. Hope you' at least gettin' it up here!" Miguel smiled, fishing in the cable.

"I'm not getting *it* anywhere," Curtis said, uneasy.

"Shit, man, you're gone for weeks at a time. I'm surprised you're not cleaning up. I would, yo."

"When? In the middle of the afternoon? Try to pick up girls at the coffee shop? Or the mall? Besides, I'm not interested." Curtis suddenly realized where this was going. "Didn't I see you talking to some high school girls in the music department right before work? Is that why you get here early?"

"It's not like that, yo! They just wanted to know what I thought of that new Britney Spears joint, but I try to tell them I'm more of a Jessica Simpson kinda guy, right? You know, they both got that southern belle thing going, but yo, Britney's got the whole, '*girl from the trailer park*' thing, right, and I'm not into that! And Simpson's more the wholesome, '*bring her home to mom*' type—plus she got those massive *globos*, you know what I'm sayin'?"

"No."

"Besides, my girl would fucking kill me—she catch me talking to some chicken-head broads," Miguel said, as if he had been in this situation before. "You ever date Spanish chicks, man?"

Curtis shook his head.

"Spanish girl catch you cheating, yo, they will castrate you. They won't even ask questions—no breakup—no divorce, man. They just cut yo' *pinga right* off! They don't fuck around, yo." Miguel chuckled to himself with a smile that radiated across his bloated, scruffy face.

Another minute of silence.

"What the fuck does '*kinda separated*' mean anyway?"

"I don't know, man. Separate bedrooms, I guess. We don't talk, and when we do, it's always about the same shit—fucking money. There just never seems to be enough of it." Curtis shook his head, growing more irritable. "Miguel, you feeding the cable or just watching me pull this shit?"

"Yo, relax, man, daaamn—it's coming, it's coming..."

It was coming, all right. A cloud of smoke hit Curtis in the face, and he coughed. The smell, undeniably familiar, immediately clarified that Curtis shouldered the brunt of their shared work.

Curtis blinked. "Is that... are you smoking a fucking joint?"

"Na, yo. But I *am* smoking this fatty boom batty *blunt* I rolled in the shitter after dinner. My god, yo, that fake-ass food court pizza give you diarrhea, too?" Miguel wafted the smoke from his view of Curtis through the doorway.

"No."

"Damn, you gotta lead-lined stomach. I can't do that shit no more. Any large pizza that cost you six bucks *can't* be good. Yo, you gotta hit this shit, man. I scored it off this fuckin' Goth kid who works over in electronics! Them weird, Goth, country, emo dudes get the best shit, you know what I'm sayin'?" Miguel held the blunt, admiring his fine craftsmanship.

"NO. Last time I smoked your shit, I had an anxiety attack and thought my heart was going to explode. I couldn't sleep worth o' shit," Curtis recalled, slightly amused. "Ended up walking around the hotel all day, paranoid."

"Yeah, my cousin gave me that shit and neglected to tell me he laced it with formaldehyde."

Curtis stopped pulling. "Embalming fluid?"

"Yeah, yo." Miguel shrugged, nonchalant.

"What? Wait, what the fuck—seriously!?"

"Don't worry, yo, it ain't gonna hurt you! You'll be well preserved, man." Miguel smiled.

"You should quit smoking that shit."

Trying not to blow his lid, Curtis took a deep breath and walked out of the stock room toward the four recently installed self-check-out machines around the corner to work on the pending software upgrade. Miguel, oblivious to this attempt to end the conversation, followed. A laptop sat where they'd set it up, connected to new technology—a touch screen terminal machine, and Curtis jumped right in to finish configuring the point-of-sale system.

"Wow, yo, this shit blows my fucking mind! Who taught you to do this?" Miguel watched, impressed as Curtis played inside the system with ease. "You look like you could do this shit in your sleep, bro."

"I could if I slept... I was training in this kind of stuff right before I left my last company."

"Hey, how long you been on this job for?"

"As long as you—six weeks."

"Na, man, how long you been working on these store data upgrade jobs?"

"Uhh, I don't know, like eighteen months or so." Curtis pulled a pack of Marlboro 27s from his utility tool belt. He needed nicotine to settle the nerves, the employee bathroom now out of reach. "Why?"

"Cause this job sucks, man. A nine-to-five job don't interest you? You know, like, normal people? I know you're licensed and shit, and you got the experience."

"This shit's the same no matter which shift it is." He shrugged, cigarette hanging from his lips. "It pays cash, and there's no one around to answer to. I *used* to enjoy the atmosphere and silence."

"Awww, you son of a bitch, yo!" Miguel laughed.

Curtis strained an awkward smile and lit his smoke.

Two

As Estelle pulled into the driveway in her gray station wagon, she was unsurprised to find that Frank had left the garage door open again. His excuse was that he would leave it open for her, which always made her happy, even though she knew the reason was usually more forgetfulness than thoughtfulness on his part. After a half-century of marriage, she was used to Frank leaving doors open, lights on, and faucets dripping, though, since his surgery, the absentmindedness—or possible blatant disregard from exhaustion—only accelerated.

"Frank, Frank, Frank, what am I going to do with you..." she muttered as she pulled up the driveway, stopping short as an orange cat emerged from within. She sat a moment, bewildered, then witnessed several trotting out of the opening, dispersing into the dark.

The garage light flickered as Estelle stepped out of the car and entered the house.

"Frank...?" she called over the unrelenting voice of a distant sports announcer. "I see you got the power back on. Sorry I'm so late—Florence wouldn't let me out the door! You missed a helluva game tonight, too. I won twenty dollars!" Estelle went on as she took off her coat, placed it on the wall-hanging hook, and headed for the living room. "Oh, Jimmy was asking for ya. Florence had some great news, too. Her grandson is opening up an Irish joint down off Route Two, over in—Chesterville, maybe? Something about *crafted beer*? Just signed a lease and everything! Heavenly, Jesus, is it loud in here. You left the TV blaring, Frank, and—what'd you do to the living room!?" Estelle picked littered items off the floor, one thing after another as she walked through spilled snacks and empty cans.

"Frank?" Estelle called as she entered the upstairs bedroom, finding it empty before proceeding through the kitchen and out the back door to the deck. Everything remained silent, with only the moonlight shining down, illuminating the still water below. She called out several more times, seeing the scattered trash outside too. Now growing a little more worried by his lack of response, she walked back inside and started toward the basement.

Estelle opened the door, habitually reached for the switch, flicking it up and down. She called impulsively for Frank before noticing a glimmer of light in the distance. Delayed confusion hit her first, followed by immediate concern as she began down the dark stairwell as quickly and safely as possible, treading lightly on each creaky, wooden step. The illumination from the flashlight shined off several stacked boxes at one end of the room, leading her in that direction. She caught the shimmer of a barely lit lamp through her side peripheral, although she couldn't identify where it was. She couldn't place anything in the darkness. Arms up, reaching out, she continued moving forward at a comfortable pace. Her left leg brushed the side of a large, cold object she quickly identified as either the washer or dryer unit. Now, she had an idea of where she was... but beyond that, the room remained a mystery. Other than cleaning clothes, she'd had little reason to ever go down there until now.

About five feet from the washer, Estelle noticed the sound of liquid sloshing under her shoes as she stepped. *Lord, I hope this machine isn't broken again!* The last thing she wanted to do was deal with a leaking appliance in the middle of the night. Annoyed at the thought that there may be a much bigger mess to clean up that she couldn't even see, she picked up the pace toward the lantern.

The light loomed within arm's reach, and as she went for it, her brown loafer snagged something, causing her to lose balance. Almost before the panic of falling into the unknown set in, she crashed down. Her left arm broke the fall, but she still hit the ground hard. The upper portion of her body splashed in the dark puddle, and her wrist popped as she cried out from the sharp pain. Thoroughly drenched, she began to quiver, slowly picking herself up. The persistent sting of her left wrist warned her she'd most likely suffered a sprain. Keeping the arm tucked under her breast, she ambled along, faintly whimpering like a wounded animal. With a shaking hand, she finally reached the lamp, picking it up with her right arm and holding it high while slowly rotating in a circle. Nothing looked out of the ordinary, with only so many visible feet ahead, but she was reluctant to continue on with pain setting in.

Finally, she hovered over the area around her feet. Now dreadfully low on fuel, the lamp lacked sufficient light, so she crouched down for a better view. At first glance, she saw a pair of shoes. Immediately, anger rose in her stomach. She had hurt herself tripping over her husband's mess. Frank would hear about this. She continued to pan, and attached to one of the shoes were pants, followed by a shirt. She needed a second or two before the pieces came together.

Estelle dropped to her knees and tugged at Frank, who was face down, trying to elicit a response.

"FRANK!! OH MY GOD, FRANK! Are you all right—what happened!? Talk to me! Frank!" Tears welled up and fell from her eyes as she struggled to turn him over, shaking him violently. He may have fallen, hit his head and drowned, or had a heart attack—but maybe she could still save him. God, please say she could still save him. Trying to move Frank's body weight with one hand proved difficult, but using her foot as a wedge, she barely managed to pull him over.

"Oh, Frank. Please, say something!" she cried, feeling him over until her hand sunk into a cold, spongy pit. Still unable to clearly discern, she pulled back her hand, taking a length of intestine with her as it unraveled.

She slowly stood, instinctually recoiling, and within seconds of the visual, a flood of recognition hit her all at once. She hadn't fallen into a puddle from a leaky washer, and Frank wasn't laying in water—it was *blood*, and it was everywhere. She motioned the lamp across her body and saw much of her canary-colored floral dress and matching sweater stained top to bottom in the rusty liquid.

She waved the lamp over Frank, revealing his mutilated torso and mangled face. The sight before her sent her into debilitating shock. Frank's lifeless eyes stared open, widely gazing up at Estelle. Most of his neck had vanished, and his head cocked to the side, mouth open, hanging by a flap of lacerated skin. She could see spine and torn cartilage, visible through his missing skin, and ragged flesh layers hung from the stripped chest and throat.

Horrified beyond comprehension, Estelle let out a thunderous, lengthy shriek that could have shattered the Gilt mirror. The lamp swung around and smashed as she slipped backward on the mess below while the pieces fell into a box, instantly igniting its contents.

Fire spread quickly, inundating every cardboard box and piece of furniture until, amid the blaze, the terrified woman could see everything in the cavernous room.

Estelle sat where she'd fallen to the floor, watching as the basement lit up around her. The flames flickered across the Persian rug, up the wall to the drying bed linen hanging overhead. Then they engulfed the curtains and window shade, sending tattered pieces of ignited material into the air. Once the heat started to reach her, Estelle snapped out of her trauma-induced trance and pulled herself to her feet, heading automatically toward the densely hazed exit before the smoke finished its consummation. She started up the stairs and moved through the house, out the front door.

A pathway of fresh air entered, and the fanned flames cut a fierce path to the propane grill tanks, an old kerosene heater, and a fuel container, which combusted in a violent uproar. The blast blew out the windows; a flare of fire violently advanced to the house exterior. The wake of the explosion sent Estelle tumbling to the ground, down the front lawn. Covered in soot, blood, and glass, she lay unconscious as flames ravaged her home, blotting out the vivid, stellar sky with the radiating smolder.

THREE

—·—

Curtis woke abruptly from the chiding sound of his Skytel pager. He quickly glanced in bewilderment at his surroundings and noticed he was sitting in the cab of his truck. The time on the dash blinked up at him: six a.m. After a few moments, the disorientation subsided. He must've fallen asleep during what was supposed to be a quick cigarette break, having finally made it outside the store. Pulling out his pager, he skimmed the message. **NEED YOU TO CALL ME. AMY.**

Huffing, he reluctantly returned the call on the beat-up, four-year-old Nokia cell—which he kept in the glove box for emergencies—before starting up his old Dodge Ram pickup and hauling out of the parking lot of the Mondo-Mart Superstore, inordinately irritated.

Home was the last place he wanted to be, especially with how behind he was with work. And the news he just received didn't help the situation. Now fighting exhaustion, he beat his hands on the wheel and cursed as he threw the stick shift into third, stomped on the gas, and headed toward I-93. Before the highway on-ramp, he pulled off at a service station for gas and a large coffee.

The radio, set to AM and turned on low, dribbled news from its speakers...

"... much has changed in the last twenty hours here on the coast, and this impending storm just keeps increasing in severity for all of Essex, Middlesex, Suffolk, and Plymouth County. Very quickly, meteorologists went from Topical Depression to Tropical Storm, and they're predicting—"

Curtis, headache returning, shut it off.

Silence.

⸻ ⬦ ⸻

Beginning to sweat, Curtis snapped off the heat and shimmied out of his jacket, using a knee to hold the steering wheel. The windows had fogged from the artificial warmth, so he cracked his and the slider in the back glass behind him. The cold outside air, about forty degrees, cleared the fog and cooled him down a bit—all while providing the perfect excuse to smoke.

The return commute was a breeze at that hour, just missing the excruciating and unruly build-up over I-93 through Boston; however, much of it traveled northbound as people headed into the city. Southbound was smooth sailing. He continued his journey home, passing Providence before heading west, a cigarette in one hand, a coffee in the other. Every few minutes, he'd put the coffee down and run his fingers through his wavy, dirty blonde hair—a compulsive attempt to try to stay alert.

With only adrenalin and caffeine to keep his eyes open, Curtis soon found his mind drifting—as it usually would—now reflecting on the Mondo-Mart project. To his astonishment, he and

Miguel had just about finished the stock room, trusting—*hoping*—he would complete the few small tidying details; though that was tantamount to giving a child homework and expecting them to complete it in a toy store. He immediately regretted leaving work.

For the better part of the last two years, he'd spend weeks, even months at a time, working third shift at various franchised department stores, converting their systems over to digital format. Hired as a journeyman by C/Z Corp, a private telecommunications company, his latest contract had situated him in Mondo-Mart, a large box store located on the north side of the Rockingham Park Mall in the Merrimack Valley, just over the New Hampshire border. Since the majority of contracts he picked up required him to travel out of state for extended lengths of time, C/Z Corp would sponsor his temporary residency in cheap hotels.

The job *had* required three tradespeople, and Curtis had been happy to hear that one of his prospective co-workers had "loads of experience." But before the project commenced, one of them had been arrested. With no time to hire a replacement, Curtis and Miguel were tasked to complete the project in eight weeks, which didn't leave much downtime. This fact immediately stressed Curtis, who'd just left a one-week break from a job where he had spent two months away in Maine. He had learned early on C/Z Corp preferred to hire unlicensed techs at lower wages, which generally left the talent pool less than desirable.

To make matters even more unpleasant, he lost the lottery of co-workers with the exceptionally *laid-back* Miguel. Though not necessarily his fault, the man's recently acquired skills just weren't on par with Curtis's. And although he did exhibit some knowledge of having labored in the field, his cavalier attitude contrasted Curtis's *balls-to-the-wall* work ethic. Sure, he was a barrel of laughs and a fun person to shoot the shit with, but he didn't instill much confidence in Curtis about finishing on time.

Most nights were the same: Curtis and Miguel would show up at the mall, either grabbing dinner at the food court before it closed or sitting bar-side at either one of the two franchised restaurants inside the complex. Curtis would choose a large coffee to go with his usual plain, alarmingly undercooked, pub burger, and Miguel would usually consume two or three beers along with a plate of buffalo wings, cheese fries, and anything else on the menu that screamed, *clog-my-fucking-arteries, yo*! And on top of that, Miguel always found time to get high—which Curtis wouldn't mind except for how Miguel slowed down for the remainder of the shift, adding to Curtis's building stress.

The days grew long for Curtis as he would lay in bed, tossing and turning. He wasn't getting great sleep to begin with at the start of the project, and now with each night that crept closer to the deadline, his sleep subsequently became less frequent and restful. He grew so desperate for a good day's rest, he actually replaced the curtains in the hotel room with blackout curtains purchased from Mondo-Mart. At most, he would drift off for two to three hours, but even then, it was consistently interrupted by the daily activities outside the hotel and within the rooms on either side of his. If he could manage it, he'd try to squeeze in fifteen or so minutes during the few breaks he allotted himself at work.

⸺⁂⸺

As Curtis hit the *Connecticut Welcomes You!* sign on the Route Six turnpike—a barren stretch of lackluster road with sprawling, hilly, heavy forests on either side for miles—he finished his coffee, dropped the cup on the passenger seat floor, and snapped on the radio. Sam and Dave's "Land of 1000 Dances" was on. Unsure of which station he'd hit, and too tired to flip through pre-sets, he just cranked the volume, then rolled down the windows further so the cold, damp breeze would blow in, the sound of deep whooshing and upbeat music keeping him alert. Soon, he drove down I-395, another empty highway in the central-eastern part of the state. Every few miles—or at least it felt that way—he'd come across a Mobile gas station and rest area, which tempted him to stop for another coffee. He shook his head each time, pressing on. He'd reach home soon.

Exiting the interstate, Curtis shot down West Main with increasing speed until he connected to Asylum Street, which, at that hour, overflowed with daily commuters. Exhausted and irritated, he just wanted to get to the house and find a bed to shut his eyes. From Asylum, the town's main artery, he skidded onto Newton Street before reaching the desolate stretch of Forest Street—a half-mile-long, dead-end road tucked away behind downtown Norwich, along the edge of the Yantic River.

His eyelids grew heavy, beginning to shut, then quickly opened as he fought his exhaustion. But each time, they closed longer and longer. He finally surrendered, reposed with his head slumped over the wheel until a deep pothole jolted him. By sheer defiance, he jerked his eyes open only to see a flash of brightness dart out from the front of his truck. He slammed on the brakes, skidding off the side of the road into the brush. A small, metal toolbox shot from the truck bed through the back glass and into the cab, flying right past

Curtis's face to bounce off the dashboard and crack the windshield. Hyperventilating, he tipped his head back against the headrest, eyes shut as he tried to catch his fleeting breath. A moment or two passed before he blinked and looked around. Shards of glass covered the cabin, himself, and the open toolbox on the floor below, from which drill bits, a spanner wrench, and various-sized sockets spilled. With a quick glance around the truck to assess the damage, his gaze returned again and again to a fresh, softball-sized spider crack in the center windshield—hard to miss. But then, movement in his peripherals, reflecting in the rearview mirror, drew his attention behind. Several cats loitered across the street around the fenced-off entrance of Laurel Hill Drive, two of which lay in the road center, staring at him, tails gently waving.

FOUR

Still breathing heavily, Curtis stepped out to see what had darted in front of him, or rather what scurried to avoid being hit. An orange tabby looked back at Curtis, paw raised, before turning to limp across the street.

"Fuck," Curtis said under his breath, then repeated it at the shattered window.

He squeezed his eyes with a thumb and index finger, took a deep breath, then glanced around. Following the trail of burned rubber from behind the truck through a haze of dissipating vapor, he saw the tabby about twenty yards from the other cats. As it hobbled toward them, it stopped once again and looked back. His heart sank, now wondering if he might have clipped the creature. He froze; a shadow loomed over his mind, almost bordering on despair, momentarily paralyzing him. He shook it off, but the sensation made him uneasy.

Calmly, he crossed the street, noticing a small trail of blood and partial paw prints. The tabby, up ahead, continued to hop along, stopping every few feet to look over its shoulder. His pace tapered so as not to startle the injured animal. Ten feet out, he dropped to all fours and crawled toward the cat, which continued to take small steps in the opposite direction. He held its gaze while it stared in scrutiny through the hairline of brilliant golden eyes; it grumbled, ears back, followed by a low, lengthy *hiss*. As he gently raised his hand, the cat cowered down, then rolled to its back, paws up in defense. From his peripherals, Curtis noticed the other cats standing from their lounged position. He wondered if they would attack or run, albeit never breaking eye contact with the tense tabby.

A foot away, he could now see the cat's affliction—a thin shard of sooty glass sticking a half-inch from the side of the cat's paw pad, difficult to spot, no less, through tufts of amber fur. Gradually, Curtis reached back with the opposite hand and, from his utility belt, pulled a pair of needle nose pliers, formerly wedged between crimpers and measuring tape.

"I'm not gonna hurt'cha, fella. I'm—not—gonna—hurt—cha..."

Another *hiss*, this one slightly more penetrating.

"Hold—still—there—little—buddy..."

The cat glared, petrified.

With considerable patience, Curtis reached with open plyers as the grumble turned to growl. They locked eyes. The second the needle-nose grazed the shard, he yanked, freeing the feline from agony. In response, it rolled out of reach and darted into the woods. He looked up to find the others had mysteriously gone as well. Before tossing the glass, he spotted traces of dried blood along the sharp edge, indicating it had been there for some time before he arrived. He loosed a strained sigh of relief.

After briefly reassessing the damage to the truck, shaking his head, he lit a cigarette and continued toward home.

The street comprised only four Cape-style houses, with a narrow strip of wooded area interspersed with lofty pines on either side of the road. Each home had a considerable amount of land surrounding it, far enough apart to maintain a decent level of privacy. If nothing else, the backyard waterfront view made the isolation largely favorable. The property at the start of the street belonged to Curtis, while the last belonged to old man Cavanaugh.

Flashing lights ahead caused Curtis to slow down.

"Christ, what now..." he mumbled under his breath.

He recognized the town constable standing center in the street. With a small-town police barracks, only seven in size, they likely knew you—and you certainly knew who they were. Troop-K, the state police, weren't far away either; their headquarters bordered the Norwich/Chesterville town line. They mostly just hid out on the interstate, ready to hand out citations for speeding down Route Eleven and I-395. Curtis, unfortunately, knew all of them.

As he approached the perpendicularly parked, black and white police cruiser, a rapid succession of visions assaulted his already throbbing head: blinding red emergency lights, cold steel handcuffs too tightly applied, being stuffed hurriedly into the back of the squad car. In the distance, an interminable cloud of grey smoke permeated over the treetops.

The constable waved him over, stepping out in front of his approaching pickup. Curtis stopped less than a foot from Constable Rick's highly polished black shoes, drably dark gray Connecticut standard uniform, and matching Stetson hat. In complete contrast (one Curtis thought to be ridiculous), a royal blue tie hung from his over-starched shirt with blue piping and gold patchwork decorating the chest and sleeves.

The tall, stocky man had to lean down to reach Curtis's driver's side window, his nametag—reading "Sergeant Rick"—catching the light. Curtis stared at the new addition to his outfit.

"Mr. Reynolds," Sergeant Rick monotoned as he tipped his hat.

"Sergeant," Curtis returned.

"We have the road closed ahead. There's been a fire on the Cavanaugh property. It's a real big mess over there. Been here since early this morning. A real, real big mess." Sergeant Rick shook his head.

"My wife called. Any word on the Cavanaugh's?" Curtis glanced at the man, then back out through his cracked windshield.

"The Mrs. was taken over to Lawrence Memorial late last night. She was unconscious. Unfortunately, Frank didn't survive. Can't exactly say what happened—the wreckage is pretty bad, but it doesn't look good—say, uh, you get in an accident? Your back window is all smashed to hell." Sergeant Rick looked Curtis up and down, his gaze lingering on the bags under Curtis's eyes.

Curtis adjusted his air freshener, the smell of stale cigarette smoke suddenly stinging his nostrils, and glanced behind him at the damage before looking back at the sergeant. "Probably vandals. I think a buncha kids were fucking around the mall parking lot all night while I was at work. Am I going to be able to get to my house, officer?"

Sergeant Rick hesitated, giving the truck a quick visual once-over before conceding. "Yeah, you should be fine up to your house. Just be careful—there's a bunch more emergency vehicles up ahead." He stepped back, watching as Curtis pulled away toward his chipped, white, two-story abode.

Curtis backed into the drive, threw the shifter in park, and sighed deeply. The house hadn't seen a coat of paint since long before he took ownership. With the coastal air levying a constant assault against the last dilapidated coating, the walls needed attention desperately—something Amy loved to remind him about. His temples pulsing, he reached for a bottle of ibuprofen in the glove box, dumping several pills into his mouth haphazardly and swallowing them without a chaser.

One of his biggest regrets was the house purchase. At the time, it seemed like the best option in a sparse market. Compared to some of the other locations they considered, the neighborhood provided a safer place to raise a family; at the time, it had also been a work commute of equal distance. Another regret, almost in comparable magnitude, was the furniture—all provided by his in-laws. If it wasn't an inexpensive, low-quality gift, it was a dated hand-me-down, and if it wasn't that, it was some high-end piece from their sold estate, now stored in perpetuity in their basement, collecting dust. Though, he supposed, things could always be worse.

Glancing over at Frank's house—what remained of it—in the distance, he tried to identify the disarray, struggling to discern much beyond the flashing lights and smoke. Then he continued to the house through the open garage, stopping for a moment to pan the sun-bleached, blue shutters on each window—another item on a long list of things to do.

Amy waited in the kitchen.

"You look tired," she said.

Her eyes traveled up and down his thin frame, burning him. Curtis shrugged, apathetic. He found himself mostly detached when in any conversation with Amy. "I'm exhausted. I should be asleep by now."

"I haven't slept either, I just got back a little while ago. Did you see Sergeant Rick on your way in?"

"Sergeant Rick? Yes, I saw him on the way in—he stopped me at the top of the street and then analyzed my truck like I'm some sort of degenerate. My blood pressure went up, and I started to have a goddamn flashback. Since when is he *Sergeant Rick?"*

"I'm sorry, Curt."

"You know… I haven't seen him since the—the damn accident. I mean, it's been a long time since, but seeing him standing there, it felt like fucking yesterday." As he stood there further thinking about it, he regretted calling Amy or even leaving Mondo-Mart. Maybe if he had waited to call until the evening, after he'd slept, she would have been less hysterical and not have expected him to return.

Amy quickly changed the subject. "Well, I'm glad you're here—it's been some night. Mrs. Cavanaugh fell into a coma as soon as they brought her into the hospital."

"I thought you said she was yelling incoherently." Curtis ran his fingers through his hair, trying to recall the earlier phone conversation.

"This is when I got to the house and found her. The whole night was just strange, Curt. There was this bang, and the power went out. Then later, I heard this loud blast, looked out the window, and saw a flash of light over their house. Giant flames poured out of the house all over, with smoke and shit everywhere. I don't even know how I found her. And she was just covered in debris, Curt, and… *blood."* Amy paused, blinking rapidly.

"Jesus Christ. I can only imagine what that was like. She was in the explosion?"

"No, but something happened there, I don't know what, but she was saying… she was saying someone—murdered Frank. And she kept repeating it until she was out. It was just the craziest thing, Curt. I have never seen such a thing in my life. I couldn't believe it."

Curtis shook his head, aghast. "Wow. So you think she flipped her shit, stabbed her husband to death, and blew the house up?"

"Well, I mean, that's a bit absurd; I doubt it. Do you know how old they are!? I'd be surprised if one of them wasn't using a cane at this point. I can't remember the last time I saw either of them, let alone Frank. I'm pretty sure he doesn't even leave the house anymore.

"But anyway, what was even weirder was that there were these random stray cats watching from the edge of the woods there across the street while I was waiting for the police, just, like, milling around. I've never seen so many—ever." Amy stood, arms folded, staring out of the window behind the kitchen sink.

"I almost hit one on the way in, in the middle of the street. They were just lying there. Like they were—on guard."

After a slightly awkward silence, Curtis, wanting to flee the room, sheepishly asked, "You okay?"

"Yeah, it was just a lot, is all. Thanks."

"I'm off the next couple days. Spoke to the territory supervisor. With this storm coming, they want everyone to be cautious. I really don't know why; it's just a bullshit tropical storm that's just going to pass through in a few hours anyway, but whatever. I need to go to bed."

"I'll be around today. I called out of work, obviously."

"That sucks you had to miss a day this early in the school year." Curtis offered as he walked out of the room, feeling slightly more composed now that he no longer spoke face-to-face. Since Amy had started in this district not two months ago, he knew she hated missing any day on the job.

She shrugged. "Wes will be excited you're here when he gets home from school. Oh, which reminds me, the basement door is jamming shut. Wes keeps getting stuck down there when he plays. If you could find time to fix it, that would be nice."

Curtis, already halfway up the stairs, didn't respond.

Beelining into the spare room at the far edge of the long hallway, he hurried past a small, three-drawer dresser—a hand-me-down from Amy's parents when they first married—and a round bedside table, barely large enough to hold the dusty lamp and pink radio clock which lay upon it. The room's décor remained an eclectic afterthought at best. But the only thing he cared about was the neatly made, quilted comforter, stretched over the full-size bed. He flopped onto the mattress, sighing with relief as his head hit the firm, cold pillow. The stifling silence, as if all the air had been sucked out of the room, almost deafened him, save for the high-frequency squeal of his recrudescent tinnitus. He lay concentrating on it—an act of subconscious meditation, which would sometimes help alleviate the barrage of thoughts and voices—his voice, an incessant narration cycling through the myriad things he'll need to consider now that he's home.

Five

Ronald Haverhill didn't respond to Cindi's screams and insults as he shoved open the screen door and stumbled out of the small, ranch-style house with a six-pack of Pabst Blue Ribbon. He flicked the end of a cigarette into the yard, then climbed into his red '92 Jeep Cherokee. The boat trailer waited for him, still hooked up from the night before, the dinghy loosely tied down.

"Ronny, you son of a bitch!" Cindi yelled through the flapping screen door. "Where in the Christ do you think you're going? I'm talking to you!"

He glanced back to see his estranged wife storming out behind him, wearing a slightly open, tattered pink bathrobe and matching slippers. Strands of her mousy brown hair slipped from her hot rollers, and the already dried seaweed exfoliating dressing that covered her face cracked with every expressive movement. The short, plump woman managed to stomp and scream full, explicit insults, all while keeping a cigarette hanging precariously from her thin lips. She was an expert, after all. As she charged the driveway, her oversized breasts heaved heavily with every step, exposing tattooed cleavage through pilled terry cloth.

"My father is expecting you at the store this afternoon to haul away all the shit behind the building, and you're about to spend the fucking day fishing!?" Cindi thundered in a raspy, panting voice. "Ronald! I need help around the goddamn house today, too! You heard the fucking weatherman, didn't you!?"

Ronald didn't acknowledge her berating onslaught as he started up the Jeep, instead cranking the stereo volume. Most appropriately, The Rolling Stones, "Time is on My Side," played. He smiled, lit a cigarette, and pulled out of his long driveway on Grant Court before taking a hard right onto Asylum Street, which ran parallel to Forest Street and perpendicular to West Main. It connected Norwich to the turnpike, and its many branches filled this corner of town with sparse neighborhoods, public schools, and recreational facilities. Whether one headed to the casino or the interstate, Asylum offered the path of least resistance.

About a mile up Asylum, Ronald crossed over to Sherman Street—a small industrial park—and took a quick right onto Yantic Dam Trail, which led to the boat launch. He slowly backed to the edge of the river, submerging the trailer, where the boat released itself and began to drift. After retrieving it, he pulled the Jeep around and parked in the dirt cul-de-sac.

Turning to retrieve his gear, Ronald frowned at the trashed back seat, awash in empty fast-food containers, crumpled cigarette packs, and miscellaneous clothing items. Rummaging through the mess unearthed a tan bucket hat, which he placed on his greasy, shaggy head, followed by a pair of black, knee-high rubber boots that he slid over his gaunt legs. After grabbing the six-pack, a small radio, and two fishing poles, he was ready to spend the morning in solitude.

Getting out on the water this particular morning had become an imperative after Ronald worked third shift last night at Ascendant Utilities—the state's largest power plant, though, considering there were only two, size was more or less irrelevant. Like most shifts, he'd been listening to news radio, and the weather declaration of a tropical storm had concerned him. Mostly, he worried several days may pass before he could get back out on the water. That also meant several days of unwanted quality time spent with Cindi, and, if that wasn't bad enough, his father-in-law, the owner and namesake of Crazy Bill's Cordials. He certainly preferred spending his day on the lake to delivering beer kegs or hauling away the broken soda cooler and old floor displays to the town dump.

Ronald stepped onto his heavy-duty, yellow Saturn Dinghy, starting the small outboard motor once he settled in. At twelve feet, the unnecessarily large boat accommodated at least four people comfortably. Ronald was the only person ever in it. Cindi hated fishing, which suited him just fine; the lake was his getaway from her and from his miserable world. Although they followed different schedules, with her working at her father's liquor store during the weekdays and he working as a security guard during the weeknights, they still saw each other more than enough in the morning and on weekends. He did everything in his power to minimize their "quality time."

Ronald steered the boat through the narrow channel, under the rusted, decommissioned railroad bridge, and around the bend. To his surprise, an empty river greeted him. This time of year, residents regularly took their boats on the Yantic or around Hock Island—but not today. The cold nipped his face, unseasonably bitter for a mid-November morning, and the air hung dry. Brittle. The river remained still, and the surrounding land looked barren of life, almost as if time had stopped. At the edge of the Yantic, not a single car even crossed the Washington Street Bridge. How unusual. As he steered ahead, however, a few properties could be seen through the vibrant foliage. On his right, he came upon the abandoned neighborhood of Laurel Hill Drive—his least favorite part of the ride out, since it always left him unnerved.

He glanced over as he passed, but there wasn't much to see through trees and high grass, save for a few faded rooftops and chimneys. He recalled taking the boat out on a freak, sixty-degree afternoon in January the previous year—the first and only time he got a good look at the properties, albeit a brief glimpse, and from afar. The skeleton of bare trees veiled the estates, and a light layer of snow from storms past covered the houses themselves, jagged icicles hanging down from the low-pitched roofs. The few visible windows were blacked out, as if they weren't there. The frozen, monochromatic landscape, with every available surface appearing frosted, reminded him of a black and white Hitchcock movie. Eerie. Unsettling. Strangely, right after he had passed, he sprung a leak and began taking on water, so he had to turn back.

Ronald also recalled hearing stories of a couple teenagers going missing a few years back—that they had kayaked over one afternoon and never returned. Neighbors along the river corroborated, seeing the teens that day in the inlet nearby. One teen did turn up about six months later. Lobster boat fishermen had pulled up a trap under the train bridge, discovering the remains. Ronald, convinced the neighborhood was cursed, wondered why the town never bothered to tear it down.

While looking for an area to settle in, Ronald steered past Hock Island, another structure he wondered why the town didn't demolish. He grimaced at the ancient, drab brick structures as he passed, then blinked, surprised to see construction. *Maybe they are finally tearing it down after all...* The boat slowed to a halt once he reached the edge of the inlet near the Yantic and Thames confluence. He considered the spot under the Washington Street Bridge prime for striper fishing. Leaning back in his seat, he pulled out his prize rod—a seven-foot Shimano saltwater jigging pole he won in the 2001 Northern Bass Open tournament in the Mystic harbor. His backup, an old Fenwick two-piece, sat waiting nearby.

Generally, his routine involved setting up both poles at either end of the boat, sitting back, and drinking while he waited. After casting out the second line, he hooked the handle under his seat, lit a cigarette, and cracked open a can of beer. He zipped his Duluth waterproof jacket, shielding the cold breeze while he took in the view.

The boat gently floated in what the townspeople referred to as the *"crack"* of Norwich—as if someone split the town right in the middle with a "Y" shaped crevice, and it splintered fifteen miles down to the Long Island Sound. From his location, the top left part of the "Y," he looked out on the town's perfect view. He could see the police station to the south, the Johnathan Black Memorial Park, and town library to the north, and directly across from him to the east was the Norwich Water Park and Mini Golf.

Closer than any of that, Ronald could see a series of flashing emergency lights just beyond the pines, starboard side. From what he could make out through the densely wooded landscape of Forest Street, an ambulance and a couple of police cars lined the road. And, craning his neck, he could just about see the Cavanaugh's charred, dilapidated structure.

"This *whole* goddamned place is cursed," he mumbled, finishing his third beer.

As he snapped back the tab on the fourth can, the fishing line tugged in the water. Ronald perked up and grabbed the pole. The line pulled away at a steady pace as he watched, waiting for the right moment, slowly reeling, stopping for a few seconds, then continuing. The line pulled stronger, the pole firmly in his grip, the boat slowly moving backward. Ronald reeled until the tension increased to the point the handle couldn't complete another revolution. The pole arched from the weight of whatever was attached below as he clasped on, white-knuckling. He sat with both feet dug into the bow for support. The boat pulled a little faster; it quickly picked up speed until Ronald found himself hauling down the inlet, water splashing in from either side.

Ronald's eyes widened, and his heart pounded as he held on, wondering what he had snagged. Shark seemed unlikely, but not impossible. The idea of tuna excited him—there was good money in tuna, also known for occasionally traveling the river.

Ronald was *hoping* for a Tuna.

The line snapped, and Ronald fell back to the bottom of the boat. After a few moments, it slowed down, drifting in circles. When he sat up, he was in an inch of icy water. He looked around and noticed he was halfway back down the inlet. His backup pole was missing, and the line on the Shimano needed repairing, he noticed, swearing to himself. And on top of that, he'd lost an expensive lure.

Five feet from the boat, bubbles slowly began to surface—small at first, but quickly growing in size and rapidity. Ronald leaned over starboard to look at the strange anomaly. The bubbles increased in diameter to an alarming size, and while his curiosity was piqued, he slowly backed away. Long, stiff barbs surfaced, two to three at a time, like dark fillet knife blades rising toward him from the depths. Chills surged through his every nerve, and without hesitation, he jumped over the seat and yanked the ripcord on the motor. It started right up, but then elevated out of the water, followed by the stern as the boat raised, sending Ronald backward over the bench. For an instant, he saw the side tubing had four wide tears, air loudly escaping, while the bow submerged in water—no, not water, but something absolutely terrifying. He barely saw it coming before everything went black.

The expansive cavity of the beast let out a mean snarl, then its jaws clamped down on Ronald as he slid headfirst into the mouth. Its large front teeth impaled his chest before he could so much as squeak. Blood gushed from his cracked breastbone, his heart bursting upon impact, while the lower teeth effortlessly crushed through his back, rupturing his lungs. He gurgled out several fluid-filled grunts, and his arms and legs convulsed as he slid under the frothing water with the beast. A rush of burgundy-fused saltwater undulation surfaced for a few moments before dissipating.

Most of the yellow dinghy sunk under the Yantic as it drifted toward Forest Street.

Six

Curtis tossed and turned, still fully dressed, sprawled across the quilted top—now completely disheveled. He turned to the crimson glow of the pink clock radio, which stared back: 6:14 p.m. He turned it on, hoping the soft sounds of an AM station would help lull him, but all he got was propagandist commentary droning on about the one hundred eighty ways for men and women to become soldiers at home in the Army Reserve. The volume was low. He left it.

Any moment he had felt himself drifting off, he would jolt awake, and the relentless burden of work would return. It invaded his brain like a freshwater parasite, slowly feeding on cell tissue, disrupting his neural network. Incorruptible, until there was nothing left. He couldn't turn it off, shut it down. Some days during his interrupted sleep, he would lay, staring into the dark, and question his career decision. An Electronics Systems Tech was not the future he envisioned for himself after high school. In fact, he didn't have much idea of what he wanted to do with his life upon graduation. While most of his classmates entered college, Curtis, confidently turning down a football scholarship to play quarterback for UConn, followed in his father's footsteps and joined the military.

He studied Ohm's Law to validate the value of current levels, voltage drops, and resistance in integrated circuits; he learned to read system elements of schematic diagrams and how to solder electrical hardware components to circuit boards; he could blindly splice coax cables and terminate delicate fiber optic telecommunication cables. And at the end of the day, Curtis wasn't eighty grand in student loan debt.

His father, a decorated Army captain, served two tours in Vietnam and was awarded the Congressional Medal of Honor for his bravery during the assault of Chau Phu. Curtis, proud of his father's achievements, thought serving his country with honor like his father was the appropriate path to follow. He went into the Marine Corps. To his unexpected misfortune, conflict erupted a few years after enlisting, forcing him to deploy overseas. He spent six months in Saudi Arabia during the Gulf War, most of which was spent in the blistering sun troubleshooting and repairing high-frequency, multichannel, portable radio communication systems along with ground/vehicular transceivers. Much of it had arrived faulty from California, and operation was a constant struggle, keeping Curtis plenty busy.

It didn't take long after stepping on foreign soil for him to realize being a soldier was *not* his calling. Physically fit for battle, yes, but emotionally, things had taken an unexpected turn. Many in his unit were either wounded or killed in the assault on Kuwait City while he took shrapnel, critically injuring him days before the war ended. Things he saw over there in that short time weighed heavily on him, forever changing his hopeful, carefree disposition toward the world. He was honorably discharged a year later.

Curtis stomped down each creaking step, rounding the corner through the family room toward the kitchen. Wes sat on the couch, fidgeting, engrossed in a television show. As Curtis walked by, he brushed the top of his shiny blonde hair.

"Hiya, kiddo!" Curtis said softly.

Wes, not acknowledging, kept his attention on the TV screen.

Amy stood at the kitchen sink, her strawberry blonde hair tied back in a ponytail and her face bare of makeup as she rinsed dishes and squeezed them into the primarily full dishwasher below. She wore baggy gray sweats and a tank top—her usual evening attire, which she'd typically throw on upon returning from work. Then, most nights, she'd spend the remainder of her evening correcting Algebra and Geometry homework while drinking a glass or two of wine. In the life of a high school math teacher, total comfort was everything.

She stood, staring out the window while scrubbing dried, burnt gunk from a large glass casserole dish. But when Curtis headed for the refrigerator, opening the door with a little pop of suction, she turned to face him. "There's a plate for ya in there if you're hungry."

Curtis slid a saucer down from the shelf, twice wrapped in cellophane—but what the transparent sheet covered, he had no idea. A viscous, brownish-white substance stared back at him over a mound of dry egg noodles, peppered throughout with chunks of what he thought most likely to be beef. The sight reminded him of the many unpalatable meals during chow time in the mess hall at Parris Island during basic training—*one-pot slop*. He grimaced, pushing the plate back on a mostly vacant shelf.

"Not that hungry. Thanks." Guilt swirled within him for turning her down, but he just couldn't stomach the sight of her cooking, let alone the taste of it. The shelf below held something far more provocative: pizza. Sausage and mushroom. There were two slices left in the large, brown box. He grabbed one; the aroma of oregano and baked crust instantly sparked his hunger as he folded the cold slice, shoving half in his mouth.

Amy turned back to her casserole dish. "How'd ya sleep?"

"Don't know if I actually did," Curtis replied, walking to the small, square dinner table against the kitchen wall, which as of late, was a junk counter covered with mail, coloring books, Amy's workbooks, papers, folders, and car keys. Anything anyone might have in their hands upon entering from the garage wound up there. In the back middle was a pile of mail, which Curtis avoided by looking at everything else around it.

"There's a bunch of mail on the table for ya," Amy called from the sink.

He cringed.

"Oh, and there's another one of those weird letters, too. You should take a look at it."

He needed a moment to recall what she was referring to by "weird letters," as he didn't want to directly ask what the hell she was talking about. He lifted the pile and sifted through—propane bill, SunTrust Bank mortgage bill, Charter Oak Federal Credit Union car loan bill for Amy's SUV, doctor bill, doctor bill, specialist bill, Mastercard bill, junk mail credit card offers, junk mail car insurance offers, debt consolidation offers, Allstate car insurance bill times two. Sure, he could've avoided the headache by just having Amy manage the checkbook while he worked away from home, or at least ask her to pay her own bills on the joint account, but he needed the distraction.

He needed to keep a sense of control, even if nothing else around him stayed within his grasp.

Then, there it sat at the bottom of the stack—opened, edges frayed as if torn open by a child on Christmas morning. But Curtis had a feeling this was no present. Nor was it something he wanted to even look at, much less discuss. He pulled it, opened it, quickly scanned the contents.

```
Mr. & Mrs. Reynolds
1 Forest Street
Norwich, CT 06360
Via Certified Mail
```

I am writing in response to the multiple correspondences we have sent out over the last four months regarding the land surrounding the Forest Street properties. The City of Norwich is wrapping up negotiations in coming weeks and is intending to sell the land for a proposed project funded by the Federal Government.

This letter serves to notify you that the City of Norwich, on behalf of Hock ADR Corp, intends to take ownership of the land surrounding Forest Street by means of eminent domain to ensure redevelopment, which is slated to begin spring of next year.

If you would prefer to avoid delay and the process of court and expenses, Hock ADR Corp would like to retain its current offer for just compensation on your house to help facilitate the process. As explained in the previous letter dated September 18, it has been estimated that fair market value of your house is $123,896; however, the City of Norwich would like to have an assessor out to determine actual value. The acquisition of this land is of the utmost importance to the City of Norwich; however, their goal is to attempt to negotiate an amicable agreement for all property acquisitions.

Failure to respond to this final notice by January 1 will result in nullification of the proposed offer followed by court proceedings with removal in sixty days thereafter. It will not be necessary for you to surrender complete possession of the estate until March 1. In the meantime, please provide a copy of your purchase agreement and a list of expenses incurred for improvements to the property to date to ensure fair market value.

Best Regards,

```
Kirsten Janson
Corporate Councilor
```

```
                    Norwich Corporate Council
              80 Hunters Avenue, Suite 823
                       Norwich, CT 06360
```

Curtis quickly stuffed the letter back in the envelope and threw it on the table with the rest of the mail. "I'll go through it tomorrow."

Tossing the pizza crust in the garbage pail, he walked out to the garage and returned a few moments later with a Mondo-Mart plastic bag, a rectangle box contained inside. He then crossed the threshold into the family room where Wes sat, still fixated, gently bouncing up and down on the seat cushion, his hands twirling by his sides.

"How's the man of the house doing, huh?" Curtis asked, sitting down next to his son.

No answer or acknowledgment.

"Whatcha watching, champ?"

The Discovery Channel logo appeared at the bottom of the TV screen, then the title flashed along the bottom as it returned from commercial: *Before We Ruled the Earth.* Curtis watched a few moments as a grisly saber-toothed tiger lurked among the dense overgrowth, stealthily trailing three cavemen.

"You know; daddy misses you *soooo* much—come here..." He picked Wes up, placed him down on his lap, and let out an overly dramatic, audible grunt. "Oh my lord, Wes, you are getting so heavy! What's mommy feeding ya, huh? I know what she's feeding you, pizza and casseroles! That's what she's feeding you, isn't it—isn't it? And from what daddy saw in the garbage: McDonald's Happy Meals!?"

Still at the kitchen sink, Amy turned back, giving a disapproving glance. Curtis pretended to ignore her, though he couldn't help but note her smile when he began bouncing Wes up and down on his knee.

"Happy Meals, Happy Meals, Happy Meals! Are you happy, kiddo? Huh, huh, are you happy!?" Curtis asked in sing-song.

Wes nodded his head, smiling, still staring at the TV.

"You *areeee*!? Good!"

Curtis dove forward, tickling Wes's underarms. The boy let out a shrill of uncontrollable laughter, rolling off daddy's leg.

With his son distracted, Curtis reached around the side of the couch, grabbing the box he'd brought in from his truck. "Daddy got ya something. Check it out..."

Wes looked over, and Curtis held up the Star Wars Millennium Falcon one-thousand-piece puzzle he had bought. The boy's little mouth dropped from his pudgy, pale cheeks, baring a smile that lacked both teeth on either side of the upper two fronts. Flapping his hands in front of him, he grabbed the box from Curtis's fingers and stared at the cover, analyzing the muddled graphic and its intricate contrast of neon colors. Against the backdrop of outer space, all of his favorite heroes stared back, the Death Star looming in the distance and of course—Darth Vader.

"Sweetheart, it's time for your bath," Amy said with a soft smile, leaning in the entryway.

Wes, ecstatic, held his new puzzle straight over his head for his mother to see, jumping up and down as if he'd just won a first-place trophy.

"Sooo cool!" Amy playfully gasped. "Come on, hun; it's getting late."

Wes and his puzzle followed Amy upstairs to the bathroom directly across from the top of the staircase. Curtis, feeling a bit dazed from lack of sleep, decided he'd go try to take a power nap. He knew he'd have to force himself up at a certain hour to maintain—or at the very least, *try* to maintain—his current, erratic sleep schedule. Before getting up, though, he stayed to watch the TV for another moment, curious as to the fate of the cavemen. At that moment, the saber-tooth neared, getting ready to pounce, before a pack of dire wolves thwarted his attack. Curtis smirked at the cheesy computer-generated graphics, then headed upstairs.

Sleep didn't pan out as he'd expected; he continued to roll around, tossing, turning. This time, he wore comfier clothes—a pair of old, faded Gold's Gym shorts and matching tank top. The brisk autumn air blew in from the river and through the cracked window, cooling his overheated body, which had always tended to run hot. Since high school, he'd slept with a fan at the edge of the bed, perpetually running year-round—especially sleeping next to Amy, who was always cold, having the heat cranked during the winter and AC turned low in the summer. Curtis, now fan-less and alone, lay awake, wishing for the soothing low hum of the motor and blades to drain out the clatter of chirping crickets pervading his bedroom.

The pink clock mocked: 9:43 p.m. Curtis rolled out of bed and headed straight for the bathroom, where he peed, washed his hands, then splashed cold water on his cheeks. With liquid dripping down his chin, he stared at his reflection in the mirror, analyzing the contours of his aging face: the forehead wrinkles and smile lines increasing in prominence, the bags beginning to form under his eyes, and his five o'clock shadow, which darkened the edges of his square chin. His electric razor remained back at the hotel. Now that he thought about it, so did his toothbrush.

The upstairs lacked any illumination save for the mild, amber glow of a night light near the top of the steps across from the master bedroom. Curtis, wanting a sweatshirt, slowly entered Amy's room and tip-toed over the hardwood floor to his closet to grab one, keeping an eye on her bed as he did so. The white, sheer curtains were open several inches, letting the soft glow of moonlight spill over her face as she slept. He stopped to admire her a moment, remembering how beautiful she was. He couldn't recall how much time had passed since he'd last seen her so at peace. Years.

Next, he opened Wes's bedroom door and peeked in. Like the one by the stairs, a night light was next to his bed—a giant, red race car. The only indication of Wes's existence, buried beneath a plethora of stuffed animals, was the snuffling snores droning from under a pile of Storm Trooper covers. Curtis smiled and shut the door.

After finishing the final slice of cold pizza—crust tossed—he plopped down on the couch. The lights stayed off, but the same moonlight that crossed Amy's bed now formed a spotlight through the tall family room window, making its way past the kitchen and out the sliding glass doors. Curtis lit a cigarette, took a deep drag, and dropped his head back, staring at the ceiling and exhaling the intoxicating vapor into the atmosphere. He slowly turned his head, taking in the space around him as if seeing it all for the first time. The chatter in his head, now just muffled, incoherent noise, darted around a hundred different intermingling thoughts. His mind couldn't seem to decide where to stop. But, he decided, he didn't mind that.

The shelf under the coffee table held many items, primarily things needing to be hidden from plain sight: magazines, coloring books, Amy's manicure kit and staggering array of nail polish shades, photo albums, remote controllers. He reached under to remove his favorite ashtray—his only ashtray, a vintage glass Amberina, blood orange and amber. It had belonged to his father, though his mother had also used it before she quit ten years earlier. Now, he and Amy mostly used the cumbersome platter as a paperweight, holding magazines in place. He grabbed it, and as he did, a series of photo albums of different lengths and sizes caught his eye. He pulled one out and began to flip through. It was the latest album—Wes's eighth birthday celebration, with Amy's parents at their beach house in Madison and all his Harry Potter-themed gifts—Legos, puzzles, Hufflepuff Quidditch jersey, etc. His mother-in-law, clad in a flowing red cocktail dress, dangly jewelry, a face full of makeup and drink in hand, was present in just about every one. *Who the hell gets that dolled up for a kid's birthday party?* He didn't much like his in-laws, knowing he was too *low class* for their pretentious tastes, especially Amy's mother. Nor did she much like him. They both dealt with the awkward discomfort by only having to see each other three times a year: Thanksgiving, Christmas, and Wes's birthday.

The next album, slightly older, held some glorious memories: the early years of the Reynolds' life on Forest Street. Wes must have been two or three years old by Curtis's recollection, judging by his size. The Cavanaughs were present as well. Half the photos had been taken in their backyard from either a Memorial Day or Fourth of July barbecue, Curtis couldn't remember which. The cookouts and gatherings all blended. He pulled a group photo from under the thin plastic slot and held it up in the bluish-grey hue of the moon. The camera must have been on a timer, he thought, because all five of them stared back, set in the front of Frank's picnic table. Wes sat top center in a patriotic red, white, and blue jumper; to his left stood Amy in a yellow summer dress and Estelle in a floral pattern. To the right of Wes, Curtis, in jeans and a tee-shirt, wrapped his arm around the hilariously shorter Frank, who wore one of those funny quipped aprons—*If You're Reading This, Bring Me A Beer*—gripping a giant, stainless steel grill fork. Plastered smiles on all.

Curtis gently shook his head, took a final drag, then snubbed out the butt against the scalloped edge of the Amberina. "Can't believe you're gone, Frank."

Seven

Curtis raked leaves and twigs into three medium piles in the backyard. With a pair of canvas gloves and a dustpan, he scooped the debris into a plastic-lined, thirty-two-gallon wheeled garbage can. Though a cool mid-afternoon breeze whipped by, the sun beat down as it began its descent, causing him to perspire. He stopped to rest, catching his breath, and, in doing so, realized how out of shape he had become. *Christ, I really need to quit smoking.* The wind blew through his hair and around his face, chilling the glistening sweat on his forehead.

New England storms could be incredibly fierce, unpredictable, and destructive—physically and emotionally. Having lived in Southeast Connecticut his entire life, most of which in Chesterville, he knew that full well. The last thing he needed was for the yard to flood, pulling his four-burner gas grill and Wes's playground belongings down a roaring Thames until they washed up on a beach somewhere off Long Island Sound. The last storm, two years earlier, sent a red maple into the rusted, metal shed behind the house, crushing all of his hanging tools, but that act of God was mostly unavoidable—his tools now lived in the garage. And as he thought about it, he also didn't want chopped wood, from that tree currently rotting at the edge of his property, to be blown through his sliding glass door window from potential high winds. *Another thing to move, ugghhh...*

He glanced around the yard to consider the myriad of tasks ahead of him. But as he prepared to get everything in order before the storm, movement on the red deck caught his eye. The one-thousand-piece Star Wars jigsaw puzzle lay on the wooden surface, along with an engrossed Wes, sitting cross-legged in an oversized Hartford Whalers sweatshirt. His fingers fluttered and flapped almost incessantly, desperately clinging to each piece he spun around in his hand before meticulously laying it down, always finding where it connected. The puzzle was the second one of the day, the first being a seven-hundred-fifty-piece Hogwarts Castle & Great Lake puzzle he had completed before lunch—a slow day for Wes. By the age of two, he churned out two or three completed hundred-piece boards a day, his one-man assembly line play style fascinating Amy and Curtis.

His spatial and visual abilities surpassed anyone in his age group, and although he rarely spoke, the second grade boy possessed the vocabulary of a fourth grader. His high marks on advanced reading comprehension tests proved this. The main problem Amy or Curtis had was pulling him away from an activity. If Wes had not completed a project come dinner time, they couldn't interrupt him without an absolute meltdown. Amy did her best to avoid such conflicts by keeping him on a daily schedule, in the hopes of avoiding activities that could disrupt scheduled events. If Wes started something an hour or so before bedtime, a real late night would no doubt follow.

Curtis, who had just tied off his sixth bag of leaves and begun to re-line the can, stared in slight shock across the yard, unable to stop watching his little boy on the deck. Sometimes he forgot how big his son had gotten. Only recently, he thought, Wes still used a car seat. That was the last time Curtis was home for any significant length of time. His mind drifted, recalling how he had barely made it home for Wes's birthday in July. On a typical day—typical for Curtis, anyway—he'd be in bed by eleven a.m.; but he stayed awake and pushed through to make time for Wes, despite being in the middle of a busy work project several hours away. On top of his late arrival, the lack of sleep made him a zombie and, worse, very moody throughout the whole party.

The guilt of being away from his family for so long set in, and Curtis had to shift his thoughts—yes, he was barely home, but what choice did he have? The jobs away wouldn't last *forever*—hopefully.

Amy walked out of the sliding glass door in a tightly wrapped towel, the cordless phone in her hand. Her hair, still dripping wet, rose atop her head in another towel. "Miguel's on the phone," she shouted, leaning over the side railing. And as she handed it over, she added, "You didn't hear it? It rang forever."

Evidently, the phone had rung fifteen times, but Curtis had drifted off in thought. A trance. He took the receiver, ignoring Amy's comment.

"Miguel, what's up?" Curtis asked, surprised.

"Aeeey, man. Everything all right over there? Yo, you fucking took off on me, like I was a teenage girl who just told you she was pregnant, and you could be one of two, or maybe three baby daddies, and now we need to go on *Maury* for the paternity test results, but I ain't heard from you since!" Miguel ranted, sounding sort of concerned between his regular bullshit.

"What the fuck are you talking about? And how did you get my house number?"

"White pages, yo. I didn't even bother trying your cell phone—I know you don't turn that shit on."

"Wh—where are you? Are you still at the Mondo-Mart?" Curtis could hear the elevator music and automated *specials* announcements in the background over some distinct chatter nearby.

"Yeah, yo, I stuck around here this afternoon to relax. And to get some more of that *herb* from that Goth dude—he also works over at this bar. And you know I live in New York, right? I can't just fucking drive back and forth like I'm going to the office, man. Plus, I met this little *niña* at the bar down the street. DUDE, she's got a tattoo of the *"bat"* symbol over her left breast; yo, she just whipped that shit out in front of everybody—and down on her inner thigh, she got this—"

"MIGUEL! You're trailing—what is the point of this conversation? I gotta get this house straightened up before this weather hits."

"Well, I was just gonna say, yo, you left your tool bag here, man. And all the rest of your shit. I didn't know if you were coming back or not—just wanted to give you a heads up, you know."

Curtis's heart stopped as he looked down on his left hand. Staring at the narrow, white strip of skin around his finger where his wedding band should be, he wondered if Amy had noticed its absence... though he'd seen very little of her upon returning. *Wouldn't she have said something?* Then he realized he couldn't say whether she'd been wearing hers.

Curtis panicked. "Well, what are you doing—are you staying or leaving?"

"Just saw that shit as I was headed out the door, man. Gotta get on the road, though. You want me to hold on to them?" Miguel offered.

"NO. Thanks, no. Umm, all right, I—uh, I'm going to head back up and grab them. Thanks for the call." Curtis sighed.

"Hey, no problem, man. I'll leave them in Simmons' office. Oh, and don't be alarmed if by chance you go through your toolbox and find a bag of..." Miguel paused, dropping his voice, and then whispered, "*cocaine*," as if anyone could hear. "That bat-tit girl from the bar left me this eight-ball, and you know I'm on probation and all—"

Click. Curtis cut the line, doubting Miguel would even notice.

He couldn't believe, after never leaving his tools on the job before, that he now had to drive all the way back to Rockingham Park, New Hampshire. But he didn't trust Miguel with the bag or its irreplaceable contents—he didn't even trust Miguel to run to the gas station for a pack of cigarettes. And he didn't trust Simmons either. Truthfully, he didn't trust *anyone* with it.

His tool bag, though expensive, wasn't anything special: blue canvas, faded, heavily worn at the edges, having suffered years of abuse. But its contents—especially considering the Reynolds' financial situation—were priceless. The bag contained thousands of dollars' worth of precision tools and specialized telecom devices accumulated over time: coax and modular test equipment, circuit testers, laser measuring, and impact tools. His Fluke Calibration and multimeter device alone cost him a grand. Then, of course, there were various cutters, crimpers, strippers, drivers.

But his tool bag also held two personal items that Curtis really did consider priceless. The first was an Oak Ridge bone handle folding knife, the last Christmas present from his father before he'd entered Webelos Scouts—the highest Cub Scout rank—in the spring of '78.

The second item, wrapped in cloth in a small, zippered pouch inside the bag's main compartment, was his wedding band.

His heart, previously stopped, exploded in his chest, thudding rapidly back to life, and Curtis scrambled to check the time on the phone. Plenty more chores remained for him to do at the house before the storm, before the long journey back, and daylight was burning. Not to mention that he still had to tell Amy, who wouldn't really understand. She would, however, most likely give him an ear full of shit.

Curtis swore under his breath and got to work. The Reynolds' had dealt with the mess storms left in their wake on numerous occasions during their time on Forest Street. But especially after the tree incident two years prior, Curtis strove to properly prepare for all probable future occurrences. Since the backyard often flooded with heavy rainfall, being so close to the river, he took the sump pump out of storage, setting it up in the far corner of the basement, where the floor sloped several inches. Over the years, even before the Reynolds purchased the Cape, the foundation had begun slowly sinking. The slab was cracked in a few places, which was of no concern to Curtis, though he did notice a more recent split during his installation. With a sigh, he added it to his long list of things to fix later. Then he fueled up the ancient hand-me-down generator from Frank inside the shed before starting in on the yard.

As he wheeled the gas grill from behind the house at near neck-breaking speed, car horns prompted him to notice Holly Hock Island, wedged inside the narrow inlet of the Yantic. Scores of vehicles started to vacate over a narrow passageway connecting the island facility—a three brick building structure that stretched the length of Holly Hock—to the opposite side of the mainland, interrupting the heavy flow of rush hour traffic on Route Thirty-Two. He found this quite peculiar; although he hadn't considered the island in years, mostly due to his recent work schedule, he had deemed the facility obsolete. With the wind slowly increasing in intensity, tossing around decaying leaves, Curtis shook off his curiosity and hurried to finish tidying.

His spine cracked as he took the deck chairs and stacked them inside the new metal tool shed, now offset behind the house; his joints popped as he rolled inside the glass table top. His once athletic frame had begun to diminish under the crumbling weight of stress, age, and lack of sleep. He wheezed, dragging full garbage containers from the driveway and into the shed as well, wondering if thirty-five was too young to be falling apart. Then he turned to the many items in the yard which belonged to Wes—scattered toys, plastic furniture, and a BMX bike all had to be put away. Lastly, and by far the most infuriating, stacks of rotting firewood waited for disposal, which meant he needed to wheel them out to the woods between the properties.

Grabbing the wheelbarrow of heavily decomposed, termite-infested wood, he carted it deeper into the brush. Sweat dripped from his stubbly face, his white V-neck soaked through and clinging to his thinning frame. Yard work kept Curtis's mind busy—unfortunately, however, not busy enough from wandering. Lately, he couldn't shut off his thoughts, and his cognizance of that fact stressed him further. His third-shift schedule had created what felt like an eternal imbalance in his circadian rhythm, which became more and more evident as time passed—indecision, memory loss, blackouts. Rage. Some days he wouldn't see daylight at all, depending on the season and how much overtime he put in. A feeling of unfamiliarity plagued him, as if he lived in a delusion.

He grunted as he dumped the wood, then dropped the wheelbarrow to quickly catch his breath. As he stood, wiping the perspiration from his forehead with a red, paisley handkerchief pulled from his back pocket, a fly buzzed by his face—followed by a second and third. He turned and looked back, his house barely visible through the unruly stretch of tall Eastern white pine between his property and the Jensen's, the elderly couple next door.

The sharp, sweet smell of evergreen trees drifting with the breeze off the river brought with it a jumbled snippet of pre-teen memories—three summers at Camp Hazen. During that small, unfamiliar window between childhood innocence and bewildered adolescence, he had found camping an exercise in self-exploration, self-confidence, and resiliency, all while building a shared connectedness with his peers and with nature. Catch your first fish, build your first fire, develop your first crush. Exhilarating. He took deep breaths, drinking it all in. *I wonder, would Wes like camping?*

The number of flies increased dramatically, and morbid curiosity drove him further into the wooded area. Brown pine needles, rickety cones, and decaying leaves canvased the twisting path, crunching under his Timberland boots along with an occasional snapping branch. Nearing the edge of the river, he looked up to roaring seagulls soaring ten to fifteen feet above as they gracefully passed; he felt as if he could almost touch them. Strange, he thought, having rarely seen one this far up the river, let alone a colony. But he could not entertain the common, New England indication of inclement weather further as the smell hit him, now surrounded by swarming flies.

He hadn't had the misfortune of coming across the familiar smell in over a decade—one he hated, one he would never forget. He sniffed again. Rancid. Maybe the pungent marshland riverbank? Having briefly lived on the Connecticut shoreline, where such smells were much more common, he knew the emanation from low tide was basically synonymous with rotten eggs. Still, he pressed on out of reluctant, morbid curiosity, keeping the handkerchief pressed over his nose and mouth.

An almost unrecognizable mess awaited him. The first disturbing image: a human head, decapitated, half-covered—the half still intact—with matted, tufted dark hair. In the top quadrant, everything from the cheekbone through the nose was missing on one side. Hollow. The face took on a waxen complexion, glossy white—a pale green hue developing around the chin and cheekbone. The mouth, blue and scabrous, slightly ajar, formed a portal for the passing of black flies through a missing front tooth. Curtis wafted them from his face, unable to avert his eyes as he struggled to identify the remains against an internal Rolodex—a subconscious cross-referencing of everyone he'd ever met in town. The frosted eye glared up at Curtis.

The torso gaped open, ripped vertically up the middle, crotch to chest, with viscera and other internal organs strewn about. Excavated. Trailing. The remains, still partially clothed with pieces of yellow fabric from a shredded jacket, littered the ground. A right arm severed at the elbow and a leg torn from the knee down—concealed mostly by a rubber boot—lay five to ten feet away in opposite directions.

The worst part for Curtis, as if any of it were tolerable, were the maggots. Fresh maggots. Tiny, rice-like organisms uniformly squirming. His stomach churned from the very sight as they discharged from every cut, gash, and gaping orifice. Within seconds, his eyes watered, and he retched off to the side, coughing, the acid burning his esophagus.

He had seen his share of mutilated men. Men who met their demise by a smattering of gunfire, men who had been in close range of an explosive device—just far enough away to suffer, if only for a few moments, conscious of their imminent end—men in pieces. But never had he seen a mess quite like this. Fragments of human flesh continued to trail ten to fifteen yards beyond the carcass.

Curtis followed the splotches of blood through withering leaves and forest overgrowth until he was about ten yards from the river. Looking up toward the marsh, he could see the stern of a yellow dinghy partially emerged in tall strands of golden reed. He stood, taking in the view of the Yantic, processing, deliberating, weighing the pros and cons—what to do—his thoughts looping.

Before turning back, he noticed from the corner of his eye a mound of dirt surrounding an oblong crater in the earth. The hole, about five feet in diameter, looked as if someone had dug a ditch and left it. Not being able to make much of it, he gave an unenthusiastic look in, which only offered infinite darkness, then kicked in a limestone teetering at the edge. But instead of hearing an object landing, he made out only a murmur of low chirps and faint scratching. In fact, the stone didn't seem to contact any surface, vanishing into the void. He squatted, inches from the opening, trying to discern the noise. Perhaps a chipmunk or maybe a kitten had fallen in. But that theory quickly proved illogical as the noise heightened, squeakier.

A massive cluster tore straight up past Curtis's face, mere inches away, fluttering and squealing as he tumbled backward, arms up, bracing his head. He lay, peering through the crossed frame of his arms, at the anomaly, which lasted only seconds. By the time he perceived what the creatures were, they had faded, dissipating into trees.

Bats...

EIGHT

Emergency vehicles returned to Forest Street, this time between Reynolds' property and the Jensen's. Four townie black and whites, a rescue truck from the Norwich Fire Department, and a coroner van. Not as many as Curtis was expecting, but he hardly minded, as his desire to avoid a spectacle had made him initially reluctant to report the incident anyway. He stood in the middle of his backyard, Amy beside, watching. Two men from the coroner's office, clad head to toe in black with matching rubber gloves, carried a gurney with a black body bag from the woods, shortcutting it alongside his house. Two officers stood by the river inside a forty-foot-roped-off area of police caution tape, wrapping up their investigating at the water's edge.

Sergeant Rick and another officer, much younger by comparison, walked from the woods up to the Reynolds'.

Sergeant Rick spoke first. "I apologize. Normally, we'd have the state police here as well, but there's a large pile-up on 395 by the casino exit involving a jack-knifed tractor-trailer—a bunch of cars on fire. Pure chaos. Just about every available emergency vehicle is over that way, helping out. Casino can't have their traffic diverted

"

too long, know what I'm sayin'?" He displayed a brief glimmer of a smirk. "How you two holding up?"

"We're okay. Do you happen to know who that poor man is?" Amy asked, her arms folded in a baggy, hooded sweatshirt that looked as if it may have belonged to Curtis. Her eyes squinted at the officers as the sun, shifting from canary yellow to a shade of dandelion gold, began its methodical descent behind Hock Island.

"Whelp." Rick paused, taking a deep breath. "Now, we didn't happen to find any identification on the remains or in the surrounding area, at least as of yet. It's, uh—it's quite a mess back there." His face twisted, as if seeing the sight again for the first time. "But by the looks of it, I'm almost certain it's Ronny Haverhill. Lives a few streets over, on Grant Ct."

Amy stiffened up, scrunching her face in confusion. "Ronny-Ronny-Ronny—why does that name sound so familiar?"

Curtis, just staring at his wife with raised eyebrows, lit a cigarette.

"Uhh, his wife Cindi—she and her family own Crazy Bill's Cordials over off Main Street," Rick explained. "She reported him missing just this morning, actually. Said he left yesterday morning after a heated argument and she hadn't heard from him since. Do either of you know him or the family?"

"I don't, but I remember Cindi from the package store. I mean, it's been a long time since I've been in there." Amy shrugged, averting her gaze to the ground. "Cindi seemed sweet, though. She and her father were always really nice."

The sergeant and the other officer turned to Curtis.

Evidently, Amy had forgotten Ron's significance, but Curtis knew instantly. In actuality, he'd just about forgotten himself until he heard the name. Not only had Curtis worked at the liquor store briefly, but he'd done some electrical work in the massive, walk-in beer cooler two years earlier. Cindi's father had given Ronny a substantial amount of money and tasked him with hiring out for the job, but Ronny, knowing he'd get Curtis for a fraction of the price, had pocketed the remainder. Instead of the two grand he had promised, Ronny ended up paying Curtis three hundred in cash and a case of white wine as an "I.O.U."

Curtis nodded. "Uh, yeah, I remember them from the store, too, but I haven't seen either of them in—years." He wasn't exactly lying.

"Sergeant, what could have possibly done that to that man?" Amy twitched, shuddering slightly.

"Oh, hard to say, really. There's a chance he could've fallen overboard—cut up by the outboard motor. With the storm coming in, a shark could be making its way up the river. Wouldn't be the first attack Connecticut's seen. Unfortunately, though, the animals have already gotten to him. Discerning anything will be tough, to say the least. Won't really know much 'til the state police can get a watercraft out and tow in his boat. The way things are looking, who knows when that'll be." Sergeant Rick removed his Stetson hat and wiped the perspiration from his forehead with a white cloth napkin—"World's Greatest Dad" embroidered along the perimeter. His constricting uniform, visibly wet under the pits and too tight for his bulking, unstructured frame, rustled with every movement, the sweat gradually expanding to either side of his chest.

"Before we head out, I'll need a brief statement. Now, you'll have to excuse me, Curtis, for asking, but if I don't ask now, someone else is liable to eventually come around asking questions. At least I can get something on paper."

The young officer stood, expressionless, hat low to his brow line, staring at Curtis with a pen and pad.

"I know you just got back into town yesterday morning. I saw you pull in with your—as you say—damaged truck from work vandals. Is there anyone that could verify your whereabouts Monday morning between eight and nine a.m.?"

Curtis blinked, taken aback by the question. "I was driving home from New Hampshire. So no."

"And how 'bout the night before, Sunday, between nine and ten p.m.?"

Curtis, flushed, glared at the Sergeant. At first, he didn't remember where he was, but as he thought about it, he did recall grabbing pizza in the mall food court with Miguel before their eleven p.m. shift. "Yeah, my co-worker Miguel."

Then he flicked his cigarette and walked away.

Curtis immediately regretted his decision to call the police, knowing he was better off minding his own business. So far, by this point in his life, the sentiment had only proven true. He figured the buzzards and whatever else lurked out there would have taken care of the remains over a few days, anyway. The corpse lay far enough away that the smell wouldn't have even reached the house. With the storm coming in, the river might flood in, consuming Ron and everything in its path, thereupon dragging any evidence downstream to wash up someplace else. And Miguel, a man with a record almost as long as his winded conversations, now became Curtis's only alibi. *Oh, totally believable.*

He then realized—he spent most of the night installing cable in the stock room with no camera or evidence at all of his evening shift. The ones that *were* there were black and white, grainy at best. *Should*

I just go sit in the fucking squad car now, or wait for a warrant? He smirked at the thought as he walked up the back steps and through the sliding door.

Amy watched her husband enter the house, slamming the slider closed, and gave an incredulous smirk. "Sergeant, you really don't suspect my *husband* had anything to do with any of this, do you?"

"Just doing my due diligence, Ma'am. I do apologize."

"What about the Jensens next door—are you going to question them?"

"We did. Or, at least tried to. The place is vacant."

Amy shot the sergeant a puzzling glance, now trying to recall the last time she'd actually seen them herself.

The sergeant returned the Stetson to his matted head. "After I leave here, I'm going to have to break the news to his wife before questioning her as well. Not much looking forward to that, I can assure you, but it does go with the territory."

Amy stood, arms still folded, staring off at the house as she wondered where her husband had stormed off to.

"But between you and me, I can count on two hands how many times myself or another officer has been called over to the Haverhill residence from a neighbor complaining of a domestic dispute. You just can't rule anything out these days, you know?" He shook his head in disgust. "Damn shame either way. That's a helluva thing to happen to a man."

"This is all so crazy!" Amy snapped back. "First Frank and Estelle, now *this*!" She took a beat, struggling to regain composure. "God only knows what happened at *their* place." Her eyes began to well, nose running as she snuffled. She turned toward the river, embarrassed by her emotional reaction. "You wouldn't have happened to have heard anything on how Mrs. Cavanaugh is doing, would you? I feel bad. I haven't been by to check up on her since she went in."

"Still haven't been able to get a statement from Mrs. Cavanaugh, unfortunately. She fell into cardiac arrest shortly after she was admitted."

"Oh my god. Is she all right?"

"She coded several times, so now they have her heavily sedated. They hooked her up to the ventilator to wait for the heart to recover."

"I still can't believe any of this is happening." Amy wiped her eyes and turned to the sergeant. "What do you think will happen?"

"With Mrs. Cavanaugh? To be honest, it doesn't look promising. Not in my experiences anyway." Seeing Mrs. Reynolds in her distressed state, the sergeant took his cue to exit, tipping his hat. "We're going to get out of your hair now, Mrs. Reynolds. If we need anything else, we'll be in touch."

She nodded, watching him and his officer walk to their car. She could just make out his words as he turned to the younger man: "Boy, what a week it's been. And to think it's only Tuesday."

NINE

Curtis took a long, overly hot shower. Leaning against the beige tile, he closed his eyes, letting the spray hammer off his flushed back. Remembering the lousy, pressure-deprived hotel shower, he smiled. How nice it was to be home. The spray felt so... relaxing, almost massaging; he really could have stayed in all night. After toweling off, he put on another white V-neck tee shirt with beige Carhartt cargo pants, finishing with scuffed, black steel-toe boots, the same ones he would wear for a shift. His wardrobe was, if nothing else, functional.

Grabbing a partial pot of coffee in the kitchen, brewed from the afternoon, he filled a tall thermal mug to the brim. The dark roast, like his wardrobe, lacked much interest; he preferred his caffeine black. Then he pulled on his matching Carhartt jacket and quietly grabbed his keys from the kitchen table, figuring Amy would call him on the road if she needed something—at the very least, avoiding an argument until he returned.

"You going somewhere?"

He spun around to see Amy standing at the kitchen counter, holding a letter. *Fuck.*

He glanced over to Wes, sitting at the kitchen table coloring a *Finding Nemo* book, then back to his wife. "I gotta run up to work real quick—I forgot my tool bag. I can't leave 'em there."

"Seriously—right now?!"

"YES."

"The police just left here an hour ago with a—" She paused, then mouthed, "mutilated body." Then, audibly, she continued, "An hour ago! Our neighbor—your friend, Frank is *gone*, his wife is on life-support, and you *need* to go run errands!?"

"I understand that—it's why I ran *all* the way back here and forgot my shit." *Try-to-stay-calm, try-to-stay-calm...*

Amy's face reddened. "You *know* what time it is?"

"No, Amy, I don't know what time it is. I don't even know what fucking day it is. I seriously don't! Do you know why—because I *work* seven days a week, and lately, I feel like I've been living in the goddamn *Twilight Zone!*" Curtis snapped, searching his pockets for his smokes.

"You know a monsoon is coming, right!?" Amy threw her shaking hands in the air. "I can't *believe* you're headed back to New Hampshire!"

"It's RAIN, Amy. Christ. Not the end of the world. There's over three grand worth of tools and shit there. I just can't leave them to be stolen." Curtis struggled to keep an even tone. He needed to clear his head—get in his truck and drive. Just a couple of hours. He didn't want to explain the importance of the tool bag.

"What about your co-worker?" Amy implored.

"He's gone." Curtis turned and charged out the front door. "I will be back in four hours, max. Everything's gonna be fine."

Amy chased behind.

"Curtis… Curt! CURT!" She barked.

"Jesus Christ. What, what, WHAT!" Curtis, grimacing awkwardly, stopped and turned around.

"What is the matter with you!?"

"Nothing. I *need* to go get my tools. That's all. What's the big deal here?"

"I haven't seen you in over a month. I haven't spoken to you in weeks—WEEKS, Curtis! I call your work phone, and it always goes straight to voicemail. No one can get a hold of you!" Amy stopped to take a breath before she continued, her tone changing from anger to desperation. "I know things haven't been going well lately. And I can't pretend anymore that nothing is happening."

"Whaddya want me to do? *This* is the job—I need to work!"

"You can get another job *here!*"

"HA-HA!" Curtis belted out, unable to stifle the rage. "What—go back to fucking construction? Break my balls for half of what I make now? I'll fucking DIE before I even think of considering that."

"What is WRONG here, Curtis!? TALK-TO-ME!" Her shrill voice carried almost all the way to the Cavanaugh's.

"I don't know what you want me to say."

"ANYTHING! Just—say—*anything*. I can't help you if you don't talk to me," Amy pleaded. "Look, I know you get really anxious around this time coming up on the anniversary—"

Curtis froze a moment, chills washing over him. "I don't want to talk about that."

"Then *tell* me what it is!?"

"Really, you want to get into this right now? Fine. Well, let me see, wh—where do I begin? How—how 'bout *we're broke*. The fucking money is—is gone as fast as it comes in! I get home to a—a—a stack of towering bills that I can't even keep up with," Curtis stammered, his stutter habitual with the onset of high distress. "And these doctors or specialists or whatever the hell—bills—on top of this *thing* with Wes that no one seems to understand. We live in—in—in this expensive, falling apart house we refinanced that we *still* can't afford the mortgage on. Christ, half the shit in there is—is your parents'. Ummm, OH, I'm on probation, let's not forget *that*, so—so the only job I can work where the pay isn't complete shit is in another state, and it hires a—a—a bunch of lazy, deplorable, ex-convicts—and I work *all* fucking night, not to mention, I'm gone for weeks on end! Good times! Now, if it's okay with you, *dear*, I would like to get my tools *before they're stolen*, and we can no longer continue to pay for this lavish fucking lifestyle."

"You think I'm having a great fucking time, Curtis!? I go to a school every day where there's fights on a daily basis. It's the worst district in the state, and I'm a glorified babysitter! I'm terrified of these kids! There's trash littered up and down the hallways that nobody cleans. Half of the teachers aren't even certified; they show up in sweatpants. They look just like the kids!" She took a shaky breath. "These problems aren't *new*, Curtis, and they affect me, too. You're just not here to see it—but *I'm* still present. I'm doing what I have to do to keep things going, to work through it. I need you here."

Curtis, now fuming, turned to walk away. He had no interest in continuing the argument he'd been actively trying to avoid, and he needed to cool down. "I'll be back in a few hours," he muttered over his shoulder.

"Oh, and that reminds me," Amy added, "you need to call the lawyer back. He's been trying to get a hold of you for weeks."

A cold twinge of anxiety crawled into his stomach as he climbed into the truck. "Are you kidding me? If you think I'm signing papers, you're out of your damn head."

"No, CURT. That's not what I'm talking about. Your lawyer. I want you to discuss the letters we've been getting." Amy slapped it against his chest before he had the chance to close the door. Then she turned and stormed into the house, slamming the door behind.

Curtis watched before sighing deeply, shutting the door, and departing.

Holding back as long as she could, Amy sat down at the kitchen table, finally surrendering to her affliction. Uncontrollably, the sobbing commenced. There weren't many days that went by where she *wouldn't* cry, as planting on the pseudo smile grew routinely challenging. If she was smiling—always smiling—then nothing was wrong. Makeup ran down her face, and she wiped the tears away with burgundy polished fingertips, smearing mascara across her hands.

In the bathroom, she blew her running nose on a long pull of toilet paper, then washed the remaining makeup from her face in the sink. Using the hand towel to blot her puffy, red eyes. She stared at the growing bags under each. Crow's feet in the corners. Had they always been there? Well, as long as she could remember, anyway. She grimaced at her appearance. Old, worn clothing. Her face. Disgust washed over her.

I could've had anybody...

Calling Amy a beautiful woman was a gross understatement. To describe her would be on par with describing a mythical creature or a work of art. Elusive. Striking. At least that's what Curtis told her his first impression was.

She'd achieved popularity from a young age with her long, wavy, strawberry-blonde hair and fair skin, her cheeks lightly flecked with freckles that only seem to emerge in the summer months. Men who'd hit on her would say she had the face of a Botticelli—also a quote from her favorite 80's Molly Ringwald movie—but she didn't quite think so, especially with her high cheekbones and strong jawline. Amy had always been a pretty girl, the type who could turn any head in a room without even wearing makeup, the type that was *never* single—or at least the type that never knew *how* to be.

What the hell had she become?

Amy returned to the kitchen, still crying, in an attempt to finish preparing dinner for herself and Wes. A bag of frozen vegetables—partially defrosted—sat in a puddle, slumped, lifeless on the counter next to the sink. Red bliss potatoes submerged in a shallow pool awaited the gas flame in a tall pot on the back burner. The savory aroma of roasted chicken filled the room as she opened the oven door for a glance. She snapped on the back burner and turned to the soggy vegetables when she spotted an unopened box of red wine tucked behind the bread bin. She tore into it.

After filling a large piece of stemware, she popped down on the couch. She put back half the glass on her first drink before noticing the open photo album on the coffee table. She peered down at the holiday picnic photo for a moment, which didn't offer any comfort—a memory of her friends who'd recently suffered in some strange tragic incident. Curiously, she pulled another album, a smaller one buried at the bottom of the stack. The photos in it, much older by about a decade and mostly filled with early date nights and day trips, brought her back to the night she and Curtis met and the honeymoon phase which followed.

One could say Curtis was extremely fortunate. Dumb luck. The two met by chance on a casual weekend night out. She had just happened to be at the end of a two-year, dead-end relationship with an obstinate restaurant owner and executive chef, who, to make matters worse, was a tyrant and an alcoholic. In her mind, the relationship was long over, even though she still clung on. The fact that she lived with him didn't help matters. Once she found her comfort zone, she stayed well cemented, so she tended to drag out relations while considering a suitable replacement.

Curtis wasn't the typical guy she'd go for, with the prerequisite of most having at *least* a college degree. Her resume was impressive, though she herself was surprisingly low maintenance. In college, Amy had dated a finance guy, followed by a lawyer and then a doctor, before moving in with the chef and co-owner of a high-end restaurant in Old Saybrook. They worked opposite schedules, and when they did finally spend time together, he was ornery, tired, and miserable from putting in a twelve-plus-hour shift—not to mention annihilated, reeking of tequila.

Amy hated the dating game and didn't relish the fact that she'd soon be right back out there. Still relatively young but growing impatient, she only wanted to settle down—but after wasting a year on verbal and emotional abuse, even she knew she hung on by a thread. Desperate, she spent the last few months of the relationship making a last-ditch effort, spending most weekend nights at the restaurant with a couple of work friends just to squeeze in some *quality time*. That's when she met Curtis.

Curtis's longtime friend, Alan Fogarty, was the Friday and Saturday night bartender. He was one-fourth of the infamous *quartet* along with Russell Foley and Geoffrey Maher during the glory days of high school. Alan was wide receiver on the football team and Curtis's close partner-in-crime.

Alan thoroughly enjoyed his friends showing up at the bar—anything to break the monotony of a long, busy, mostly aggravating shift. The inordinately demanding, pretentious shoreline clientele always managed to strike a throbbing nerve. Of course, that was hardly difficult to achieve; they only had to walk through the front door and sit at his bar. The people that came in having never worked a *real job*, as he'd always say, would sit there and look down upon him—or at least, so he said. He also loathed the executive chef—as many people did—"with the fire of a thousand suns," he also used to say, and in requital, he took it upon himself to hook up his regular guests and his friends, as well as himself. Management had a feeble, inconsistent system of keeping inventory, and no one would miss a half-bottle of Absolut on a busy Saturday.

Curtis would arrive toward the end of dinner service, and Alan would pour some heavy-handed cocktails—their poison of choice: vodka—before being cut from work. Then they would proceed to hit up the local dives, especially their favorite, The Donkey Barn Tavern—an old, wooden-panel sports bar with no heat, no A/C, no tap beer, and no credit cards. And it was *always* full, day and night, with the liveliest bunch of townies that side of the Connecticut River.

Amy, who usually visited on Saturday, decided to come in on a Friday by a curious twist of fate, as she had her mother's milestone birthday party to attend that weekend. On her way out the door, she stopped and walked back into her house, deciding to forgo this particular trip. It was late, and she was tired. She then proceeded to go anyway, not wanting to break her streak of effort. And after an exhausting work week, she needed the getaway, however brief it may be.

She grabbed the last open seat at the bar, which happened to be next to Curtis. Alan knew Amy well, introducing one to the other. Basically, he'd introduce her to just about any of his male regulars, in the hopes she'd go home with them—just to spite his boss.

Curtis had this cynical and self-deprecating sense of humor with a snarky wit, which kept Amy on her toes. She loved a guy who, when she dished out the teasing, could really give it right back to her. The chemistry was instant. He was just a fun person to be around and very outgoing, totally different from her previous, much more rigid suitors. He wasn't jaded by a demanding, stress-inducing job, nor did he spend half the week at the "office"—and although he didn't have a board certification in neurology or have to take the Bar for his job, he was successful. And there was ample money in the trades.

The things they had in common were almost endless, albeit simple, with dining out and attending concert venues among some of their favorites. They both regularly followed the new wave genre of alternative rock music, frequenting venues such as Toad's Place in New Haven, the Hartford Civic Center, and The Meadowlands. They would spend an entire weekend at the casino, which had a lot to offer—dining, comedy shows, live entertainment. Of all activities, they mostly loved to eat—which was maybe why Amy had fallen for a chef—and, having an eclectic taste for food, they frequented all styles of ethnic cuisine. The only argument they faced was over which restaurant to go to. In summer, they toured local wineries during the day and finished the night up at a craft brewery. And once in a while, on special occasions, they liked to lay on the concrete jetty along Saybrook Point, smoke a little pot, and stare into the unbounded galaxy at twilight. The view to Long Island sprawled out, infinite.

Amy's parents seemed less enthusiastic about her decision to "abruptly" leave her boyfriend and immediately move in with Curtis. Amy rarely acted on impulse before, which concerned them, especially considering he wasn't really her "type." So, shortly after Curtis came along, her mother began to give her a hard time. Every chance she got, the older woman would pointedly ask what Amy was doing "wasting her time," expressing that she was "too beautiful and too smart" to settle. Hearing about their quick engagement and subsequent marriage especially displeased her mother, while Amy's father, the reasonable one of the two, trusted his daughter would always do what was best.

Amy had seen a lot of wealth and status by the time she reached twenty-five—still naïve by some people's standards—and she didn't need a lifetime to discover the real secret to life. At the end of the day, she just wanted to be *happy*; and with Curtis, she had never been happier. Compared to other guys in her life, Curtis embodied manliness. He was tough, rugged, rarely clean-shaven; he was affectionate, companionate, and had just the right amount of emotion without coming off as needy. His physique, built like a college athlete, made her swoon; she found keeping her hands off of him incomprehensibly hard. Whether prim and proper in a three-piece suit or dirty and sweaty from the day job or gym, the sight of him instantly turned her on.

Curtis captured the unicorn. She fell fast, and she fell hard.

Amy drained a second glass of wine.

Then the unfathomable happened—something Amy saw happen to other people. Something that could only happen to other people: people on the news, people in the movies, people in a realm outside of her own. But, that night, her husband was involved in a car accident. On his way home from his furtive after-work pitstop at The Donkey Barn, he had fallen asleep at the wheel, exhausted from a twelve-hour day on a Cat 5 installation job at a new time-share development inside Sound View Manor—a prestigious resort, spa, and country club one town over in Westbrook. And he'd killed the other driver. She was irrevocably devastated, and the walls around her began to crumble. She hated that, after his phone call from jail, she was instinctually more concerned about how her parents would react to the news, or worse yet, how it could affect *them*.

With his bail at fifty-thousand dollars, she couldn't just ask her parents for a loan. So disgusted by her husband's gross negligence, selfishness, and lack of consideration for those around him, she wondered how she could have let this disruption happen, grossly unaware of how long it'd been going on. A busy woman herself, she had been blinded by housework, schoolwork, and spending every available minute beyond that with Wes and his increasing developmental needs. Amy avoided visitation, only speaking to Curtis over the phone when essential during his three-month respite at Corrigan Correctional until his plea bargain and subsequent release. Though his friend at Russell Foley's law firm represented him, thankfully reducing the cost of representation, in the end, the expenses still drained the majority of their savings.

Fired from his telecom company, Curtis had to take odd jobs, mostly labor jobs, where people weren't concerned so much with police records and would compensate you any way they pleased. First, he worked at Crazy Bill's, where he became acquainted with Cindi, her family, and Ronald. The dull gig didn't pay well, but dealing with a bickering, alcoholic family stressed him to the point of walking out the door in six months. Having quit drinking also made working around alcohol too much of a temptation. He tried his hand at construction in many areas: masonry, roofing, flooring installation, but again, the pay was mediocre—half of what he was earning previously before OT. He was unlicensed, cheap labor, and working in ninety-degree heat didn't suit him well. Not to mention that his growing temper on the job made him less desirable for subsequent contract work.

At one point, three years into *their* sentence, Curtis and Amy both found themselves out of work for a brutal three-month stretch, right before Curtis found C/Z Corp. Two parents out of work. Stress levels soared, and the resentment piled higher and higher. Amy felt trapped, sharing her bed with a perfect stranger... until eventually, she wasn't. At some point, he'd drifted into the guest bedroom, which suited her fine. Everything he did annoyed her—his mannerisms, his incessant smoking, his oblivious attitude, his constant bitching about work or lack thereof, and his racked-up credit cards and towering bills—all with a fuse that grew shorter as the months progressed. Amy finally broke down, reluctantly asking her parents for a hefty loan to pay the mortgage and keep food on the table. The money came with their unyielding disapproval, as they urged her towards divorce, pleading for her return home, which only broke her heart.

Protecting Wes, who needed his father in his life, now more than ever, was her only priority, despite being uncertain of the current state of her marriage. But she *refused to* fail at it; it just wasn't in her. And although Amy wasn't entirely infallible, everyone eventually has their breaking point. Even she.

TEN

As he hauled up I-93, Curtis ripped drags off a cigarette, glancing back from the road to the letter. I-93, no matter what time of day, suffered from congestion. And at this particular moment, the tail end of rush hour, he sat almost at a standstill as he approached the Tobin Bridge and tunnel, trying to pass through Boston. He thought I-93 may very well be the worst highway in America, and the fact that it traversed one of the most densely populated cities in the country validated his theory. *I don't understand why they haven't redesigned this fucking highway!* Automobiles ahead abruptly stopped every ten to twenty feet, the red flash from taillights catching the corner of his eye, and he kept slamming on his brakes, trying to finish the letter.

Curtis dialed the law office on his quickly draining, low battery cell phone, hoping there was enough juice to at least finish the call. After the office picked up and patched him through, he sat waiting on hold, his mind darting around the argument with Amy. The guilt of what transpired gave him an unsettling feeling in the pit of his stomach. On an average visit, they'd be too busy avoiding one another for a fight to ensue, but this was something much different—much different. He had only seen such an aggressive spark to her otherwise calm, benevolent demeanor once before, and its return startled him.

Attorney Russell Foley finally picked up his line after an abnormally long hold time. "Curtis? How's it going—hey, did you really just tell my assistant you needed to speak with a '*Mr. Raw-dog*?'" His tone sounded unamused.

Curtis smiled, highly entertained by the old nickname. "You mean you don't go by that at the office?"

Russ sighed. "No. Nobody refers to me by that here. We went over that last time we spoke."

Curtis loved to give Russ a hard time, especially now, since he'd gone *soft*. They'd been friends since the tenth grade, a time when Russ *was* the ball breaker, before finally coming into his own, finishing school, and settling down with a girl he met first year of law school, now his wife and the mother of his triplets. Many nicknames had been thrown around during their adolescence, some worse than others, but *Raw-dog Russell* had stuck—branded due to his allergy to latex and his tenacity of persuading women to sleep with him through high school and college. Curtis had always found that impressive considering Russ had terrible acne and a profound overbite until his mid-twenties. His ability to debate had started at an early age. And, unfortunately for Russ, Curtis refused to let it go.

"My apologies, *Raw*. So, what's going on? You seem busy over there. You gotta minute, orrr…?"

"Uhhh, yes—yeah, I can talk, what's up?" Russ said, the sound of shuffling papers echoing through the phone.

"Amy faxed you a letter a week or so ago, she said?"

"Umm, let me look. Yes, yes, she did. Hold on…" He called over to his receptionist and asked about the letter, as if he had forgotten it came. After a few moments of more shuffling papers, he spoke into the phone once more. "Yup, yup, I have it right here. What is it you want to know?"

"Well, how 'bout, what the Christ does it mean!? It looks like someone wants to buy my house? They must think I live in the projects. Did you see what they want to give me?" Curtis laughed.

"Yup, okay, now I remember. Yeah, she sent me this almost a month ago. I looked into it. This particular letter is an offer on the house, but it's only the beginning." Russ warned.

"Whaaa—whattaya mean?"

"Well, I've seen these letters before. It looks like there's a private enterprise looking to purchase the remaining properties and the surrounding land around your property."

Curtis blinked, flabbergasted. "Uh... okay?"

"It looks like they already started." Russ said, flipping through pages once more. "There're the two houses on your street already vacant, and it looks like they've been targeting your other neighbor, uhhh—Cavanaugh? They made some sort of offer to him three months ago."

"Really? I didn't even realize the other families moved." Curtis wondered how he hadn't noticed, especially with the chaos of the Cavanaugh incident.

"Yup, they did. They took low offers for whatever reason and moved. But all of them were longtime homeowners, though—no mortgage to worry about, right? Now, I'm guessing this is the first step. What it looks like they might consider if you refuse to sell, of course, is to take legal action to try and force you and your neighbor out."

"What? They can't fucking force me out of my own house. What are we in, Russia? No. I owe twice as much as what they want to give me. Did you see that shit? And then what, I'm supposed to finish paying a mortgage on a house I don't even own!?" Curtis gripped the steering wheel with such force, his knuckles whitened.

"They've done it before, dude. If you don't take the offer, they're going to try to use the power of eminent domain to seize your property."

"What in the curious fuck is that?"

"What? Eminent domain?"

"Yeah. That." Curtis's mind went blank—so infuriated that he could no longer think straight.

"Basically, it's the legal taking of property, generally by a state or a government municipality for what they call *public use*, which ultimately translates to anything they deem worthy for the benefit of economic development," Russ explained.

"They can do that!?" Curtis huffed, bewildered.

"It's the Federal Government—they can do whatever the hell they want. It's not terribly uncommon. It's just that you don't really hear much about it."

"What about *my* rights?" The cigarette fell out of Curtis's mouth, rolling down his shirt and onto the floor. He bent down, grabbed it, then resurfaced, slamming on the brakes, skidding out of the lane onto the shoulder. The traffic had slightly let up, moving at twenty miles per hour, then the car in front of him had abruptly stopped, leaving him mere inches from colliding. The phone dropped, but Russ kept speaking as if nothing had happened.

BEEP! BEEEEEP!

"GO AND FUCK YOURSELF!" Curtis yelled from his window as the car behind him laid on the horn. "Sonova-cocksucker..."

"You all right over there, man?"

"This fucking bullshit Boston traffic is going to be the death of me, I tell ya."

Russ chuckled. "Deep breaths, buddy. Deep breaths. Well, anyway, that's the beauty of the Fifth Amendment, my friend. It sure as hell wasn't meant to benefit the taxpayer. Well, maybe initially they were. These clauses were written with enough loopholes, so they can be basically bent to their will."

Curtis smiled with disdain, exhaling cigarette smoke. "Heh... land of the free!"

"With the constitution, there's nothing the government can't destroy, my friend. But anyway, I digress... you don't remember when all that eminent domain stuff happened? God, when was it, eight, maybe nine years ago? It was big news, man."

"I moved here seven years ago." Curtis lit a fresh cigarette with the tip of the one he had just finished.

"The whole thing was such a huge, goddamn disaster, the Supreme Court subsequently made it very difficult for any entity to seize private property."

"Where was this?" Curtis had a hard time believing what he was hearing.

"Uhhh, give me a second to think..." Russ flipped through a few more pages. "Yeah, they had a concise time frame to vacate, too. Actually, I remember I had a potential client who told me some people completely trashed their places, left behind cars, all sorts of shit. They didn't even bother shutting their front doors when they left. He told me he heard some families didn't even take *anything*.

They took the check and just took off. His name was Lavigne, and I only remember that because his family owns that popular seafood restaurant on the Old Saybrook shoreline—you know, that place Fogarty got fired from for all those after-hours poker games."

"Wow. Yeah, I remember." Curtis grinned. "Best lobster rolls on the shoreline."

"Yup. So Lavigne came to see me for representation—he'd just moved in the year before and dropped like thirty-K in renovations. He was not happy."

"So, what happened?"

"I didn't take the case. My small firm isn't equipped to take on big pharma. I felt bad. The guy had a pregnant wife and two young kids. I remember now—it was the neighborhood of Laurel Hill, if I recall."

"Laurel... Laurel Hill? You mean that deserted street right down my road!?"

"Uhhh, yeah, that's right! You're right by the old Hock Pharmaceuticals, aren't you?" Russ recalled. "I don't really remember the details, but basically, they forced the people out of their homes, paid them very little, then did nothing with the land. I believe the facility shut down not long after. There was some sort of accident, then hundreds of people lost their jobs, I think? They have the New London office, which they originally built as a replacement, anyway."

"Really? From what I saw this week, it looks like the island is in full operation," Curtis recalled.

"I don't think it ever really closed completely. It was originally a government-run facility back in its heyday, and for whatever reason, *they* closed operations, and a pharmaceutical company moved in.

Look, I gotta get going. I need to close up this office and send everyone home before this storm comes. Call me if you receive any more letters or anything you feel that is of a threatening manner. Take care of yourself."

"Thanks." Curtis tossed the cell phone in the passenger seat.

ELEVEN

Parking took ten minutes, which was entirely *too* long to find a sufficient spot, and then, of course, as soon as Curtis stepped out of the truck, the rain started to come down. He ran through the automatic door, straight into bedlam, and screeched to a halt, taken aback. Lines of shopping carts blocked the corridor, snaking around the corner to the check-out area while additional carts pooled in front of every aisle, trying to reach any register as the PA system announced Mondo-Mart was closing in an hour. Curtis squeezed through the jam, pushing through hordes of consumers who frantically bought up merchandise as if the end of days had come. He couldn't believe the panic as inconsiderate passersby repeatedly bumped him from either side. The uproar nearly blotted out the PA announcement, which warned, yet again, of the imminent closing, instructing customers to *please finish purchasing items.*

The Mondo-Mart Superstore—a New England chain—loomed vast before him, a massive all-in-one department store, grocery store, and electronics powerhouse similar to and in direct competition with Target Stores. The main difference was in theme color, with Mondo-Mart's theming forest green. And in addition to its many convenient, self-indulgent offerings, Mondo-Mart came equipped with an in-house coffee chain and express fast-food pizza eatery, because God forbid that you *ever* left. This particular location had two levels and walking through gave Curtis anxiety—not only from the crowd, but from knowing there was much more work still needing to be finished. At the moment, he just wanted to find the escalator up to Simmons' office.

Curtis, subconsciously utilizing his knowledge of Ohm's Law, managed to locate the path of least resistance—down the frozen food aisle along the far-left side of the store. He squeezed by one very homely, morbidly obese lady, watching as she wheeled a cart full of gallon ice cream tubs and frozen meals with one hand while dragging behind a screaming, ginger child with the other. People around him stockpiled cases of water, flashlights, extension cords, batteries of any and all sizes, canned goods, bread, milk, eggs, toilet paper, you name it. Curtis could never comprehend, which drove him mad, why people bought up crazy things like milk, eggs, and other perishable goods, *especially* ones that required refrigeration. *If that power goes, and it certainly will, that's just a fucking waste.*

Shaking his head, Curtis walked behind the Customer Service desk, wedged inside an inlet between *Home Goods* and *Electronics*—it too had quite a line—and entered a back room with an empty employee lounge and three small offices, one of which was the general manager's office. The plaque on the door read *GM - Orlando Simmons*. Curtis pushed the knob, finding the room empty. He figured with the store this mobbed, Simmons must be out on the floor, putting out patron fires.

Tempted to look for the tool bag and make a clean break, he stepped in, but Simmons emerged from around the corner, beaming ear to ear. Tall, dark, and lanky, the man always dressed to the nines.

Curtis found his outfits impressive, albeit always—ALWAYS profoundly over the top. Simmons kept himself deliberately clean-cut; his frosted-tipped dreads twisted into a high bun and canopied over a skin-tight fade and a strategically cropped goatee. He then finished the look with black, square-framed, non-prescription eyeglasses. The blush and rose, paisley bow tie said it all as he sauntered over to Curtis, hands resting on his hips.

"Tsk, tsk, tsk, Mr. Curtis. You never, never, *NEVER* leave your tool bag at the Mondo-Mart!" He waved his index finger with a smirk.

"Hi, Mr. Simmons," Curtis mumbled, slightly embarrassed, but more so distracted by the man's shiny, lime-green suit.

"*Please!* How many times do I have to tell you—call me *Orlando*!" He smiled, enunciating. "And don't you worry, suga'—I kept them safe under *my* desk, uh-huh."

"Oh... okay. Yeah, sorry, I was in a bit of a rush. Had a family emergency and left them behind. I feel so stupid—I *never* leave my tool bag anywhere."

"*GASP!*" Orlando touched his chest with over-exaggerated shock. "Well, I hope everything's all right! You look very tense. Come on in, sit down, we'll talk about it." He motioned toward the inside of the office as he walked in.

"OH... um—I really, I uh—I can't. I should really get back on the road with this storm coming and all, you know?" Curtis stammered, trying to be polite but also honest.

"Oh, I completely understand. It looks like it's getting bad out there! Well, if you change your mind, my door... is *always* open." Orlando patted his shoulder, then lightly squeezed it. "My, my, you are a strong one!"

"Uh, thanks, Orlando. I'll keep that in mind." He shrugged, looking for a segue out of this conversation. "Hey, uh, why is everybody going nuts out there, buying up the whole store?"

Simmons laughed, shook his head, and sat down behind his immaculate desk, consisting of only four items. In one corner sat a twenty-inch, flat-screen computer monitor; in the other, situated beside a phone, rested a sizeable at-a-glance calendar—blank. Centered directly above the calendar stood a Newton's Cradle. Lounging back, Simmons reached across the desk, lifted a shiny ball bearing, then released it.

"Remember the Blizzard of '78? Oh, what am I talking about—you're *way* too young to remember that." Orlando giggled. "This happens anytime, every time, it's projected to rain longer than *a day*. They're like scared children out there. That's why I hide in my cozy little office with my essential oils and my meditation CDs."

Curtis shrugged. "I'm not that young."

The nation had arrived to work that February morning in 1978 with rain and walked out to four feet of dense snow, with wind drifts ten to twenty feet high by the day's end. Some, who managed to leave work early to "beat the weather," ended up trapped in cars on the interstate. They would spend days buried in shallow, snowy graves before being dug out by cross-country skiers and snowmobilers, the only ones able to reach them, either to be rescued or found dead, having succumbed to asphyxiation. The coincidental New Moon had brought in massive tides, resulting in coastal flooding. Merciless waves lassoed thousands of shoreline homes out to sea, while explosive cyclogenesis crippled the Northeastern seaboard, leaving it in a perpetual state of darkness. *That* was the epitome of a natural disaster, which Curtis would never forget. He, like many, had spent the surprise catastrophic nor' easter—or "Storm Larry," as it had been coined—grossly unprepared, literally trapped at home for weeks.

"I actually do remember," he continued, focusing on the pendulum. For reasons unknown, he began to feel a little more at ease. "I missed school for about fourteen days. Had my ninth birthday during that time; we were shut-in."

"Bet that was nice!"

"It wasn't. I lost my father that week," Curtis said matter-of-factly. The bearing swung, smacking the stationary ones, mirroring the effect on the opposite end. As he stared at it, the clanking impact of each return rose in a slow crescendo.

Orlando gasped. "Curtis, my god, I—am—SO—sorry!"

"It's okay. It was a long time ago. My parents couldn't get to work, you know. There was a mountain of snow in front of the door. I remember them complaining about lost wages the entire time for days. And we had one TV, and sports and news seemed to *always* be on. And I remember being so bored, just sitting on the couch. I think my father started to get cabin fever or something, so he forced his way out to begin shoveling, and out there, he had a heart attack. My mother went to go check on him, and he was just face down in the snow.

"Thankfully, by that time, the main roads were somewhat drivable, so we didn't have to wait long for the ambulance, but it didn't matter. The EMT said it was pretty instant. He had been dead at least two hours." Curtis, still staring at the cradle, shook his head to release himself from the grips of his trance. He couldn't believe he had just said all that to Orlando, but there was something oddly comforting about the strange man. Whether just joking or being awkwardly flirtatious, his personality always felt authentic.

"Sorry to hear that," Orlando murmured, his face somber.

Curtis nodded, slightly embarrassed, and turned to exit. "Life goes on, right?"

"Amen, honey. Hey, do me a favor—tell Miguel to *call me*." Orlando giggled and motioned the telephone sign with his hand up to the side of his head.

"You got it," Curtis responded, slightly bewildered as he walked out of the office.

"He is such a trip that one! I don't know how you get any work done with him around?"

Yeah, I don't either...

Before moving beyond Simmons' office, Curtis quickly opened his bag, grabbing the folded cloth inside the pouch. The gold wedding band gleamed under the lambency of fluorescent lighting, as pristine as his wedding day. He'd never been a fan of wearing it, to begin with, having developed a habit of subconsciously fidgeting with it, inducing a new distraction. He'd take it off while at work to protect it from scratches and for safety reasons; its electrical conductivity made it a dangerous object to wear, which provided the perfect excuse to be relieved from its constraints. Mostly, it irritated the hell out of him while constantly working with his fingers. His complicated and confusing marital status hindered him from returning it to its proper place each day after work, and, knowing he wouldn't return for several weeks, he'd decided to just keep it off.

He slid the ring on, then reached back inside the pouch, pulling out his father's Oak Ridge bone handle folding knife: four inches of stainless steel tucked away into a textured ecru handle with

CCR engraved on the side. The blade, slightly tarnished from decades of sporadic use—mostly from his early teen years in the boy scouts—was his oldest possession, the only thing preserved from childhood. He pushed it in his back pocket.

CCR, Curtis thought, his initials and also those of *Credence Clearwater Revival*, his father's favorite rock group (though he mostly listened to *Elvis, Jerry Lee Lewis, Little Richard*). He now wondered if that was a coincidence, though he didn't believe in them. Though he'd retained only sparse childhood memories over the years, he briefly recalled, at either six or seven, a period of making weekly dump runs. His father's eight-track cassette tape had filled the cab of his 1970 crimson Ford pickup with the swampy bayou sound of country, rhythm, and blues. "Bad Moon Rising" was always his favorite.

Curtis quickly moved through the store, which seemed slightly less chaotic than when he first arrived, but the store's front remained as busy as ever. Shoppers in front of him nearing the exit began to slow down, bottlenecking, so he stopped to check his work pager, wondering if Amy had tried to reach him. The pager wasn't even on. Seeing the weather appearing to worsen while reassessing the panic-stricken crowd, he began to worry about whether she and Wes were safe. He should have stayed, he knew, even though he'd prepared the house best he could. Stubborn as he was, he questioned his decision to run all the way back—but his anxiety hadn't given him a choice. It rarely did. His heart sank into the pit of his stomach, and he wondered what was now in store for him when he returned. The last time he truly felt this way was after his arrest, and he thought for sure he'd be divorced. She hadn't spoken to him for an entire month thereafter.

Hordes of the intolerant, urgently entering or exiting, pushed shopping carts into a traffic jam, pervading any available sidewalk space outside the front entrance to avoid pounding rainfall. A middle eastern family with a heavy, older gentleman yelling at his children in a language Curtis recognized as Arabic nudged past. *He shuddered.* Others pushed on either side of him as they shoved through the doorway chute like cattle. With his patience increasingly wearing thin, Curtis finally looked to see what the holdup was. His hands began to quiver. The street slowly pulled away from his peripherals. He needed OUT.

"MOVE!" snarled the woman next to him.

"Huh?" He mumbled.

Curtis turned, recognizing her as the obese woman with the cart full of ice cream. Her face, inches from his, was covered in massive, oozing boils and black, pulsating lesions. Her pallid lips cracked open with dried, umber scabs crusted over. Her teeth, stained green and tinged with black mucus, dripped from her broken lips down to her tatted cleavage, protruding from a torn, form-fitting *Hello Kitty* tank top. Dried blood had caked over her flaky scalp under matted clumps of black, greasy hair. The face boils self-lanced, viscous, whitish orange puss dribbling from the surface. The most terrifying thing was her eyes, irises frosted over, with bloodshot sclera glaring into his soul.

"MOVE WHILE YOU *STILL* CAN!" She thundered in a deep, raspy tone. Black saliva shot from her mouth, splattering across Curtis's face.

The color drained from Curtis, and his heart rate shot up, a bitter chill shivering through him. Frantically, he dropped the pager and tool bag, then collapsed, gasping for air, trying to assimilate what stood before his panicked eyes, which had since gone black after vertigo struck—bright confetti bursting across his line of sight.

"Mister, are you all right? Mister?"

Curtis, on all fours, sucked back several deep breaths. After a few moments, he grabbed his belongings, standing up slowly—still lightheaded. And, with a delicate glance, he looked back at the lady.

She stared at him with profound concern. "I was talking to my son. Sorry to startle you, Mister. I said, MOVE IT!" She continued to yell and drag her screaming child behind her. Her face, though adversely unbecoming, seemed ordinary. Other than a bulging, hairy mole, her skin gleamed, spotless, and her eyes—a blue hue. Her hair, medium brown and straight, sat just above her shoulders. Other than having the appearance of a welfare case, she looked healthy.

Curtis forced his way through the unrelenting crowd, shoving an elderly woman's shopping cart entirely from his path and knocking it on its side; round, gallon-size water jugs rolled into the parking lot. The wind gusted, sending the rain showering down at different angles as he ran to his truck, trying to avoid the downpour, albeit without any success. Drenched, he jumped into the cab and closed his eyes to catch his breath. Heavy, persisting rain pelted the pickup, the sound resonating as if an entire choir was sitting in the bed, performing a snare drum solo. *That wasn't real, that wasn't real, that wasn't real, that was not fucking real.*

Curtis knew that his stress levels had risen dramatically in recent weeks, and, in addition to body clock sensitivity, progressive insomnia had finally begun to affect him adversely. He would spend restless days laying in the hotel room after work, with the curtains drawn and a bedsheet over him for added hindrance to incite unconsciousness. Mostly, he'd drift along in a seemingly perpetual state of lucidness—a fine line between two distressed worlds, never really knowing if he slept. And suddenly, he'd be in the middle of a somewhat hyperbolic interpretation of his current, cursed life: at home arguing with Amy, who'd be in tears; cowering in a room, terrified; or stuck inside a cloudy Mondo-Mart stock room, inordinately frustrated with a maniacally laughing, smoke exhaling Miguel. But the worst was when he would get trapped in a version he most feared, and the voices would come—the jumbled, incessant cries for help. Begging. Pleading, as he would stand by, paralyzed. Powerless.

But it wasn't until now, this moment, he became cognizant of his altered perception of reality and the resulting repercussions manifesting from his latent subconscious. He no longer knew if he was grossly under-rested or heavily overworked—physically, mentally. Could he even differentiate between the two? He did know one thing...

The visions were back.

TWELVE

Amy poured herself a fourth glass of wine as she sat, grading papers in front of an empty dinner plate at the kitchen table; the oven-stuffer she had prepared before Curtis decided to leave, now rested in brown congealed liquid, picked apart, and pushed to the side.

A bottomless box of wine had sat handy on the kitchen counter for months, wedged between the microwave and an over-filled wooden bread bin. One box contained four bottles worth of wine, and, until recently, she had found herself going through one at *least* twice a week. The problem—well, she hadn't seen it as much of a problem, not originally—was that with a box of wine, she could never discern precisely how much she consumed. She preferred a crisp, New Zealand sauvignon blanc, but since storing boxed wine in the fridge proved difficult, she had switched to pinot noir, which was just as light and didn't need to be chilled. Then, she had stopped drinking altogether.

But tonight, when she returned to the kitchen, crying, she'd spotted the last, unopened box of Corbett Canyon, sitting beside a stale loaf of Wonder Bread, and staring at her longingly. She had stared back.

Tree limbs, barely visible through the downpour, swayed outside, stretched back and forth by loud, tenacious winds. She watched the rain come down in buckets, whipping the windows and sliding door; the intensity came and went in waves. The sound reminded her of a jar of marbles endlessly spilling onto glass. Strangely soothing. The hour started to grow late, and she repeatedly looked back to the digital stove clock and her cell phone, now concerned for Curtis—who remained out there, somewhere, with the weather taking a turn for the worse.

In the living room, Hartford's local news aired with the volume on low, discussing every facet of the current weather development: inches of downfall, property damage, power outages, storm projections. Amy would glance over but kept losing focus, with the alcohol taking its proper effect. Last she knew, officials had issued a flood warning for most of the state, with the shoreline in a flash flood watch. The screen, slightly blurred from her perspective, had since blared some new, much more pertinent information. What was initially branded as a tropical storm had been remarkably upgraded...

Her jaw dropped. "A fucking category-three hurricane?"

A fifth glass.

As the alcohol absorbed and began to distort Amy's perception of reality, her mind raced uncontrollably. She could no longer concentrate on schoolwork; she kept reading the same blurred equations on one student's quiz over and over. All she could think about was how she couldn't take much more of Curtis—his blatant disregard for her feelings, his status quo mentality. Maybe it was finally time to reach out for help. But hell, who? The only people she knew to turn to were her parents, and she was *not* going to prove them right, showing up with her tail between her legs.

Besides, considering Wes made wanting to leave Curtis difficult. There were too many moving parts, and making a decision such as this, that could drastically alter their lives for better or for worse, wasn't something she could do to her little boy, no matter how bad things got with her husband. Still, she couldn't stop thinking of the possibilities. What mainly troubled her—and she hated that this thought was even a thought—was whether she could find another man that would support her and a son with special needs. Who would welcome that burden?

In her drunken state, she recalled the night she gave birth, and, at that moment, discerning she could never love anything in this world more. Named after Curtis's father, Wes had arrived three weeks early at six pounds, ten ounces, with curly, light blonde hair and bright blue eyes. He never cried, always slept through the night without issue. A perfect baby. They were lucky—or so they thought.

The concern began when Wes hadn't formed vocabulary by his first birthday. By eighteen to twenty-four months, he said a couple words here and there, but to those around, he appeared to have a developmental deficiency in comparison to other children his age. By the time he started mastering puzzles, his limited vocabulary comprised around thirty words. Initially, she thought maybe he suffered from shyness, a phase of which he'd soon grow out. Unfortunately, as reported by the school psychologist halfway through kindergarten, that assumption proved incorrect, and Amy found herself—by herself—searching for answers. Curtis had just left for a three-month job in Boston, leaving her to deal with the leg work. Although Wes exceeded all intellectual and standardized testing with high marks, he remained socially apprehensive, and his reticence forced him into special needs programs, mostly occupational and speech therapy. The out-of-pocket expense to treat Wes soon surmounted what Amy's insurance covered, and Curtis didn't have coverage with his present employment situation.

Amy's eyes grew heavy; five glasses of wine and the exhaustion from being up since five a.m.—dealing with unbridled chaos at school—began to take its toll. She wondered where Wes had gone, turning toward the empty living room. For a moment, she considered going to check his bedroom, but everything felt heavy, as if a lead weight anchored her down. Unable to keep her eyes open any longer, she passed out at the kitchen table on a pile of papers.

Wes, lost in his own element, played in the basement, a common nightly occurrence. He spent hours down there in the dim lighting, engrossed in make-believe. For an eight-year-old, he had quite the collection of action figures; if he didn't have one in his hand, he instead held a controller for a video game console or an implement for drawing or coloring. However, nothing made him happier or more focused than completing puzzles or—his absolute favorite thing to do—building with Lego bricks. An entire universe existed in Wes's bedroom, consisting of Harry Potter and Star Wars sets. Surrounding the movie-themed scenes lay an entire city block with a police station, firehouse, theater, bank, hotel, and an assembly square. The little town provided another reason for his frequent adventures in the basement; his bedroom had little space to walk, let alone play. Still, the crowded upstairs space possessed its advantages, allowing him to bring every character into one giant, blended universe, an amalgamation of fantasy storylines. He loved having Godzilla stomp through downtown Lego City, swallowing up little brick men while an army brigade of GI Joe men rolled in to save the day, aided by Spider-man and the X-Men.

On this particular evening, Wes decided that he would build a fortress large enough to support himself and his action figure universe, using the highly secluded, wide-open space of the basement. He brought blankets, building blocks, and cardboard boxes downstairs, cutting and carving the latter to replicate housing and building structures. Then he stepped back, admiring the elaborate structure in the far corner of the room.

The basement lacked sufficient lighting, but it possessed a good deal of space with high—though dingy—ceilings and wall-to-wall concrete, between which sat the washer and dryer unit, a workbench, and myriad storage boxes filled with years' worth of junk. An old sofa sat under a layer of dusty sheets on one side of the room, creating a snowy mountain for his X-Men to climb, and the Chastains' high-end mahogany furniture accumulated on the other, with a round dining room table, a buffet hutch with wall unit, and a grandfather clock all forming potential landscapes for toy battles. Near his city, his dad's pump, which he'd been instructed not to touch, stood in its sinkhole—currently, the Lego mines.

The rain beat fiercely overhead, continuing to fall in buckets. A stream of water permeated Forrest Street, flowing down, pooling in front of the Reynolds' house—the storm drains overflowing. The basin of the Yantic rose, ingesting the mainland foot by foot. The wind gusts blew seventy miles an hour, slamming into the houses again and again, as if to rip them from their distressed foundations.

The river, finally reaching the house, began flooding the basement—and Wes's multiverse fortress happened to be erected in the very spot where the unleveled floor sloped. Unrelenting water pooled around his cardboard buildings and scattered toys as the "mines" kicked on. Wes beamed, more than excited to include the growing puddle in his game. Superheroes took to underwater battles with sinking ships full of Lego men, who suffered unmerciful deaths by drowning. The rising tides formed the perfect environment for Godzilla to emerge with furious vengeance, setting down on Lego City, swallowing up GI men on a path of destruction. The limitless ocean expansion allowed for intersecting storylines between various characters, creating an integrated macrocosm for them to live.

Pure bliss.

The "mines," now submerged and mostly forgotten, stalled out, and the rising water level accelerated. The back wall heavily perspired, thin streams gliding down from the bottom of the window frame. A faint scratching noise beyond the wall caused Wes to briefly take notice, but with the knocking and rattling sounds of the rain and the wailing of heavily shifting winds, the noise proved difficult to discern. It would start, and he'd look up; it would stop, and he'd continue his game. But soon, the noise increased, becoming loud enough to pique his curiosity and deflect his attention from aqua-zilla. He dropped his toy, which disappeared under the swell, and sloshed through the water toward the wall. A coin-sized piece of concrete chipped off, falling into the water, followed by a few more, splashing—*plop*—*plop*—*plop*, as they landed.

Then, it cracked. Wes backed up slowly, watching the wall. The four-foot, horizontal fracture spider-webbed down to the floor and up to the window frame before shattering, spewing clods of rock and silt in every direction. The breach in the foundation caused the boy to trip over himself, moving out of the way. He fell back into the rapidly accumulating flood pool.

A surge of pressure came forth, releasing from behind the aperture, mud, and concrete spilling out. Wes lay, almost submerged, watching as water rushed past him, fearing that the entire side of the house was giving in. Unfortunately, his predicament was much worse and more terrifying than he could have ever expected. What emerged from the slushy deposit froze him in his place.

A muddy muzzle, followed by a head with large, white ovals, rose from the murky deluge. Wes stared in horror as clouded eyes gazed back at him. The broad, almost round snout twitched, loaded with long, translucent whiskers; its front teeth protruded from its mouth, long and gleaming, tapering down past the jawline. Its maw opened wide, letting out a vociferous *squeal*, which in turn, Wes reciprocated, each resonating through the house.

THIRTEEN

Amy jumped off the chair as if hit with a shot of adrenaline. The wine had thoroughly sedated her; she must have nodded off. Still disoriented upon waking, her brain struggled to catch up as she panned the room for Wes. The screams continued in rapid succession. Amy, now in a panic, darted through the house, then upstairs, into each closed bedroom, yelling for her son. She stopped to catch her breath, panting and nauseated with anxiety, the room partially spinning on an angle. She couldn't tell where the shrieks came from, but they sounded increasingly unnerving, growing dire. Just as she was about to lose it, she suddenly realized where he must be.

The basement door hung slightly ajar, and after she flew down the upstairs staircase for a forceful entry, it swung open, then slammed shut behind her. Amy stopped short on the landing, gripping the railing at the top of the hollow, wooden steps. She couldn't believe the scene before her, and she froze, scanning over the havoc, which resulted in a momentary lapse as to why she first ran in. Wes didn't appear to be anywhere amongst the stacked clutter. She hollered for him, cautiously maneuvering through the frigid water.

A squeal directed her focus across the basement, where she saw some... *thing* emerge from beyond the foundation into the flood. Amy's eyes widened in disbelief; her jaw dropped, fear electrifying every nerve. Her throat tightened, shortening her breath and preventing her from screaming, although like hell, she tried. All she could do was swiftly glance around for Wes. The lights began to dim, and the room fell silent. Finally, she spotted her son, standing on the rattling buffet hutch and shaking violently, debilitated by shock. Amy darted over, quickly pulling him off, and aimed back toward the door. Wes tightly wrapped around her torso as she fired up the stairs and pulled back on the doorknob—only to slip right off. Stumbling backward, she tripped down the few steps, landing in the shallows. Her head smacked the cement, the water alleviating only some of the impact. Squeezing Wes with one arm, she rolled over and sprinted right back up the stairs.

Her wet hand grabbed at the knob again, shaking it vehemently, but it wouldn't budge; two hands came next, but still nothing. Surging with trepidation, she whimpered, peering back over her shoulder, cursing erratically as she shook the door.

It was jammed.

The beast fully emerged from the muddy debris, quickly closing in on the stairs. Amy could hear it grunting, sloshing through the water as she turned to search for something, anything. A metal folding chair sat close by, up against the side of the staircase. She bent down and grabbed it, her son still clinging to her side. As she came up, the beast lunged at her, mouth open, and Amy fell back against the arm rail, the end of the chair lodged in its squealing orifice. She held the jaws back with everything she had, screaming, while the beast tried to advance forward. It thrashed, missing her legs, striking the wooden support beams of the steps with protracted, razor claws, tearing away the bottom planks. Amy slid down a step as a shallow blow from a swipe struck her calf through wet denim; she screamed out in pain. Quickly twisting the chair, she cocked back the beast's head, thrusting it off the staircase, losing her shield in the process. The beast fell into the rising water, and Amy made a blind run for it.

Hurrying across the flooding basement, she searched for a place for cover, her son still hanging on to her for dear life. A small pantry cupboard, connected to the upper wall and running lengthwise above the workbench, caught her eye. She climbed atop the bench and opened a cabinet, yanking everything out to the water. With a sudden strength she had never imagined, she managed to pry Wes off, immediately boosting him into the opening. Then, shutting the door behind him, she looked around for an elevated spot to fit herself. One section of the ceiling had metal rods running perpendicular across wooden boards, storing kayaks, skis, and other awkward sporting equipment. She leaped from the bench to a dining room table, then to the hutch, where she reached for the rod.

The beast sprung from the murky flood while Amy pulled herself up, missing her legs by mere inches before falling back to the water, empty-handed. It rose on hind legs and clawed at the wall, slicing through the soft rock as it reached for the ceiling. Amy grabbed a plastic oar, repeatedly jabbing the creature to prevent it from gaining footing. It slipped back under and was gone. She huddled, trapped in the rafters, freezing, dripping wet, shaking, wanting nothing more than for her husband to return.

Then, the power went out.

Fourteen

Curtis reached Norwich in darkness. Though he drove in four-wheel, the wind slammed against either side of the truck, causing it to sway. The viciousness of the weather worried him; he had never driven in such chaos. But beyond the disquiet of the dreadful weather conditions, his own stubbornness frightened him most of all. He knew the second he pulled out of the driveway; leaving was a bad idea. The idea of potentially poor driving conditions and possibly another automobile accident concerned him enough, but the repercussions of leaving after a blowout with Amy scared the shit out of him. He opened a fresh pack of cigarettes and lit one to calm his nerves.

Driving through what the radio had just deemed a hurricane, and nearly suffering a mental breakdown at his workplace, didn't much help either. He fought a constant internal battle—a battle often lost to abated restraint. Making justifications and shifting blame elsewhere always seemed easier, safer than asking for help. And as much as he sometimes wished to show a little vulnerability, such as this very moment, he found himself unable to stand up and face his subconscious, unable to shut out that little, detrimental voice inside his head.

He couldn't see a single soul on the road. Not surprising. One would have to be out of their goddamned mind to be out in this shit. The bright lights of his truck only shone so far, allowing Curtis to just barely avoid driving through fallen branches and busted tree limbs, albeit while speeding forty-five miles per hour. Powerlines and traffic lights swung wildly in the blotted night sky. The rain had let up a bit by the time Curtis reached Forest Street. He searched for the glow of his house as he drove down, but saw nothing, as if he had passed into a void. He thought back to the afternoon and couldn't remember if he had fueled the generator; he thought no, he must have. *Maybe Amy doesn't know how to use it?* The notion immediately agitated him.

The garage door stood open when he pulled up, lights shining in. Everything inside looked wet, as if someone hosed out the room; the workbench and everything on it—drenched, as well as the metal shelving that housed his electric tools. His face flushed with anger as he peered through the cracked windshield. Grabbing the Maglite from the glovebox, he stepped out into the mini stream covering the driveway and sloshed through the muddy lawn to check the generator's fuel line. Seeing it was full, he started it up and headed back toward his home, stepping into the kitchen.

"Amy? Any reason you're sitting in a dark house? I had the generator all set up in the garage there," Curtis said calmly, desperately trying to keep his cool. "What are you doing—Amy!?"

He grabbed a dish towel hanging from the oven handle and began drying his hair, then threw his wet jacket on the back of a chair in the dining room, where he saw the finished, yet abandoned, dinner. He picked up the boxed wine, light in his hands, and stared at it, exhaling deeply.

While he paced through the house, the rooms slowly began illuminating. Assuming Amy had passed out, he walked up to the bedroom to check on her, feeling relieved that the argument wouldn't continue—at least for tonight. When he saw an empty bed, he turned for Wes's bedroom, which soon yielded the same vacant space. Starting to panic, he called her cell phone, which immediately went to voicemail.

"Amy—you here?" Curtis yelled. When he reached the bottom of the stairs, he called out again.

"Down here," a muffled voice called back from below him.

"Amy? Where are you?"

"The basement door is jammed!"

Curtis, now annoyed that his wife locked herself in, sauntered over to the door and pulled at the knob. He couldn't get it to budge. "Damn it. Why were you down there, anyway?"

No response.

"Amy?"

He heard a scraping sound, crumbling rocks, and then a shriek.

"Amy!? What's going on in there!?"

Now concerned, Curtis yanked at the knob, vehemently trying to shimmy it open to no avail. He decided his steel-toed boot was the next best solution and stomped the door—a handy tactic learned in the Marines. It began to crack after a few swift kicks, but he kept losing footing with the stairs in his way. He backed up as far the landing would allow, and, with his shoulder, he laid into it, busting through the door with such force that he fired down the broken steps, crashing into the water.

He found footing and stood up, water streaming off his body. In shock from the cold, he gasped for air, puzzled.

"Jesus Christ! What—what the fuck happened down here? Amy!?" Curtis yelled, looking around the room for her, but more so assessing the damage.

"Curtis!" she called out from somewhere in the darkness.

He glanced back and forth, taking shallow steps forward in the nearly waist-high, murky flood.

"I'm—I'm up here!"

"Huh?" Finally, Curtis looked up and saw his wife spread across the metal beams. "I don't—What—what the hell are doing up there? What is going on *here*, Amy? Wh—Where is Wes!?"

"LOOK OUT!" Amy screeched, pointing her finger out.

At the opposite end of the room, the barbed back of the beast emerged, slithering through the pool.

"WHOOAA!" Curtis bellowed; his eyes fixated on the creature. "What—*is*—that!?"

"Curtis—get us OUT of here!"

POP!

The basement window shattered inward, the pressure of the flood thrusting its way through, and a cascade of water came rushing down.

Curtis hurried toward Amy. From under the rising flood, the beast rose, towering over him, piercing, white eyes staring as water rolled off its spiky, frizzled coat. Curtis froze, replete with incredulity, mostly dread. It snarled with deafening ferocity, saliva flying from its mouth and hitting Curtis in the face as the creature swatted downward at him. He ducked backward but tripped over a rolling object. Dark water flooded over his eyes as he fell, submerging himself. While down, he reached blindly through the murk for anything in proximity, searching his sunken environs for some form of protection. Within arm's reach lay the object that sent him down—a fire extinguisher, now his only option as the floor trembled beneath him. In a matter of seconds, the beast bounded over and pounced on top of Curtis, pinning him under the water while its savage jowls snapped inches from his throat and face. Grabbing the extinguisher, he pushed into between himself and the beast's cavity, hindering the attack with all his might.

Blood splashed out from his pinned torso, absorbing into the fabric of Curtis's shirt. He struggled to roll out from the beast's clutches, taking a wallop against the shoulder blade that sent him sailing forward. Using the momentum to run to his workbench in search of something more advantageous, he tore open every drawer with both hands, pulling out the contents and flinging them left and right. In the depths of a top left drawer sat a dingy, red pipe wrench—he grabbed it. Under that, he found a large flat-head screwdriver—he grabbed it too.

A loud crash drew his attention to the other side of the room. The metal pipe beneath Amy had given way, sending her and the sporting equipment clattering into the deluge below. The beast shook its head, heaving the extinguisher, and moved in for her as she stood up, choking and struggling to pull drenched hair from her face. Curtis sprinted, unable to avert his gaze as he threw himself toward his wife. Amy, having just uncovered her widening eyes to see the beast closing in, ducked down and grabbed for the first object in reach—a ski pole. She jabbed at the beast, thrusting the tip into its upper front leg. From behind, Curtis plunged the screwdriver into the hind leg, trying to draw its attention, then proceeded to strike it with the wrench. Howling a prevailing, crepitant squeal, the beast turned to Curtis.

Without looking away from the creature, he yelled to Amy. "Grab Wes and get the fuck out of here!"

The creature whacked the wrench from Curtis's clutch, easily ripping flesh from his hand and forearm. Quickly, he reached behind for a floating wooden plank, blocking another incoming snap. The creature snarled, inches from his face, spewing a thick, matted liquid from its musty orifice. He held the plank in its mouth, using all his might to push back, but this *thing* was just too strong. Blood coursed from the exposed muscle down the back of his arm, trickling onto his neck and face.

His gaze flicked to Amy, crying so hard she could barely breathe as she trudged through the flood. Gasping for air between her whimpers, she pulled a catatonic Wes down from the cupboard, his dead weight falling into her arms. Even from this distance, his skin looked pale, almost translucent, in complete contrast to his sallow eyes. Amy caressed their son's cold, damp little face, saying his name over and over, but Wes remained unresponsive.

Curtis blinked, stepping toward his little boy, but the beast pressed its advantage, driving him backward through the room and up against a cube shelf, knocking its contents to the water. Over the beast's shoulder, he could see Amy take a few deep breaths, then climb up the broken steps with Wes draped over her shoulder, exiting the basement.

An old emergency kit floated in the debris, and Curtis reached for it with his injured hand while the other held tight to the plank still wedged in its jaws. From inside the canvas pouch, he pulled a road flare. He needed two hands for a few seconds but couldn't risk letting go, the beast splashing in the flood before him, barely at arm's length. But when the mighty mouth snapped through the plank, lodging the jagged pieces in its maw, Curtis seized his chance to light the fuse. He struck it several times with the scratch before it caught, and as it ignited, he stuffed it behind the block in the beast's jarred mouth.

The beast screeched and squealed, thrusting itself in and out of the water, creating a grungy whirlpool around Curtis. It backed away before submerging into the dark, where red sparks flashed, but only for a short time. Curtis grabbed another flare and struck it. The brilliant light shimmered off his glistening face as he held it in front of him, white smoke emanating. The door out beckoned, though quite a walk away; in fact, he couldn't have been farther from leaving. Slowly, he paced through the misty lagoon toward the exit. Along the route, he picked up a can of brake cleaner floating by—light in his hands, nearly empty, but certainly better than nothing.

The discharge from the broken window had begun subsiding, and the basement water tapered at waist level. Just then, the generator stalled out, and everything went black, his flare becoming the only source of light. *Oh, fuck, no...* From the center of the room, Curtis heard movement from every direction. His body sank into shock, quivering; his arms shook as he defensively held them out in front. Floating objects collided, and water currents splashed against stationery items, sending him in high alert circles, peering in a different direction with every modicum of noise.

Curtis could see the way out through the red haze, and his blood pressure rose, his heart pounding in his heaving chest as he drew deep breaths. Myriad thoughts surged through his mind within a matter of seconds. A part of him doubted he would leave the basement alive, while another part of him wanted to accept that fate. And as that logic passed, he realized none of his affairs were in order.

In actuality, *nothing* was in order. What kind of man would leave a woman with *this* burden? And then there was Wes—

Before another thought could develop, Curtis fell back under the water, yanked down by a tight grasp around his right leg while he fought to pull himself free. The spark from the flare lit up the froth enough for him to identify the rawhide, fire-hose-like object around his calf as a tail. Curtis's boot slid off, releasing him, and he made a break for the exit as fast as his legs and the impeding flood would let him. As he reached the steps, the snarling beast cut him off by the side, tearing through the bottom tread of the staircase.

Curtis held up the flare and pushed down the aerosol plunger, firing its contents through the spark. A burst of flames ruptured straight at the beast. It howled in agony, retreating from the unexpected napalm effect. But Curtis didn't look to see how long his plan worked. He just threw himself up the broken steps and out of the basement.

FIFTEEN

Curtis, sitting at the table with a dish towel pressed to his arm, stared out into nowhere.

"What are we gonna do!? What are we gonna do!?" Amy cried hysterically, pacing around the kitchen, trailing dirty water from her saturated clothing. "Why the *hell* aren't they answering the phone!?"

In all the mayhem, the beast must have destroyed the junction box, leaving the landline dead. The house's cell service was abysmal; it was hard to connect a call even on a good day. And to make things worse, the cell phone battery wouldn't stay charged long enough to get a call out, even with the temperamental generator running. The few times the phone had connected, no one would pick up the other end.

She slammed the cell down on the counter. "What if that *thing* gets inside the house and tries to kill us?"

Curtis shrugged. "I got this if it comes back."

On the wooden surface before him lay an old twelve-gauge pump shotgun he'd pulled from the closet. He didn't know if the beast was still there, but he'd pushed the love seat from the dining room against the top basement door in case it tried to make its way up.

"We can't stay here! We can't fucking stay here, Curtis! We need to LEAVE! CURTIS!"

"How? Where do we go!? There's a goddamn monsoon out there!"

"OH, *is* there, Curtis!? I thought it was 'just *fucking* rain'!?"

Amy snatched up the cell phone again, trying to dial, but her hands shook so hard she could barely hold it. The "no signal" tone beeped. She tried several more times—*beep, beep, beep*—before slamming the phone down in frustration, continuing to bawl.

"It's probably a good thing we can't get through, anyway," Curtis rationalized. "I mean, what the fuck are we going to tell them—a monster broke into our house and tried to kill us? You know how *absurd* that sounds? The local police don't like me in this town. All I need is something to give them an excuse to break my probation and throw me in fucking jail."

"Curtis, what are you saying?"

"We... we can't tell anyone about this. This is just fucking nuts!"

"Are you out of your mind, Curtis? We need to report this. *You* need to get to a hospital. We need to get our son, who's still passed out on the couch from shock, and leave this place!"

A long, silent pause ensued. Curtis grabbed a second dish towel, holding it tightly to his arm to try and stop the bleeding, but it easily soaked right through.

"Christ, Curtis..." Amy grabbed another dishtowel from the counter and a box of gauze from under the sink, which they'd bought when Wes fell off his bike, scraping his knees the previous summer.

Curtis pulled off his wet shirt and let Amy clean and bandage his shoulder.

"I think I know what that thing was." Curtis thought of Ronald, now wondering if he'd crossed paths with the beast.

"Huh?" Amy said, clearly focused on taping the bandage perimeter.

"I can't remember what they called it, though. It had a funny name. They'd tell tales of a beast that was known to roam the woods in southeast Connecticut back in the '50s and '60s, mutilating farm animals. Stories of campers that had gone missing—found mutilated, you know, shit they say to scare ya right before bed."

"What?"

Curtis blinked, a little surprised. "Didn't you ever do girl scouts or, uhhh—summer camp? People telling tales around the campfire; scary stories of urban folklore?"

"No, Curtis," Amy said in her no-nonsense tone, clearly uninterested in hearing anymore. "Whatever that thing is, it's still in this house, and I'm not staying here."

Curtis stood. "Thank you."

He hugged Amy long and hard, and while doing so, tried to recall the last time he touched his wife. Her delicate frame stiffened, then relaxed into his, soft and damp; he could faintly smell the sweet scent from her facial moisturizer underneath the musky river water. He didn't want to let go.

"Once this shit calms a bit, you're going to head to your parents' house," Curtis said, his voice serene. "I'm going to take care of this *thing*, and I'll be there later on."

Amy, without question, nodded her head.

Not long after, he pulled his truck out of the driveway, watching as his wife lay Wes—now conscious, wrapped in a twin comforter—across the back seat of her SUV and climbed into the cab.

The rain still pounded heavily, but the wind speeds had diminished enough to make a safe passage.

Curtis sat back at the kitchen table and lit a cigarette, preparing for his mission: to go down and kill the beast. His arm, now wrapped in gauze, continued to bleed. He stared at the bloody towel and dirty dishes, then over to the piles of folders and notebooks—Amy's work things. As he ashed into a burgundy stained glass, a manila folder wedged between two notebooks caught his eye: "Dr. Patel" written on the tab. Not recognizing the name, he opened it. Inside lay pages and pages of handwritten letters, mostly scattered sentences and paragraphs with entire sections crossed out with pen. All in Amy's handwriting. Underneath, he found one that appeared complete.

PART II

Sixteen

The impact reminded him of sparring practice during his first weekend at boot camp, like he had been slugged in the face by a sixteen-ounce boxing glove—shock and disorientation. His eyes opened briefly, just enough to see a bright white flash before the burning commenced, followed by tearing and profound throbbing. When his eyes fully opened, a white haze of dust canvased the inside of the pickup's cabin—stifling, asphyxiating. He struggled to pull in fast, shallow breaths, the taste of iron flooding his mouth as he coughed up thick clumps of blood. It oozed down over his swollen lip, dripping from his stubbly chin. Warm liquid also trickled down the side of his face, and he touched his head. The sticky redness coating his fingers revealed he bled from there, too.

Fully alert now, Curtis sat up, spotting a cracked windshield and driver's side window shattered. Smoke billowed, intermittently blotting the pale, ambient streetlight. The airbag deflated, and the dust settled, but he still struggled with limited sight; his face growing numb as he sat in malaise. An accidental glance in the bent rearview mirror revealed a likely broken nose. He then saw the slit in the corner of his forehead that was beginning to bruise, swollen from having cracked against the door window.

The engine had died, but the radio, alive and well, still played music, producing the truck's only light source. Station 102.9 blared golden oldies, though Curtis never listened to this station and didn't even recall turning it on. The Genies' "Who's That Knocking" eerily played at a low decibel through the cabin.

Disoriented, he opened his door and climbed down from the cab, stumbling into a dark stretch of sparsely lit highway. Crushing shards of glass with every step, he turned to assess the damage to his brand-new pickup. The hood bent upward through the middle in the shape of a cone, which had prevented Curtis from seeing out upon waking. The driver's side front panel crumbled in on itself, with the aluminum bumper bent around it. The grill looked torn in half, with one part embedded into the radiator as it continued to surge ashy, grey smoke. The headlights had disappeared entirely, as if the truck never had them, while liquid trickled from the undercarriage and drained ahead. Curtis turned to follow the stream of fluid pooling fifteen feet or so ahead, beside the rear end of a BMW.

The other car lay slumped halfway over the shoulder, perpendicular to his truck. The length of the driver's side had caved in, with both side windows popped, the side mirror missing, and the roof bent inward. Fragments of glass, plastic, and metal littered the street for a distance. He squinted, struggling to determine the car's color—white, he thought—with much of the paint scraped off, replaced with smudged pigments from his pickup. Pieces of the truck's grill had lodged in the door and side panel. One headlight flickered.

A cold, dense chill propagated through every nerve in Curtis's shaking body. There was no way he was just involved in a collision, and certainly, he could not be responsible. In utter shock, he followed first instinct: to look around to see if any other automobiles were involved or maybe had witnessed and pulled over roadside. Apart from the two vehicles, the street looked empty. The need to check the car for passengers then dawned on him. He walked over, trembling, terrified. It was too dark inside to see, and the door, crushed into the frame, couldn't be opened. He remembered he carried a flashlight in his glove box. He grabbed it, flicked it on, and walked back over.

At first glance, he saw the blood on the door—but when he shined the light inside the cabin, he nearly fell over backward.

"FUUUUCK, NO, NO, NO, OH, JESUS CHRIST!" Curtis cried. "This isn't happening. This can't be fucking happening!"

A long patch of crimson-stained hair gleamed in the light. He couldn't identify the figure, but they slumped over the passenger side seat. With the opposite side of the car thrust up against the guardrail, slightly suspended from the ground, the bent railing blocked his path to the door.

He grunted, straining to open it regardless, before realizing he would need to switch tactics. Using his foot, he peeled the door, binding it to the twisted rail. Though only allowing minimal access, the strategy provided a sufficient entryway for Curtis to reach in. He brushed aside the disheveled, wet hair and saw a woman—her face glazed in a streaming, viscous fluid. Curtis reached over for a pulse. Nothing. Blood leaked from the laceration on her forehead onto the beige leather of the bruised upholstery. Curtis pushed his hair back in a long sweep—a nervous habit—smudging blood across his head, then slowly slipped out of the tight opening to lean up against the rail, staring at the woman.

The spins came furiously, followed by profuse vomiting. Curtis panicked, realizing the severity of the situation and the fact he'd just left a bar—a half-hour away—*and* may be intoxicated. Between the pain from smashing his face and the reeling disorientation, he couldn't quite tell. But how; he only had a few Coronas. Right? He tried to recall the evening's events, but for some reason, he couldn't remember leaving the bar—or intended destination, or even where he *was* exactly.

Curtis accepted that he needed to flag down help. Walking awkwardly into the street with his flashlight and looking in either direction, he saw the small roadside sign for I-395. The median divider had been ripped open, the metal twisted up and over the other side. Walking through it, he began piecing together what had happened. He couldn't fucking believe it. Somewhere, at some point, he must've blacked out or fallen asleep and crashed through the center barrier, veering off onto the other side of the highway. *And what fucking shit luck to hit the only other car on the road!*

There wasn't a soul in sight. Curtis spun around in circles looking back and forth, trying to think. *Shit, maybe—just maybe this woman has a cellular phone or something in her purse.* He partially squeezed back into the BMW and searched around for anything. The glove box held nothing, save for piles of fast-food napkins and a few CD cases. The passenger seat floor contained two dirty food storage containers with silverware and a brown banana peel. He then turned to the woman, meticulous not to touch her again as he inspected around her person. A leather bag caught his eye from the backseat, along with empty water bottles, folded blankets that had spilled, and small containers of essential oils. He reached back, grabbed the bag, and brought it to his lap. The light, wedged between his chin and chest, shone in as he fingered through.

Crystal Nolan was her name, as indicated on her driver's license, which Curtis had in his hand along with other credentials. Crystal worked as a massage therapist at Mohegan Sun—Connecticut's *other* casino. She belonged to a coffee club and a local gym; she liked frozen yogurt, and she had two cats. She was young—around his age, and she was pretty. Combing through further, he found a makeup bag with nail files, clippers, lipstick, and birth control. Along the bottom lay loose change and a pack of Virginia Slims. The side pocket of the purse looked more promising.

Curtis unveiled a Motorola StarTAC cellular phone. He flipped it open, hand still trembling, pulled up the antenna, and dialed 9-1-1. Norwich police answered, and Curtis reported the accident, though unable to give a proper location. He was told to sit tight, and that they'd dispatch authorities down the Interstate. Curtis lowered his head and took several deep breaths, phone still by his ear, debating whether this was a good time to call Amy.

A hand reached up, grabbing his arm. Long, sharp nails pierced his forearm, breaking the skin. The pale, ulcerated hand drew arterial blood, which oozed over damaged, black cuticles. Curtis shot up, screaming. The woman shot up from her slumped position, inches from his face, and glared—her eyes sunken white. Opaque. Vapid. Her mouth fell open, unnaturally wide, exposing her dank, black orifice, and olive green, fractured teeth that individually fell from black gums. Blood streamed down her forehead over hollow, lesion-covered cheeks. Her hair darkened, first from stained blonde to an inky, brittle twine, and then to a sludge binding texture.

She pulled Curtis in and snarled, "DON'T LET ME DIE!!" Blood spattered from her mouth, beading his face.

"DON'T LET ME FUCKING DIEEE, CURTIS!!" She wailed, head violently shaking.

Her piercing, foggy eyes disintegrated, liquefying into a white, pus-like substance that drained down her boney face. Her skin exsiccated, every ounce of moisture in her body sucking out as her complexion quickly blackened, then decomposed. The crisp, rotted flesh split around the cheek and eye sockets before breaking from the fractured skull, crumbling to keratinocyte dust. Jaw still open, still *wailing*, her skeletal remains clung to Curtis—frozen, staring into her ocular cavities. The front and back windows imploded, sending thousands of shards screeching in.

***

Curtis woke. He shot up—*screaming*, chair flying backward, crashing to the floor, and then dropped to his knees, hyperventilating, gasping for air. Minutes later, after catching his breath, he slowly stood up and looked around. He was in his kitchen. *What the fuck is happening to me?* Racing to the bathroom, he opened the vanity behind the mirror, shuffling through products and medications, knocking them out of sight. With shaking hands, he picked up an expired bottle of benzodiazepines and dumped several pills in his mouth. The faucet cranked open; his hands cupped water to his mouth. He swallowed. Cold sweat dripped from his forehead.

Those words. Those words she used were so familiar...

The visions, triggered by bouts of insomnia and anxiety, began after his return from Iraq. Prescribed opiates for pain from shrapnel lodged in his abdomen and hip escalated them. Excessive drinking for pain amplified them. A half decade of variating antidepressant, mood stabilizer, and benzodiazepine cocktails left him emotionally paralyzed. Detached. Eventually, something just clicked, and the visions subsided. Amy's arrival had been the antidote.

The visions had made a vicious return; he was now sure of that.

Seventeen

Lightning crashed and rain pelted the windows; the lights continued to pulse in and out. Dawn had nearly arrived, and the eye of the storm had finally passed, leaving only the remnants of a fading thunderstorm.

The shoddy bandage job on Curtis's arm, now soaked through with blood, needed a change. He grabbed a tube of superglue from the odds-and-ends drawer in the kitchen next to the silverware, then pulled off the butterfly bandages, separating each slit. Four precise lacerations glared back at him: clean, one deep, needing sutures. With the meaty palm flesh and forearm side exposed, he could see ribbons of moist, pink muscle fiber beneath. The oozing had stopped, but thin strands of blood continued to leak from the corners with each movement. He grew instantly queasy and light-headed at the sight, so he sat at the kitchen table. Pulling the cap off with his teeth, he squeezed the bottle across the incisions and held them shut. Then he disinfected, re-bandaged, and covered up the area with a roll of woven gauze. While he cleaned himself up, he couldn't help but relive the conversation with Amy before she left—the curse of a wandering mind. Then he recalled the letter once more, which he had already read several times over...

Dear Curtis,

I'm not entirely sure what my intentions are in writing this letter, beyond therapeutic, but the idea was to just put words to paper. I don't really know where to begin. First and foremost, I am unhappy. This should obviously come as no surprise. I know you're unhappy, too. Most of all, I'm just hurt. I feel broken and alone. I feel like I've been completely abandoned to raise our son all by myself. I have had several months to sit with my thoughts about our marriage, and this letter has seen many iterations as I struggle to find the right words. And as I sit here writing this for the fifth time, I always come to the same conclusion in the end.

You probably haven't noticed the few times you've seen me, but I've put on this happy exterior because it's the only way I've been able to get through the day, to combat these feelings of immense sadness and an emptiness that have left me just numb. Work, the nightmare it has turned out to be, has at least redirected my anger and kept my mind occupied. It's allowed me to feel a little more independent in your absence and has given me a sense of purpose I forgot I was missing for so long.

The numbness is just as physical as it has been emotional. As much as I'm embarrassed to admit it, I need to be honest with you and myself. I have been drowning myself in wine just about every weekend since I can remember. Sometimes even during the week. Some days I'm not even sure how I've made it work—but I know everything came to a head about three months ago, just after you'd left for Maine. Wes locked himself in the basement. I could barely stand when I heard the screams, but I pushed my way through the jammed door and fell down the stairs, smacking my head on the cement and knocking myself out. Wes thankfully called 911, and Sergeant Rick showed up with the EMT and helped me out.

I've wanted to tell you this for so long, but I couldn't bring myself to. I was just too fucking embarrassed by this whole situation—mostly for the fact I had let it get to this point, where I found myself drunk, neglecting my own son like a total piece of shit, and also allowing myself to be abused by you in this way. Wondering now, if I had told you, how'd you react? With anger? Or worse. Silence? The silence kills me.

Anyway, I was fine. Ended up with a couple stitches and a mild concussion. Rick knew I was intoxicated and could have caused trouble, but he didn't. I think he just felt sorry for me. I know you don't like him much, but I am ever grateful to him—because that day scared the shit out of me. Not just my behavior, but the thought of dying and leaving our son without either parent. I needed that clear wake-up call.

Somewhere along the way, we just stopped communicating. I feel mostly responsible for allowing that to fade. Showing your "feelings" never came easily to you, especially in the beginning, but when you did, I got to see the man I fell in love with, the man I knew I wanted to raise a family with. I understood your initial reluctance to do so (and even more so now, regardless of my feelings on the matter), but then when Wes was born, I saw the look in your eyes of a man in love.

Remember when we met, I told you all I ever wanted in this world was to be a mother, have kids, and raise a family? It's all I've thought about since I was a young girl. I thought WE wanted this, remember? I always wanted to have more children. And the longer I wait, the more difficult it will become. I sometimes wonder if maybe we just rushed into things. You were so transparent when we met that I thought you knew what you wanted. Or maybe it was just what you thought you wanted. Or worse, you just told me what I needed to hear.

A wave of remorse washed over Curtis; he knew he wasn't the same person that returned from the Gulf War, leaving some of the *crazy* on the back burner early in the relationship. He thought he'd have time to figure it out—the delusion of time and how much of it one believes they have control over. At the very least, he thought they'd spend a couple years getting to know one another, living life, exploring the world, though a small part of him also feared he'd never change and end up just wasting her time. He never knew for sure if he wanted children, especially with his debilitating anxiety; now even more anxious, and having a son with special needs, he couldn't fathom planning for another. But things don't necessarily go as planned; time is *not* always on one's side—for Curtis, it seemed to mostly work against him—and within a year of dating, Amy became pregnant. And their love ultimately made the decision.

I've watched us slowly spiral downhill for the last five years with much regret. I was scared. More so, I was weak. We both lost our jobs and hit rock bottom, and I didn't know what to do. And I found myself escaping, focusing my effort on Wes and his ever-growing needs. Then all of a sudden, you got a job! And you were lucky enough to get hired doing what you're good at, and I was so excited for you and for US. I thought maybe that would help you start to feel good again. I obviously didn't think all our problems would be solved, but it seemed like a positive step for both of us. I hoped to get a piece of my husband back. Then, what started as being away for a few days turned into weeks, then months, and then you just VANISHED. My husband didn't return. When you did come home, you stayed stuck someplace else. I tried so many times to talk to you, and you just refused to let me in. I didn't know how to help you. Your patience dwindled, and I found myself walking on eggshells, wondering what was going to set you off next. I really don't know any easy way to say this, but you scare me, Curtis. I no longer feel safe in this relationship, and that is a real problem.

I worry about Wes and what he sees when you're here on a tirade. Your son is confused and doesn't quite understand why you're gone all the time. And it doesn't seem to matter what I tell him. I just find him in screaming fits, breaking toys, and calling for his father. He's a very strong little boy and getting harder to restrain, which absolutely rips my goddamn heart out every time I have to do it. Nothing in this entire world is more important to me and keeping him safe is my ONLY priority.

I understand things are really tough right now, and I know you've been busy with work, but I believe therapy would do you good. For two years, I've suggested time and time again that you speak to someone. But you still haven't even made the effort to look into it, have you? I've been seeing Dr. Patel myself now for almost three months, which is how I've found the courage to start writing my thoughts and feelings out on paper. Wish to God I started sooner. I have been wanting to share that with you, but I can't even remember the last time we had a conversation. I can't remember the last time you've asked me anything pertaining to what's been going on in my head or, at the very least, how I'm feeling. Not even a disingenuous, "how are you?" Nothing. But your refusal to see someone only tells me you don't take our marriage seriously, though part of me hopes it's nothing more than your head getting in the way.

I can go on and on, but the bottom line is that I am so sorry for whatever this is that's come between us. I'm sorry for not trying harder, Curtis. I know it's been a really rough road, but I'm not angry. Not anymore. I don't hold blame for anything that's happened. I love you and will always love you, but I also can't be a fixture in the background anymore. I've gone through a lot to get to this place, where I finally found the courage and the strength to make one of the toughest choices in my life, and it completely breaks my heart to say it. I NEED to move forward with life.

Curtis hung his head, his eyes beginning to well. A chill overwhelmed his entire body—a cold but mild electric shock to the system, a sickening chunk of ice in his stomach. Reading those words over and over didn't change the feel of daggers piercing his heart. How foolish of him to think that this way of life wouldn't eventually come to an end, that he could continue blindly, ignorantly down this morose path. That a woman like Amy would continue to sit by his side 'till death do you part.'

I've tried to write a version of this letter where I don't mention the past, but I can't seem to find any way around it. In my heart of hearts, I know the root of your problem. You don't talk about it, but I've known you for nine years, Curtis. I know you better than you know yourself. I know it still hurts you, and I know you've never been able to say her name. I think it would do you good to visit her. Tell her how you're feeling. Ask her for forgiveness. And please let the healing process begin. Find a way to forgive yourself.

Love always,

Amy

Eighteen

The moment Amy left Forest Street, she pulled a heavily scraped, silver Nokia cell phone from the overnight bag in the passenger seat. Her hands still shook as she flipped it open and scrolled through the contacts on the small, green screen. The rain came down hard, smacking the windshield while the wipers oscillated at full speed. Having never been changed, the shoddy blades could only smear the water across the glass, making seeing that much harder. The streetlamps had blacked out, and the headlight visibility only stretched twenty or thirty feet. Amy found it difficult to keep an eye on the road and search her phone for her parents' number, having to keep dodging fallen debris. Leaves, branches, and in some cases, fallen trees of different lengths and sizes littered Route One. Downed power lines and street signs provided the biggest hazards, forcing her to make some minor detours; however, she mostly just drove over everything that crossed her path.

Once she reached the interstate, the rain began to let up—slightly—and Amy felt a little safer. Unable to spot a single automobile on the road, she began to worry about what would happen if she got into an accident en route to Madison, a good forty-five-minute drive south. Her gaze flicked to Wes, still sprawled across the seat, completely wrapped. His face remained ghostly white, his eyes open, empty, staring out into the dark.

"Wes, baby, we're going to be okay." Amy tried to be as reassuring as possible, albeit still completely terrified herself. "Mommy's taking us to Grammy and Grampy's summer house. We're going to be safe there, sweetheart. Mommy won't let anything happen to you, okay, honey?" She reached into the back seat to rub Wes, but she could feel only the thick, bulky comforter. She dug until his cold little hand emerged, then gently squeezed it.

The highway opened, and the lanes widened; she approached the Baldwin Bridge that expanded over the Connecticut River. Though the road remained dark, Amy decided this was the safest time to try to make a phone call. She found the number and dialed out, noticing one battery bar left—as if her anxiety wasn't high enough, she realized she'd soon be without a phone. The line rang many times before someone finally picked up.

Cecilia Chastain popped the cork on a frosty bottle of a 1983 Cristal Brut she unearthed from the cellar fridge. She pulled two flutes from the Cherry wood cabinet above the white marble kitchen counter next to the sink. The hiccups came suddenly, but that didn't stop her from pouring a full glass. Matching white marble surrounded the butcher-block-top kitchen island, with four white leather bar stool chairs where she sat. She slid over a crystal ashtray, opened a Louis Vuitton leather cigarette case, and pulled a True 100 from a fresh pack. After lighting up, she removed a dangly emerald drop earring from each ear and placed them on the counter, followed by a matching necklace.

In a tight, black, fishtail evening gown, Cecilia pulled incessantly at the fabric around her belly—a hail Mary attempt to squeeze into it, even before the night of dining and drinking to excess. Her husband, Harold, who had entered the room in a black tuxedo, loosened his red bowtie and removed his silver cufflinks while Cecilia poured him a glass.

"Oooh, the '83, huh? You shouldn't have..." Harold teased as he kissed Cecilia on the head.

Cecilia smiled. "Oh, nothing but the best for you, dear."

"What a long night, wouldn't you say?" I can't believe what time it is!" Harold said, impressed by how many hours he managed to make it past his bedtime, as he pulled a cigarette from the leather case and lit it.

The phone rang.

"Who could be calling at this hour?" Harold said disconcertedly, checking his silver Rolex before sliding off the bracelet band.

"Give me it," Cecilia demanded with an arm reached out and a waving hand.

Harold picked up the cordless phone from the base and handed it over. Cecilia recognized the number on the caller ID, but to whom it belonged didn't immediately register. Though not in much of a condition to carry a phone conversation in her inebriated state, with her elated mood, she answered.

"Hello?"

"Hi, Mom," Amy said—her voice breaking up. "You and Dad okay?"

"Amy! Oh, honey, we're fine. Southern Florida didn't see much of the storm. It rolled through overnight and was gone by morning. Looked like it did quite a bit of damage in the Carolinas, however. *Hiccup*—oh, excuse me, my lord!" Cecilia said after a large sip from the flute. "Your father and I just got back from the country club a little while ago—Harold, it's Amy." Harold smiled and took his drink to the outside deck. "They do a post-Presidential electoral banquet the week after every election, and I'll just say, what a celebration. The Governor was there with both senators—more politicians in a room than I could honestly stomach, but your father was very excited—another four years of Bush!" Cecilia hiccupped, then stubbed out her cigarette and lit another.

"That's good," Amy said, her voice trembling.

"Sweetheart, you okay? You don't sound right."

"Yeah," Amy said lightly, wiping the tears with her palm. "I'm okay. I'm on my way to Madison with Wes." She barely finished the sentence as more tears streamed down her flushed cheeks.

"Oh, honey… What happened—you gave him the papers, didn't you? Your father and I have been waiting for this. What happened—did he hurt you, Amy?"

"What? No, Mom, it's not that. I'm fine. The storm was incredible up here, and the house flooded, and we lost power—"

Cecilia hiccupped again. "I told you, honey, I told you not to marry him. Your father and I warned you, dear. We knew it couldn't last, and this day would come. I just don't understand—you are such a sweetheart, Amy. You're so smart"—*hiccup*—"and you're so beautiful! You could have had anybody…"

"*Mother*…" Amy bemoaned.

"You know, a few months ago, before we left for Palmetto Bay, guess who we ran into? Daniel Haynes—*esquire*. Remember you dated him through almost all of college? If you didn't catch the 'esquire,' he's now a—I think he said, *partner*—of some law firm in Stamford—or Stratford—or, Christ, I can't recall now." *Hiccup!*

"*Mother...*"

"Doesn't matter, not important. Anyway, he's *so* handsome, and more importantly, he's *single*. He asked quite a bit of questions about you, dear. Why *did* you break it off with him?"

"Mom—PLEASE!" Amy shouted.

"Honey, your father and I are just trying to look out for you. You're *thirty-four* years old. You're so young and vibrant and should really take this opportunity to explore your options before you end up at forty, and it's *too* late—cause I'll be honest, we women do not age gracefully, and I don't want to see you alone, and unhappy."

"This is definitely NOT the time to be discussing my personal life or anything else, Mother!"

"There is never a good time to talk about these things, honey, but if they go unaddressed, then they only cause more stress down the road. You can't just sweep this under the rug like you have everything else the last couple years; we did not raise you to ignore your problems. Let me just tell you what's happening: you are experiencing dissonance right now, Amy, completely normal dissonance." She hiccupped again, then cleared her throat. "We all sometimes make these unnecessary justifications that keep us walking in, well, circles, perpetuating the same mistakes, over and over and over. You don't need to live this way!" Cecilia's tone quickly changed to one of contention.

"Oh, great, now I get a goddamn therapy lesson? I'm not one of your pretentious clients, Mother. You do this *shit* to me every time you drink—which incidentally is just about every time I speak to you!"

"We feel so badly for you and moreover for poor Wes. Our only grandson, born with a disability that no one understands. I know this did *not* come from you or anyone on *our* side of the family, dear. This environment he's in cannot be helpful for his well-being. The focus needs to be on *him*, Amy."

Cecilia had crossed the line. For the most part, Amy put up with her mother's forced involvement in her life—including the generic advice likely recycled from years of working as a cognitive behavioral therapist—but she did not particularly appreciate her mother speaking of anything regarding her family, *especially* when she's been drinking.

"Do NOT tell me what to do with Wes!" Amy snapped. She went from shaking with fear to shaking with rage. Wes *was* the most important thing in her world, and she refused to entertain her mother's continuous suggestive assessments of his life. "And I am just calling to let you know WE are headed to Madison to stay at the house for a while."

"Why are you getting so worked up, Amy? Your father and I—"

"Look, I appreciate what you're trying to do, but I don't need any more advice on the happenings of my life! I don't need marital counseling. I don't want suggestions on how to raise my son. And I don't care for you always pointing fingers at my husband!"

"Sweetheart—"

"My phone is about to die; I'm losing the signal anyway—I have to go. Bye, Mother." Amy snapped the phone closed and flung it in the passenger seat. She looked in her rearview mirror to check on Wes, who remained utterly still, continuing to stare off.

Still not a single person on the road, Amy finally reached her parents' exit. Darkness shrouded the entire trip, diminishing any confidence she had that the house would have power; by the looks of it, the whole town had blacked out. Similar to Norwich, leaves, tree branches, and fallen power lines littered the streets. From the damage Amy assessed on her journey, she suspected most of the state would lack electricity for some time.

The summer house sat in a small, seasonal community off Neck Road, located behind a family-owned deli on Route One. A thick, fallen tree obstructed the beginning of the street, so Amy parked the SUV at the deli. She slumped Wes over her shoulder and held him with one hand while using the other to hold the flashlight. The rain had let up to a light drizzle, making the walk more comfortable, or rather, less uncomfortable, considering the sixty pounds of dead weight in her arms. To her surprise, some houses had electricity, the distant, dull roar of generators audible as she approached the family cottage.

The Chastain's purchased their cottage in 1974 for forty-thousand dollars. The current market value of the modest two-bedroom had since surpassed three hundred thousand. They saw the value increase considerably each passing year, and after ten years, they moved to a larger house in town while using the cottage—until recently—as an academic rental. Two years ago, they decided to semi-retire and sold their house to buy property in South Miami. Amy's father, formerly an Emeritus Professor of Literature at Yale University, transferred to the University of Miami, where he taught two classes: Mad Poets of the Nineteenth Century and German

Fiction of the 1800s. Her mother moved her practice to an office in their Art Deco-style home in Palmetto Bay, where she kept only a handful of clients—just busy enough between lounging at the beach and by the country club pool. After the spring semester in early May, they would return to Madison for three months, then back up in winter throughout the holidays. But for now, the house looked dark. Empty.

Amy reached the cottage and walked up the long driveway, wet and out of breath from carrying Wes. Bending down near the front steps, she picked up the fake brick that contained the spare key to the house. Upon entering, she habitually hit the switch to turn on the kitchen light. Nothing happened. She sighed at the dark room, placed Wes on the living room couch, and walked back to the kitchen to the odds and ends cabinet, pulling out four battery-operated lights disguised as candles. They provided minimal illumination at best, but she preferred any dim glow to the otherwise black room.

Amy, still dripping, went for the liquor cabinet next. She pulled out a dusty bottle of hundred-proof rye whiskey and poured two fingers into a square rocks glass. Without wincing, she threw it back and poured another. She'd bought the whiskey, Curtis's drink of choice, herself, putting it there specifically for him. The bottle hadn't been touched in some time.

She picked up the cordless phone—already clinging to life on its backup battery—on the counter to check the line for a dial tone. Hearing the beep, she scrambled to call Curtis's cell phone, which went straight to voicemail. She then began to dial 9-1-1 before hesitating at the last digit, unsure of what to say. She couldn't explain any of the night's events. Besides, she wanted to believe that whatever Curtis planned to do was the right decision, to trust in that—now knowing she could. She replayed the incident, surprised, even excited by how he took charge and put himself in way of the creature for their safety—a glimmer of the man she remembered marrying.

After pouring a third drink, Amy joined Wes on the couch, who put his head on her lap and soon fell asleep. She ran her fingers through his soft, blonde hair, sipped her whiskey, and stared at the blank television screen across the room. All Amy wanted now was her husband.

She waited.

NINETEEN

The zigzagging, heavily wooded trail behind the home on the farthest corner of Coit Street ran about the length of half a football field, its boundary ending by the cul-de-sac on Forest Street, in front of the Cavanaugh's residence. Or what was left of it. That's where Mallory Luske's Yorkshire terrier ran, broken free from the confinements of her fenced-in backyard. The storm's high winds managed to dislodge several posts of the aging, four-foot-high, white, vinyl picket fence, just enough for Balki Bartokomous—named after her favorite '80's Mediterranean sit-com character from Mypos—to squeeze under. But, of course, this wasn't the first escape Mallory witnessed since she, as a recent empty nester, had brought the puppy home ten years earlier.

The first escape occurred a year after the adoption, right after her diagnosis of emphysema and subsequent early retirement from Southern New England Telephone. The terrier slipped from its leash-tie and scampered into the neighbor's yard, hiding under the porch. This happened a few times—the pooch was crafty. A month later, she put up the fence. She loved her new family member, who made her happy. Or as happy as one could be, now bound to a ticking clock from a progressively debilitating disease—one that eventually robs one of who they are, physically, mentally. Now, with whatever remaining time she had left in the world, she just wanted to enjoy its company.

She was ready.

She'd just finished putting in a solid thirty years of her career, only having to take a short leave of absence twice—both times the company went on strike. Being part of the Union made job security possible during three decades in a fickle phone company, saving her from cutbacks each time. The magical round number of thirty also had its benefits—a pension, and she'd just reached top salary in her management position, having worked her way up from a mere phone operator. Had she not fallen ill during the imminent threat of another strike, thus accepting a buyout at the end, she might have sucked it up and stayed a few more years, if only to earn a little more money.

Thirty years was also the length of time she'd been burning through a pack and a half of unfiltered Lucky Strikes a day, only switching to Merit lights during the nine months of her pregnancy. For Mallory, falling victim to the smoke's unyielding detriment at such an early age—forty-seven—seemed too short a time, even considering her inordinate dedication to Lucky Strikes. But scar tissue from her two-month spell with whooping cough as a baby, which she'd barely survived, acted as an accelerant. A slow burn. The addiction increased dramatically after her husband, a pilot, vanished during a classified mission in the Gulf War, leaving her to raise their teenage daughter, Evelyn, alone. She smiled at a picture of the three of them hung by the back door as she ambled by. Evelyn, now married with two kids of her own, currently resided two streets over on Pearl.

Opening the door, Mallory entered the backyard to let her fur baby in from his five a.m. piss. "Balki!"

Her heart sank at her inability to find him, followed by a rise in blood pressure, irritated—with him at first, but then mostly with herself. In his defense, he had been out about a half-hour. Too long. The flashlight only shone so far when she had let him out, the dark hiding much of the aftermath from the hurricane. The time now neared dawn, pressing away from the deep violet skies of nautical twilight, entering the blue hour—the period before sunrise.

She shuffled back into the house. She needed some time to get to the front door, as she always did. She moved at a snail's pace through the candle-lit room, taking her time so as not overexert herself—a difficult thing to avoid, in her condition. In her right hand, she carried a hand-held compressed oxygen tank with clear tubes running along her back and up and around her face, with a nozzle tucked under each nostril. The low growl of the bag and a steady hiss of gas pulsing with each inhale and exhale filled the quiet kitchen as she ambled to her porch door. The gear weighed a bit heavy in her hand, having just been replenished from a large concentrator tank, which lived in the corner of the dining room. "The junk room," as she called it. The room contained storage of anything and everything she might need on the daily to avoid having to move very far throughout the house: mainly clothing, reading material—books and gossip magazines—and snack food, both hers and Balki's.

She slid on calf-high duck boots and a faux fur hood parka, first walking out the front door where, on an ordinary day, her view would stretch to the far end of each corner. Quiet greeted her; the homes on either side of the street appeared deserted, devoid of life. Defunct streetlamps hung from powerless utility poles. Infinite darkness. A broad, red oak had fallen on her neighbor's property, blocking the debris-covered street, and another had fallen further up in the opposite direction. She called for Balki several times from her front landing, clapping her hands and gazing up and down the road. Standing. Waiting. This went on for minutes until it dawned on her where he'd run off to the last time. Frank, while harvesting cucumbers and cherry tomatoes for his "world-famous salad," had found Balki chasing a cat in his backyard the previous summer. She recalled how sweet the man was to drop everything and venture through the neighborhood, going door-to-door in search of her dog's home.

She began her slow trek through the damp woods, flashlight in one hand, oxygen in the other. The wind, heavy at times, and the uneven sprawling terrain of tarry mud, prevented her from moving at a favorable pace; she needed to stop every ten to fifteen feet to catch her breath. Drops of cool rain, filtered down through evergreen needles, landed on her wiry, salt and pepper hair as she ambled with a light wheeze, beginning to perspire in her brown winter coat. The scent of wet pine clung heavy, lingering; she could almost smell the strong woody musk emanating from below the earth. With each rest, she called for Balki for as long her struggling diaphragm would allow. Her efforts only returned the melodic chirps of rising robins and the delicate rustling of woodland creatures, venturing forth from concealment from the storm. The forest—alive and breathing.

Lightheadedness, setting in from oxygen deprivation, prompted her to reconsider her search, and she wondered how much further she could manage. Still, anxiety loomed at the thought of worst-case scenarios: a tree falling on Balki, or maybe a coyote attack, or worse yet, carried off by one of those new fisher cats—not cats at all, but vile weasel-like creatures known to prey upon small animals, crying before they killed. Disturbing and unmistakable. She recalled hearing the blood-curdling wails of a fisher cat from her porch on many a night. The thought of abandoning the search tore at her weak heart, but she knew she verged on entering an internal forbidden ground.

Just as she turned back, eyes welling, the infectious yaps of a small dog materialized. Chills crawled up her back as her pulse quickened, invigorating hope, empowering her to continue on.

"Balkeee! Balki, where are you, boy!"

Through a break in the trees ahead, she spotted the Cavanaugh's house; her mouth dropping as the building slowly manifested. She recalled hearing sirens and seeing smoke beyond the trees the day before yesterday, when she'd let Balki out, then seeing the quick snapshot on the channel eight morning news. But seeing it in person, before dawn, seemed a whole new and haunting experience. In disbelief that this could happen in her own backyard, she slowly panned the debris cluttered yard and dilapidation wrapped in caution tape, taking a moment to consider Frank and the harrowing experience this must've been for his wife and family. But within a moment, Balki's yaps grew emphatic, almost vicious.

Mallory continued to holler for Balki with strained breath, picking up her pace through the driveway. Around Estelle's station wagon, the oxygen tank started to feel heavy in her raw hand. Halfway around the back, she came to a halt—startled by the view of the Yantic, which had transformed the Cavanaugh's property into a partially sunken island. Hearing the barking again, she flicked her flashlight to the left. At the end of the beam, just behind Frank's shed ten yards ahead, she caught sight of her terrier's silky, blue and tan coat holding ground near the edge of the flood, staring off, yapping.

"Balki, get over here, right now!" She clapped, slowly stepping ahead. "Balki! Do you hear me, boy?"

A shadow rose in front of her dog, tough to delineate from the undulating, dark river, and surrounding brush—especially with only a sliver of azure sky to provide contrast. Instantly, she considered a bear, and without rationalizing the potential danger, she dropped her oxygen tank to free up a hand. Her only instinct, to get her dog away from whatever loomed ahead, sent her scampering toward Balki. Staggering.

The beast squealed in Balki's face, attempting to paw forward, daunted, hesitant of this tiny, eight-pound barking creature blocking its path.

"BALKI, GET OVER HERE!" She gasped.

Unable to inhale enough oxygen to compensate for energy exertion, she sensed the earth beginning to move beneath her with every step—the wavering effect of vertigo setting in. She clapped vehemently, trying to get the dog to turn around, at which point, he finally did. Only for a moment.

Balki recognized Mallory, his master, and barked happily, excited to share his fantastic discovery. Turning back to the beast, he saw only the blue hue of a vast skyline beyond Hock Island, melding the surrounding woods and the river's drab surface. His churning vision ascended awkwardly, mere seconds before fading to black.

Mallory gasped, watching her terrier's decapitated head hit the water. A wheezing shriek followed, fading almost as quickly as Balki's life, with her lungs wholly depleted in a matter of seconds. She couldn't move, unable to even suck in a quick breath, much less scream at the grotesque sight—a gaping palate of dripping teeth and swollen, blistered flesh—as the beast advanced. Frank's yard now spun in lopsided semicircles, and she collapsed, lungs seizing while she scrambled to reach back for the unattainable oxygen tank, only a foot or so away. She felt a swift pull of her leg, unable to sense much more of the sharp pain as her body went into shock. Suffocating, like she'd just ran a mile and now struggled to catch her breath, though through a plastic straw. As the beast dragged her over the wet, cold earth, her only refuge was grabbing Balki's furry remains before her last vision, that of Frank's deck, submerged in the icy flood.

TWENTY

The Mega Home Improvement Warehouse over on Route Eighty-five by the old indoor shopping mall bustled the morning after the big storm. Many of New London County's residents had their work cut out ahead of them. According to the reporter, which droned from an employee's personal radio as they stacked four-by-eight plywood sheets onto a large flat cart, the damage inflicted by the hurricane had devastated the northeastern seaboard.

"... 'Connecticut, Massachusetts, Rhode Island, and Maine suffered moderate damage with power outages and ten fatalities in total'—wow, that's if you want to call thirty million dollars 'moderate!' Around two million people are without power, with no certainty of when it will be restored. The storm hit Massachusetts, Boston specifically, hit worse than its surrounding states with massive flood damage; the estimations near one billion dollars. Can you even believe these numbers here? New York and New Jersey took the brunt of the storm with catastrophic devastation. And you're just not going to believe any of this—there are over thirty deaths and an already estimated three billion dollars in needed repairs. The Jersey boardwalks have been torn apart—half of it just washed right out to sea. New York's subway *shut down for the first time in history, having succumbed to saltwater. Coney Island's Wonder Wheel—GONE! It's just—gone, folks! The Cyclone roller coaster, demolished, like a ship drove right through it..."*

Curtis, staring at sheets of frosted plate glass, listened to as much as he could stomach before interrupting to ask about sump pumps.

While most shopped to pick up supplies to aid in their own home repair, Curtis had something else in mind. He walked up and down each aisle with his own large, flat cart to search for his project items. He picked a wet tile saw with an assortment of cutting blades, dumping it on the cart. A bag of cement followed. Then he headed to the metal aisle. Curtis found a seven-foot-high panel with a two-gauge steel pipe—indestructible—and took five. Along with that, he needed socket screws, hinges, corner joints, corner caps, and draw wedges.

He looked down on his supplies, suddenly reminded of the motto that shaped his life. *Be prepared, son... be prepared.*

He didn't know if his sump pump was clogged or just plain shit out, but he happened to see one left on the shelf: a ¾ horse-powered motor, capable of removing approximately forty-six hundred gallons of water per hour while operating twenty-four hours straight. Curtis stopped a moment and did some quick math. Expensive, the pump seemed a tough sell even for the most desperate consumer. But if he wanted any chance of clearing the basement in a timely fashion, he'd need it. After asking a store clerk, he discovered two additional pumps, tucked away in storage but available for purchase. Lastly, he grabbed a carpenter's mask and a pair of heavy-duty gloves.

The check-out line loomed, astronomical. Every lane backed up all the way through the store aisles. People stood with blue shopping wagons and flat carts loaded with electric tools, lumber, shingles, and other roofing materials; some even held toilets, sinks, and countertops, as if the storm provided the perfect excuse for home renovation.

Growing impatient as he stood with the flat cart, Curtis looked back and forth to the lines surrounding his, wondering if—*hoping that*—another moved faster. He began to perspire. Inching closer, he saw what, or in this case, *who*, had held up the works: a pint-sized elderly man behind the register, clad in royal blue with apron and matching cap, with *Mega Home Improvement Warehouse* splashed across both. He smiled, his grin wide and crooked, and his bushy, white eyebrows shifted up and down like caterpillars wriggling below the cap's perfectly straight brim. Sweat dripped from Curtis's forehead at the man's incessant chatter with each patron, the walls seeming to close in around him as his mind flashed back to Mondo-Mart the previous evening. The cacophony of commerce slowly drained away, heightening the thumping of his beating heart.

Lub-dub... Lub-dub... Lub-dub... Lub-dub.. Lub-dub.. Lub-dub.. Lub-dub.. Lub-dub, lub-dub, lub-dub, lub-dub, lub-dub, lub-dub, lub-dub...

He closed his eyes, shifting his focus to breathing—drawing deeply, holding, releasing completely, over and over and over and over...

"Hiya, sir, how are you today?" The chipper, old man behind the register asked.

"Huh?" Curtis opened his eyes, finding himself in front of the register.

"I said, how are you doing this fine morning?"

"Fine," Curtis uttered, slightly puzzled. "Thanks."

"Some storm we had last night, wouldn't you say!? Gonna make this a year to remember, eh? Hope you fared okay? Whoa, looks like you had an accident there!" He chirped, looking at Curtis's bandaged hand from his jacket sleeve.

Curtis shrugged with his uninjured shoulder, not looking up. "Just some flood damage. Could've been worse."

"Yup, that sounds about right. Flooding has just been devastating all over the east coast, my lord! Have you seen the damage?"

Curtis shook his head.

"Say, whatcha putting together over here, an aviary, somethin'?" The old man asked curiously, now noticing what he rang up.

"Something like that."

"God, I love exotic birds. Once had a Hyacinth Macaw, long ago. Most majestic creature you've ever seen—feathers the most vivid color blue, like a moonbeam in winter sky, I tell ya."

Curtis, expressionless, shuffled through his wallet for a form of payment and pulled the *emergency credit card*. He almost hesitated to hand it over but instead smirked and tossed it on the counter. The old man finished the transaction, and Curtis began to push his flat cart.

"*You think that'll stop what's comin*?" The old man grumbled in a familiar monotone.

Curtis stopped and turned. "Excuse me?"

The old man smiled. "I said, thanks for stoppin'. Come again!"

"Thanks," Curtis said, slightly muddled. He gave the old man a second look before turning to exit the warehouse.

"A strange one, that one is," the old man mumbled audibly, moving to the next patron in line as Curtis shuffled away.

Curtis didn't trust the police, and certainly not after the events that had transpired the last few days. He didn't know how much time he had until Sergeant Rick came snooping around again to question him, to passive-aggressively intimidate him until he cracked. And his story of a monster-in-the-basement would only get him locked up, or worse—sent up north to the psych ward in Middletown. The only thing to do was capture whatever this thing was and turn it over to the police. Or destroy it.

Curtis didn't have a computer, so he headed to Otis Library on Main Street to access the World Wide Web. As he entered, having never been inside before, the large, three-story brick structure intimidated him. But the space seemed cozy and mostly empty, save for two elderly female librarians behind a central station and a couple of patrons, equally as old, sitting on comfy La-Z-Boy chairs reading *The Day*. He asked to use one of the computers, and the librarian, preoccupied laminating book covers, deadpan, handed over a ticket with a login code for the row of desktop computers located in the back corner of the main floor.

The library was one of the few buildings in town with electricity, due to its high-power generator. Through the windows he passed, Curtis could see flooding from the Shetucket River, a branch of the Thames, slowly receding. With the water level so high, he could barely identify the Yantic and Shetucket Rivers' convergence—as if the Thames had furiously and unforgivingly swallowed up the inlets, creating one expanded, direct route all the way down to the Long Island Sound.

There was much research to be done. Curtis started with tips for his project, which didn't take much time; he found an ample amount of Do-It-Yourself carpentry sites and forum discussions.

Next came the current issue of residency. He doubted Amy would ever return to their house after the previous evening's events, and with what Curtis was planning to tackle, it might soon become inhabitable. Staying with his in-laws was out of the question, so he looked at several apartments in the area. He found many other properties close by, or at least within New London County—most inexpensive, but also situated in regions stricken with high poverty rates, full of low-income housing. Not ideal. Still, New London County *was* by the water, which Curtis liked.

New London City, along with Norwich and the rest of the county, had been on a rapidly progressive downturn in recent decades. The dissolution of industry was a shame—the slow demise of what was, at one time, home to one of the busiest and oldest whaling ports in the country. Starting with commercial fishing, followed by a boom in shipping and manufacturing industries, the city had become a hotspot after the Second World War with people migrating from worldwide to work here. It wasn't Boston, and it surely wasn't New York, but this area in Southeast Connecticut had something the other cities didn't—a sense of community.

However, the turn of the twentieth century brought the beginning of the end. With the advent of petroleum and gas, the need for oil derived from marine mammals diminished. The textile industry thrived during the next half-century. Many manufacturing companies either ceased operation or moved overseas through the 1960s and 1970s, due to labor costs and increasing technological advancements. After deindustrialization, urban decay set in around various parts of New London, Groton, and Norwich. Families moved from the area in search of work and the rents dropped, poverty ripening. Shells of abandoned, graffiti-splashed factories remained prominent throughout the county, a community eyesore all along the water-front.

New London County was one of the largest in Connecticut, more rural than the others but with a slightly urban feel. The county housed a small airport, a pharmaceutical company, a military sub-base—the US Navy's primary sub-base, mind you—a waste treatment facility, and a power plant. For what was otherwise a quaint, shoreline fishing community, New London offered a wide variety of amusements, chock full of marinas and tourist attractions. But the beaches—stretches of beach towns down the Connecticut River and along the Long Island Sound that seamlessly spilled into the neighboring Rhode Island—*that's* why you lived here if nothing more. Curtis, who had lived in the county most of his life, considered it his home; no matter how many negative boxes were checked, he couldn't really imagine being anywhere else.

The lights flickered sporadically as Curtis browsed online, sipping his cold, bitter cup of coffee while his eyes grew heavy. The mental and physical exhaustion grew tougher to shake, especially with the return of the hallucinations from his past now eating at him. Unable to distinguish his visions from reality, he struggled to trust what he heard and saw.

He could no longer stare at the computer. Inability to turn his brain off yielded procrastination, a loss of focus. He needed to walk around, maybe get some air—and a cigarette. Always a cigarette. Stepping out the back door of the first floor, he jarred it open using a coin from his pocket wedged in the latch. The cool, dry air blew through his hair while he gazed at the waterfront landscape, or what remained of it. Despite the overcast sky, a crystal-clear view greeted him. Seagulls drifted over the river to Holly Hock Island with the deviating winds, shifting his attention. The island didn't appear to be affected by floodwater, due to its high elevation—a preventative measure for such disastrous events, for sure.

From this point of view, Curtis could see a massive hole on the back end—a foundation, the bare, metal, bottom bones of a new structure erecting. Other than a dump truck and a backhoe, though, the place appeared abandoned, much like many of the county's old commercial structures. He exhaled deeply, snubbed out his smoke, and went back inside.

⸻⟡⸻

The unfriendly librarian gave a disinterested wave of the index finger toward the three hundreds section of the non-fiction stacks along the back of the first floor. In a raspy monotone, she said, "390."

Jesus, I think it's time for this lady to retire. Probably been here since the day this place opened...

After browsing the shelves for a few more moments, Curtis finally found what he searched for. *Connecticut Folklore* was quite old, thin, a black cover with red spine, the corners were frayed considerably, and the outer page edges heavily yellowed. He opened the book, thumbing through from back to front, too impatient to start with the table of contents, if it even had one. Full-page illustrations intermingled with disbursed text—not quite reference material and certainly not very comprehensive, but fascinating, nevertheless. He flipped through several sections: psychological and descent into madness, serial killer and home invasion tales, nature and monster myth, paranormal, and the occult. He didn't realize—better yet, couldn't fathom—how many strange stories the *Constitution State* had to offer.

Headings included: Haunted New Haven Town Green; Built Over Cemetery—Stones Removed, Dead Remain; Cursed Indian Land of the Kowalski Farmhouse; Sawmill City Melon Heads—Family of Cannibals; Jewett City Vampires—A Tuberculosis Curse; The Long Island Sound Serpent. Then, there it was: The Norwich Norwaukus. The short passage included a brief history and description of the creature.

The Norwaukus has been described as having the fur-covered body of a grizzly bear and a face similar to a bat or rodent, with bare feet and a long, hairless tail and possibly horns or "thagomizers," as seen on the backside of a Stegosaurus, protruding from its head and torso. The white-eyed creature has been rumored to be blind, but could not be verified, as no encounter has been officially documented. First spotted in the mid-1950s by farmers witnessing the mutilation of cows and livestock... Curtis skipped down. *Has been considered responsible for thirteen disappearances of locals over a two-decade span, three of whom were found in the woods in 1957, brutally mutilated at their decimated campsite. Seven policemen on horseback hunted the beast, but the search did not return a single clue. Before entering, one of the terrified men quoted the John Muir passage, "And into the forest I go, to lose my mind and find my soul..."* Curtis turned the page. The picture of the Norwaukus—a cartoon-like drawing—didn't quite seem to match the creature Curtis saw in his basement; however, the size definitely seemed accurate. He figured whoever drew the image must have based it on whatever had been described by the few farmers who claimed to see it. *This is ridiculous...* Curtis shook his head, then shelved the book.

Amy's letter kept returning to the forefront of his mind, leaving him in a fog of disquiet. It formed a burgeoning hole in the pit of his stomach—an ulcer—deteriorating, as he slipped and slid through its sour wake, racking his brain on ways to repair the perpetual damage. It was likely too late, but if there was a chance, now would be the time to at least finish what she'd asked and research the goddamn pharmaceutical company. Since the internet was at his fingertips, he needed some understanding of this strange island facility and why it had chosen to rob his family of their home.

Curtis came across a digital archive rich with historical information; the search soon sent him down a rabbit hole of facts he couldn't pull his overactive brain from. The first article of interest had details on the creation of Hock Pharmaceuticals. After skimming through pages of text, he learned that it was developed by the United States Department of Agriculture before the end of WWII, and it was intended to be "the technological solution" to the advancements the Germans were making, which seemed unexpectedly light-years beyond the US. After the war, it became a research facility before growing into the pharmaceutical market in the 1970s. Digging slightly further back, he discovered that a century ago, it had been a U.S. military installation called Fort Hock, and before that, the island had been purchased by the son of the Governor of Connecticut in the mid-1600s for a barrel of bread, a fur-lined coat, and basket of fishhooks.

He also found several dated clippings regarding Aldrich Douglas, a British native and top scientist at the company, about his appointment to CEO in the late 1980s, followed by a biography and a list of impressive accolades. From what Curtis gathered, the brilliant man graduated top of his class from the University of Oxford, going on to become the youngest to earn a Copley Medal and the Nobel Prize for his work in biology and chemistry. Curtis couldn't find much else on Aldrich dated after the mid-1990s.

The last collection of articles delved into the eminent domain, Laurel Hill, and the decommissioning of the pharmaceutical division. An unnamed entity associated with the facility had conceived the plan to develop beyond the island in 1991. A concept drawing of the finished facility included an anticipated completion date of spring 1997. The artist depicted several tall buildings along the inlet's perimeter—currently Laurel Hill—with the smallest gap between the island and the mainland connected by two bridges, one for automobiles and one for pedestrians. Other structures surrounded the facility, including an exquisite garden and a large, round fountain with statues on either side. *How fancy...*

Curtis clicked to open a low-quality MPEG video from a local news affiliate broadcast, titled "Interview with Douglas" dated November 1995. Both parties' accents made the short, vague clip slightly less discernible; however, he found the news reporter's southern drawl quite charming.

"Good evening. This is Rachel Estridge with WTNH, here on location in Norwich outside of Hock Pharmaceuticals, and I have with me here Dr. Aldrich Douglas, who has just been appointed CEO of this booming facility. He's here to talk about some new and exciting changes happening in the years to come. So, Aldrich, congratulations, first and foremost, and thank you for being here with us. Can you tell us a little about what we can expect?"

"Rachel, dear friend, thank you very much! Indeed—very exciting things are happening here at Hock in the not-too-distant future. After years of extensive planning, and receiving a generous donation, we

break ground in the spring, and development will be underway as this aging facility gets a major facelift."

"Well, the island looks great from here, Aldrich."

"Thank you, yes, much of it will be internal. Being a small island, things tend to wear quickly, being so close to saltwater."

"What can you tell us about your research?"

"My team and I have been undergoing extensive research trials, and we've had some major breakthroughs in the fight against infectious disease that I'll go into more detail very soon as they develop. Fascinating things underway."

"That's all you can tell us!?"

"Of course not! The expansion will facilitate all of our new areas for vast exploration, where we can advance our biological research development program—a world-leading powerhouse that will be the future of this country, and dare I say, lead to the inevitable eradication of cancer!"

"Wow, that is quite a statement, Aldrich. Inspiring news. We'll have to follow up with you after it's complete. This is Rachel Estridge—back over to you."

Curtis came across eminent domain in a related article and found it linked to extensive commentaries on the subject. He clicked through page after page of information, taking in everything subjectively and with great discontent. He couldn't believe what he was reading, skimming old court cases all with unfavorable outcomes. *The notion that the fucking federal government and state could seize your property—private property for "public use" goes against everything the constitution is supposed to stand for. You're worked like a goddamn mule in this country, you pay these ridiculous, bullshit, high taxes, you try and raise a family and do your best to survive by playing by the fucking rules, and your own people can swoop in and take your fucking land right from under you?*

The last clause of the Fifth Amendment, also known as the Takings Clause, limits the power of eminent domain by requiring compensation for property seized for public use—known as *"just compensation."* For the residents of Laurel Hill, that meant fair market value for their property. Unfortunately, the Laurel Hill residents suffered yet another painful blow as the fair market value was at an all-time, extraordinary *low*. At the time, the waterfront view of a pharmaceutical company wasn't considered *attractive real estate*. Original owners formed at least half of Laurel Hill's population, and to just up and relocate after four undisturbed decades proved extremely difficult. Young adults primarily composed the remaining residents—family members who basically inherited property. Curtis, thinking back on the decision to purchase *his* house, started to put the pieces together. The deal on the place was outstanding, all things considered, but he grossly overpaid in hindsight.

Some of the residents fought back and brought suits to the town and state. One young, newlywed couple, who had moved in the year before, made it as far as the Supreme Court, four years after the fact. Curtis continued to read, drinking another coffee graciously provided by the library. *Lavigne vs. City of Norwich* was the particular case. The plaintiffs, Matthew and Lauren Lavigne, brought the suit in front of the state of Connecticut, stating it had misused its power of eminent domain. The Lavignes had argued that the vacant lot formerly known as Laurel Hill Drive, now reserved for economic development, did not meet "public use" requirements as stated in the Fifth Amendment. Additionally, he argued it unconstitutional for the government to seize property from one individual and transfer it to another individual or corporation.

Matt's grandparents had left the house to his parents when they passed, succumbing to carbon monoxide poisoning in the winter of 1991 due to a clogged chimney flue. Matt's folks had recently retired, living their early golden years on Marco Island, off Florida's Gulf Coast. They signed the deed over to Matt, who made the house his dream project. He expensed over forty thousand dollars in renovations to prepare for their *forever home*—money which he had painstakingly squirreled away in his twenties, money he hoped to recoup from the court proceedings.

To his misfortune, the court ruled with a 4-3 decision in favor of the City of Norwich. With the promise of tax growth, city revenue, and ample employment opportunity, the justices ruled the project economically viable for *public use*. Matt's forever home was gone. Forever. Despite the misfortune, the Lavignes appeared to be doing just fine. A quick internet search affirmed the restaurant was not only open but thriving with a second location upstate.

Curtis knew that Eminent Domain had its place. When it benefitted everyone as a community—highways, railroads, school systems—the concept made total sense. But this private corporation corruption seemed like something else altogether.

Curtis dug further. *Why was this land left to waste? Why in the sweet fuck did this company kick everyone out of their homes, then pull out? Pieces of shit...*

Interestingly enough, he came across a scandal involving a large construction outfit from New York City. Hock Pharmaceuticals had invested ten million dollars upfront for the project, which began in the spring of 1996. One month into the project, the Federal Bureau of Investigation seized the company, known as Enzo Corp, for a laundry list of criminal activities, including extortion, trafficking, and numerous capital and felony murder counts.

Hock lost their ten-million-dollar investment and couldn't obtain additional financing from any institution, thus forcing them to scrap their development project. A few more articles surfaced that headlined: *"Fire on Holly Hock Island,"* followed by *"Hock Pharm & 1,200 Jobs to Leave Norwich."*

Later that year, a lab explosion and fire on the rear end of the island caused the death of four employees, including Aldrich Douglas. That incident, followed by the recent expiration of tax incentives, resulted in the government closing shop in Norwich and moving their research department elsewhere. Many employees, low-level all the way up the executive chain, lost their positions while a select group transferred to the newer sister location in New London. Hock Pharmaceuticals filed Chapter 11 in 1997, selling off its remaining assets, including the New London location to the Chindōgu Corp, a private Japanese research company.

He tried to delve further into the rise and fall of the Enzo Group, however, the only information offered was that the business had been established in the 1940s by Italian businessman, Lorenzo Passerini. The few articles he managed to find suggested his family may have been under scrutiny dating back to the nineteenth century with alleged rumors of ties with organized crime.

He couldn't find much history of Laurel Hill online, so Curtis asked the seemingly dispirited librarian to help dig up old newspaper archives, which she did, albeit indifferently. Large, dusty, antique leather-bound books stored the collections, some of which suffered from red rot and other effects from time. After some tedious hunting and careful handling, an old clipping surfaced, unveiling the Laurel Hill estates' completion from *The Day,* dated September 21st, 1955. The headline read, "*The Neighborhood of Tomorrow,*" and depicted a wooden street sign with a half-page size, hand-drawn ranch style home underneath. Other clippings followed, spanning four months detailing the local housing projects and land deals. Then, he turned the page to an article that almost floored him.

Enzo & Son's Construction Co. —the same company that contributed to Hock Pharmaceuticals' demise—had built the neighborhood of Laurel Hill in the summer of 1955. Lorenzo purchased the land for pennies on the dollar, with plans to expand other neighborhoods around the Yantic, building affordable housing to rent. Not long after completion, and for reasons unknown, he sold the properties to a shrewd, local land developer, who then unloaded the properties at highly inflated prices with duplicitous practices and *clever,* innovative marketing.

In 1956, many people just didn't know any better—naïve to a fault. In the years following WWII and the Korean War, when people saw billboards advertising "*The Neighborhood of Tomorrow*" in the land of opportunity, they figured they best get in while they still could. And there was no better time, as families flooded in to meet the manufacturing companies' high employment demand. The increasing desire for automobiles, the highway interstate's inception, and new government mortgage plans encouraged the post-war sprawl to suburbia.

The Ranch became the pinnacle of minimal traditional style housing construction. The compact house with a cost-effective structure could be built on a very modest lot with a shallow foundation slab. Yet the broad, rambling façade, built-in garages, and long, ribbon windows made this style house quite an attractive place to live, composing the fourteen-plot community of what became Laurel Hill Drive.

The flickering lights above Curtis dimmed low. He blinked hard and twitched as if waking from a trance, glancing up and around. The library was empty. Silent. Even the staff appeared unusually absent from their station. A static *snap* followed by a dull hiss brought his attention to a fading monitor screen. The library's generators had stalled; the brownout forced all computers to simultaneously shut down.

Clearly, it was time to leave.

TWENTY-ONE

The burned, apricot glow of the nightfall horizon peacefully lingered as the truck backed up the driveway into half the garage. Curtis pulled the material he purchased at the warehouse from the bed and hauled it inside.

His first order of business: set up the sump pumps in the basement—and he didn't look forward to it. With the shotgun in hand, he quickly inspected the space from atop the landing in front of the busted door, uncertain if the Norwaukus was still there. All seemed quiet. Carefully, he climbed down the broken steps and jumped into the waist-high lagoon as if he had entered the cabin of a partially sunken ship. The shock from the raw cold sent chills through him, a quiver, waking caffeine-numbed nerves. The water gleamed, black. A thin layer of dust coated the still surface, with many of the Reynolds' possessions submerged beneath while other small items delicately drifted by.

A school of tiny fish swam just below the dark surface as he inched toward the back. Several light splashes drew his attention to a couple of frogs jumping in from his workbench. He drew in deep breaths, shivering, panning the room, still in utter disbelief; what used to be the basement was now an ecosystem for aquatic life—a swamp. A slight, salty aroma lingered in the stale, musty air.

He needed some time to get everything connected, and after he finished, he sporadically returned to check and make sure all the pumps ran. Twenty feet of an inch-and-a-half hose were rigged with duct tape to each pump, fitted for maximum efficiency to rapidly expel water. With each trip down, he noticed the water level slightly dropping, still having a ways to go. With no reason to wait, he got right to work on the next thing on his list.

Curtis turned the dial to Radio 104 on a little AM/FM stereo found inside a partially destroyed, water-damaged storage box—the only salvageable item inside, and at the immediate moment, the most important. The station played 311, a favorite band of his and Amy's. The song reminded him of the grandiose Radio 104 Festival at The Hartford Meadows Pavilion he'd attend every other summer. The one where he proposed to Amy. He sighed, remembering that romantic evening. Other delectable tunes followed as he started to get into the project. The Red Hot Chili Peppers played in the background, then Blur, Collective Soul, and Everclear—all bands he recalled seeing, barely. Three sheets to the wind, as they say?

In his two-thousand-square-foot Cape Cod-style house with limited space, in need of considerable renovations, the dining room seemed like the most practical place to tear a giant hole in the floor. He dragged out the rarely used eighteen-inch, oak IKEA table they received as a wedding present from Amy's parents. Curtis fucking hated the constant reminder of how frugal his in-laws were—only gifting cheap furniture or old hand-me-downs. The chairs followed. And while he was at it, he pulled out the matching glass-door cabinet buffet chest and gaudy Oriental rug from underneath.

Curtis drew a rough outline on the floor in permanent black marker. He slid a fresh blade in the tile saw, plugged it in, slid on his goggles, and of course, lit a cigarette. Painfully, he carved through the pristine, aged oak top board, carefully removing it intact. Then, with little regard, he tore through the floorboard, slicing through each joist as sawdust filled the room. Lastly, he removed the insulation, exposing the watery chamber below.

He spent the remainder of the evening constructing the metal enclosure. To ensure the security of every joint, Curtis welded each groove and each corner. He bolted large industrial hooks into the dining room ceiling, running the length of the house to the end of the family room. He fastened twenty-four feet of an inch-and-a-half diameter braided rope with a galvanized metal thimble end loop to the cage by a large carabiner. The rope fed through the ceiling hooks, with Curtis using the staircase pillar as a support to pull the rope, lifting the cage from the floor.

Curtis hadn't given much thought to what he was going to do once he caught the Norwaukus. *It definitely killed Haverhill, no doubt about that there. But, Christ, could there be others?* The house was lost—that much he knew for sure. At this point, causing an "electrical fire" would be the best option to recoup enough of the insurance money to pay off the goddamn loan. Though fraud offered a viable option, he knew bad luck always conveniently followed two steps behind him, and he'd be scrutinized by the local police if *his* house went up in flames. Plus, if Sergeant Rick returned asking questions, trying to find any way to possibly make Curtis accountable for the recent deaths, burning down the house might be off the table. *FUCK*. Another thing to dwell on. Curtis could go back and forth all day weighing options, but he didn't have time.

Clear the mind. As far as he could figure out, trapping this creature remained priority one.

He worked diligently, stopping only for coffee and a quick smoke. Before he knew it, night fell. The exhaustion reached him, but his mind wouldn't shut off—at least not long enough for him to pass out as he plopped down on the couch. As usual, sleep eluded him. No surprise. Regularly drinking four to eight cups of coffee throughout the day didn't help, either. He couldn't remember the last meal he'd had, or if he'd eaten at all, for that matter. This thought worried him a bit, so off to the pantry he went.

Though the thought of eating actually caused him to salivate a bit, which he felt good about as he shuffled through the shelves of boxes of pasta and canned goods, he found himself too tired to actually cook anything. The pantry housed bags of mixed nuts, mini snack packs, and fruit gummies that he assumed Wes took for lunch—none of it appealing. Instead of Doritos and cheese puffs, bags of veggie chips and sleeves of rice cakes filled the snack corner. *Is Amy on some sort of diet?* The thought fleeted as he turned his head to find treasure. A jar of peanut butter caught his wary eye, which he grabbed along with a loaf of Wonder Bread before making his way to the living room. He sat for a moment, staring off into nowhere, and ate, dipping dry, folded slices and scooping up chunky PB in silence.

The generator barely produced enough energy to run the pumps and lights, but oddly, enough juice remained to still run the television. Curtis pulled out the sliding drawer of an oversized, plywood entertainment center—that housed the equally oversized Panasonic TV DVD/VCR combo—sorting through the VHS cassettes stored within. He popped in one labeled *Florida - 1999.*

The first video in the loop showed a trip to the magical world of Disney, where he'd taken his wife and son. Since Curtis had never been and always wanted to go, and Wes was finally old enough to enjoy it, he figured it was time—and well overdue, as their first trip since the honeymoon. Amy had come up with the idea, actually; she'd been many times as a young girl and cherished any opportunity to return. By the time they reached Disney, she seemed more excited than *they* were. Curtis had supposed there were other, possibly, more satisfying options to consider. Aruba? Europe? But he had still enjoyed the trip. How does one weigh islands or foreign countries against a twelve-minute boat ride with puppets singing "It's a Small World," after all?

The splotchy video, shot from a large, clunky Panasonic camcorder—the size that held the actual VHS tape—showed every scene in sequential order with hard cuts from Bradley International to the Disney resort, through the parks. He couldn't believe how happy everyone appeared—the huge smiles, the laughter—the synergistic bond among the three palpable even now. Seeing the enchantment in his son's eyes in this mystical kingdom made him melt, and he smiled at the screen, watching them travel from park to park.

Next came a dolphin show at Sea World and riding the Trolley Train in Seuss Landing at Universal Studios, infused with random, choppy editing, before cutting to Fantasyland. A blissful Amy rode the Mad Tea Party teacups with her happy little boy. The excitement in her was unmistakable—nothing more prizing than to be a parent, sharing the best moments of your childhood with your kid. When the ride ended, she stepped out of their yellow and pink striped cup, picking up Wes, swinging him around in the air while making noises like an airplane. Curtis marveled at the precious expression on his son's pudgy, little face as he giggled shrilly, beaming ear to ear, mouth full of baby teeth.

In the following cutscene, Wes took a photograph with all his cartoon heroes, then immediately after, ran into the arms of six-foot giant Tigger, squeezing him with every ounce of his small being. Curtis laughed. Quite some time had passed since he had felt that much joy, or even had a real reason to smile—an emotion long since departed. At that moment, he could sense innocence in his young son, pure bliss. The feeling had eluded him since his birth, and long before that, his own childhood.

His eyes welled with tears as a sudden sadness washed over—an emptiness he doubted could ever be replenished, knowing it had been over five years since they'd gone away. He missed that feeling—one that only develops over a time—one of familial discovery, traveling uncharted territory, building those eternal memories. He wanted to go back, fearing now he was too late. The thought of another vacation, whether theoretical or not, died away as his thoughts flitted back to his current financial—more so, marital—situation. Such a trip may never again be a possibility.

Pacing through the living room, he managed to watch hours of family footage, hoping the images would subsist long after within his latent mind. On TV, their family became jubilant and engaging—an expression of life he thought to be most advantageous. Birthdays seemed like Christmas, and the weekends looked like holidays. Family barbeques and day trips to Mystic Aquarium and the Harvest County Fair appeared routine. Each day felt as consequential as the last, and for that happy, smiling Curtis, each day would conclude with a quiescent mind. Utter bliss.

Watching his past, Curtis cried long, and he cried hard, to the point where he could barely breathe, sucking in quick breaths between each wail. The cheerful people on the screen had become strangers. Unrecognizable. A family existing in a fantastical world, a land of illusion. Where were they now? Living in some alternate, branched timeline, somewhere split off from his own universe. His wife and son were his world, all he had left, as he was finally able to see the years spent—wasted—pushing them away.

TWENTY-TWO

Curtis woke. He didn't quite know if he had fallen asleep or just plain blacked out, having no recollection of time passing, but the sun poured in from the family room window over his face, causing him to squint. He slowly sat up and glanced at his surroundings, almost forgetting how he got there. The couch, now just as filthy as he, had a trail of dried, muddy footprints leading up to it from every direction—something he hadn't noticed the previous evening with the lack of sufficient lighting. *Fuck it...*

He lit a cigarette, followed by a morning piss and a trip down below. The sump pumps had lived up to their reputation, and the water looked low enough for him to finish his project.

Curtis measured and drilled through the seventy-year-old, wet, granite surface, then slowly carved a six-inch-wide slit around the diameter of the seven-by-seven space he created, thankful for purchasing the wet tile saw. Switching to a hoe, he dug down about a foot deep to break up its contents, shoveling chunks of stone and dirt into a large, wheeled garbage can to be pushed to the basement corner. He came across the sheet of frosted plate glass on his way out, which he used to cover the broken window. Everything looked good, so Curtis decided a test run would be in order. He untied the

171

rope, releasing the trap through the dining room floor. The heavy contraption weighed enough for it to drop straight down without much sway, right into the groove. Perfect. Curtis smiled.

Bang! Bang! Bang! Bang!

Curtis stopped, then turned to look behind. From where he stood, he could see through the dining room and past the family room, all the way to the front door, where the heavy knocking originated. Without moving—without breathing, he waited, perfectly still. The room fell silent. Almost. As if the air had been depleted, the only sound, a low, steady hum, came from the mild tinnitus in his left ear.

Several seconds later—

Bang! Bang! Bang! Bang!

Curtis slowly walked to the door, where, through the cream-colored curtain which hung from the sidelight window, he saw a silhouette standing. With two fingers, he gently pushed the fabric aside just enough to peek out. He could barely see the figure outside from this angle, and he strained for a better view.

Bang! Bang! Bang! Bang!

"Mr. Reynolds—hello? Is anybody home?"

The voice sounded familiar, as if he had recently heard it, but he couldn't quite place it. Curtis remembered his truck, still parked partially inside the open garage, so he doubted he could delude whoever this was. To avoid arousing further suspicion and interruption, he reluctantly responded, opening the door about a foot just as a fist went up to knock again.

"Mr. Reynolds..."

"Sergeant? What a surprise." With a quick look behind himself and back to Sergeant Rick, Curtis closed the door several inches, so only his face remained in the doorway. His eyes squinted in an adjustment to the incoming light.

"Sorry to bother ya, uh, did I come at a bad time?" Rick stood awkwardly in the doorway, his gray uniform slightly disheveled, as if he'd been in the same clothes for days.

"Uh, no—no, of course not. Um, what—what can I do for ya?" Curtis discreetly glanced beyond the officer's shoulder to see if anyone came with him, but he only noticed an empty Crown Victoria cruiser parked curbside.

"You okay?" Sergeant Rick asked with a slight wince, looking him up and down. "If you don't mind me sayin', you, uh, look like you crawled out of a swamp, there."

"Huh?" Curtis looked himself up and down. "OH! Haha... yeah, yeah—just uh, doing some mild reno' work. Basement flooded."

"Yes... well, I was just passing through the neighborhood, stopping door to door to ask a few questions. You see, we got a 'missing persons' report for a woman who lives nearby." Sergeant Rick pulled a photo from his pocket and held it in front of Curtis. "This here is Mallory Luske—went missing yesterday morning. She lives over beyond the pine there on Coit Street. You seen her?"

Curtis's eyes squinted more to better view the photo, in which Mallory sat on her porch with Balki in her lap, smiling; her oxygen sat next to her on a side table, a tube running around her face.

"Uhhh, no. No," Curtis said, looking back and forth from the picture to the officer, waiting for the uncomfortably long silence to break.

"Hmm..." Sergeant Rick put the picture back in his pocket. "I was afraid of that. Her daughter, Evelyn, who lives nearby, went over to check on her after the storm—make sure she was all right—and noticed neither she nor the dog was there. Called late last night to report it after waiting it out to see if she'd return. I had one man along with her family checking the woods earlier, which turned up nothing."

"Huh…"

"Suppose this wasn't the first time either."

"Hmm?"

"She'd taken off before without telling her daughter, who reported her missing the year before after the last hurricane. Ended up leaving with the neighbors, who we're now trying to get a hold of. Well, who knows, right? Is the Mrs. around? Maybe she might have seen her?"

"Yeah, no, she ran out with our son to—get some groceries, but, uh, I can definitely ask her when she returns if she—she'd seen anything."

Another uncomfortable silence…

"I'll tell ya, it's been so crazy around here since the hurricane struck down: the damage, and the loss of power everywhere, roads blocked by fallen trees, houses too, personal injury, *plus* all of the regular problems we face on a daily basis—domestic disputes and the like. The phone's been ringing off the hook at the station, and we're short-staffed as it is here. I've been at this all morning by myself in between tending to other calls." Sergeant Rick lamented.

Curtis wondered how the sergeant even made it to work every day. In the now three instances he'd seen the officer, he appeared utterly morose, as if he'd experienced all the horrors of the world during his seemingly short tenure patrolling the county and now couldn't take anymore. Curtis almost felt sorry for him. And as he began to think about how to get out of this conversation, the Sergeant's shoulder radio interrupted.

"*Sergeant Rick, come in, please,*" Central Command prompted.

"Rick here."

"*Sarge, we have a report of a 10-91V at Black Park, a 904A on Route Twelve near the brewery, a 10-90 at the brewery, and continuous calls are coming in for 11-65/11-66 and a 909C in various parts of town, mostly up and down Asylum, and that's all.*"

"Sweet Mary, mother of holy Christ," Sergeant Rick said softly to himself, shaking his head. "Mr. Reynolds." He began to turn, then stopped midway. "Oh—I almost forgot. Mrs. Haverhill—Ronald's wife—when I spoke to her, she happened to mention he owed you quite a significant amount of money for some freelance work a while back?"

"Yeah?" Curtis said almost inquisitively, waiting for a follow-up question or comment, though not in the mood to entertain.

"Just find it curious, is all."

Curtis stared at the sergeant—his blood pressure rising.

"Hmm... welp, you have yourself a good rest of your afternoon, Mr. Reynolds. I'll be in touch." He tipped his hat, turned, and walked to his car.

TWENTY-THREE

The Reynolds' kitchen freezer didn't contain much to bait the beast, so Curtis drove down to the butcher off Main and picked up a side of venison, which he also purchased with the emergency credit card. He figured something a bit gamey might do the trick. The butcher, happy to offload his inventory, gave Curtis a good deal, as he struggled with keeping the perishables at a consistent temperature with his feeble generator.

A shower and change of clothing seemed in order. Curtis cleaned himself up, slipped on another white V-neck undershirt and cargo pants, then made a fast run to the only convenient store with power. After acquiring a cup of gas station coffee and a pack of cigarettes, Curtis had everything needed for a stakeout. When he returned, he placed the meat dead-center of the seven-by-seven spot along with two packages of cured bacon and a pint of peanut butter for good measure. He grabbed the radio, pulled up a chair, and sat front row, looking down into the giant crevice that was once his dining room floor while sipping his coffee and lighting a smoke.

Time was lost on Curtis. In between cigarettes and piss breaks, he'd get up to stretch, walk around the house, raid the cupboard for nourishment. He feasted on junk, mainly consisting of animal crackers, fruit gummies, pretzels, and cheese—basically everything Wes would bring to school for snack time.

Almost forgetting about the outside world, he stepped out the front door for some breezy, fresh air, lighting a cigarette with the end of one just finished. Well, outside smelled fresher than the dining room, anyway. A waning full moon sat in the clear, bright sky, just above the glowing fir treetops between Forest Street and downtown. As he put the cigarette to his lips, movement caught the corner of his eye, directing his sight to the main road. Down the street, which he could just about see from the reflection of his front stoop light, an animal sat on the center line, watching him. He walked to his truck, still backed into the driveway, and snapped on the headlights, which dissipated as they reached the street, creating a shadow near the little black figure, which was his only indication it might be a cat. Eerie.

Curtis made a few cat-calling sounds and patted his thighs, hoping to maybe elicit a response, but the cat did not reciprocate. He turned off the lights and walked back to the stoop. From what he could see, it appeared to be a black cat, which reminded him of the one his mother brought home on his ninth birthday. Though mostly in response to his father's passing, she clearly thought the critter would help cheer him up. He did enjoy having a new friend, but his involvement in boy scouts took up much of his free time, and in the years to follow the animal took a backseat as he found other things to occupy his time. In the end, the cat became his mother's best friend. Just as well—her husband's passing hit her much harder than Curtis. She, more so than her son, ultimately desired companionship.

Continuing to enjoy the breeze, he glanced periodically back to the street, each time noticing a new feline friend joining the first stray. By the time he finished, more critters than he could instinctually count occupied the pavement. Curtis, weirded out, snubbed the end of the smoke, backed into the house, and shut the door.

More time passed as Curtis sat. The hours began to feel like days. The radio continued to play, now tuned to 102.9's Golden Oldies for reasons unknown, but he left it. Despite the fact he couldn't recall changing the station (which no longer surprised him), he found something about the rockabilly sound of southern rhythm and blues relaxing—the mix of harmonious tones threading gospel and the melodic lines of doo-wop together had formulated a style that defined a generation. His father's generation. And although Curtis was born in '69, technically raised in the 70s—the age of hair bands and metal—he could appreciate early rock.

The copious amount of coffee consumed kept sending him to the bathroom. He went, pissed, washed his hands, and splashed cold water on his face. In the mirror, he stared at himself. The bags under his eyelids sunk dark. Heavy. A gleam of light in the reflection caught his tired eyes. He looked up to see three cats sitting on a high shelf where the towels lived. The sight didn't faze him, and he just stared.

They stared back.

The Cellos, "Rang-Tang-Ding-Dong," began to play from the dining room.

"*Who—are—YOU!?*" The cats sang out in unison.

"I—am the Japanese Sandman," Curtis replied, somberly, in the mirror.

"*You lookee like a Japanese Sandman!*"

Curtis turned to an empty shelf and exited the bathroom, back to his nest. The radio batteries depleted; The Cellos faded out.

Some time had passed, and a rustling broke the stale, damp silence that filled the house. He quietly inched toward the opening, careful not to make a sound. On his hands and knees, he crawled to the pocket, gently peering down into the gloom below, dark even with the dim shine from the hanging 60-watt bulb.

Squinting, he discerned an object stirring through the wet room, moving closer and toward Curtis's line of sight. It picked off small chunks at a time with its hands, backed out of sight, and noisily devoured each piece of sticky deer flesh. He struggled to tell for sure what he saw, but its textured, full torso became visible—long, curved barbs protruding back. They quivered while it ate. Curtis watched this sequence of events while waiting for the... *thing* to stay still. He wanted it distracted, eating through the top layer of meat before he released the trap. And he waited. This *thing*, suspicious, untrusting, moved in and out with precision. Curtis, anxious, watched it work its way through most of the food, now fearing he'd miss his chance. Needing to take his shot before it was too late, he crawled back to the staircase, stood slowly, and pulled the rope from the taut position—causing it to slingshot through the room, dropping the heavy crate to the basement floor below.

Before he could even wonder, the immediate thrashing below indicated success. He'd captured it. The Norwaukus, frantic, scurried back and forth, colliding with every barrier. Each time it struck, the force would jolt the cage, dislodging it from the carved groove meant to keep the contraption secure. Curtis, alarmed, jumped down through the opening, landing across the top to try and hold it in place. He held tightly with a bar wrapped in each white-knuckled hand as each collision thrust him in a new direction. For a moment, he regretted this decision, realizing he didn't fully understand what this thing was capable of—there weren't more than a few feet of space between him and it. The Norwaukus jumped from its hind legs; spikes shot through the top as Curtis let one hand go, rolling back to avoid being impaled. The enclosure raised, tipping to one side, and with maximum effort, right at that last possible second, he flipped over, grabbed the far edge, balancing out the weight. The cage dropped back down.

The thrashing continued, but gradually weakened with each minute that passed, until the shaking lightened enough for him to safely get down. The beast staggered, swaying left to right. The light remained too dim for Curtis to get a good look at the *thing* that attacked him, terrifying nevertheless behind those bars. It snarled, deeply exhaling, then fell to its side.

Unconscious.

He passed the flashlight over its head. Looking at the bat-like face directly horrified him. The pudgy, wide, swine-like snout covered in long, rigid whiskers formed the uninviting forefront of the beast. Attached to the short muzzle came four protruding central incisors—two long, tusk-like teeth extended down past the jawline, with two shorter protruding from the mandible, all tinged yellow with pink, streaky blotches. Behind them, he found a row of small canines, top and bottom. Teeth and gums looked slightly exposed on one side of the mouth, surrounded by twisted hair and black, roasted flesh patches; slight ulceration contoured the jaw and neck. The ears seemed as ample as they were round on either side of its head, poking through tuft fur.

Curtis, out of breath, smiled, proud of himself for dosing the peanut butter with the old half-empty bottle of benzodiazepines from the vanity. He had trapped the Norwaukus.

Unsure of how much time he had, Curtis hurried to work on the final touches. He rolled the wheelbarrow from the shed to the basement, dropped in the bag of cement, and ripped it open with a shovel. With some of the leftover puddles of floodwater, he mixed the sandy material with the shovel until it reached a thick, muddy consistency, then filled in the slit he had drilled out earlier, sealing in the cage. Two industrial-size floor fans helped aid in the drying process. For added security and final peace of mind, he finished by anchoring the bottom edges with a few pieces of scrap metal, using a masonry drill bit to seal it into the foundation.

Curtis grew drained, exhaustion hitting him, hard, out of nowhere. Barely making it back up the stairs, he plopped down on the filthy couch, staring at the blank television screen. The cable box flashed a green 12:00 a.m., as it usually did, and in the absence of outside light, this possibility proved plausible. Soon his eyes finally closed. But they wouldn't stay that way. They never did. Every time he'd begin to transcend the living room, he'd jolt awake. At times, he felt as if hours had passed, though only a few moments had. But, eventually, the hours did pass. Curtis, giving up on sleep, snubbed out his last cigarette in an overflowing ashtray, took the shotgun out of the closet, and went downstairs.

He stared at the thing in the cage, still laid out, barely identifiable. Several swift clinks across the bars with the spade of the shovel brought no response from the Norwaukus. Wondering if maybe he'd killed it, Curtis decided to poke it with the back of the handle. Apprehensively, he took a swift jab at its side, then quickly stepped back.

Nothing.

Curtis began to lay into it, driving in the staff. He managed to push the beast onto its side, exposing its face and upper body. The mouth fell open, baring teeth and tongue. The smell emanating from its orifice smacked him in the face, causing him to choke and gag. The head rested against the side of the steel bars, its ear partially protruding through.

An anomaly caught his eye as he glanced over its unsettling facial features. He reached in with two fingers, while keeping as safe distance as possible, and lightly grasped the veiny flesh of what appeared to be an ear, giving it a slight twist. To his surprise, he unveiled a series of letters branded along the curved backside of the flap. He inched in closer to make out the writing, but he couldn't quite put together the tag. Curtis spoke each character aloud as he deciphered them: **L-O-T, 0-0-1, H-O-C-K, A.-D.-R....**

The shovel jerked, knocking Curtis back, then snapping in half over the cage bars as the Norwaukus shot up. It shoved its snout in between the bars, viciously chewing at the steel rods. Curtis stepped back and waited for the thing to settle down. When it did, he finally had the chance to take a good look at the creature.

He slowly and cautiously moved toward the cage, eyes fixated on *it*. It stood on all fours, staring back. Even in a cage, it loomed. The size of a young black bear, maybe five feet long, head to hind. The large head was attached to a short, stout body, with no apparent neck separating the two. Its stubby limbs bore grayish-pink, scaly feet with long, narrow, translucent claws. The tail stretched about as long as its body, tapering down to the tip and scaled, much like the feet. Black and brown frizzed fur coiled the head, frame, and limbs. The back happened to be much more interesting. Running from head to rear, the hair grew thicker, lengthier, and barbed—almost quill-like. Light shades of white and grey—patterned chevron—comprised the salient topcoat.

Faint stirring outside caused Curtis to glance up and around. Shadows beyond the frosted plate glass trotted past in both directions, wildly tapping, digging, scratching the side of each wall. Copper dust emanated from the fissure between the window frame and the eroded foundation. The surrounding phenomena drew his attention for a moment as he prepared himself, unsure of what may follow.

After a long, silent pause, Curtis turned back to the creature. It stood still, staring back with those terrifying, clouded eyes. Cold. Vacuous. Never in his wildest dreams could he ever imagine the existence of something as strange and as heinous as what loomed in front of him. He looked into the shiny, white orbs and came to one conclusion—abomination.

Curtis picked up the shotgun, broke it open, and loaded two shells into the chamber. Pulling back on one, then both hammers, he lifted the barrel to eye level. The gun fixed at the beast's head. His breathing grew heavy; his heart rate increased. Both hands trembled, and the shotgun shook. Curtis, trying to keep steady, gripped tighter, only making the tremors worse. The Norwaukus, not moving, kept its gaze fixed on him. The heavy breathing turned to hyperventilation, and he lost control.

He pulled his finger off the trigger and lowered the weapon, gasping for air. Tears ran down the side of his face; he let out a deep howl, fell to his knees, and broke down in uncontrollable sobbing. The feeling almost suffocated him, and he sucked back air to catch his wheezing breath. Looking back at the creature, he realized they shared commonalities. He, too, had been created, so to speak, to kill—had killed, indiscriminately and without remorse. Maybe *he* was an abomination. But he imagined this *thing* must feel scared, alone, mostly confused… he knew not his purpose in this world.

Icy cold water splashed his face, beading down his patchy beard scruff, neck, and chest. A few more handfuls of water cleared his eyes and pushed his hair back. He grabbed a towel off the rack and gently dried his face, watching his reflection in the bathroom mirror. A disheveled wreck stared back—a shell of a human. Ten years had gone by overnight. A pouch of violaceous skin bowed from under each sunken socket, surrounding each bloodshot, steel-blue eye.

"What the fuck… what the fuck am I doing?" He asked himself, looking into dilated, sable pupils. His hands grasped the sides of the sink as he leaned in. "Who the hell are you?"

A tear rolled down his cheek.

"Who am I?" His reflection returned, confused. *"Who—are you? Well? Who the hell are* you*!? Look at yourself. What the fuck have you become? You worthless piece of shit—you're nothing. Without* them, *you're nothing. You don't deserve them. You don't deserve this life."*

"Shut up." Curtis hung his head, unable to look back.

"Whaddya gonna do when she's gone? Huh?"

"Shut—up."

"You think she's going to settle for a guy who can't even pull the trigger? That thing almost killed her—your son. Now it's your pet? You know what you need to do."

Curtis squeezed his eyes shut and tightly gripped the edges of the sink; his body started to quiver. "STOP!"

"You're pathetic. It's no wonder they all hate you. You should have done her the favor and just let that thing fucking kill you."

"GET-OUT-OF-MY-HEAD!" Curtis screamed, panting heavily.

"Curtis..."

He slowly, reluctantly opened his eyes—then shrieked, utterly mortified.

Crystal's pale face reflected inches from his, staring—eyes frosted. Her wavy blonde hair, saturated with blood, clung to her cheeks and bulging, broken neck. Her mouth dropped open. Curtis stumbled backward, arms braced, fearing she may come at him through the mirror. He hit the split barn closet doors, cracking the rungs, before sliding down on his ass.

There, he sat, shaking, head between his legs.

TWENTY-FOUR

Through the dry, temperate, evening air of the base camp, moaning and wailing echoed. The noise intensified with every passing hour, filling the several parallel Temper tents erected as temporary barracks. Each tent contained sixty cots, half occupied, with vacancy steadily diminishing. Soldiers dropped one after the other. Some men lay unconscious, while others writhed in agony. Those lying down remained too weak to move, save for leaning over the side to vomit. The ones with enough strength to manage a beeline to a toilet seemed equally out of luck.

The latrines stayed unceasingly occupied, backed up with interspersed lines of distressed men waiting their turn. Some didn't make it; they savagely raked away sand with scooped hands and dropped trousers, defecating where they stood. Fear and panic struck the First Company of the Seventh Marine Infantry Regiment, stationed on the Qatar Peninsula.

Forty-eight to seventy-two hours earlier, a handful of soldiers began to show signs of illness upon returning from assignment in Kuwait City. The First and Second Marine Divisions, along with the First Light Infantry Battalion, had just achieved victory after a long, arduous, four-day firefight to drive the Iraqi troops out of Kuwait.

The First Company of the Seventh Regiment concluded the liberation with an unexpected skirmish at the Kuwait International Airport, thus ending the Gulf War.

Several troops reported flu-like symptoms and indigestion at the base, which they disregarded as a probable twenty-four-hour bug. But the sickness soon magnified, moving swiftly through the unit. By day two, an epidemic had arrived, and the symptoms only continued to worsen overnight.

Navy physicians arrived on scene, clad in white, disposable hooded coveralls, face masks, and goggles. They examined the first group of symptomatic men, who had been temporarily quarantined in a private barracks. X-rays were taken, blood tests were administered and expedited.

The aviation medical examiner ran down a luminous clearing between the barracks and into the medical tent. The relatively small space contained a handful of fully occupied cots with soldiers hooked up to intravenous lines. A small, mobile counter with a built-in sink and cabinet held medical supplies, centrally stationed in the room. A silver radio lay at the edge with a 1950s cassette tape in the deck playing Little Richard's "Keep a Knockin'" at a shallow volume. Entering at such a high speed, the examiner knocked over a tray with surgical tools and startled a physician, who was using the equipment to clean up sutures on a soldier's leg.

"Are you all right, Private Reynolds?" the physician asked her patient, hurriedly picking instruments from the ground.

"Doctor, I need help over here," another physician yelled. "HURRY!"

The examiner grabbed a clipboard, skimming over notes. "What do we got?"

"Rise in heart rate, acute respiratory failure. Body temperature keeps dropping. Patient has been producing blood-filled sputum," the second physician reported.

"This man is going into septic shock. Get me a respirator and prep the IV. We need to clear this room!"

Curtis watched the physicians move the soldier to a gurney. His head rolled to the side, blood leaking from the nasal passages. Many ulcerated lesions marbled the surface of his now unrecognizable face, exposing raw subcutaneous tissue as if he had been blowtorched. The perimeter of each lesion glared with a pink hue, which blended a crusted pigmentation of yellow, burgundy, and brown at its center. Other parts of the skin, more notably the arms and hands, hid behind raised vesicles that oozed clear liquid.

"Doctor, is that man, okay?" Curtis, alarmed, watched as they wheeled the soldier away.

"We need to leave the room, sir. Please come with me."

Curtis, masked, picked up his crutch, limped out of the barracks, and entered another with the few uninfected. He had arrived at Qatar's base earlier in the day, awaiting evacuation aboard an amphibious warship docked outside of Bahrain in the Persian Sea. At this last stop before leaving Saudi Arabia, he just required a final examination. Now, in shock, he lapsed into a trance as he stood staring at the men on cots. In the quiet room, many of them sat reading or playing cards. Some appeared to also have received some level of medical attention. The silence, along with the cocktail of drugs circulating his bloodstream, sent him back to a moment of quiet two days earlier...

An explosion—thirty yards out. Tearing skin—sharp. Pain—everywhere and all at once. Ringing ears. Deafening. A Lock-

heed SC-130 transport aircraft, plunged into the ground, killing everyone on board along with several ground troops. The surrounding men, including himself, lay speckled in shrapnel, surrounded by a smoldering blur of twisted metal.

Curtis snapped out of it—his heart beginning to race. Shaky, and uncertain what just happened, he hopped out of the tent, sucking in a few lungfuls of cool, arid air and waiting for his pulse to temper. With one crutch wedged under the right pit, he lightly limped around the barracks to clear his head. The surrounding chaos managed to divert his attention as well as pique his curiosity.

He peeked his head inside a nearby tent. The First Lieutenant stood viewing a handful of chest radiographs against a dim lamp inside the near vacant command center. A Warrant Officer and Corporal clad in arid camouflage fatigues stood silently nearby, awaiting the examiner's return. The barracks stood in slight disarray, as if business had abruptly stopped, everyone leaving posthaste. Deserted radio equipment rested on sand-dusted folding tables lining the perimeter of the tent. A heavily marked, six-foot map of Southwest Asia hung from a wall behind a row of large cathode ray tube computer monitors and desktop towers floating in a pool of scattered paper.

"Jesus, what do we have here, huh? What is it that we have here!?" The lieutenant questioned, flustered, staring at the radiograph. His sun-blistered face glistened below a low brow, arid-camo cap. "Why are my men dropping like fucking flies!?"

"I have never seen anything like this, Lieutenant." The symptoms appear to be all across the board here—we can't keep up! We don't have enough goddamn hands here. We need to call in the medical team from the carrier." The Corporal said, wiping sweat from his forehead with a sleeve.

"I just spoke with Command; they're not sending anyone in or letting anyone out. They're shutting this base down until they get answers. Now, what is it? This airborne? Chemical? Is it contagious? None of the other companies are experiencing anything of the sort." The frustrated lieutenant drank hard from his mug, splashing watered-down coffee in his salt and pepper mustache.

"I mean, it rained for weeks in the Asir Providence a few weeks back. Some of these men were stationed there. This could very well be a rampant virus caused by a contaminated water supply. I've seen that before." The Corporal offered with a tentative shrug.

The lieutenant, still viewing the radiograph, turned toward the entrance. Curtis, afraid of being seen, moved on.

Further down, peering into some windows, he recognized a few faces—soldiers from basic training, years prior on Parris Island. He entered the barracks cautiously. The cacophony of hacking and coughing reverberated through the tightly closed-off space. Men sprawled out on cots, some on the ground, some completely unconscious. The air thickened, stale and oppressive, with circulation restrained. One soldier in a white crew neck and lower fatigues sat upright on his cot, coughing blood into a rag, dog tags clinking. His skin looked dull and clammy, and his eyes, dark, sunk slightly back into their sockets. Curtis moved closer, noticing his hands, arms, and neck peppered with a series of tiny, vesicular blisters.

"Hey, *Mcfly*!" Curtis called in his best Biff Tannen impression, pulling off his face mask. "I thought I told you never to come in here..."

"Curtis! Aw, man, I shoulda known it was you—you're the only one who calls me that." Marty laughed, then coughed.

"What can I say—I love movies," Curtis said, almost morosely, looking his friend up and down in disbelief of what he was seeing.

"Better than what my mom calls me—she calls me *Martin*. Ugh. What are you doing here, bro?"

"Just wanted to say, 'what's up?' I saw you guys through the window. I haven't seen you or any of the guys here since basic."

"Yeah, bro. We've been stationed here in Qatar since August. Longest six fucking months of my life, you know what I'm saying?" Marty said, continuing to hack crimson mucus.

"Everyone?" Curtis peered around the room.

"Na, half these guys, maybe. The rest just showed up over the last few weeks. I think some moved in from the west. Some from the north—I don't know. But most of them were in Kuwait City the other day. What a fucking shit show that was, man. You?"

Curtis smiled. "I heard about the engagement, man. *Ho-lee shit.* A hundred enemy tanks blown to high hell in under two minutes."

"Awe, it was fucking insane, bro. Glad it's all over. Time to go home." Marty coughed again, wiping some mucus from his lip.

"I'm hearing that," Curtis said, distracted. "What's going on around here, man? Why's everyone look so fucking sick?"

"I don't know, bro. This shit hit everyone after we got back in from the firefight at Kuwait Airport. I was there. Something wasn't quite right about that whole situation. There were fucking hours and hours of gunfire exchange, right, and then all of a sudden, there was some sort of underground explosion, it sounded like. Smoke and shit poured out from the sewer and cracked asphalt. The enemy retreated, and the fighting ended," Marty recounted. "You?"

"Huh?"

"What's *your* story?"

"Was stationed in Dhahran for a bit, 'til the scuds came in and blew it all to hell. Next came Khafji, which they also blew to all hell. Then Kuwait..."

A lengthy pause ensued.

"I don't know how the Christ I've made it through, man. God-damn miracle, I think." Curtis shrugged, abridging six months into a few sentences.

"Barely. You look banged up, bro."

Curtis giggled at the irony. "Took a large piece of fuselage to the thigh—thirty stitches." He pulled his pants down and un-wrapped the gauze bandage, exposing puffy, bloodstained skin and a hook-shaped, scabbed laceration surrounded by contiguous nicks and gashes up his torso to his neck. Fifteen stitches wrapped around his lower left abdomen and oblique.

Marty looked astounded. "Jesus Christ! You' lucky you ain't dead. That just looks fucking awful—*cough, cough*." He hacked a nugget of dark blood into a rag. "You know, I've been laying here, wondering—why I joined this shit—why the fuck I'm here. Ugh-hh..." He sat upright, taking in a long wheezing breath. "Why'd you enlist, bro?"

"Ummm, my father, mostly, I guess. He served two tours in Viet-nam."

"Yeah, I guess that makes sense. Had an uncle die in 'Nam. You'd think that would've deterred me."

"My old man apparently couldn't get enough. It's funny, he, uh, served one tour, came home and knocked my mother up, and then returned to serve the other." Curtis smiled.

"Yeah, but you knew what a shit horror show that war was, man. And your old man who was forced into the draft was lucky to walk away from it. Fucking lucky. Why the hell would any sane man sign himself for this shit knowing there'll always be some war erupting around the corner?"

"For me, it was after I found one of his medals in a storage box. I must've been six, seven—my mother told me this story about when he got separated from his unit. Now, he never talked about the war. At least not around me. So, I never got his perspective. But my mother said he wound up walking for, like, days by himself—lost, right? Somehow, he ended up coming across the Capital during, uh—a firefight, where these two battalions of Viet Cong fought, attacking the locals and bombing buildings and shit. So, instead of walking on in search of his people, he decided to stick around. He snuck in and hid out in one of the villages with some of these terrified locals. And each day, he'd sneak into the city and rescue two people here, four people there, ya know?

"The turning point was when the local Vietnamese Army noticed what he was doing and joined forces with him. Together they ended up rescuing the Province Chief and his family—wife—children, held hostage from the Viet Cong. Crazy, right? This one man fucking inspired them to fight alongside him. They gave him the Congressional Medal of Honor for that." Curtis looked down, now realizing how much he differed from his father—how his time in war was conversely different.

"You know, I asked my mom years later, I said, why didn't he just keep walking? You know? He had a wife and a newborn back home waiting for him. Why did he risk *everything* to go in and help these people out? And all she said was, 'because he could.'

"Sounds stupid, but after that story, I thought he was the coolest thing growing up. I just wanted the chance to feel what he felt—to maybe bask in that glory—to actually make a difference."

"Hey, it's better than the reason *I* joined. It was either this or construction, ughhh—I'd much rather be hauling stone right now." Marty smiled, then paused to cough. "Maybe these people we're fighting got it right."

"What's that?"

"Religion is big around here, man—that Quran stuff is serious. They fucking live by that. The Day of Reckoning—the resurrection of the soul and all the eternal spiritual and physical pleasures. Maybe life *don't* start 'til after you're dead."

A brief silence fell among them.

Marty winced; his eyes watered. He dropped his head into his hands, not bothering to fight the tears. "I don't wanna die," he choked out.

"You're not gonna die," Curtis reaffirmed, terrified of his own fate. "They're gonna figure out what this is and fix it. There's a huge medical team coming in. They're gonna fix everybody." His words sounded hollow, uncertain of what would happen—though, from the looks of it, he doubted Marty would ever leave that base.

Marty wiped his face with the bloody rag. "You think that'll stop what's coming? They can't just *fix* everybody." He desperately reached for his friend, his nails squeezing into Curtis's arm. "Don't let me die, Curtis. Don't let me fucking *die*!"

Hearing the naval physician staff coming into the barracks, Curtis slid on his face mask and slipped out the back as they entered. Less than six hours later, he stepped on a gunboat headed to a Carrier outside Bahrain. The ominous conversation he just had with an old friend left him restless for days to come.

The spectacular, last vision of the dissolutive territory didn't offer much comfort or hope as he watched the burning of hundreds of oil wells from aboard the carrier. An inferno of infinite geysers blazed marvelously, a volcanic rupture from the desert ground flaring into the night sky. Black smoke billowed over each spout, canvasing the Kuwait coast. The glow of scorched earth became the only beacon of light over the dark ocean for miles. He watched it recede, blotted by the horizon.

Curtis woke.

TWENTY-FIVE

F rank Cavanaugh's property stood the most prominent of the four on Forest Street. The one-hundred-twenty-year-old two-story Cape was also the first built. Initially constructed for the General of Fort Hock, who resided there with his family well into the early 1900s, the house had seen several renters since the fort's decommissioning after the First World War.

After returning from Korea, Frank purchased the home for a modest price from a government subsidiary looking to unload some of its assets—the deal of a lifetime. Its previous renter, an elderly woman from New Mexico, had gone missing several years before, leaving the house unoccupied until her legal declaration of death. Frank, who had an affinity for antiquities, welcomed the fully furnished house. He made several impressive modifications in the 1980s to the kitchen and dining room, including the alluring sliding glass doors—which he had cherished as an outlet to his handcrafted cedar deck, where he'd enjoy a smoke and drink.

From where Curtis stood, one would have difficulty discerning a house, much less a little piece of Connecticut history. He attempted to recall the last time he'd visited here. Almost impossible. Snippets of past gatherings flashed by, but mostly from what he had ascertained from the photo album, which still sat open on his coffee table. The once familiar space, albeit now from a lifetime ago, seemed utterly foreign as he walked up to the front yard, stopping a moment to survey the land. He glanced over at two Bush/Cheney '04 signs, gently swaying at the edge of the lawn—the only thing the fire didn't seem to reach. Estelle's station wagon sat in a thin layer of water splotched soot in front of the garage, a faded and disheveled Snoopy plush, morosely hung, head drooped from the front grill. If he hadn't known otherwise, by the aftermath of the hurricane and the scattered, charred house debris, he would have thought a tornado passed through.

Among the rubbish, he spotted strewn pieces of furniture, tools, torn cardboard, household cleaning products, kitchen appliances, busted tableware, and shredded newspaper scraps. Sheets of decomposing leaves and broken branches sparsely veiled the property. Every piece of litter had a degree of singe that may have pinpointed its proximity to the blast—the ones closest to the house, now unrecognizable. The land still had the eerie smell remnant of a recently snubbed-out bonfire, even though several days had passed since the incident.

The morning wind ruffled his hair as he crossed the debris field to the back of the dilapidation. The flood had essentially receded, the river regaining much of its splendor while Curtis stopped to admire the landscape. Frank had the perfect view of the Yantic and Thames confluence, clear out to the tip of Hock Island on the left and on the right, the Washington Street Bridge up high running across, dissipating just beyond the public library. Curtis totally understood how the Cavanaugh's could spend almost half a century—a lifetime—here, at the end of a partially hidden street, tucked away from the world. The amber glow of a newly rising sun emerging behind Norwich began to push out the light blue layer of civil twilight, evaporating the bright, starry ocean of night sky high above. He lit a cigarette and took a moment to watch the sunrise. Spectacular.

As he turned back, flicking the butt, he looked down at a familiar object in the grass. He did a double-take, almost instantly recalling where he'd seen it—a photograph. Rick's photograph. As soon as he recognized the portable oxygen tank, he knew—he knew precisely where Mallory Luske "went missing."

Curtis stepped over a large, gaping box that once housed a television, making his way into the front entrance—a partial standing frame with no door, blocked by a thin wrapping of yellow barricade tape. The one-third of the house still standing contained the kitchen, living room, and attached garage. The back wall of the kitchen, where Frank's prize glass doors still stood, was visible from the front yard. The glass, clear as this crisp November day, exposed Frank's dull yet unscathed deck.

A colossal breach on the first floor of the house also exposed the basement. Curtis decided the safest way was through the garage, where he entered, followed by the kitchen. Everywhere he stepped, he found some object he had to be cautious of so as not to trip or roll an ankle. He crossed through the kitchen and climbed over a fridge to get to the living room. Frank's drab recliner sat unblemished in its natural spot—the corner of the living room next to the front window, side facing Curtis. Not even an explosion could blot out that ghastly tinge.

Glass popped under his boot as he walked past the fireplace. Out of curiosity, he bent down, brushing away charred wood and dead leaves to unearth a picture frame. Behind the cracked glass lay Frank and Estelle's black and white wedding photo; he found a handwritten date of *June 1954* on the back. Curtis moved some more of the rubble and found Frank's military portrait, dignified in his black uniform and white cap. The eagle with double insignia stripes on his sleeve patch indicated he was a Petty Officer, Second Class.

In the years they'd known one another, Frank never spoke about his time in the military—even though he knew full well Curtis had served in the Gulf War. Curtis appreciated that fact, as he neither wished to swap stories. He remembered when he and Amy first arrived in the neighborhood—when they had ample time—they would have Frank and Estelle over for monthly cookouts. The Cavanaugh's didn't have close family, and Amy, who had summers off, would always suggest having them over. Despite the multigenerational age gap, Curtis didn't mind so much; he enjoyed listening to Frank drone on about antique Victorian furniture and carpentry, while Amy would get an earful from Estelle on their many grandchildren.

Frank would invite them over to his yard for his "World Famous BBQ," which would commence during summer holidays, with Memorial Day as the grand kick-off. The Jensens, along with the Millers—the retired inhabitants of the remaining property—would gather, with each bringing a dish or two of their own. Though not the typical neighborhood community Curtis envisioned upon moving to Forest Street, the gatherings provided that little something—a familial camaraderie that had been missing from his life, with his grandparents passing before his birth and his father dying when he was only eight. Spending time with Frank especially gave him a sense of what it may have been like—could have been like—had his father survived. And even though Wesley Reynolds had been gone from Curtis's life for a quarter century now, Frank made a suitable surrogate parent.

Years had passed since they gathered for an occasion, a holiday dinner, or a board game night. And as Curtis thought about it, one of the last conversations he had with Frank was regarding much-needed electrical work, mainly for some bad switches he said he'd try to find time to investigate. *Was it the basement?* That conversation occurred several months ago, at least. A sense of guilt spilled over him, mournful, and he wished he had spent a little more time to better know his neighbor. The fact he would never see Frank again unsettled him.

Curtis carefully walked around the friable hole where the dining room once stood and through the basement door, still barely attached to the frame. Most of the basement's effects fanned out along the room's edge, much of it piled upon itself. The ghastly scene took him aback, and he struggled to imagine what had transpired here—at one time, this had been a room in his friend's house. Now, with everything torched and covered in wet leaves, not to mention resting in a foot of black flood water, analyzing the room's contents proved difficult.

He kicked over a slumped cubicle shelf blocking the stairs and entered. Barricade tape surrounded the washer and dryer where Frank's remains were recovered—a disquieting sight. He walked around the taped-off section, clearing a narrow path toward the workbench, where another cubicle shelf had fallen. A collection of porcelain teapots remained in one of the cubbies, along with cups and saucers, all tarnished with soot. Among blackened china, a glimmer of gold caught his eye—a thin chain, draped over the side of an open Georgian kettle. He lifted it out to reveal a pocket watch, which gently dangled before him. Though tough to open, either from fire or old age, he managed to pry the latch with a thumbnail to expose an equally tarnished and cracked face. Behind the door he found a one-word engraving: *DUNKIN*. Along with the rest of the junk, he figured the couple had picked up the watch at a flea market or backyard estate sale where it probably—*definitely*—should have stayed. Oddly enough, and to his delighted surprise, it still functioned; Curtis watched as the seconds hand tick-tick-ticked away.

The cubicle shelf lifted out of the way with ease, baring a sizable English tool chest underneath. Opening it—with the toe of his boot—revealed an assortment of equipment sheltered from the fire. Inside, under a pile of hammers, measuring tapes, handsaws, and electric drills, he recognized a particular piece of equipment he then recalled lending Frank the previous year—an ICS petrol-powered chainsaw, one he specifically purchased to dismember that pain-in-the-ass red maple.

He gave it a quick once over, and then yanked back on the starter grip, springing it to life. The visceral sound of the motor reverberated through the scorched chamber, permeating the dry air with smoke. Stretched along the back corner of the room sprawled a vast pile of debris. The billiard table covered most of it, fused in place by the fire. He jerked the throttle on the saw, giving it enough gas to rip into the lifeless table game. While it may have been burned up, it remained a well-built, durable apparatus.

The saw blade seamlessly shredded into the maple veneer cabinet through the walnut top slate; burnt red felt and chipped wood flaked onto Curtis. Billiard balls spilled, splashing into the shallow, rolling around his feet. He placed the saw down nearby on the skeletal, metal remains of the sofa and proceeded to pull each half of the table apart, the pervading black dust causing him to hack. He cast aside an old Schwinn bike and a few heavy, steel containers with broken china, leaving a tarnished, shattered Gilt mirror against the wall. He pulled back the mirror, unveiling the thing he searched for, suspected, even, yet profoundly feared...

The hole.

PART III

Twenty-Six

—•—

Eyes open and neck kinked, Curtis picked his head up from the back cushion of the couch. Out of habit, his eyes gravitated to the time first. The cable box on the entertainment center was blank; combined with the tranquil atmosphere of the room, it indicated the generator had stopped. Daylight had arrived, and that was all Curtis knew. *I should find that watch Amy got me for our anniversary—buried someplace in the closet, perhaps.* The cell phone on the coffee table wouldn't turn on either, signaling a dead battery. In fact, it had been plugged in since the night of the storm, ready for whenever the generator would kick on, but it still hadn't held a charge. *Fucking things never stay charged. And why do they keep making them smaller?* Curtis flung it back on the table, and it slid off the side.

His mind turned to Amy and Wes, now curious since the phone appeared to no longer function and his pager died in the basement flood. He wondered if she had tried getting through, concerned for him. She hadn't heard from him in—well, who even knew how long. Time, finally, had become irrelevant. However, he reminded himself, she must be fairly familiar with his silence already. The storm was "Tuesday," according to Sergeant Rick, whenever that was—weeks, months, half a decade, maybe. Sure felt like it. Regardless of time, a sensation began to surface over him, a former void—he missed them.

Light pierced the room through the front window, glaring off his stubbly, hollow face. He had no recollection of sitting down on the couch, let alone sleeping. He floated somewhere between reality and a dream, a type of subconscious state of delusion, with no way to discern one from the other. His post-traumatic stress had resurged, so maybe none of it was real: the house, the Norwaukus, the vivid dreams. Perhaps he *had* drifted into an infinite state of hypnagogia.

In any event, he needed to finish what he had started. He'd now confirmed this thing killed Frank, Ronald, and likely that poor woman, Mallory—God only knew who else. He needed to call Sergeant Rick and put an end to his inquiries. He needed to get back to his wife and son.

His headache returned—the eternal hangover which lingered for days, sometimes weeks in variable intensity, though he hadn't had a drink in years. Today's hammered on, incredibly intense, almost as debilitating as a migraine but without the dizziness or nausea—just pain. When he sprang up from the couch, tiny golden sparks fired from the back of his eyes, filling his peripherals, but only for a moment, as the blood rushed down to other parts of his body. He popped four ibuprofen, lit a smoke, and headed straight to the basement. As he got down and took the corner, small pieces of rock caught the corner of his eye. He looked up, following the trail of torn slab leading to the steel cage. The basement was somewhat dark, but he could see twisted bars, and some of his clips which held the cage to the floor had been dislodged—a clear indication of a struggle he couldn't believe he slept through. Slowly, he approached the contraption, picking up the flashlight next to the folding chair along the way. He flicked it on, shining it in.

The cage shone back—empty.

The cigarette fell from his mouth, his jaw dropping in disbelief as he approached the vacant cell, looking in, only to find a massive hole surrounded by dirt and chunks of stone. The Norwaukus must have exploited the fragile granite floor while Curtis blacked out. Dread and hopelessness poured over him; he couldn't face his family after another tragedy—another disappointment—and he wasn't leaving Forest Street without this creature, needing to find it before it discovered the neighborhoods beyond the stretch of separating pine.

For a moment he considered the shotgun, but in his mind's eye he emptied the barrel at the rampaging beast, then fumbled, trying to reload—mauled down. A flashback looking up at the beast pinning him under the flood made him quiver. *Those empty eyes...* He saw the chainsaw, swung the strap over his shoulder, ran upstairs, into the dining room, and peered into the floor opening—a tunnel. He jumped down, landing atop the cage, one foot sliding between the bars; he grabbed the edge, catching his balance. Pulling open the roof hatch, he dropped in, straddling the wide opening. The flashlight passed over for inspection, but only darkness greeted him. He hesitated a moment, wondering how deep the hole could be, but also, more curiously, where it may lead.

He entered the four-foot opening without further thought, sliding down six feet on an angle, scraping against sharp rock and twigs. The ground, cold and damp, squished beneath as he inched his way forward on all fours. The flashlight shone ahead, barely penetrating the void. He took each step cautiously, knees and hands sinking in the spongy soil, knowing he'd be trapped if this thing happened to appear. After several yards of crawling a steady incline, a narrow strip of light pierced the tunnel before taking a hard turn downward. Curtis's sudden surge of valor diminished; a sliver of rationality struck him. He pushed his hand through the breached surface and dug himself out of the ground, where he made it as far as the back-yard.

Beyond the property, leading into the wooded area, the ground raised up in sections, slightly breaking at the top, similar to a ground mole, albeit about three feet wide and much more unnerving.

Into the forest I go, to lose my mind and find my soul...

Curtis followed the trail, which often grew difficult from the dead foliage and hurricane debris that canvased the land. As he pushed deeper in, something felt a bit off. The formidable woods stood tranquil; neither a bird nor cricket to be heard. Squirrels and other woodland creatures had ceased rustling through the trees. The air stood still. Silent.

At last, the trail narrowed and faded along the edge of the river. Curtis glanced at his surroundings. Thirty yards ahead, upon a short but steep incline, ran a long segment of eight-foot-high chain-link fence. The crown of it bent outward another foot—a feature designed for added security. Beyond the wire mesh lay the desolate estates of Laurel Hill Drive.

Was the Norwaukus inside?

A rectangular, corroded concrete slab lodged in the hillside caught his eye as he neared. It was an old, French-style storm drain with a two-foot diameter opening in the center, veiled by perennial weeds and blackberry brambles. The silence finally broke. Curtis heard faint rustling from within, almost elusive. Slowly, he crept up with the Maglite, peeking into the black cavity. The lambent light only shone so far, leading Curtis to be extra cautious, though decidedly curious. A few passes with the light and nothing. He turned it off, waited a bit, shone in again. This time the light captured an irregular glimmer deep inside, one that reflected various pairs of tiny, shifting, chatoyant orbs.

Hmm...

Thick, rusted line posts ran every ten feet as he followed the length of fence up to the edge of Forrest Street, which ended with a chained and locked double gate. For a moment, Curtis considered how many times he had driven by the street without regard, oblivious to its existence. Knotweed and honeysuckle grew on either side of the weed-infested, cracked asphalt, patchy and brown, exposing their skeletal limbs. Dutchman's pipe wove in and out through the square mesh, dangling layers of faded lily pad-like leaves concealing the mysterious beyond. To the right, arched over a crumbling cement slab, hung the faded, oval, wood placard, splintered down the middle.

Welcome to Laurel Hill.

The locking mechanism and link chain guarding the entrance appeared considerably corroded. Clearly, no one had opened the gate in quite some time—by Curtis's guess, since the day the city sealed it. One swift thrust from a piece of roadside quartzite, and the preserved lock effortlessly shattered, falling to the ground. The double doors creaked open.

The street of Laurel Hill began with an abrupt slump but continued as a long, gradual, curving decline that ran down to the base of the Yantic River. He couldn't see the properties from the street top, but as soon as Curtis made it over the hump, the first estates emerged. He walked gradually down through the unfamiliar territory, taking in the epitome of a land long forgotten by time—dismissed by much of its surrounding world, lost in plain sight. And although feared by some, Curtis soon revered the space, finding an unmistakable beauty to the neighborhood. The dilapidation sort of reminded him of a particular Charles White landscape painting he'd seen hanging from the white walls in his in-law's family room, albeit much more fantastical.

The houses, single-level ranches, stood seven on either side in almost too-close-for-comfort proximity. Ominously similar, each one mirrored the one across from it, with the color and the number stenciled on the front door offering the only discernible difference. Each simple setup possessed a broad front-facing gable, low-pitch roof, massive chimney, and two-car garage. Perhaps the most prominent feature was the spacious front bay window, each with a central six-by-six panel construction, side windows double-hung. A short, white picket fence separated each yard, not all of which remained standing or intact. Busted rails hung haphazardly over deeply scratched pickets.

The symmetrical front yards overgrew with slumping hazel grass, patchy green weed, and dandelions in bloom. Hedges under front windows had erratically sprouted while perennial vines crawled the façades, weaving floral patchwork and forging a path. Kudzu interconnected each yard, devouring any object it rivaled. A subdued, deflated soccer ball peeked out amid the proliferation. A blend of freshly decaying leaves littered each lawn, masking where one ended and another began, spilling into the lackluster road, while ragweed and goldenrod sprouted from asphaltic fissures and cracked curbs.

Red maples lined the street and hung high above the landscape, arms stretched across, exposing nearly bare limbs. Burned leaves of bittersweet orange and geranium lake scarcely clung to frangible branches. Limbs had grown to such lengths that they began to conform to rooftops, squeezing shingles and bending gutters. A thick branch grew inside an open kitchen window in one house, wrapping around a ceiling fan; fallen leaves canvased the linoleum. Barren and uninhabited, the street stood completely still, not even a bird passing between the trees. In fact, Curtis could see no woodland creatures at all.

Quiet.

Forty-nine years of seasonal New England weather had taken its toll on the homes of Laurel Hill. Just about every one had its original pastel-colored finish, now faded and chipped. Layers of dirt had fused to lower parts of the aluminum siding, between areas that weren't covered by shrubs. The dingy, smudged windows looked dark, difficult to see in. The derelict dwellings' interior couldn't be viewed clearly from the road, but Curtis suspected everything inside rested under blankets of dust, dirt, and leaves blown in from seasons past—black mold and mildew from years of rainfall forming on the walls and ceilings, flourishing throughout. Colonies of lime-green moss densely grew across countertops, floors, and into living rooms with delicate vegetation, where bushels of golden ferns sporadically erupted. Tangerine sporophytes casually clung to exposed chimney brick, down back walls, and along frosted windows.

Looking in the few broken windows, Curtis could see some places still had furniture left behind, carelessly abandoned. Couches, television stands, and free-standing lamps lay dormant in family rooms. Others had kitchen sets and appliances with countertop accessories—a heavily molded, plastic dish drain, or a corroded, under-counter electric can opener. He even saw a house with a table partially set for three—eaten, discarded. A stained coffee pot remained plugged-in inside number four, with remnants of a morning past.

Telephone poles with streetlamps attached ran defunct power lines down, connecting each unit. Juice hadn't traveled through those cables for some time. Curtis noticed one draped across the street, likely fallout from the storm, as he walked over it and up to a mailbox, opening the latch out of curiosity. To his surprise, mail sat inside. He pulled a couple stiff letters stuck together—utility bills and a dried-up, wrinkled newspaper from *The Day*, dated September 1995, which broke apart in his hands. The bills were addressed to Mr. & Mrs. Matthew Lavigne.

He walked further, noticing a driveway with an actual car sitting in it—a silver, five-cylinder, VW sedan, tires flat, resting on bent rims. In another property, perched above sagging bluegrass and red sorrel, lived a decrepit, concrete birdbath with severe scaling; it overflowed with a murky liquid. Behind it, at the edge of the woods, a sun-bleached garden gnome stared at Curtis through a refuge of crumbling straw.

An open door suddenly piqued his curiosity as he sauntered up the covered walkway. Cautiously, he took each concrete step, then walked over the small porch landing. The royal blue door, with three rectangle windows set diagonally, stood half-open, leaves trailing in. He gave it a slight nudge, the rusted hinges creaking as he stepped inside.

A bat fired out the moment his head crossed the threshold; a sudden, high-pitched screeching pulled him backward off the landing, into the front yard. The noise quickly heightened, evolving, becoming more phonetic; it resonated through his body, torturing every shot nerve. The screaming deafened him, like squealing tires inside his throbbing head. He squeezed his eyes shut and grit his teeth, wincing as the sounds of dying men pierced his eardrums. His hands gripped his ears, hoping the pressure would stop the voices. They continued in unison, echoing down the line, cascading from every open window and empty doorway.

I can't help you. I can't help you. I'm sorry. I'm sorry. I can't help... ANY OF YOU! I am SO fucking sorry!

Saliva dripped from his open mouth, hands quivering, but no words would come out. He just repeated lines of remorse inside his head over and over and over, fighting until the noise eventually subsided, and he found himself cowering, head between his legs. And just like that, it ended. He took a moment to catch his breath before standing, wiping away tears with the back of his hand. Then, cautiously, he continued.

Halfway down the street, an eerie feeling of being watched struck Curtis. A cold sweat trickled down his forehead; he stood, body still shaking, on high alert, anticipating the emergence of the Norwaukus from the dense overgrowth. Turning a quick three-sixty, he saw nothing, heard nothing, save for the elevating rhythm of his own jabbering heart. *Jesus Christ, what the fuck is happening to me!?* A breeze picked up, shuffling crisp leaves gently down the street, and he realized he stood alone, in the middle of a ghost town. He smiled warily, shaking his head at his own paranoia.

Curtis took another step forward before *they* caught his eye. Out of nowhere and without warning, they appeared—the forsaken inhabitants of this barren wasteland, encompassing the land around him in all shapes, sizes, and colors. They were many, and they were beautiful.

Had they been there this whole time?

Little, inquisitive heads cautiously emerged from the brush. More began to materialize beyond the properties; they popped out of bushes, jumped from tree limbs; others appeared from under the Volkswagen and inside its cabin. Silhouettes of pointed-eared bodies climbed into hazy bay windows, fighting to get a glance at their new visitor, and oh, were they ever curious. Another slinked out through a front door opening, rubbing up on the frame, bushy tail in the air. Narrow, whiskered faces peered out to investigate from the curbside, oxidized storm drain.

He looked around, turning his head, slowly surveying the space. Twenty, thirty, fifty... that quickly doubled, then tripled. Curtis couldn't believe what he saw before him.

My god, there are hundreds!

Generations upon generations presented themselves. Some, friendlier looking, he suspected were once domesticated, founders who claimed this unoccupied territory. Some seemed more rugged, native to the land; never having laid eyes on a human, they hung back, suspicious, though nevertheless fascinated. Some, he imagined, were just outlaws who had drifted in overtime—feral creatures who had found acceptance, a tribe, a sense of belonging.

He marveled in the splendor, a diverse array of colored fur: solids, bicolor, and calico; striped tabbies, spotted tabbies, ticked tabbies, and lynx; torties and torbies and color-point patterns; whites, blacks, reds, blues, and browns, as well as chocolate, cream, lilac, and cinnamon. Some were tipped, some were shaded, some were smoked; some had mittens, some wore buttons and some lockets; some were tuxedo, and some were harlequin. Long hair, short hair, and every hair in-between presented themselves, some with long tails, some with stub tails, and others with no tail at all. An elite few looked purebred, while the majority appeared mixed.

Curtis stared, surrounded and scared to move. Would they attack? He knew if they did, no one would ever find his remains—they'd say he'd mysteriously *taken off* like Mallory Luske. Making a run for it seemed tricky; these animals were sure to be quick on their feet. With no sense in further deliberation, and with only one thing left to do, he took a step forward. As he did so, the crowd parted. One of the feline inhabitants approached Curtis. A harlequin white, domestic long-hair with a patch of grey atop its head entered the ring, its chest as broad and full as a lion's mane. Long tufts of fur protruded from in between the footpads of each mammoth paw. The poufy tail gleamed, magnificent, reminding him of a lambswool duster swaying above as it walked. The little fellow looked as if it had been around a very long time. Judging by the size, it also appeared well-fed. It stopped in the middle, about ten feet from where Curtis stood, staring up, examining the trespasser.

This must be the ruler of this land…

He gently squatted and took a knee, slowly extending his right arm. A breeze shifted down Laurel Hill, rustling up foliage. It blew through the animal's thick, alabaster coat; the sun's reflection shimmered off its fur. It stepped forward, casually but confidently, stopping just close enough for Curtis to make contact. With three fingers, he very softly caressed the top of its head, down around the neck, and finished by scratching under the ear. The eyes closed, the snout puckered, and the tail stood straight up and quivered. For a moment, he imagined the animal became cognizant of a life long past. Clearly, although it had been without a master for some time, part of it still yearned for human companionship.

The harlequin king looked behind and back at Curtis, granting permission to pass. It then trotted off, vanishing through the high grass, though not before stopping to take a final look at its new guest. Curtis stood up and peered around one last time, and just as mysteriously as they appeared, the cats all vanished, save for one orange tabby—with a slight limp.

Curtis recognized it immediately. It trotted down the street a bit, then stopped, looked back, and waited. Unsure of the reality of what he witnessed, he shrugged, then opted to walk after the tabby. It kept moving, stopping only to quickly check back, leading him to the bottom of Laurel Hill. Beyond the houses, at the end of the street, stood a cul-de-sac, which lay along the river's edge.

A peculiar, round, concrete structure protruded three feet up from the asphalt in the shape of a well, which the tabby hopped upon, walking around it. With a solid metal gate sealed with a lock and a layer of oxidization, the thing looked definitely out of place.

"Look out, fella..."

The tabby jumped down as he ripped the cord on the chainsaw, instantly searing the locking mechanism. He pulled the gate open, with much effort, breaking the seal. A suction released, as if he'd opened a refrigerator door, air rushing out, stale, cool. Inside, metal planks lead below. The flashlight indicated the descent stretched around twelve to fifteen feet, and without hesitation, he climbed down. A loose plank gave out about halfway down and sent him falling to the cold, stone base, landing on the chainsaw, reopening his wound, and sending his flashlight rolling. He yelped in agony, then lay silent, catching his breath, staring up at the bright, round opening above, before picking himself up from the ground.

The cylindrical tunnel, seemingly composed of granite, looked deep and dark. A succession of tiny, red indicator-type bulbs ran down the ceiling's center, faintly dimming through an age of dust. At the end of the tunnel, one hundred feet in, stood a Mesker galvanized steel door. To the side he found a disabled keypad panel with a card reader. Curtis hung his head in defeat and sighed, fearing the journey had come to an end. Upon further inspection of the surroundings, a light bulb flickered on.

Twenty-Seven

The diamond chain of the five horsepower saw effortlessly scored the concrete wall beside the steel frame. He snickered as he cut through the stone, thinking back to his new feline friends. *Were they even real?* He felt a rush of adrenaline: excited, anxious, bordering neurotic. He forged on, entering forbidden territory—no-man's-land—wondering what he'd find beyond those walls, and as a vagrant no-less, an anomaly, with his stubbly face, white shirt, and khaki cargo pants covered from head to toe in grime. Not to mention, his wounded appendage. Blood trickled down his vibrating hand as he cut. He smirked at that, too.

He cut a hole just big enough for him to squeeze through, after kicking out a few loose stones, and entered a large room, sporadically lit with low emitting fluorescent lamps along the wall. A couple of workstations and long countertops that held a couple bulky computer monitors lined the room, reminiscent of an office. One side of the space contained cardboard boxes, storage containers, and random equipment stacked to the ceiling. Walking closer, he could see a faded, splotchy *Property of Hock ADR* stamped on each box's side. Rows of metal racks with shelving held dated medical devices, lab equipment, and endless boxes of manila file folders containing decades of records. Whatever this room had originated as, it was now a repository. To Curtis, it was a basement.

Curtis shone the flashlight up the wall, across the ceiling. The pigment gradually shifted from light to dark along the backside, presumably from smoke damage. Black soot dripped down the wall, thick as tar, staining the peeled sheetrock. A double door opened to another stripped office space and laboratory, completely consumed by smoke and intermittent fire damage. Dust particles drifted through the light stream, landing on gray cobwebs, which overlay abandoned furniture. The smell of mildew permeated the damp room. Puddles gathered on uneven surfaces from a slow, post-hurricane water drip. Clearly, no one had been down there in years. The floor above, at ground level, looked sealed off, likely from the accident years prior.

The opposite end of the lab had another steel door with a non-functioning card reader—*Experimental Laboratory* printed on the sign beside. A thin ray of light emanated from under it. Firing up the saw, Curtis carved a wide entrance into a more illuminated corridor. A fine dust of mortar and cement filled the air, coating the man behind the saw. This fact struck him funny, and he developed a compelling case of the giggles for reasons beyond his comprehension. He kicked out the blocks and ducked under, through the opening. Uncontainable laughter and excitement swept through him as he revved the throttle of the saw, hoisting it up above his head, and advanced down the hall. The thin line of sanity and madness he teetered began to shift in the latter's favor.

The end of the short corridor opened into a wide open, dark space. With a chainsaw revving in both hands, Curtis entered, triggering the motion sensor. The lights flickered on in succession in three main areas. To his mouth-dropping surprise and absolute horror, he saw something utterly incomprehensible and altogether unimaginable. He killed the throttle on the saw and dropped it to the floor next to him, letting it slip through his fingertips.

"Fuck. Me," he muttered, eyes wide, scanning the room. This was *no* hallucination.

Before him sat an entire colony of the elusive Norwaukus. Curtis deduced this secluded section of the domain must be some type of deranged, underground, synthetic ecosystem. The structure descended further below basement level, at depths beyond what he could see. A ten-foot-high, titanium-reinforced polycarbonate sheet encased the viewing area, displaying and shielding the front of the terrain. On the far-left side, built into the wall, stood a four-by-four, square, metal double-door, which contained a feeding area—it likely opened electronically with some kind of a hydraulic mechanism. Curtis stepped forward slowly, approaching the glass to get a better look. The terrain level contained ground soil with wood chips and scattered rock. The back of this ghastly aquarium possessed a structural formation—a burrow of sorts, with a trove of intertwined strands of dead marsh salt grass and turf, with milkweed silk, flossed throughout. Chips of tree bark and fern moss completed the bracken tapestry. Nesting inside the fortification lay the abominable creatures. They seemed primarily dormant, nestled on top of one another.

Curtis watched as they slept with only a six-inch-thick sheet of glass between the Norwaukus and him. For an instant, in a demented sort of way, he found them to be captivating, even slightly mystical. He touched the glass with his left hand, gently moving laterally, panning the habitation. Suddenly, he spotted an opening eye. A head rolled to the side and up, glancing at his figure through the pane. His body quivered with chills that crawled up his spine; he froze, staring into those empty, white spheres. They looked just as terrifying from a distance, and any moment now, there could be many pairs. Without regard, a moment later, the creature rolled back, lids closed.

He noticed walls dividing the habitation unit into smaller sections as he moved along, still keeping his eye on the Norwaukus.

WHAP!

Curtis stumbled backward, tripping over a wheeled instrument tray; its contents crashed down around him. Up against the misty glass stuck a fleshy ring of retractable tentacles erratically tapping. His eyes fixated, his breath catching as he picked himself off the floor. He struggled to see beyond the dense, hazy build-up, which surrounded what appeared to be a two-foot-wide, bilaterally symmetrical organism with twenty-two rose-colored projections. But as the mist dissipated, it revealed something viler—a creature, dark-haired, stocky. Black, beady eyes stared from behind the fleshy ring that protruded from its snout. Its paddle-like, scaly feet looked colossal, visually disproportionate to the body with long, broad claws. It stood on hind legs, head-to-head with Curtis.

He pulled a clipboard out of the file holder alongside the display and flipped through the pages. *Star-nosed mole...* having never seen one, he had no idea such an animal even existed—he certainly never expected to stand in front of two hundred pounds of one. Moving to the cubicles along the room's perimeter, he searched and emptied every accessible desk drawer and opened every file folder. As he shuffled through, he came across diagrams and experimental data—some with accompanying photographs. Pictures of porcupines, raccoons, South African springhares, and something called a naked mole-rat soon filled the desk; he even found a separate file on armadillos. He couldn't discern much of the jargon, but specific terms, *DNA Replication* and *Clone,* jumped out, giving him a narrow idea of what he had entered into.

"What the fuck *is* this place...?" He dropped the file, stepping backward until he had a broad view of the entire habitation.

Yes, these creatures were, if nothing else, deadly—but abominations? Designed and conditioned for God only knows what... But, as far as he knew, they didn't kill to kill. They killed to survive—the innate and divine right of all creatures in this world. It wasn't their fault they were brought into this shit existence. Fuck. What about us? Were we at fault for our own? Curtis decided one thing for sure: they should be exempt.

After a quick examination of the lab, Curtis located a rectangle panel on the far side, near a double door with frosted glass. He smiled at the touchscreen, with which he felt reasonably familiar since working with them in recent months, installing them throughout Mondo-Mart. Pulling the Oak Ridge folding knife from his back pocket, he unscrewed the panel and opened it, displaying the circuitry beneath. With the blade, he dislodged the tiny battery, then shorted the circuit, resetting the system. He didn't need long after browsing through the screen's options to find the selection he wanted. He hesitated, closed his eyes, and tried to consider an alternate, viable option, but ultimately, in his mind, there was really only one answer, no need for justification.

"Fuck it," he muttered.

Curtis hit the release.

He didn't know what happened in this facility, a stone's throw from his backyard, and nor did he want to, but his erratic brain raced with endless questions, scenarios playing out with what these creatures were bred for—none of which he found settling. He smirked, knowing whoever was responsible for this experimentation would soon find out what he'd done.

The containment doors opposite the lab slowly slid open with a dull roar from the hydraulics. He backed away and watched as yellow emergency lighting flickered throughout the unit. Beyond the confine, inquisitive eyes opened, and they began to rise. Curtis grinned and turned back down the corridor to make a quick exit. As he approached the carved brick, he came to a halting stop, greeted by a familiar, disfigured face. The Norwaukus nudged its head through the hole.

Fuck...

Without thinking, he spun around, bolting back up the corridor through the habitation lab and double doors into a long, narrow hallway, where he reached a set of steel double doors. Frantically, he pulled at the handles, to no avail. The Norwaukus pushed through the lab doors and leisurely paced the hallway with its sights set while Curtis, back against the door, watched it advance. Its glistening, red nose pulsed, whiskers twitching—white eyes squinting low. Globs of saliva dripped from the side of its charred, open mouth, hitting the floor behind a trail of something else Curtis noticed—his heart sunk. He squeezed his eyes and waited, sweat dripping from his forehead. The Norwaukus had followed his blood from the tunnel, and he knew it.

A light above the door lit green, and the wall panel buzzed, opening one side and sending Curtis falling through. He slid in, and the door auto shut. Without assessing his new surroundings, he picked himself up and started running. The hall resembled a hospital wing, but with laboratories instead of patient rooms. At the intersecting corner of each wing stood a station for personnel. Winded, he stopped to look around, heart pounding. The wings all looked eerily similar—pastel blue and bare; small square signs on the walls vaguely indicating their purpose: *Office, Laboratory, Research, Closet, Bathroom.* It was quiet, way too quiet, and this was no time to wander. He needed a way out. What he needed was a—

And there it was; he saw it, hanging from the ceiling at the far end of the corridor—a green exit sign with an arrow indicating: *left.* He ran straight for it, taking the corner at high speed.

THUD!

Struck in the chest, he flew somersaulting backward, face slamming on the linoleum as the wind knocked out of him. Four men clad in black coveralls, tactical vests, and low caps surrounded him; one had clotheslined him, while three began grabbing at limbs, pressing his face to the floor.

"NO, NO, NO, NO! NOOOO! Get the fuck OFF ME!" Curtis bawled, gasping for air, squirming, trying to get loose.

"Stay down on the ground, and stop moving, or I *will* fire upon you!" A guard asserted, Beretta M9 in hand—a gun Curtis recognized well, similar to his sidearm in Kuwait.

Curtis sent a guard backward with a boot heel, thrusting his body around, trying to roll from their clutches. Another guard caught an elbow to the cheekbone. Quickly, they climbed back on top, wrestling Curtis, shouting as he continued to scream over them.

"Let me fucking go! You don't know what you're doing!" Curtis pleaded.

Though struggling, the three men managed to flip Curtis on his front, arms pulled around his back. One guard leaned on his neck; another dug his knee in the middle of Curtis's spine while he slipped on double-looped, thick cable ties.

"One…" The gunman started.

"NO! You need to listen to me!" He continued to fight his way loose.

"Two…"

"Shut the fuck up!" A guard yelled.

Curtis howled—his face beet red. His anger melted away in a surge of unmitigated terror as he looked up. "WE NEED TO GET THE FUCK OUT OF—"

A snarling *grunt* belted out, and blood from the gunman's shoulder socket surged, his arm tearing into three segments with the bone snapping. The infliction sent the Beretta firing a single shot, bursting through the cheek of the guard over Curtis. His face blew open, lips and upper palate crumbling away as the rupturing exit wound splattered the wall; his mandible swung open, exposing oral mucosa and a hanging tongue. Teeth and bone launched into the wall slate as the guard slumped against it.

The gunman experienced three seconds of profound shock, gazing, mouth open at the lacerated, fibrous connective tissue dangling from his exposed bicep, before the Norwaukus pinned him down by two scaled feet and rendered his esophagus. Opaque fluid spewed from his open mouth and neck in pulsing spurts as he gargled bubbles, trying to scream.

Curtis rolled over and crawled backward, kicking out with his feet until he hit the wall. Head fragments and blood spattered on the side of his face and upper body while he watched in horror.

Another guard froze in fear, witnessing the mayhem. He reached for his sidearm, hand trembling, as four broad, razor slits carved through his face, from his forehead down past his neck, popping the right eyeball and splitting the nose. His hand locked around the trigger and fired through the holster into his right foot and floor. Surrounded, then mauled down, he stood no chance.

The guard to his side suffered the same fate, but not before discharging his sidearm and erratically firing aimless rounds. Three shots plunged in one Norwaukus and two in another. Before he could squeeze off a fifth, he had been wholly taken. The large central incisors of the Norwaukus pierced the top of his head, splitting through the skull base and severing vertebrae. The lower incisors simultaneously tore into the throat, decimating the trachea, and with one swift motion, the man's head disconnected from his body. The creature scored through the armor with brisk strokes almost instantaneously, scratching into the chest and heaving Kevlar, fabric, and flesh, followed by chipped rib and moist colon.

By that time, Curtis was up and running.

TWENTY-EIGHT

He had no idea how many of these things there were out there—five? Seven? Too many. One unlocked passageway led to a stairwell, which he burst into, taking steps up to the door leading to the next floor. Locked. Gasping for air, he paced back and forth on the landing, trying to process what just happened. The exit had not led out as expected, and he was now trapped in a strange building on a forsaken island, unsure of what lay ahead. If nothing else, he did feel a little safer knowing those *things* remained on another floor. Hands still tied behind, Curtis, back to the door, ignorantly yanked on the handle repeatedly, knowing damn well it wasn't going to open. Noticing the keypad panel, he grabbed the folding knife from his back pocket, cut the cable ties, then wedged it under the metal frame and pulled it out. After rewiring the board, he cut the ground wire to short the circuit, which unlocked the door with a click.

Several more clicks followed, as every door in the corridor un-locked.

Unsure of which direction he should be heading, he pressed for-ward cautiously along the left wall, hoping for a sign. He saw just as few indicators on the second level as the first, and the hallways stretched on, identical; however, fewer doors lined the walls, all obscured by frosted plate glass. A security guard crossed the far end of the corridor, so Curtis ducked back against a door on the left, the frame barely concealing him. As soon as the guard passed, he opened it and slid in.

The door tag to the right read: *Papilio.*

Soft lighting flashed on in one section as he entered. Flickering noise caught his attention as he moved along the dark edge of the room. He stopped to listen. The sporadic flickering gently pinged beyond the solid void, which felt smooth as his hand ran across it. Glass. With his hand against it, he walked until he felt a rough surface that housed a dual switch. He snapped it on.

The other half of the room sprang to life under fluorescent, amber luminosity. Curtis's eyes lit up, captivated by the view before him. *My god, there must be hundreds—hell, thousands!* Ubiquitously fluttering, the brilliant iridescence of butterfly wings glimmered as they moved, a vast variety of exotic creatures: Monarch, Sapho, Blue Morpho, Purple Emperor, Ceylon Rose, Chimaera Birdwing, Swallowtail, Buckeye, Luzon Peacock, Tiger, Marble, Glasswing, and the list went on. The light hit each one differently, creating a prismatic effect, endless, unrestrained colors—some so bright, Curtis raised his hand to shield his eyes.

Vegetation, high grass, and flowers covered the bottom of the habitation, from which the butterflies emerged. An enchanting plethora landed on the glass, flaunting their broad wings, delicate bodies, and curious antennae in front of Curtis. He put a hand on the glass as if to touch one, and several Blue Morphos gathered in his palm, wings delicately twitching. Never in his life had he experienced such a sight, a true essence of beauty. He pulled away, backing up to take it all in.

Next, Curtis entered a well-lit laboratory off the butterfly room, with a workbench encompassing the room's perimeter. Several stations had the same devices and tools—microscopes, hot plates, graduated cylinders, tongs, flasks, and test tubes. Each had a laptop station with large duo-external monitors. A currently absent staff clearly utilized the pristine room. Personal effects occupied each station: framed pictures, themed calendars, coffee mugs, earbud headphones, cellular phone chargers.

An open connecting room on the far side contained a six-foot-high, sectioned saltwater reef tank that ran the room's length, filled with exotic fish. He recognized the busy skin patterns of colorful Mandarin fish and various styles of Tang. Peppermint Angelfish and Basslet fish, identified from a nearby plaque, resided in their own section, hiding under lime-green trumpet coral and dimly lit corners. Schools of mini Dottyback zipped from the right corner, zig-zagging magenta and yellow past Curtis's wide eyes. Clownfish cautiously emerged from the porous, rocky crevices of white aragonite rock, which overlay most of the bottom, some immediately seized by the protruding dorsal spines of a hunting Lionfish. Its many fan-like pectoral fins churned, sweeping the ground as it passed.

The bottom of the tank looked just as fascinating as the fish it housed. Canary lace coral sprouted from beneath the dense sparkling substrate, polyps branching out as tiny underwater trees. Otherworldly Galaxia, a stony, radiant creature of metallic green and red, lay, sheathed with long, crystal bulb-tipped tentacles swaying with the current.

He smiled at the rainbow, tie-dye splashed seahorses, delicately floating in pairs, tails interlocked, changing color. Mostly translucent, their internal matter glowed, as if filled with tiny electrodes that lit up their thistly bodies. The tiny sea creatures seemed almost mystical, and he paused to admire them for a long moment.

In the next interconnected room—the outside door labeled: *Invertebrate/Cephalopod*—many large, liquid-filled glass tanks ran floor to ceiling. The sparsely lit space spread out much like the butterfly room, save for the highly illuminated tanks with a fluorescent, royal blue sheen. Box jellyfish hovered desultorily inside, moving intermittently. Curtis was in awe of the enormous, deadly, cube-shaped carnivore, longer than he was. With its translucent body and glowing filament through the top of the malleable bell, it almost resembled a light bulb. Long, thin tentacles floated underneath, the lighting giving the creature a turquoise hue.

Another tank, populated with the infamous Man O' War jellies, fascinated him even more. Although, according to the sign, they weren't invertebrates or technically jellyfish, they remained part of this aquatic display. They possessed a curious design with their sailboat-shaped, gas-filled bladder bodies. Myriad tentacles flowed—a long, purple-tinged, venomous thread coiling from its center—with its base saturated in a blue hue with a carmine tincture outlining the edge of the sail shape. A vivid galaxy of mulberry and burnt orange fibers, which composed the underbelly, streamed down like confetti.

The dimly lit main tank, built between two levels and taking up the most space, contained the elusive giant squid. Curtis only saw a flash of eight mahogany, suction-cupped arms twist past his face beyond the dark liquid, dropping to the floor below.

The adjacent room had tanks with extraordinary, deceased creatures. The door tag read: *Mesozoic & Misc.* The faint scent of formaldehyde and other preserving chemicals lingered overhead as he walked through. He saw two, and three-headed reptiles, amphibians, sea mammals, and fish separated into various individual-sized and shaped containers. The fluid in all the displays glowed dandelion, giving its contents an all-the-more ominous demeanor. The last spectacle was, by far, his favorite—more terrifying than anything he's seen on this journey, save one living creature, while strangely having an aura of mysticality. Even deceased, the being in the vat, labeled *Plesiosauria*, gave him chills.

Suspended in water, the massive reptilian-like creation hung high in a cylindrical, copper base tank with its broad, flat, scaly body and stubby tail. Its long, slender neck and narrow head curved up and over, facing Curtis, mouth open, exposing needle-thin, procumbent teeth. Two pairs of paddle-like limbs drifted in the surrounding, silky liquid. The horizontally striped skin had paramagnetic properties and sparkled, emitting a different pigment dependent on how the light hit it. Every few steps he took, the metallic gems changed color, like magic. The creature watched with sad eyes as Curtis walked past.

He came to an exit door, which stretched into a long corridor, decidedly ending the field trip early to find a way out. His eyes darted front to back, side to side, conscientious, creeping through the unoccupied wings on high alert. Each hallway blended into the next, and with no windows to the outside world, he had no idea where he was in relation to anything else. Even more confusing, he couldn't find any exit signs. No indication of a way out. Downstairs was definitely out of the question. Going up another flight didn't seem rational—not that *any* of it did.

After a couple of short corridors, Curtis entered an expansive, sectioned room with hanger doors, a location for shipping and receiving. His heart rate shot up excitedly; he ran towards it and hit the green plunger. The mechanism fired, and the pulley system loudly creaked. The door inched open as the light pierced his feet, pants, and chest. A cool breeze gently pushed by, filling the space around him. Eagerly, he ducked under the hanger door, stepping out, but then stopped short, dreadfully greeted by a formation of unwelcoming assault rifles. He raised his hands, but only to block the beautifully blinding sun from his eyes.

TWENTY-NINE

A my paced back and forth in the kitchen, cell phone—partially charged—in one hand, running her fingers through her greasy, disheveled hair with the other. She'd been dialing Curtis's cell phone all morning, which kept going straight to voicemail. Days had passed since she'd left Norwich, all spent wondering when he would walk through the door. After the first day, she wasn't quite concerned, even though she wished he had just left with her to begin with, but she'd been in no frame of mind to make any logical decisions, much less argue with her estranged husband. She tried his cell several times on the second day, which at least rang, indicating the phone at some point held a charge. So, she figured, he must be okay. But then she wondered why in the hell he didn't return a call and instruct her as to what to do, or, at the very least, check in to see if his *wife and son* made it out safely?

Wes, whose face returned to a color reminiscent of a young boy's, sat cross-legged on the floor between the couch and coffee table eating a PB&J with the crusts cut off, staring at his silhouette reflecting off a blank TV screen. Every so often, he'd look over at his mother anxiously walking circles. She spoke in low tones, having a personal conversation with herself—repeatedly asking where his father was and why he wasn't picking up the phone, using a few other terrible words she hoped Wes couldn't hear. Finally, Amy decided to give it a break and sat down on the couch next to her son, firmly placing the phone down on the table with an audible *whap*.

She closed her eyes, then took a deep breath, letting it slowly out. Wes watched this go on for minutes, until his mother finally turned to him.

She put her arm around him and gently kissed the top of his head. "How's the sandwich, sweetheart?"

Without acknowledging, he continued to eat, grape jelly staining his upper lip.

The days remained quiet since arriving on Neck Road. Too quiet. She wasn't surprised; silence was to be expected, considering most of the neighborhood had gone south for the winter. She had left the house only twice: once to get her car, along with picking up some groceries and a car phone charger at the corner market next to the deli, and once earlier today to take a stroll around the neighborhood to view the damage while Wes napped. The exceptionally slim roads, barely capable of accommodating one car, let alone two, meant that someone would *always* have to pull off in the grass during two-way traffic. Amy had found herself stepping into a yard a couple times to let one pass.

The adjacent street from the cottage led straight down the beach, narrowing, eventually ending as a driveway for a large house on stilts in the sand, perpetually under construction since being abandoned some time ago. Much like the neighborhood, the beach hid beneath littered branches and a few thin trunks from trees that had washed up. Withered seaweed lettuce with scattered crabs and firm jellyfish in the early stages of decay veiled the white sand; the tangy scent of ammonia and brine lingered. A refrigerator, partially buried at the edge of the shore, caught her eye; the current, still choppy from the storm and on its way in, gently crashed against it.

"The Long Island Landfill," as Curtis referred to it—the lifeless body of water wedged between Connecticut and Long Island, runoff from the Atlantic—trapped whatever would flow in; at least twice a year, the towns would have to close to the public due to a random, high concentration of toxic bacteria in the water. But Amy didn't care—she never did—staring out, taking in the beautiful beach view that stretched for many miles all the way down to Saybrook Point. She recalled many evenings standing in this same spot and watching the harmonious glow of orange and pink skies reflecting off the shimmying water. New England sunsets were something to behold.

The beach.

She spent much of her life here—here—at this beach, as a young child and for just about every summer since middle school, when her parents stayed for three months in between academic rentals. Sure, they could've charged an exorbitant amount of money and really cleaned up renting it weekly to vacationing families from New York City or Hartford or from wherever people look to escape, which many other residents on neighboring streets did, but she was glad her parents hadn't. As she surveyed the landscape, a barrage of memories—snippets of images, things she hadn't even thought of in decades—flooded over her, a flash before her eyes.

The fourth of July, especially—always a banner day on Neck Road. Street-wide gatherings, depending on where one lived, of course, started mid-morning with homeowners setting up their yards with large, square, canopy tents, folding tables, and chairs, not to mention 120-quart plastic coolers, big enough to store a body, all for a day of celebration, a day of barbequing, a day of gleeful inebriation. Lawn games of badminton, bocce, and lawn darts littered backyards, even some horseshoes—*Jesus, when was the last time anyone's seen a bocce ball or a horseshoe?* The shrill laughs of children echoed through each closely connected yard, splashing around in small, plastic kiddie pools. And the music. Loud and resonating, it carried all the way to the water. People would actually rent bands to play festive classic rock ballads until the sun fell behind Long Island.

From as early as she could remember, the fireworks display from a barge water vessel off in the sound would put on the most spectacular display of fireworks she'd ever seen—other than Epcot, of course—but, much like bad pizza, even a lousy firework show was still pretty damn good. She found something amazing in its simplistic splendor—something about the cascading burst of multicolor flare gracefully willowing down, a phosphorescent palm tree, against the starry backdrop of night sky, slowly dissipating over the cove of dark ocean as the metallic smell of pluming sulfuric smolder lingered in the sultry summer air. And, as an adult, fireworks remained just as captivating, even invigorating—promising, perhaps—more on a subconscious level, much in the same way some choose to see each New Year's Day as their *new beginning*. The view all along the coastline, even as far as Long Island, fifteen miles out—if you could believe it—showed a celebration of magnificent, illuminating propulsion.

The beach held many memories. Probably most significant, her innocence, generously given away to Paul Buckley in the wee hours—also on July fourth, summer of '86—a boy she'd been *dating* since middle school, when dating meant making out inside the two-cinema movie theater on Main Street and loitering at the Surf Club at town beach or the campgrounds of Hammonasset State Park, where the cool "older kids" would hang out, with other coupled friends. After four committed years, she felt the time had come. He was a sweet boy, whose parents moved him out west Junior year, breaking her heart. After six months of exchanging letters, he vanished. Moved on.

For a moment, she wondered where Paul was.

Amy fast-forwarded through years—too many years—of drinking Bartles and Jayme's wine coolers and smoking Merit 100's with her two girlfriends, Megan Walker and Liz Mitchell, sunbathing with Hawaiian Tropic Tanning Oil until they turned a shade of dark caramel, which they managed to succeed by mid-June. By then, her face scattershot into a hundred thousand tiny freckles, as she always did in the summer months, with her hair washing out to light apricot. A teenage Ann-Margret.

Jumbled flashes rolled by—sitting in the sand smoking pot with Curtis, then kayaking around the cove with her fiancé while pregnant, then massaging suntan lotion all over the pallid, soft arms of her smiley three-year-old in dinosaur swimmies. Then Wes, adorably sitting on a sandbar, digging wet sand with a red, plastic shovel before desperately dumping its contents into a matching pail. These images remained slightly fresh in the back of her mind.

She wondered how she could have spent so much time away from it. The ocean—unfathomable. She had the view of the river behind her Forest Street abode, but it wasn't the same, not by a long shot, even without that ghastly centralized island, obstructing what could have otherwise been a possibly picturesque view. And now, why should she have to, all things considered? Four years of college aside, this beach is where the best years of her life lay. Right then and there, it hit her. She knew she wasn't going back to Forest Street.

⸻ ⬗ ⸻

The silence broke as Amy noticed, from the living room window, the faint sound of a screen door opening. Her neighbor, exiting the house, stepped into the backyard with a large pail and rake. She got up to look out, excited—another human.

"Daddy?" Wes said, now standing and looking at his mother.

Amy turned—her mouth dropped. She walked over and squeezed him tightly.

"No, sweetheart, it's not daddy." She kissed his face, bracing him in her arms. "Daddy—daddy is..." Amy couldn't bring herself to tell her son another lie. She stood immediately, looking back out the window for a moment. "Be right back, honey, just stay here, okay?" With haste, she made way through the front door into the neighbor's yard.

"Amy, is that you, dear?" The elderly woman asked, dropping branches into the pail. "I had no idea anyone was home next door."

"Hi, Anne." Amy cautiously smiled. "I didn't know you were here, either, uhh—"

"Yes, well, it wasn't a planned trip, unfortunately. Flew in yesterday to make sure the house was still standing! Had to make the rounds, you know, visit my daughter and son. My lord, did you hear the news said we could be without power for *two weeks!* Can you believe that!? Good thing I'm here another day or two," Anne said, now raking sticks.

Amy started to rock side to side, looking back at the house and then to Anne. "Oh—I uh, didn't hear that—wow, that's insane. Um—"

"You know, my daughter's in Long Island. I swung in on my way from LaGuardia, and things there are so much worse—no power either. And did you hear about Coney Island?"

"I—I didn't—" Amy grew impatient.

"The whole park is underwater! Pictures of the Cyclone roller coaster sitting right there in the ocean, a sad, sad shame—oh heavens, and that haunted house and some of the other attractions that washed out to sea."

"Huh—oh wow—uh—"

"How are your parents, dear? You know it's funny, they live an hour away from me in Florida, too, and we never seem to cross paths, not even up here! I do miss talking with your mother—such a classy lady. Last I spoke with her, she was moving her practice down—"

"Anne! I'm sorry, but I'm actually here to ask you a favor if you wouldn't mind. I'm in a bit of a bind here," Amy finally squeezed in. "I was really hoping I could ask you to look after Wes for me for just a little bit. I can't seem to get a hold of my husband, and I really need to drive back to the house, and—and Wes, he can be a little sensitive when it comes to sudden changes, and I'm going to be really quick and don't want to disturb him."

Anne, at last, stopped raking up sticks, now giving Amy the up and down. Amy winced, knowing she hadn't slept in days, clad in a wrinkled tee-shirt and pink sweats with her face colorless and eyes puffy.

"Are you all right, dear?"

"Every—everything's fine. I just need to get home." Amy looked back at the house, where Wes stood in the window, looking out.

THIRTY

Two guards led Curtis by his arm into an office, sat him down in a black, leather guest chair, then departed. Confused and distracted by the elaborate interior, he barely noticed the guards leaving. The broad room contained a long, rectangular, red mahogany desk in its center, which housed two flat-screen monitors, multi-line telephone, and two-way radio. Neatly stacked files sat in the left corner, immaculate. At the center edge lay a double-sided retro clock, entangled in a wiry, bronze frame, each busy face containing a world globe encompassed by Roman numerals. The time—illegible.

The ample space reminded him of his trip to Disney's Animal Kingdom—a safari motif. Tall potted plants, ficus trees, indoor palms, and yuccas lined the perimeter. Various pieces of carved wood, ivory, crystal statues, and porcelain trinkets sat displayed behind glass shelving between the jungle foliage. On one shelf, set behind a small glass plaque, he spotted two gold coins—a Copley Medal and Pulitzer Prize. Various framed credentials vertically lined the wall between. Though hard to read, they appeared to be degrees—one, a Ph.D. from the Massachusetts Institute of Technology in Cellular and Molecular Neuroscience, another from the University of Oxford.

Faint snapping drew Curtis's darting eyes to a magnificent, white cockatoo, which sat undisturbed on an open perch in the far-right corner. It watched him with turquoise-rimmed eyes, clicking its marbled, gray beak.

A wall made entirely of glass overlooked another enclosure behind the desk, brightly lit, sky blue. In front of it stood a man in brown slacks and a white oxford shirt, his hands interlocked behind him as he looked through the pane, his back facing Curtis. Curtis sat, fidgeting, wondering what he'd gotten into.

After a long moment, the man, back still turned, broke the extended, awkward silence. "You mind telling me how you got into a guarded, government research facility?"

Curtis picked a bit of grime off his face with his fingers. "Government research facility? I thought this was a dead pharmaceutical company."

The man chuckled under his breath. "I'm afraid, dear friend, you've been mistaken."

"I'm not your friend."

"No. You're Curtis Colby Reynolds, neighbor across the river. Husband of nine years to Amy Chastain-Reynolds. One son, eight years old, with *special needs*. Former military; served in the Gulf War. Arrested five years ago for vehicular manslaughter, given six years' probation. Works odd jobs to keep a failing marriage afloat. You see, I know a great deal about *you*, your neighbor, Mr. Frank Cavanaugh, *former* resident of Forest Street..." The man rattled off as if reading from a folder.

"You plan on writing my life story?" Curtis snipped, though his jittery tone betrayed him.

"Not quite. However, if I were, this could be the concluding chapter."

Curtis blinked. "You're going to kill me?"

"But how could I? You're already dead. That's how you ended up here, am I right? Besides, after what you've seen, I couldn't very well let you go now." The man turned his head, exposing his right profile. "You know exactly what we do here?"

"Aside from creating weird, fucking hybrid rodents?"

The man smiled.

"Yes, I do apologize for your visitor there. It killed two of my men and escaped during transport—so sad. They thought they were shrewd, trying to smuggle it off the island. Somehow, they managed to kill the power while mid-transport to its new habitation unit, deactivating the electronic locking mechanisms and causing all sorts of unbridled chaos. The creatures were mostly incapacitated but getting them back in their proper places proved a bit dicey nonetheless, I must admit. Eventually, we got the power on and scrambled to get everything locked down, until further problems ensued. Reactivation caused a power surge at this aging facility, temporarily browning out half the town!

"Not fully understanding what they had in their cargo, the thieves never made it off the island. I was able to eventually track the van to the bottom of the Yantic. I really should have pulled the alarm then, but after this venal act, I started thinking. I was curious—wondering what this thing would do, now left to its own devices.

"You know, by circumstance, it came into existence—turned heads upstairs—and just like that, along with the world's worst, fortuitous creations, we were off and running."

"We? You keep saying, *we*. Who's *we*?"

"The men upstairs, old boy! The men who run your country. The country you and your ancestry fought so admirably for. Of course, then, *they* fought for a different world."

"Nothing wrong with this country. I'd give my life for it any day." As Curtis said this, he wondered—for a split second—if he actually believed the words that had just left his mouth.

"But you already have. You know who I am?" The man said with an air of importance, turning to face Curtis.

The left side of his gnarly face glared, disfigured from his forehead and down around his ear, all the way beyond his neck. Curtis winced at the sight, reminded of the awful wounds and diseases he'd seen overseas. Most disturbing of all, the man's left eye had clouded over from retinal damage. Dead. It reminded him of the eyes of the Norwaukus. But something else about the man seemed familiar...

He needed a second or more before he registered where he'd seen that face, partially unrecognizable with the heavy burns.

Curtis blinked, astounded. "You... You're Al—Aldrich Douglas."

The man stood and looked at Curtis. Still well-kept, he kept his slacks and shirt tailored, fit, and pressed. But in all other ways, he appeared quite different from the video clip. Older. His hair shone bright auburn, slightly curled, and combed back with a high sheen. A streak of white ran along either side of his head just above the ear line, matching the hair on his chin. The beard and mustache he wore looked thin, trim, but they failed to conceal much of his heavily scarred complexion.

"But... you're—"

"Dead?" Aldrich finished. "That was the idea. After the accident, we sold off what was left of the company, and I assumed a different identity, staying here to run a private research facility. I do projects for your government, which in turn keeps them pacified and off my back."

Aldrich pulled a box from his desk drawer and opened it, revealing a hand-carved, eagle's foot, Meerschaum pipe. Curtis had never seen craftsmanship quite like it—as intriguing and splendidly unique as the man who held it. A thin, black stem ran down from the mouthpiece to the feather-shaped saddle around the intricately scaled tarsus shank. It molded seamlessly into the golden-brown bowl, tightly gripped by thickly etched curved talons.

"I don't get it."

"Are you familiar with Nanobiomaterial? No, no, of course, you're not. Would you ever guess the wing of the Central American Morpho butterfly has natural properties more advanced than any current technology? I kid you not. These aposematic creatures have this innate ability to absorb solar energy—a natural insulation. Their wings, like shingles on a roof, can quickly and easily cast off water or filth—a self-cleaning system that's ultra-thin, lightweight, and, moreover, highly flexible. Then, when combined with these extremely durable cylindrical molecules called carbon nanotubes, they create a composite—a hybrid structure—which becomes highly conductive when heat-activated—capable of replicating DNA on its surface! It's really quite marvelous, I tell you." Aldrich, leaning on the edge of the desk, struck two matches on the heel of his beige, polished shoes and lit the bowl of his Meerschaum pipe, pulling back on the tip and emitting a flow of Savinelli smoke.

"I'm gonna be honest, I didn't get much after *butterfly*. What's your point?" Curtis said, headache returning. He massaged his forehead with his thumb and index finger.

"Imagine going to the doctor and being flawlessly diagnosed by digital technology rather than some elitist, alcoholic—and if you're even lucky—Ivy League graduate who's more concerned with their bottom line and their quarter-million-dollar student loan debt, rather than your health? To find cancer long before a symptom was ever noticed?"

Curtis stared in silence.

"No? Or perhaps electronics is your thing? Instead of carrying around a laptop or your shoddy internet flip phone, you could *wear* your computing device. Stay perpetually connected to the world! Pictures, music, and GPS sewn into your favorite suit—purse—watch—or even applied directly to *your* skin."

Curtis shrugged. "Who the hell on God's green earth would want to stay connected to the internet twenty-four-seven?"

"Ah! Environmentalist, are you? Perhaps you'll like this—a renewable energy source! The tech would also improve and enhance solar photovoltaic cells, which can convert light energy into electricity. Go green! It would eliminate the need for nuclear power. Perhaps, save the planet? Hmm?"

"Hmph..."

Aldrich smirked. "Unfortunately, your government is only interested in the research of the microscopic scales located on the wing of these fluttering anomalies to improve their military reconnaissance and surveillance—more efficient modular assault vehicles, I suppose." He sighed, defeated, trailing off in a *can-you-believe-it* tone.

"I'm sure it's in the best interest of this country. They know what they're doing." Curtis said—a sense of uncertainty in his tone.

"Oh, *surely*, you can't be this naïve. This is the only land where the people in charge of protecting its citizens are the ones actively killing them! The list is terrifying! Obesity—an escalating problem in this country. The Western diet has decimated over a third of the population with your hormone-induced beef and dairy, genetically modified vegetables, flame-retardant sports drinks, and artificial food coloring. They took the arsenic out of rat poison and repurposed it in your local market chicken to keep that delicious *pink* look. Mmmm! Systemic pesticides sealed into your seasonal fruit with ursolic acid *wax,* and parents wonder why things like Autism and ADHD have gone up eight-fold in the last ten years. And don't get me started on the colony collapse of honeybees..." Aldrich lectured.

Curtis perked up a bit.

"Two and a half times more is spent on health insurance in the United States, and our life expectancy is one of the lowest in the first world. Formaldehyde isn't for just dead bodies anymore; it's a nutritious part of your cattle's diet and an ingredient in your wife's mascara and makeup! And natural disasters? I mean, how much more irresponsible can you be after dumping thirty million gallons of crude oil in the ocean then using a much more highly toxic chemical to clean it up!" Aldrich smiled spiritedly.

"And the corn; oh, the corn, corn, corn—fields and fields of your precious *Franken-corn*. My god, it is in everything, isn't it?! Not only is it fueling your imperialistic, gas-guzzling auto, but you brush your teeth with it, wash your hands with it, and you coat your prescription drugs with it. It fraudulently sweetens up all the processed food on your dinner table, the side dish to your delectable, sweet cob, and the protein they're even stuffing your livestock full with. I bet that heart-healthy, farmed salmon sounds mighty tempting right about now, doesn't it, old boy?"

Curtis glared up as Aldrich moved in, hovering over, his shit-eating-grin infuriating. He imagined grabbing Aldrich by his scrawny, scarred throat, and in doing so, he noticed the top two buttons of his shirt were open, revealing a tubular key underneath, hanging from a thin, silver chain.

"Breast cancer—on the rise—but no one *dares* question the ingredients in their broad-spectrum lotion they liberally lather on by the tube-full only to protect themselves from *another* cancer! Those pesky rays...

"It's amazing—quite comical, actually—the things that are banned even in the most undesirable parts of the world are yet deemed "*safe*" here—or just otherwise hidden or disguised with an ambiguous term." Aldrich backed away.

"Look, I really don't give a shit about any of this. I'm completely fucking exhausted, and frankly, I'm tired of listening to your bullshit." Curtis said, ultimately defeated, rubbing the corner of his eyes between the bridge of his nose.

For a moment, Curtis glanced around the room, surveying the many objects on display in the office's well-filled space; the cockatoo perked up, outstretching its brilliant white wings. He turned to view the door, curious if the guards stood outside of it—waiting. What if he drove the tusk of an ivory elephant statue—the one on the desk over the files and used as a paperweight—into the back of Aldrich's head, then made a break for it? While contemplating the assault, he tried to remap the direction from the hanger door to Aldrich's office. Six armed guards had escorted him under the middle building, up to the third floor. Even though he knew the buildings were interconnected, he figured one thing for certain: he was far from the tunnel which led him in.

"*Melioidosis*," Aldrich said, moving about the room, hoping to regain Curtis's attention with his terse comment.

"What?" Still in a daze, Curtis couldn't quite understand what he heard—or if it was even English.

"Whitmore's Disease, as it's known in some parts of the world. Severe headache, abdominal pain, difficulty breathing, sore throat, disorientation, and in some cases encephalitis, necrotizing pneumonia, bloody sputum, and the most distinguishing and horrifying pustular skin lesions. In most cases, it's followed by septic shock leading to death in two, maybe three days tops—if you're lucky. A third-world endemic, mostly in Southeast Asia, Africa—the Middle East—a bacterium commonly spread by contaminated soil, water, even rodents. Fortunately, when contracted naturally and with early diagnosis, the prognosis is generally positive. Fourteen years or so ago, we were able to synthesize a bacteriological version."

Curtis looked off to the side of the room as he tried to piece it together.

"Didn't realize you lived a stone's throw from the company which created it?" Aldrich flashed a wide shit-eating grin, now perched at the edge of his desk once more. "I've come to discover, during my little investigation into the *misfortune* that is your past, you happened to be stationed in Qatar during this little experiment. What. Are. The odds?" He shook his head.

Curtis paused for a moment. A vision of his terrified friend, Marty, immediately came to mind, and soon after, so did the barracks full of sick, writhing soldiers, all of whom sprawled out on their cots in agony.

Curtis could barely breathe. "Why?"

"Well, they had to test it, of course! And what better way to do so than on foreign soil during times of war. Perhaps it helped secure your victory. Had the Iraqis not pulled out of Kuwait City but instead escalated the severity of the situation, your government would've had carte blanche to go in and eradicate all threats by any means necessary. Instead, the war fortuitously ends, and a "foreign deployed" biological weapon turns into nothing more than an ordinary, deadly virus—and you've got three hundred dreadful soldier deaths swept under the rug in vain by the people you made a commitment to serve and protect. The few and the proud, I suppose."

"All those people..." Curtis squeaked out, fighting back tears and a surge of rage.

"A drop in the bucket," Aldrich offered gingerly. "They've been at it since the First World War! Although primitively back then—but they haven't stopped, you see. They did it in Korea in the 50s; they did it all through Vietnam; they tried it in Cuba with toxic turkeys in the 70s; bloody hell, they even tested aerosol on *volunteers* of American soldiers from the Seventh-day Adventist Church. Well, I mean, *they* were primarily targeted and basically coerced due to their impeccable health standards—no alcohol, and all that. I must admit, even *I* don't trust a man that doesn't enjoy the drink.

"Nixon may have called a *truce* on the race to develop biological warfare, but the wars of the future won't be fought any longer with an arsenal—or by soldiers. And the implications of nuclear weapons are far too dangerous and destructive to ever be utilized favorably; there's no real winner at the end of that scenario. They'll be fought quietly—covertly—undetected and without reproach. It is inevitable—next year—the year after—who knows when; millions of people will succumb to some novel virus that will run rampant, and the world won't even bat an eyelash as to who's accountable."

Curtis sat for a moment glancing around the room, eyes glassy, then directed his attention back to Aldrich. "What the fuck is this place?"

"Ultimately, we're the center for animal and disease research. Aaand we dabble in *pharmaceuticals*. You know, they originally developed this place after the Second World War in response to *UFO sightings*?" He shook his head with raised eyebrows and a sardonic smirk before carrying on.

"You see, Curtis, The Berlin Wall may have been torn down, and the Soviet Union dissolved, but the Cold War has never really ended. How could it? The Great Powers of the world are each trying to preserve their own way of life by preparing to eradicate the next. I know you know what I'm talking about—you've tried it yourself, am I right? You witnessed the horrors—the reality of what this world has to offer. You got out early—lucky. Except subconsciously, you still live with it. While most of the rest of the world gets to sleep at night *blissfully ignorant*, you—quite literally—don't get to." After a moment of silence, Aldrich continued. "You *are* correct about one thing..."

"Huh?" Curtis uttered, wholly inundated.

"They *know* what they're doing. Cancer is projected to rise over fifty percent over the next twenty-five years—two and a half million cases per year by 2030. I present them with a vaccine, and all *they* want is the source of its creation for their own intemperate purposes." Aldrich turned back to face the glass wall, waving his hand with pretentious flair. "Cancer!? HA-HA! It could be eradicated like smallpox or polio."

Another few moments of silence fell as Curtis sat conflicted, his head about to explode. The vein on the side of his temple pulsated. This was his Hell, and he just wanted it to end.

Aldrich turned. "Ever seen a naked mole-rat?"

"One of *your* monstrosities?" Curtis implicitly guessed.

"No, I'm afraid these hideous, little vermin are of their own conception. I've been studying them for years. Their cells produce a high molecular hyaluronic acid, making them impervious to cancer. These hairless little monsters have an overcrowding gene that prevents cell division, resulting in skin production with a high elasticity level—resistive to pain sensitivity. For them, it's perfect for underground tunneling. They can withstand a very limited supply of oxygen, and they possess the ability to maintain body temperatures in extreme weather conditions. Its cousin, the star-nosed mole, also has quite the complex system."

Curtis snickered.

Aldrich, disconcerted by the interruption, shifted into a more pretentious tone. "If you fancy that, I've got a whole bunch of fun little tidbits! Its fleshy, star-like protrusion, highly sophisticated with its twenty-five thousand sensory receptors, can move at lightning speed, but most interestingly, it can detect earthquakes and bypass electromagnetic fields, and *BLAH, BLAH, BLAH*—it's not bloody important!" Now inches from Curtis and leaning over his chair, Aldrich took a breath, his face flushed. "The takeaway here, Curtis, is that those genes, combined with the defensive composition of other Rodentia, ultimately become a provocative killing machine." He slowly backed away.

A large, sinuous shadow cast over Curtis as he sat, leaning forward in the chair, then a school of fast-moving tropical fish caught his eye. He glanced up at a massive substance crawling across the glass: a Horned Sea Star, thirty feet in diameter. It gleamed with the red tinge of a setting sun; black, conical spikes, single filed, branched across each of its tapered arms. The room beyond the office wasn't another *room*, but a towering aquarium.

"You allowed this thing to kill my neighbor and attack me and my family?"

"That was mere coincidence and just good timing." Aldrich shrugged, having regained his composure. "They're very instinctual creatures. I regret not being more careful—we're usually on our game over here. Been more than thirty years, though, since an escape has occurred. That one was on a much, much smaller, pinhead size scale, which was a bit hard to notice! A tick—and that little bugger hitched a ride home with one of the lab techs who lived over in Lyme. It had been quite a bit of time before anyone even noticed. An outbreak in town, which subsequently spread all over Southeastern Connecticut, became our only indication before the pandemic. Unfortunately, containment was futile. Nothing a little antibiotic couldn't clear up, however. Boy, do they still like to give me grief about that one!" Aldrich chuckled.

"What does any of this have to do with me or my house?"

"Of course, my plans are a bit more indecorous, if you will. Once I am able to seize your property and that of Mr., uhhh..." Aldrich snapped his fingers, blanking on the name.

"Cavanaugh!" Curtis interjected, enraged.

"Right, right, sorry—Cavanaugh's property, seeing his wife didn't quite pull through—I'm going to finish what I started a decade ago. Eradicate Forest Street and that decrepit Laurel Hill estates and just develop *out*. I just closed a deal on the land opposite the island, alongside Route Thirty-Two—another representation of the dying American dream. Norwich will be home to the largest pharmaceutical and government research compound in the world. And *you*, dear friend, have I got the job for you!" Aldrich puffed away on the pipe. The sweet smell of tobacco permeated.

Curtis stayed quiet, contemplating possible options for escaping, none of which he figured would end well for him. He tried to recount his steps, but his head, now pounding, drew blanks. A rush of nausea came over him; his stomach wretched from lack of nourishment. With his nicotine concentration dwindling, a craving emerged. Unsure how much more of Aldrich's rambling he could tolerate before exploding, he fantasized about taking his chances and running straight out the door. Then suddenly, it hit him, and he knew then it was over—he had forgotten about *them*. Even if he could get away, he'd have to somehow thwart any armed guards through the multi-level labyrinth of corridors and laboratories, and then there was still whatever savage *things* may be roaming the facility.

"Are you familiar with the term, *Ningen*?" Aldrich's tone became cryptic. "In old Japanese folklore, these mythological entities roamed for centuries beneath the icy waters of the Arctic and North Pacific. Inebriated fishermen aboard whaling vessels claimed to have spotted such beings over time. Part of the *Yōkai*, or spirits, as they're called, they help form a class of mystical creatures I find profoundly fascinating. They're often described as being whale-like, with smooth skin, but are also said to have a humanoid structure—head, torso, almost fin-like appendages, and gills."

Curtis shook his head.

"Ningen is Japanese for *human*. I've been waiting for the perfect specimen to blend their DNA with, and I think I've just found it." Aldrich sat on the edge of the desk, pipe in hand, and looked at Curtis. "*You're* my Ningen."

"You're out of your goddamn mind," Curtis uttered.

"Think about it! You'd be doing yourself a grave injustice going back to your sedentary existence. Existence?" Aldrich chuckled. "Everything you believed in, your deceptive government, the false sanctity of marriage, the concept *if you work hard and play by the rules, the good lord will reward you...*" Aldrich shook his head, displaying a more sympathetic tone.

Curtis looked up at Aldrich as if, for one delusional second, the man made sense.

"What good have you done? That poor, poor, young therapist whose life was taken unjustly. And her executioner, a morose drunkard behind the wheel, and his lawyer friend from grade school using PTSD as a defense. The guilt *eats* at you, doesn't it? Restless nights. I know why you *really* work third shift for months and months at a time. You don't *want* to be home, do you? Plus, you think you'll ever get to rejoin the workforce with that record? And the medical attention your son needs doesn't come cheap; I know this. The insurance your wife would receive would be enough for them to start over. Start fresh..."

And finally, there he sank, brought to his knees. Curtis looked down, conflicted; something inside began to whisper, almost persuading him to actually consider the offer this madman proposed. Though he realized, by this point, that Aldrich attempted to bait him, it didn't make anything he said less true; his marriage verged on divorce, basically over already. But what if this *was* the solution? He knew following the events of the last few days, his body and mind had reached a point of anguish he couldn't possibly come back from. How much longer could he bear to carry on?

Amy and Wes passed through his thoughts again; were they worried about him? They had to be. It had been days—he wasn't even sure how many—but long enough to cause concern. What would they think if he suddenly vanished without a trace—if they walked into their home and found it inexplicably destroyed? They, too, had seen the Norwaukus; there was no way this madman was going to allow them to move on.

From below office level, a fifteen-foot albino Manta-Ray ascended halfway and hovered in front of the glass, looking in the office. It gazed through the giant, rectangular structure, exploring the scenery—a floral backdrop: mini-fridge, multiple work desks, ceiling, and desk monitors—all surrounded by tall plant life. The wide, open mouth gently rippled, and its horn-shaped, cephalic fins oscillated in front of it, water entering and passing through its delicately swaying ventral gills while the ray viewed the two stagnant creatures on display.

Curtis, stunned at what had just surfaced over him, stared into the eyes of the magnificent being.

"You'd be making the ultimate sacrifice for science. The hallucinations, the pain... don't you want the pain to go away?" Aldrich continued, convincingly validating.

Curtis looked up at the man, eyes bloodshot, glassy.

After a moment of silence, a frantic voice buzzed from the two-way. *"Excuse me, Doctor...?! Sir?!"*

"Yes, go ahead," Aldrich spoke into the transceiver.

"We have a problem down in Sector 2-D!"

"What is it?"

"You need to get down here and see this!"

THIRTY-ONE

The lights flickered synchronously with a mild tremor as the elevator slowly descended. The carriage, small and unpleasantly dated, displayed faux wood paneling wedged between thin strips of mirror. Curtis, uncomfortably wedged between five others, wondered how far down they could be going; the time stretched on, almost as if they weren't moving at all. When the elevator finally reached the bottom, a lengthy pause ensued. The steel door opened, and two armed guards exited, followed by Aldrich, Curtis, then two additional guards. They proceeded down a wet corridor, sloshing through a thin, clear puddle and stopping at a room labeled: *Aviary*.

"Where is all this water coming from?" Aldrich asked, turning to one of four guards standing in front.

The guard shrugged. He opened the door, revealing a bloodbath of carnage. Prisms of feathers lay strewn about, and torn pieces of exotic bird dripped off every surface, as if they had been dissected with a table saw. None of them appeared eaten, only indiscriminately mutilated for nothing more than being in the wrong place at the wrong time. Six-foot high true-flight stainless steel cages dangled open, ripped apart, with piping fragments bent and scattered along the floor. A pandemonium of parrots, macaws, and cockatoos had been instantly obliterated, not knowing what hit them.

Curtis's mouth hung ajar as he glanced around at what remained of the aviary. He tip-toed through the red, swirling water around pieces of beak and talon to a rigid hole, which exposed an adjacent room where four additional guards investigated. He touched the viscous fluid oozing down the edge of the opening.

"Everything is wet down this way, sir!" The guard in the other room announced.

"*Sir?*" The two-way buzzed.

"Yes, go ahead."

"*Sir, we found something in the west wing over in 2-H!*" The guard proclaimed.

The water source seemed to near as the group kicked through the shallow stream, which grew several shades darker as they approached. A long walk down a secluded side corridor led to 2-H, where four additional guards stood. The double doors were missing, and the center frame bent inward. The sign above the gaping opening read: *Mechanics*. Walking in, Curtis saw the mechanics' room stood adjacent to buildings two and three, seeming to house the island's control system. A distribution of piping and valves interconnected the boiler, HVAC, sprinkler, electrical system, and back-up generators. The intricate piping, at one time possibly white, had darkened to a golden shade of brown filth. The highly dated system crisscrossed up the wall, covering the lofty ceiling of this dimly lit room.

They entered a recently excavated 2-H. Beyond the boiler drums, littered with tile and rock, massive holes led under the surface; a steady stream of bubbling water discharged from each opening. A round, center support beam, partially chipped away, revealed slash marks that ran all the way to the ceiling. Twelve baffled guards stood in the room, along with Aldrich and Curtis staring at the ground, the water level slowly rising.

From a distance, a disconcerting creak echoed, the sound of twisting metal reverberating. It pulsed through the men, who now stared at each other. The room tremored like an earthquake aftershock followed by a lengthy, thundering clatter. Everything went black for an instant. A red glow from emergency lighting filled every structure of the island. An industrial panic alarm began to sound off, loud, obnoxious—another dated system. Everyone turned in circles, glancing up and around, confused with unequivocal concern.

Before anybody could say a word, a transceiver broke the tension.

"Sir, the inside of building-three has just... it just collapsed!" The guard over the two-way revealed from his security footage.

"Well, how can that be bloody possible? What in Sam Hill is happening, please tell me!?" Aldrich replied.

"I tried to investigate, but I can't access any of the exit doors, Sir?!" He panicked.

Aldrich shook his head, looking worried. "The doors seal shut in response to any subversive or incendiary intrusion."

Another guard opened communication. *"Sir, I—I'm over in section X, an—and, I don't even know what I'm looking at!? The—there—there's blood all over the place, and—and—and men down!"* The guard rattled on.

"Calm down—tell me exactly what you've got there. How many men?" Aldrich, now concerned.

"I—I—I do—don't know. There are just—just body pa—parts a—all over the place, sss—sir! I'm having a—a—a difficult time

getting through—through. Half of the first floor has caved in through the—the—the ceiling, and the place is—is flooding with water!"

A faint discussion could be heard from the other end of Aldrich's two-way before the guard returned.

"Sir, apparently, there's been a breach in the habitation unit."

Aldrich, wide-eyed, turned to Curtis.

"What have you done?" He said in utter shock.

At a loss for words, Curtis looked at the guards, who stared back, rifles raised, then back at Aldrich. As he opened his mouth to speak, a terrifying scream unleashed from a guard's mouth as he fell to the ground, toppled by a Norwaukus. The creature gnawed the flesh clean off the side of his face with a single bite, exposing skull, cheekbone, and hollow eye socket until the predator backed away, snarling, leaving its prey convulsing.

The rest of the guards turned and opened fire. The muzzle blast from each shot lit the room, giving the guards quick snapshot glances at their attacker as it advanced. The Norwaukus, keeping pace, howled as each successive round struck it. It must've taken twenty or thirty before it managed to reach one gunman, pulling the rifle away with protruding incisors. The guard stepped back and reached for his sidearm as the animal coiled in defense from the heavy artillery. Gunfire continued to ring out until magazines emptied, leaving a haze of smoke dissipating between the pulsing red illumination.

Curtis, squatting down, slowly rose, shaking hands over his ears. This covering didn't do much good, as both ears still rang from the excessive noise; the blaring alarm didn't help either. Everyone stood in a moment of silence, since the Norwaukus hadn't moved from its coiled position. The guards, just as fearful as Curtis, watched for a moment in shock. Replacing their magazines, the guards slowly paced toward the creature, guns raised.

Suddenly, the gunman with the sidearm propelled backward, slamming against the wall. He looked down at the four-foot barb impaling him below the rib cage, choking out a few last blood-soaked breaths. Another barb split through a guard's quadriceps, severing the femoral artery and exiting the rear, while one more pierced the face, slicing through half of his skull from the nasal cavity and out the side, taking brain matter and skull fragment along with it. Kevlar Quills landed in succession in the pipes, walls, and floor, causing panic, sending everyone in a different direction. One guard fell straight down, his scream muffled, vanishing below the water.

"Come with me!" Aldrich proposed, making a beeline out of 2-H, through the corridor wing leading to a stairwell.

Without hesitation, without much choice, Curtis followed right behind. In that moment, Aldrich seemed the safest option—anyplace away from the rampaging *things*.

Aldrich pulled a chip card from a leather sheath and ran it along the reader, overriding the system and releasing the door, muttering all the while. "My men are being slaughtered, and now my creation—my lifelong work is being destroyed. Years of intense research, years of development and planning, years of loyalty, devotion, and moreover, ambiguity... everything... it's all coming undone!"

Looking over his shoulder, Curtis saw three beasts emerging from the dark. They trudged through the flood, hemming in the guards and covering any means of viable escape. Low growls from salivating, open mouths slowly advanced, backing the guards into one another. United, the men loaded fresh magazines and raised their rifles.

The creatures took a cue from their brethren and coiled—spiked balls—preparing for crossfire. Like massive sea urchins, they boxed the men in.

The distant echo of shrill screams between rounds of gun blasts followed Curtis during his ascent. And before he knew it, he found himself back in the office. The lighting inside looked as standard as before, but the panic alarm now blared in the background. The anxious cockatoo squawked on its perch, wings flapping.

"Wha—wha—what are we doing here?" Curtis, heaving, rested his hands on his knees, trying to catch his breath.

"We need to put a stop to all this." Aldrich hurried behind his desk and unlocked the bottom drawer, pulling out a metal lockbox. With the key around his neck, he unlocked the container, bearing another key. He punched a few buttons on a keypad at the edge of the desk, activating a two-by-three section of wall across the room to reveal a control panel. A layer of the desktop slid open eight inches, uncovering an additional panel. Curtis gasped, astonished by the level of tech before him—especially compared to the dated systems in the sealed-off section of the facility.

"Come, we haven't much time." Aldrich tossed Curtis a key.

"What am I doing with this?" He asked, staring at the key.

"That keyhole in the wall panel—put it in there." Aldrich pointed, then turned on the desk device and slid his key into the microswitch lock.

"What is this!? What are we doing!?" Curtis grew anxious; the sweat dripped from his grimy face as he followed orders.

"It's a fail-safe. Now when I count to three, we both turn at the same time. SAME time, got it?!"

"Fail-safe!? What do you mean, fail-safe? What's a fail-safe!?"

The alarm suddenly grew deafening.

"The only way anyone is getting out is when the national guard shows up to open the doors, and by that time, there'll be nothing left. They can never know what we've done here... ONE!"

Curtis, just then, realized the severity of the situation, not wholly wanting to believe it as he looked around the office with wide eyes. "You're gonna *blow up* everything?"

"Not everything. If we're lucky, it may be just the island."

"Aren't these *things* already destroying the place? You can't detonate a—a—a goddamn bomb! The—there are—are people living out—outside the—the—the island!" Curtis sputtered, feeling the rise of a panic attack.

"The blast will mostly be contained within, an imperative to vaporize the paper trail and everything inside these walls. This company at one time supplied the Groton submarine base; people will assume that with the remaining radioactive material buried under the island, an *accident* was *bound* to happen... TWO!"

Faint gunfire reverberated in the distance. Screams echoed.

Curtis looked down, his hands began to shudder. "What about us!? We'll be killed, too!"

After a short pause, Aldrich gazed up at Curtis. "Then, so be it, old boy..."

The man gave him a curt nod. "THREE!" Aldrich turned his key and hit the trigger switch.

A split second of silence followed as anticipation filled the room. Aldrich flinched, then noticed the alarm, which continued to chime. They both continued standing there, fully intact. The man lowered his head, releasing a sigh of immense disappointment.

"TURN—the—key," Aldrich snipped, his tone growing frustrated.

"I—I can't," Curtis admitted. Putting a stop to the mayhem here and now was one thing, but destroying part of Norwich seemed quite another. He also had a strange feeling—a worry, that his wife and son remained in Norwich.

"For God's sake, this is your one chance for vindication—to finally be a man and do something with your life. SO TURN THE BLOODY KEY!"

"No."

From the unlocked drawer, Aldrich pulled a shiny, silver Colt Python and pointed it at Curtis. "Turn the key before I shoot you and find someone alive left to turn it."

Aldrich waited several seconds, then cocked the hammer to illustrate his sincerity.

"You're fucking mad," Curtis snarled.

He smirked. "Dear friend, I'm a *scientist*."

Curtis froze. This was it. He closed his eyes, braced himself, and envisioned Amy and Wes in his final moments. The videos came to mind—vacation; his beautiful wife holding his smiling, elated little son, gently swinging him around in her arms. Curtis didn't deserve her, and he knew it. And although he may not have been able to give her the life he intended or was capable of, he was just happy to have been in it. A tear ran down from each eye. He was not about to use his final moments on earth detonating a fusion bomb in the middle of Norwich.

As he waited for the end, a deep, heavy scraping vibrated over the room, interrupting his thoughts. His eyes opened, slightly relieved. Aldrich and Curtis both stared at the ground, following the sound to the glass wall. A crack formed in the center and rapidly progressed, fracturing outward. A thundering POP sent the floor beneath them falling away, split straight down the middle. The three-level, office-sized aquarium burst open, sending a deluge of saltwater chuting down each crumbling level. Both men plummeted to a shallow pool on the basement floor.

⁂

What Curtis didn't know, and the rest of the staff didn't consider—except for Aldrich—was the sophistication of the star-nosed mole. Aside from its incredible innate abilities, it possessed very practical physical qualities, having water-repellent fur and being the only mammal able to breathe underwater; they were also the fastest tunneling creatures known to man. Upon being released from captivity, the mole made its way underground through the floor breach drilled out by the creatures, which in turn gouged away the concrete structural support girders on their path of destruction. The mole then erratically tunneled through the island, scrounging for food and weakening the structures above until Aldrich's office collapsed in on itself.

Thirty-Two

Amy made it in record time, firing off the exit and flying down Asylum while nervously tapping at the steering wheel. Defunct streetlights hung above, with traffic steadily building halfway down. The stop-and-go confusion between each intersection, horns blaring, only made her more anxious. While waiting her turn, she decided to try Curtis's cell again—a futile effort, and she knew it, but it distracted her from the congestion and the fact that she wanted to scream a list of violent obscenities out the window.

She managed to keep her thoughts even most of the ride up, despite her looming anxiety of what she may find upon entering her house. Holding back her dark thoughts as long as she could, she took the round to corner at the end of Asylum, and with Forest Street in her line of sight, she finally surrendered to the barrage of horrific "what ifs," prompting a sudden realization that her husband may have had no intention of returning to her and Wes. *He wanted us out of that house, and I didn't even bat a fucking eyelash.* Suicide? Was that even a question?

As strong-willed as she knew Curtis to be, the idea seemed a virtual impossibility—unfathomable. *Wasn't it?* The further she dug, as she couldn't stop her spiraling now, there *was* something different about his demeanor when he returned home. Something disquieting, beyond his physical, seemingly gaunt appearance. He was completely detached. Volatile. Cold. An empty shell, dolefully running on autopilot. Something plagued him, something more than what one would consider a natural progression, emotionally—if there was such a thing—of a slowly decaying marriage, now dangling on the frayed end of a thread.

The shotgun. The shotgun had sat on the table, along with a number of other hazardous tools and sharp objects. The shotgun worried her. She *never* liked having it in the house. Garage asphyxiation in his truck—a more time-consuming process, however. Just enough time to dwell on life's ill-fated hand, smoking one last cigarette in the driver's seat before fading to black. Like falling asleep. Then there was the basement. *I forgot about the fucking basement.* Drowning. Tortuous, painful drowning below the murky flood, lungs burning. Suffocating. Or the goddamn creature. Maybe he went back for the creature, and it mercilessly finished him off—or worse yet, he let it.

Why, why, why the fuck *didn't I* make *him come with us!?*

She advanced Forest, taking the corner at an unsafe speed, then stomped on the gas, accelerating to almost sixty miles per hour before reaching the house, driving into the front lawn. The garage stood open, and Curtis's truck lay dormant, half sticking out, which made her hopeful. Garage asphyxiation was out.

"Curtis!" Amy shouted forcefully through the front door. "Curtis, you here!?" She quickly glanced into the living room and kitchen before running up the stairs and checking each room. She came back down in a flash, through the living room, abruptly stopping after kicking his cell phone, which shot through the kitchen. She glanced around. Dried mud tracked over the once gray carpet into the kitchen, canvasing the linoleum with the haphazard checkered print of a size twelve boot. The dinner plate, crusted with dried sauce and two gleaming leg bones, still sat on the crowded kitchen table next to a pile of blood-stained bandages, an open tube of superglue, and a wine glass—similarly stained—with fruit flies swirling inside. Her letter lay underneath.

Oh, fuck no.

Dime-size drops of blood dried around the table's edge and tattered the floor amid black boot prints leading to the kitchen sink. Without even a moment to process the disconcerting imagery before her, as well as the newly flooding thoughts of Curtis's discovery, she followed the trail from the kitchen into the dining room, where nothing could have prepared her for what was next. Her mouth dropped as she glanced at the dirty dining room chair and an ashtray full of snubbed butts. Looking up, she saw the taught rope leading from the staircase, along the ceiling, straight down into the dark opening. Her heart rate instantly shot up, thumping under her breastbone and radiating up into her dry throat; it belted in each ear. Her hand trembled over her mouth, still ajar, as she slowly moved to the edge of the gaping hole in her floor where the dining room table and carpet once lived, fearing what she would find below. From the corner of her eye, she saw the floor top, in pieces, stacked in the family room alongside the other furniture piled on one another.

Struck with terror, she imagined her husband at the end of that rope. Eyes misting, she inched forward—not wanting to proceed, but somehow, pulled by sheer force toward the hole. Peering down, a pungent smell smacked her in the face, triggering instant tears and dry heaving. The odor, rancid and unfamiliar, forced her to turn away without looking, now convinced Curtis was not only dead, but dead for days. But she needed to be certain. The wind pulled from her chest as she fought to steady herself, trying not to linger on the thought of viewing her husband in a state of advancing decomposition. She gasped for air, tears running down her face. Crying felt like suffocation.

Amy lumbered down the stairs, her pulse quickening and her eyes continuing to well. She still struggled to breathe, sucking in rapid lungfuls. She couldn't even begin to fathom what had happened here, but she prayed as hard as she could. *Please, God, let Curtis be alive and not at the end of that rope.* She pushed open the broken door, which creaked on its busted hinges, and to her surprise, the flood was gone. She blinked hard and looked up. To her tentative relief, a mostly empty room greeted her, save for the ambiguous, large steel cage—top open—and the giant hole in her foundation tunneling down. With a slow spin around the room, she saw only the sump pumps and large fans. No Curtis. The smell of pervading rot grew heavy. Oppressive. And although she didn't see her husband suspended from her dining room ceiling, seeing the broken shovel and shotgun didn't provide much consolation.

After checking the rest of the house and the backyard, she jumped back in the SUV and crawled down the street, scanning yards of vacant properties as she rolled by. She hit the dead-end, circled around, and doubled back, stopping at the Cavanaugh's to view the aftermath for the first time. With that level of destruction, she couldn't do much else. Still, a bit reluctant, she walked up the littered yard to the opening where the front door once stood, peering inside. Birds fluttered out from the heavily sooted fireplace, exiting above, while a few barking squirrels wrestled through the living room foliage.

Carefully, she walked inside, but only so far—far enough to get a good look into the charred opening below and see the crumbled hole in the foundation. Shocked, she covered her open mouth, unable to fight the tears any longer as they streamed down her cheeks. Deeply saddened, she still couldn't comprehend what had happened here. Just earlier in the week, she had kneeled over her neighbor—her friend—Estelle, in a state no person should ever have to witness another human being in, especially one for whom they care.

Desperately out of options, without any shred of mental fortitude left, Amy couldn't think of what else to do other than call for help. Her home was destroyed; Curtis was now missing; enough was enough. She hauled up Forest, cell phone in hand, trying to keep an eye on the road as she dialed. The moment she hit SEND, something darted out in front of her; she slammed on the brakes, skidding up about twenty feet. The phone fell to the floor, sliding under the gas pedal.

"JESUS CHRIST!" She gasped, grabbing her chest, pulse racing.

Whatever had run across was gone, but sitting directly in front of her in the middle of the road was a cat. Staring. She stared back, panting, trying to catch her breath. She then watched as the feline turned and trot into the open gate.

"Hello, 911 emergency? Hello...?"

Amy, heart rate now steadily dropping, glanced down at the phone.

THIRTY-THREE

Curtis jumped from the lagoon and squawked, gasping for air, his arms raised to avoid falling debris. Thick, gray particles and heavy smoke pervaded the basement's main wing, making it difficult to see in any direction beyond a few feet. He pushed through the raw, waist-high water behind a corner security station for cover, coughing and choking on the dusty mist; behind him, several grainy, achromatic monitors flickered and fluttered with their limited view of the facility. An office chair came crashing down, bouncing off the countertop, jolting him back as it rained other small objects.

He stood in malaise, quivering, breathing heavily, unable to fathom what had just happened. A pressure had amassed inside his spinning head from the fall, his hearing partially obstructed. The blaring alarm had softened between the high-pitched ringing and the dull roar of breaking ocean waves penetrating his saturated eardrums. A lengthy screech echoed high above, which drew his attention up as the cockatoo emerged from the dissipating haze, soaring past him and down a corridor, fading into the void. It then dawned on him: what else from Aldrich's office was down there?

This section of the facility looked mostly dark, save for the red glow of emergency lighting and the narrow strips of sunlight crisscrossing through broken windows on upper levels. Much of the building's interior remained intact, but Curtis didn't plan to hang around and wait for it to go. He inched his way into the corridor in search of a clear path out, with every step over something submerged, shrouded in darkness. Among the drifting debris, he saw Aldrich's card sheath floating nearby a mound of crumbled rock with no sign of him.

Curtis, continuing to choke on the polluted air, didn't know why the structure was folding in on itself—nor, more concerningly, how much time he had before the rest followed. He grabbed the chip-card and moved down the only open wing, dredging through the flood as fragments of the first and second floor continued to sprinkle over him. Bodies of quilled guards drifted past while he scanned for an exit. The corridor split off with one wing blocked by rubble, driving him down a long hallway. Schools of fish brushed by his shaking legs, which startled him every time. Halfway in, he slowed for a spinous mound in the middle of the floor. The arched back of a Norwaukus protruded from below the frothy, red surface. He slid back against the opposite wall, watching cautiously, but it didn't move as he sneaked by.

The exceptionally long, narrow corridor lacked any windows or doors, save for one wide, metal gate in the middle with "Emergency Personnel" stenciled across. Curtis, confident it was locked, tried the round, silver handle anyway, then kept moving. The double doors at the end were jammed and took an effort to push open. Taking a couple deep breaths, he laid his shoulder into it, using almost every bit of strength left inside. The momentum sent him stumbling into the rose glimmer of the sparsely lit area, stopping short. An alarming, dripping, reptilian mass greeted him; its head pounded his chest. Terrified beyond rational thought, his only instinct was to scream—a sonorous *shriek* rippling through the island as he lost footing, tumbling backward. At second glance, and to his tentative relief, swaying from the ceiling, was the body of the brined, somber plesiosaur, liberated from suspended animation.

"Jesus fucking Christ!" He belted out, picking himself off the floor.

The wing had minor flooding compared to the previous, but it didn't make passage any easier. Sporadic damage from the collapse left gaping holes on upper levels, as if explosive materials had been aimlessly detonated. Scattered rubble, office equipment, wooden planks, and shattered glass barricaded the east wing, all veiled by a thin layer of dust that lingered in the dense air, making seeing difficult. Curtis took shallow steps, analyzing everything as he inched through the fog.

The west wing card reader activated, but the jammed doors provided no means of entry. That didn't stop him from trying; he kicked the door repeatedly until he lost balance, sliding down into the water. A dead end—but at this point, he saw no point turning back. He sat for five minutes, huffing, waiting for his pulse to drop—waiting for a spark of energy, which arrived in a small burst as he pushed from his feet, sliding up the door for balance.

Across the hallway, he leaned against the corner station. Fighting the urge to panic, he wondered if this could be *it*. Was asphyxiation going to do him in? Other than a pocketknife, he lacked any means to defend himself, basically fair game for whatever lurked in the dark. If, by some slim chance, the National Guard showed up and pulled him out, there was no going home—that too was a death sentence. He giggled at the thought of pulling rank on them.

His body continued to quiver, though he couldn't feel anymore; everything had gone numb. Instinctually, he reached in his pocket for a pack of cigarettes that wasn't there—he smiled, eyes becoming heavy.

Save for the muffled alarm from afar, and the variating water drips from above, splashing off solid surfaces, the room remained virtually quiet. Tranquil. The mild swishing of water in the near distance soothed Curtis; he imagined kicking through the clear, warm ocean current over silky, soft sediment during low tide near his in-law's house—an amalgam of summers' past. The noise grew in intensity, but he felt no need to look.

"Curtis, honey..." The voice echoed.

"Huh?" His head lightly lifted, eyes barely open.

"Curtis, look at me..." A hand gently lifted his chin.

"Amy—is—is that you? How—how'd you find me here?"

Curtis struggled to focus, squinting to see Amy standing in front of him. A modicum of adrenaline rushed through him; however, his eyelids dragged, the iron weights trying to shut him out.

"Curtis, look at me, baby—look at me!" She caressed either side of his face with her palms.

"I'm sooo tired, honey. I'm so..."

"Curtis, don't fall asleep, baby—wake up! Wake up!" She grabbed his shoulders and shook him, then pressed her face to his.

"I can't—I can't anymore. It's over. I fucked up—I fucked up, Amy," he mumbled, consciously holding his own head up now.

"Hey..." She pulled back to face him, trying to get his attention. "Your son and I need you, Curtis. *I* need you..."

Curtis finally blinked up at her. Though slightly blurred, she looked as beautiful as ever. Her bright, emerald, upturned eyes stared desperately into his.

"I was a horrible husband, Amy. A shitty father. A drunk. A murderer. A deplorable piece of shit…"

"Listen to me—listen to me. *None* of that matters anymore, Curtis." She held his face, using her best authoritative tone. "None of it. *All* of that is in the past. Do you hear me?"

"I ruined your life, Amy." His eyes welled, tears slipping down his sooty cheeks.

"I wouldn't be here if that were true. I love you." Amy pleaded, her eyes now tearing too.

"Not for much longer, though, right? You want out. And I don't blame you. You want more than I can possibly give you. You and Wes are better off without me." His head hung, embarrassed by his own words. "You should start over."

"Look, you are a good man, Curtis. Yes, you fucked up, but that doesn't dictate the rest of your life. Now, you have to make *yours* meaningful. That's the absolute *least* you can do. Do—you—understand? What happened was an accident—an accident! You have to forgive yourself, honey—you have to."

"I—I can't…"

"You have a son, Curtis. You have a son that needs you—who can't grow up in this world without his father! And all—I—want is the man *I* married back!" She pushed onto his wet chest. "I know he's in there!"

"I can't take it anymore, Amy. I can't do it. The headaches. The nightmares. I can't take the nightmares anymore. I don't want this anymore…"

"We can getcha help, Curtis. We can always getcha help. This doesn't have to continue for you forever. There are options; you just have to be open to it..."

"I—I—don't know, I—"

"Do you love me?"

Curtis nodded.

"Do—you—love—me!?" She shook him gently.

"Yes, I love you, I love you." He could barely look at her.

"Then—come—back to *us*!"

He shook his head. No sense in arguing anymore.

"Look around, Amy... there's no way out of here." He glanced around the corridor, still devoid of any overlooked area or means of egress.

"Bullshit. *You* are not a quitter. Never have been..." She backed away. "I'm sure you'll figure it out, honey. Just—follow—the—"

Faint yelling, squealing—almost agony, from beyond the barricade on the east side drew Curtis's attention. He looked back, and Amy vanished. Slowly, he pushed himself away from the counter, stumbling toward the barricade. The screeching chatter and hacking increased as he neared, climbing up a vast pile of gray brick to pull back shredded drywall and insulation. Under the debris, he found a jagged opening. He pushed his head through and saw the poor, dirty cockatoo perched upon an exit sign, squawking, flapping its ruffled wings. The hole looked tight, not quite wide enough for him to slide through—but it needed to be.

Entering headfirst, he climbed in, crawling on his belly over a cracked office desk. Frayed rebar sticking out from a piece of broken flooring ripped into the side of his torso, and he groaned. Spotting another piece of rebar ahead, he pulled himself through, wincing all the way until the space widened on a downward angle. He swung around to gain footing on a couple of smashed computer monitors but slipped on a shifting brick, crashing down and rolling into the water. The fall scraped up both arms, reaggravating his previous wounds, now completely exposed to the dusty air and murky puddles. Startled by the noise, the cockatoo flew off around the corner. Following behind, Curtis located a strangely illuminated hallway, glittering with shifting, fluorescent grains of neon pink, green, and blue emitting from below the water's surface. Cautiously, he proceeded on the radiant path, keeping tight to the wall, until he crossed a solid mass low to the ground—a guard, mostly submerged, sitting slumped over. Against his better judgment, Curtis thought to check for life, potentially hoping for another hand on board to help vacate the premise.

"Hey!" Curtis yelled, giving the guard a shove. "Are you all right? Are you hurt? Hey, man!" His tone grew a bit more forceful, but with no response, he crouched down to push the guard back out of his slump.

Curtis jumped back. A translucent, gelatin substance coated the guard's face and throat, trickling down his torso, which, too, emitted light. The guard collapsed under the water, and Curtis took another glance at the path before him.

My god... He shook his head.

They were jellies, and they casually floated all around him—thin, cable-like, oral arms swaying languidly, mere feet from his legs. Their chemical energy exuded bioluminescence, lighting up the wing, a vibrant spiral galaxy of interstellar dust and gas, which he found slightly advantageous, albeit profoundly deadly.

A startling yet familiar POP shook Curtis, and he instinctively ducked down as a lab window by his head imploded. He didn't stop to look or even think and shot down the hallway, praying not to make physical contact with the venomous pulp. The soft, translucent bells bobbed gently while tentacles drifted dangerously past Curtis's legs as he stomped through. Around a corner, down a hallway, he reached a door and swiped the card, which returned a red blip followed by a buzz, denying entry. Another firecracker POP rattled in his direction, making contact with the door and ricocheting mere feet from his head. Hands shaking heavily, he successively swiped the card, waiting for green, but it just wouldn't take.

"Where you going, old boy!?" Aldrich's voice rang from the distance as he fired another bullet from his Colt.

The round exploded into the key panel, disengaging it, inadvertently opening the steel door. Curtis burst through and kept running through the endless maze of unbridled fear and structural devastation, silently hoping, praying, for a sign. Though raised in the congregation, he hadn't spent much time in church since high school, other than for his wedding and father's funeral. Since then, he'd only regarded religion when pondering if there actually was a God—except the last time, the only other time, he'd asked for a sign, as he bled out behind a torched commuter bus. His ambivalence hadn't prevented him from making a series of promises—vows, mumbling under his breath. And now, though still not a religious man, he couldn't help but think of God at that very moment. If He was out there, now—now was the time for intervention.

"You know, I can't let you leave," Aldrich continued, walking nonchalantly through the jelly pond.

Curtis took a corner, trying to shake the unhinged man from his tail. He approached the end of the dilapidation, where fallout looked minimal, and climbed over to access the other side of the wing. The next door he pushed through led him to an area he finally recognized. Torn human remains spread the length of the hallway, lying in about a foot of water. The same guards who'd held him down earlier. Another gunshot sliced by, quickly followed by a second, splitting through a corner wall as he turned, searching for those first double doors. Stained walls with dark spatter and smeared footprints against the red corridor glow led the way.

Finally, there they stood. One remained closed, while the other, cratered, hung by a hinge. Curtis continued into the habitation, stopping at the partially submerged chainsaw, winded, trying to suck in cleaner air, and for a moment, contemplated picking it up. After seconds wasted deliberating, he determined the power tool wouldn't do much against a man with a gun and continued down the corridor to his man-made entrance, ducking through into the sealed-off section of building three. Pitch black greeted him—no emergency lighting, no blaring alarm, no lethargic fluorescent bulbs. Remembering his Zippo in his back pocket, he pulled it out. He knew it would barely produce sufficient light, but it had to do.

Where—where—where the fuck are you? The sooted cubicles and lab walls all looked the same, and he began to worry he had walked in circles. The lighter's flame provided only the most minimal visibility—inches, not enough to prevent him from tripping. A wheeled desk chair caught his leg, and the Zippo shot from his hand and slid several feet down the hall, out of a doorway. Frustrated, he let out an audible noise, flinging the chair from his way. The opening led into the office. Straight through the center of the room, he scanned for the entry point, hurrying forward with one hand out in front of him. He brushed against a high structure, identifying it as a service desk by the dusty, lifeless monitors. A creak from the back of the room drew his attention, stopping mid-step, lighter in front—the butane flame flickered, reflecting off his face. Immediately realizing the lunacy of the decision to pause, he pressed forward, picking up the pace.

From the corner of his eye, he spotted a glimmer of light piercing through the dark gap. He'd found the exit. In no time, he raced back inside the tunnel. The structure here appeared compromised, liquid steadily dripping from the stone's fissures—but the bright, white sun shone down dead ahead, illuminating the path, while the crisp, clean outside air penetrated his sooted nostrils and filled tired lungs as he ran forward, water kicking up behind. Reaching the end of the tunnel, he jumped and grabbed a plank to ascend from the island of madness. But before he could reach the next step, a .357 slug ripped through his trapezius muscle, exiting under the clavicle into the stone. Curtis fell backward, landing in the puddle below. Motionless, he lay, staring up at the brilliant, round opening.

Almost made it.

THIRTY-FOUR

—·—

Curtis rolled around and sat up, gripping his upper chest to apply pressure to the open wound while he watched Aldrich saunter over, gun by his side. The man's previously fitted shirt rustled, torn by his shoulder, and blood soaked through the white fabric, running down his chest and arm.

"Valiant effort, old boy." Aldrich looked to the skylight. "I see you found one of our initial attempts for expansion. This tunnel was only the beginning of what was to come... and when the dust finally settles, it'll serve as all that's going to be left." He looked down at Curtis. "I wish you would understand this is for your own good."

Aldrich raised his gun with a sad smile. Curtis, breathing heavily, closed his eyes.

The gun's hammer snapped. Curtis flinched, then slowly opened his eyes. Aldrich squeezed the hammer again but struck only an empty chamber. No rounds remained to fire. Curtis barely had enough time to feel relieved from the second attempted shooting when a crescendo of splashing water materialized, followed by the reverberation of a deep, low *growl*.

From out of the misty shadows trudged the disfigured Norwaukus. It stopped and grunted at the two figures in its sights, sending shivers up Curtis's spine.

"SQUAAACK!"

From behind, the cockatoo soared overhead toward the light, wings spread wide. Swiftly, the Norwaukus reared up on hind legs. With a quick SNAP of its jaws, the bird disappeared in the creature's clenches. White feathers floated behind, falling from its scarred mouth.

Without hesitation, Curtis flew up the steps and crawled out the open hatch.

Aldrich turned to look at the animal—his crowning achievement. This terrifying yet beautiful creature he perfected looked more impressive than he could ever have imagined. Years of development. Years of research. The vision of the future—of what could have been. The vision of what could still be... he moved toward it gradually, hoping maybe it would recognize him. And why—why wouldn't it? He raised it, cultivated it from a pup. If only he could perhaps gain its trust, he could take control of it; he might change what was to proceed. Forget the island. It was gone. The panic button was hit, and either way, the cavalry was coming.

The Norwaukus stopped and leered at its maker with curiosity. It could sense a serene familiarity in the man standing before it, continuing to inspect, snout quivering, nose snuffling. But something utterly divine filled the air, causing instant salivating. Once the scent of blood was detected, the thirst took hold, and the Norwaukus lunged through the tunnel.

From the top of the well, Curtis watched as Aldrich turned and climbed the ladder, hustling up, step after step, until he reached the corrupt rung. It gave out from the stale rock, falling as he stepped through. Curtis smiled. A quick adjustment to loosen the plank on his way up proved just enough to prevent Douglas from exiting the tunnel, leaving him to tend to his creation. Hanging from the plank above, Aldrich tried to regain balance, but the weight, too much, sent him and the rung crashing down. He jumped from the murky pool back to the planks to restart his ascent when the beast's central incisors penetrated his calf through the fibula.

The Norwaukus yanked back, pulling Aldrich to the ground. He kicked the animal with his free leg until it released him, then scurried back against the wall. Without pausing, the snarling beast went in for the kill. Aldrich wailed with everything he had before his voice cracked, throat severed. The Norwaukus encased its mouth around his neck and face and squeezed, crushing both skull and spine. The jaw, along with mutilated throat muscles, pulled away, tearing from the tendons as the beast withdrew. Red fluid discharged—a flash geyser from Aldrich's mouth; his lifeless, clouded eye popped from its socket and slid down the side of his scarred cheek.

Curtis stepped back from the well, satisfied that the scientist was, in fact, dead. With the mayhem finally ended, he looked up at the bright blue sky, took in one long, deep breath, and cried out in rejoice. At that moment, he couldn't have been more ecstatic to be standing in a condemned neighborhood or even more appreciative to be *alive*. A cold, light wind blew through his damp hair and filled his lungs as he took a moment to gather himself before starting the climb up Laurel Hill. Time to go home.

He turned—astounded...

Amy stood at the top of the street. *Wait—what is she doing here!? Could it really be her?* Too far away to be sure, he squinted, eyes still adjusting to the light. But as he began to walk, he could just about see her face and that soft, delicate smile—that beautiful smile, which lasted mere moments before washing clean away.

"CURTIS, LOOK OUT!" Amy shrieked, pointing behind him.

Curtis's newfound smile turned to grimace, coming to a halt between the first set of properties at the bottom of the hill. He glanced, wide-eyed, over his shoulder, then slowly turned to face the snarling menace standing in the cul-de-sac. Its teeth, stained red, glared back at him, flesh still clinging from its charred mouth.

"You gotta be kidding me," he muttered.

The Norwaukus charged up the street. Curtis took a couple steps back, trying to quickly consider a potential escape scenario while only drawing blanks. Deep down, he knew he was out of options. The Norwaukus, faster than he, neared in no time at all. Knowing he couldn't possibly outrun the beast, much less defend against it, he watched and waited.

Suddenly, a mass influx swarmed the street as the forsaken inhabitants of Laurel Hill emerged from every direction. They poured out from broken windows and open doors. Many made their entrance from the rusted storm drain, two or three at a time. The high grass split and crumbled under the feet of an unbounded brigade of furious felines. Curtis looked around, blinking as they rushed by. Waves of cats brushed his leg, causing him to lose balance. Trying to move away, he fell backward, arms up, bracing his face. Some hurdled right over, some just trampled with little, cold paws striking him all around.

They hit the creature in clusters, several at a time. The Norwaukus growled, shaking, and flung the attackers from their grips. They bit and scratched at the limbs and torso, some kicking out their rear legs, laying into the scaly flesh. It managed to catch one here and there with its front teeth, launching them as others attempted to jump at its head. The Norwaukus stopped in its tracks, unable to proceed forward from the heavy assault. Little critters, too anxious to fight, hissed and spit from the sidelines. The massive feet of the beast swatted, knocking them in bunches into the air as they tumbled to the ground, then proceeding on their intended course of action.

Thorns fired heedlessly from the Norwaukus, attempting a defense; one struck inches from Curtis's head, another made it all the way up the street, plunging into the passenger door of the Volkswagen. It sat up on hind legs, continuing to swing and claw at them, but there were just too many. Its tail briskly swooped in, hammering them backward. Taking a beating, many limped off to lick their wounds, while others attempted swift digs at the beast and ran back to hide before darting out to attack again. Soon, the strays sensed the weak spot and moved into the exposed underbelly of the beast. Before long, the exhausted creature's defense diminished, and its throat became the final target. Only a few constricting bites sent the life of the Norwaukus spilling out over Laurel Hill.

Without pause, the cats scampered off just as they arrived, abruptly and with haste. Amy finally reached Curtis as he stood and turned around, watching the last of them dematerialize, one little kitty stopping to swat a blue morpho. For an instant, he spotted the King sitting in a nearby bay window. It returned a cordial glance, then faded into the dark. And just like that, the neighborhood became desolate once more.

Amy threw her arms around him, and he held on, in fear of collapse. A kaleidoscope of exotic butterflies swept through, down, and around them before dissipating into the autumn sky as Curtis turned to the grunting beast, watching it expel its last breath.

THIRTY-FIVE

The young man entered Sandy's Garden Center on Main Street in the bustling town of Branford after driving forty-five minutes out of his usual way home from work. Construction paper turkeys in Pilgrim hats swayed in the glass door, advertising fresh harvest pumpkin bouquets and festive cornucopias of assorted blooms. Long lines curved around the front check-out counters as he worked his way into the inordinately busy store, brushing by ignorant shoppers, their arms full as they headed for the exit.

For a gardening store, Sandy's had a very chic aesthetic, filled with high-end items from plants, tools, and equipment all the way down to modern décor, woodcrafts, trinkets, and unique antique finds. Behind the building stood an equestrian farm—a camp for youth horseback riding and competition training. The young man felt a bit out-of-place, bordering on self-conscious in blue jeans, a black hoodie, and a backward Giants cap—not to mention the giant, empty pet carrier in his left hand.

He had been searching for weeks for an all-black, male kitten with very little luck until calling Sandy's. Though ecstatic to hear they had one, he had little hope it would be precisely what he was looking for. But another perk to the shelter was that the rescues came fixed and with all their shots for just one hundred dollars—quite a bargain in his mind.

He strode briskly through the maze of vegetation and floral arrangements, nervous but excited, looking for assistance. The aisles stretched on, twisting and turning, and he quickly lost his way, ignorantly walking in circles.

An opening appeared that he hadn't previously noticed, a corridor beyond the wall of assorted vegetable seeds and obscure gardening tools, which, upon entering, exposed a room much more extensive and even more confusing than the previous. A girl in a *Sandy's* apron stood at a nearby display, adjusting plants.

"Excuse me," he called out, relieved by the sign of employee life.

She looked up, pausing from stocking the wiry, metal table with pink-edge jade succulents. "Hi. Do you need help?"

Coming closer, the young man realized she didn't look more than twelve years old, though, on her apron, she wore a name tag: *Bailey*.

"Uh, yeah, you work here?" He felt silly asking but wanted to make sure.

She grinned, looking happy to be helpful. "This is my mom's store."

"I called earlier about the black kitten. Is there a shelter here, somewhere, orrr...?"

The little girl, seeing the carrier in his hands, beamed. "Yes! Follow me—I know a shortcut!"

She took his hand and led him out of the maze, across the garden center. They walked through a narrow greenhouse with isles of various vibrant ornamentals, some of which the young man recognized as being poinsettias, chrysanthemums, and pansies.

Geez, if this is the shortcut, I don't wanna know the other way, he thought, looking around, trying to make a mental bread trail.

The other side opened to an area that appeared much like the front entrance, though much less congested; two women stood behind check-out counters with a station for building floral arrangements nearby. As it turned out, the "shelter" was just several rabbit-sized cages made of galvanized poultry netting, all arranged in the center of the room with *Forgotten Felines* written above on a colorfully hand-drawn paper sign. Thirteen cats of all shades and sizes sat on display, incarcerated, stacked on one other.

In a cage of its own, off to the side, lay the little black cat he had inquired about. The little girl opened the cage and pulled the furball out, handing it to the man.

"My god, is he just the most adorable thing, or what!" He held the cat cradled in his arms, smiling, then looked at the other cages, noticing at least two kittens contained together in each. "Why is he all by himself?"

"He doesn't get along with the other cats. But he's very friendly." She smiled before running off.

One of two older women behind the counter approached the young man to see if he required assistance. "You must be the young man who called about the black cat. We were starting to get worried—he's been here quite a while."

"Oh wow." The young man paused, now slightly concerned there was something wrong with the animal. "Why is that?"

"Oh, I supposed some folks just have a *thing* about black cats for whatever reason, silly as it sounds." She shrugged, sticking her hands in the pocket of her brown overalls.

"Huh... How old is he?"

"We suspect somewhere around six and nine months."

"Really? Hmm..." The kitten looked bigger than he'd expected, but when he stroked the silky feline fur, it purred, curling, eyes closed, against his right arm and chest. He smiled. "I noticed this isn't much of a shelter. Did you guys find them in the neighborhood or something?"

"Oh, they come from all over. They don't stay very long, though, which is nice. Of course, with the exception of this guy," she explained, waving down at the black cat. "These ones here just came over from the eminent domain."

"Oh," he replied, wondering if he was supposed to know what that meant. "Uh... what is the eminent domain?"

"Eminent domain? It's an old, abandoned housing project in Norwich, up by the old Hock Pharmaceuticals. Since all the animal shelters seem to be overrun at the moment, we've been getting a lot of strays down this way lately from around there."

"That's crazy. So the strays just moved into the empty houses?"

"We don't think so—maybe some. Most of the people when they moved apparently just packed up and left. And we suspect some actually just left their pets behind."

"Really?" The young man blinked, surprised and a bit hurt to hear such a thing.

The woman somberly nodded, reaching over to stroke the black kitten. "Yeah. It's so sad what happened over there. I imagine they were probably outside cats, but still, I just don't know how you can do that to an animal."

After an initial inspection, and of course, being licked, which made him smile, the young man made his decision.

"He's perfect. I'll take'em."

Curtis, standing at the check-out register, looked back, overhearing parts of the exchange while purchasing a harvest bouquet of spray roses, Peruvian lilies, gerbera daisies, and orange carnations, along with a separate arrangement of one-dozen pink roses. He paid for the flowers, then on his way out, stopped by the caged felines. They all appeared on the young side, many fast asleep. A cute orange and white tabby stood up and stuck a paw through an opening as if to greet Curtis, so he extended it back, shaking the furry foot. He smiled.

Curtis glanced at his watch—an old anniversary present—and realized he'd have to hurry if he were to make it back to Yale before the end of his lunch break. He'd made a few stops to prepare for the long holiday weekend; however, he'd yet to pick up the apple and pumpkin pie per Amy's request, instead, stopping for an arrangement at Sandy's. The roses—the intended purchase—held their own special sentiment, though he thought a floral centerpiece for the dining room table might add a nice touch.

———⋈———

Miguel swung open the door, slamming it behind him as he entered the metal panel trailer parked outside the Sterling Memorial Library, supplies in hand. He tossed two boxes of spooled CAT-6 cable in a corner and dropped a bucket of assorted tools and electrical tape, creating an audible *thud*, which echoed through the hollow space.

"We're just about all wrapped up, Boss!" Miguel stood very proud in his disheveled uniform of beige cargo pants and navy flannel, hands resting on his hips. "Yo, some of us are goin' over to Louis' Lunch, for some of those *bomb-ass* Wonder Bread and onion, bloody cheeseburgers, then maybe over to that Mory's bar for some cerveza. Yo, you wanna go?"

"Ummm, no, not today. Gotta few more errands to run for tomorrow to help the wife prepare for an exciting day with my in-laws!" Curtis ended on a sarcastically chipper note, not even looking up from his computer screens. He sat, barely visible, focused, in front of two large monitors behind a pile of paperwork in his hollow office on wheels. Before wrapping for the long weekend, orders had to be placed for their immediate Monday arrival as things tended to get held up this time of year. Purchasing supplies, dealing with logistics, and keeping track of invoices was his primary job function now, and he was okay with that.

After the probation lifted, Curtis could not have been happier to have found a telecom company in New Haven County, which disregarded their background check, wanting to give him a chance, and thus allowed him to return to consistent first-shift work. After all, his resume *was* quite impressive. Yale University had a massive contract for a digital convergence in their aging Gothic Revival and Georgian architecture, and for the last year and a half, he'd been at the helm of the telecommunication department managing the fiber optics team. It was a long-term, state contract with plenty of overtime, and as a bonus, he was able to hang out with Miguel, whom he was able to hire.

"Yo, you know this is the biggest drinking night of the year, right!?" Miguel pointed out.

"I haven't had a drink in eight years. Besides, isn't Mory's a prestigious, *members-only* alumni club?"

"Yeah, yo, don't you know the history of that place? Birthplace of *The Skulls*, yo, that secret organization type club where the founding fathers of this nation and some of the greatest minds of our time like Albert Einstein and Walt Disney were influenced!"

"I don't think that's accurate."

"And yesterday, I was talking to this little niña, outside the Repertory Theater, right? She wants to be an actress—I think her parents might be celebrities, you know? And she was saying, at Mory's, they drink these delightful, multicolored, champagne cocktails from these giant, hundred-year-old, silver trophies, and groups of people stand around chanting and clapping until they finish it, and when they're done, yo, GET THIS, they *put—that—shit* upside down on their fucking *heads* and spin it around, yo!" Miguel laughed.

Curtis shot Miguel a sharp, incredulous look.

"And have you SEEN the señoritas on this campus, bro!? My GOD!" Miguel put his fist in his mouth.

"I *so* regret hiring you," Curtis groaned, disgusted.

"Come on, man, ha-ha! Oh, that reminds me, I've been meaning to ask you—my parole officer is gonna call you, and I need you to cover for me. I gotta take a few days off and head to Vegas with my cousin, yo. See, there's this UFC fight coming up, right? And he knows a guy who knows this *other* guy—"

"Miguel! OUT!" Curtis picked up the closest thing in arms reach—a rubber band ball—and launched it across the trailer, barely missing Miguel who scurried out the door.

THIRTY-SIX

Instead of instinctually getting off Madison's exit, Curtis stayed south on I-95 for another fifteen minutes until reaching Old Saybrook. He merged onto Route One from the off-ramp, then jumped on to South Main Street, passing the restaurant where he and Amy first met, along with a few other old stomping grounds from his youth. His favorite, The Donkey Barn, which at one time brought pleasant memories, now only served as a reminder of his mistakes. Watching it pass out the window, he wondered whether coincidence or some grotesque twist of fate forced him to drive by it the one time a year he visited.

This particular year was no different from the previous, but suddenly, and for no reason, it dawned on him how much of his life—essentially, the best thing to ever happen to him, and conversely, quite possibly the worst—all wrapped around this one town, a town he never lived in. Nevertheless, he still grew uncomfortable with each return, and he continued lost in thought, his anxiety increasing the closer he became.

Cypress Cemetery was the largest gravesite to be built on the Connecticut shoreline, and one of the last, "*morbidly*" located, as Curtis would say, directly across from the new middle school on College Street—a stretch of road leading to the waterfront of Saybrook Point. Curtis pulled into the entrance and drove straight down, stopping alongside the rotary in the middle of the grid-style layout. The land spread out, wide open, the grounds well kept. A small black cherry tree grew in the corner of each section, the scaly branches mostly bare. Bulbous beech trees lined each center with horizontal limbs stretching from their rippled trunks; fresh purple leaves littered the shade grown beneath each.

Curtis stepped out, and a cold breeze blew by, around his neck and through his sleeves, sending chills. He zipped his sandstone Carhartt jacket, then slowly spun around, surveying the property in awe of its immaculate beauty. Other than a few still squirrels watching, he walked alone. The school parking lot stood empty. Not even a car drove through the eerie quiet.

With each visit, he'd notice something he hadn't the previous year—this time, a small, fenced-in area across the grounds near the front entrance. Wrought iron bars of chipped black paint, three-feet high, enclosed a number of markers—older headstones, delicate, some dating back to the early 1800s—heavily eroded, mildew engrained, some so dark they looked illegible, worn down by salted sea air and decades of acidic rain. It seemed the only space the groundskeepers neglected—tough to work around, Curtis imagined. Foot-high strands of orange grass covered the rectangular plot. The year before, he'd been surprised by the many small American flags interspersed throughout the cemetery, which marked the final resting place of residents who fought in wars long past.

Curtis walked deep into the grounds, almost to the end, when he reached his destination. For a moment, he marveled at the picturesque marshland view from where the breeze emanated; just beyond lay the oceanfront properties, which ran along the edge of the point. Above and across the ocean, the beaming sun began to make its descent behind the shadowy edge of Long Island.

He gazed down at the bevel marker of Salisbury Pink granite, curved roses etched on either side of the inscription. It read:

IN LOVING MEMORY
CRYSTAL NOLEN
MAY 8, 1968 – NOVEMBER 22, 1999

Behind the stone was a dusty, white ceramic vase containing an arrangement long expired, which he replaced with a dozen roses, fanning out fuchsia buds, dispersing baby's breath and Italian ruscus, until it looked perfect. He squatted down, eyes closed, whispering under his breath for a minute or two.

The wind picked up, and the sky turned a deeper blue as the sun fell. The melodic chirps of Golden Finches broke the silence, fluttering from a cherry tree ten yards from where he knelt; brightly hued variegated leaves floated down from the branch. One bird flew directly over his head, landing on the tip of a three-foot obelisk stone behind Crystal's, and for a moment, it glanced at him before once again taking flight. Quickly, he checked the time on his Movado, not realizing how long he'd drifted in thought. He pulled one rose from the vase, laid it across the square stone on an angle, and gave the marker one last touch.

THIRTY-SEVEN

"Doctor Aleia, thanks for returning the call—I know you're very busy; I appreciate it." Curtis, sitting at the kitchen table in front of a laptop, held the cordless phone in hand and his mouse in the other, attempting to multitask organizing bills on an Excel spreadsheet, writing checks, and answering the phone.

"Curtis, glad you had a few minutes to talk! I know it's been a few weeks since our last scheduled appointment—*well* overdue for our monthly meeting, and with the long weekend ahead, we'll be heading into December, and things begin to get hectic around the holidays." The doctor said, audibly rummaging through papers. "So what's going on?"

"Just got home from my yearly visit with Crystal. Was a day early, though. Didn't think I'd be able to get out that way tomorrow."

"Good, good. How'd it go?"

"You know, a lot of feelings. But good, I suppose. I kind of dreaded the trip down, like usual, but when I am there, I feel better. It gets a bit easier each time... but I still can't really control the flood of thoughts and emotions. I spoke to her a bit, though. Said the usual, you know, the stuff we talked about. Begged her forgiveness. Said a few prayers. Made my promise. Then, just sat there for a while with my thoughts, wondering if maybe she'd answer. I know—silly."

Curtis hesitated, wanting to mention the goldfinch, but didn't.

"Well, it's not all that silly. But good. And that's all you can do, Curtis." The doctor paused, audibly thumbing through pages. "How have you been sleeping? How are the dreams? As I recall, the last time we spoke, you felt as if you were beginning to relapse—having, uhhh, unfavorable visions?"

"The dreams... the dreams, they don't ever seem to go away. Not really. Just maybe change invariably, in intensity, ya know? But they're always the same. You know, we've talked about them before. The Gulf War. The car accident..."

Curtis paused.

"The monster in the basement?" The doctor interjected.

"Been a long time since I've had that one." Curtis smiled, leaning back in his chair. "And it's weird, cuz I'll go six—seven—eight months without—without even having a dream, at least from what I can remember. And then, all of a sudden, and without any reason, I'm up in the middle of the night, sweating, heart pounding, having a goddamn panic attack, and then I'm just *up*. Sometimes, I pop a pill—it helps, but I really hate taking shit. Then, I'm waking up my wife, who also works early in the morning, and *that* makes me anxious."

"What are they like?"

"Uhhh, they're just so... vivid. It's the only way to describe them. They're so *real*; when I wake up, it takes me a—a while, sometimes a good half-hour—hour to completely pull myself out of them. It's like that *in-between*, ya know? When you're awake, you know you're awake, but you still feel like you're living in at least part of that world you just imagined. Hell, there's some days—the dreams kinda just linger. I might need the whole morning to take my mind off it and realize that *that was just a dream*—you don't live there. And sometimes, it's days where I just feel *out-of-place*, so to speak, like, unfamiliar in my own surroundings. Like that feeling you get when you're a kid, you know? And you move away from home for the first time for summer camp or whatever, and everything just feels *strange?*"

Curtis sighed, shaking his head. "At the end of the day, I always know I'll snap back, and it'll be fine. But some days I have that fear—that the visions will happen, and I'll *have* no control. My mind, *stuck* in my mind. I know—irrational." Curtis stared off, imagining that possibility.

"The mind is a powerful thing. And many people don't realize it—the things one can trick himself into believing. Remember, Curtis, *we* have the ability to exert some control of our dreams from within. We can change the characters—change the plot, by telling ourselves that 'this is just a dream.' Envisioning the scenario as you're lying in bed. It can help elicit a positive effect. Repetition is key, though."

"Oh, like, uhhh... what—what's it called—image—something therapy?"

"Image Rehearsal Therapy, correct. Take the frightening aspects of the dream and put a less frightening spin on it—change it in *your* favor. And keep rehearsing it. You'll notice the difference. Are you practicing some of the exercises before bed, you know: deep breathing, meditation?"

"Not as religiously as in the beginning, but when I can. Sometimes at the office, I can squeeze maybe ten minutes in. It's tough. I know I should be better." Curtis, feeling ashamed, scribbled circles on a napkin.

"It's okay, it's okay—don't beat yourself up over it. I know you've got your hands full over there. It's been a long road. Remember, when we first met, you were coming in twice a week for almost a year? Now, after what, three years, if I'm lucky, I see you once, maybe twice a month. You've come a long way, Curtis. You're putting in the work, and it's paying off, right?"

"It definitely is. You know, you were right about envisioning something positive before bed. Sometimes, if I'm lucky, I have this one dream—every once in a while. And it's always the same—it's kinda nice, actually..."

"Curtis, I apologize; I have to cut it short; my next appointment just arrived. I want to hear more about this, though. If you'd like, we can touch base Monday, or I can just schedule you in, same day and time, as usual at the beginning of December?'

"Totally. Yeah, December's fine. Anyway, thanks again, Doc—appreciate it."

"Happy holidays, Curtis. See you next month!"

Curtis put the phone down and opened a browser window on the laptop, and as he did, Amy slowly entered the room. He clicked back to the spreadsheet.

"Just checked on Wes. He was *not* doing his homework. Caught him playing Xbox with his headset on." She smiled, leaning against Curtis, rubbing his opposite shoulder. Her belly bumped him, protruding through black tights and a slouchy, gray knit sweater.

"Yeah... he's a real chatterbox, that one." He looked up, rubbing her stomach.

"That's not funny." She kissed his head. "I do hear him joining the conversation a little bit here and there, which is nice."

"Those new classes he's in are doing wonders, huh." Curtis turned to the laptop, glancing at the month's expense, then back to Amy. "You know what *would* be nice? If Gram and Gramps would stop charging us rent!" He said in a sing-song way to Amy's belly as if speaking directly to his unborn child. "How's our little girl doing?"

"Fussy—oh, she's kicking up a storm in here! And maybe tomorrow, *you* can propose that offer!"

"I think I'm growing on her, hun. Remember last summer, she responded to me with more than two-word answers at Wes's birthday party?"

"Now, if only you can win my father over." She kissed his head again. "I'm headed to the couch—my feet are killing me. Beautiful flowers, by the way."

"I'll come in in a few. Just need to just finish up here." Curtis opened YouTube in the browser. The website's left side revealed a search history with previously viewed videos: "Hurricane Decimates Hock Island," "National Guard Investigates Hock," "Mammoth Star Fish on Montauk." He clicked on a video in his personal account—CReyCRey_69—"Long Island Sound Serpent Found!" He watched, again, as the short news broadcast displayed "shocking evidence" in the form of a very distorted, barely watchable cell phone video clip.

Choppy, quick movements, likely captured by an excited cameraman, showed a large commercial fishing net hanging from a winch, portside. In addition to a ton of squirming striped bass and bluefish, inside, the decomposing, partial skeletal remains of the Plesiosaur glared through the netting. Seconds later, as the fisherman commenced reeling it in, the line snapped, falling to the ocean.

The glow from the computer screen shone off Curtis's face as he smiled.

Though a rough transition followed the events on Hock Island, the recent year had made a world of difference for the Reynolds'. The financial stress was finally subsiding as Curtis started putting money away, no longer having to worry about an overpriced rent or a depreciating mortgage. He reported the flood damage from the hurricane on their Forest Street home and used the insurance money to pay off most of the loan.

Amy's parents decided to stay in Florida regularly, essentially giving her and Curtis the summer house in Madison for a fraction of its worth. They were lucky to be in a quiet, shoreline, family-friendly neighborhood where half of its residents were gone nine months out of the year. The home had been updated in the last decade to accommodate the Chastain's lifestyle, and to the Reynolds' fortune, the furniture happened to be much nicer, too.

Amy had reluctantly finished out the school year in New London if only to compensate for the looming resume gap in her past. Luckily, despite the hefty commute, she rarely hit traffic traveling northbound on I-95. Angry, honking cars always backed up southbound toward New Haven and beyond, so she was, at the very least, grateful to be headed in the opposite direction.

Come August, she'd made an easy transfer to the local middle school. The new district, ranked number two in the state for *"safest school district"* and number four for best places to teach, was only a two-mile commute through a neighborhood on the other side of Route One. In the same school, Wes, now in the fifth grade, participated in an advanced special needs program offered by the district. The top-notch special education department focused on helping him master the building blocks of relating, communicating, and thinking. Though a long journey still awaited them, Curtis and Amy took delight in how much their little boy's social skills slowly improved with therapy.

Curtis shut the laptop lid and walked into the living room where his two ladies awaited.

THIRTY-EIGHT

On his way to bed, Curtis stopped to regard the Charles White painting on the edge of the family room wall. Cecilia had a thing for realism and naturalism in art, lining the house with seasonal, landscape oil paintings. She found them to be relatively tranquil—one of the few things on which she and Curtis could agree. *Nature* was his favorite. The scenic scape comprised two wide, red maples with a narrow stretch of road in between, partially veiled with rustic, fallen leaves. Variegated leaves from overhanging limbs camouflaged the surrounding area, a ray of light casting through a break in the trees, shining down over golden overgrowth. He pictured cats rustling through foliage and playfully rolling around in tall grass.

He was happy to have stopped at the garden center on his way home, as it made him curious. Laurel Hill and Holly Hock Island weren't something he had thought about in a long time, not that he would or even *could* ever forget. Thankfully, he hadn't suffered any long-term mental backlash or fits of waking up screaming from the horrifying experience, even though some nights were occasionally restless. But tonight, as happened every once in a great while, he lay in bed wide awake, thinking about Laurel Hill's forsaken inhabitants. He wondered if they were okay, or if maybe they had been discovered by vandals or local punk kids looking for a place to party. Hell, they made it a decade on their own, right? They could handle some kids—they'd certainly dealt with the Norwaukus. Smiling to himself, Curtis closed his eyes, picturing his furry friends.

Curtis reached the edge of town, making his last turn onto the street between the pines, and slowly drove around the bend. It was all still there, just as he'd left it. Although Forest Street had been long since abandoned, life still teemed here, evidenced by a moderate overgrowth of grass with tree branches extending into the street. Sweeping woodlands ran from the top of the road to the edge of the river. Vegetation veiled his old Cape, along with the other empty properties—even the Cavanaugh's dilapidated heap. Plants obstructed the view all the way to Holly Hock Island, or rather what remained, but that too had been completely deserted.

Curtis stopped the truck, stepped out of the cab, and walked across the street to Laurel Hill's entrance, barely visible from the main road. The breeze from the river chilled him as he zipped his sandstone Carhartt jacket. Thick, leafy vines forged their way through the space, weaving through each chain link of the gate, around the side, down to the valley. To his surprise, the wooden sign still hung above, also wrapped in Perennial.

He thought about the last day he had been here and the strange events in the months that followed. The last time he saw the feline inhabitants, they gathered around at the bottom of the street and watched as he dug a hole and buried the body of the Norwaukus. In his eyes, this misunderstood creature deserved a proper burial. The felines couldn't have cared less, and not long after, some even dug and squatted. On his way out of the preservation, he secured the gate with a new lock.

The remaining buildings of Hock Pharmaceuticals had collapsed on that fateful day. The island completely flooded, flushing debris and other material into the river. Curtis had assumed the catastrophic demolition neutralized every living thing inside by lack of interest from the local news, which only briefly mentioned the incident. The unpredictable hurricane that took out much of the eastern seaboard accepted blame for Hock Pharmaceuticals' destruction. Apparently, no one found it strange, or even questioned, that men in black suits and National Guard members covered the remnants of the island in the weeks that followed.

Curtis understood why nothing came to light in the papers or the news, and he wasn't surprised. But at the same time, concealing a national incident in someone's backyard, he thought, would be a little tougher to get away with. After all, it was Southeastern Connecticut—a tourist spot where the population triples between Memorial Day and Labor Day—not some desolate stretch of *Farmville*, Nebraska. He did smile, remembering the news coverage about a year ago when a group of children discovered the "*mammoth spiked starfish*" that washed up on Montauk that summer. Several locals managed to tow it back out to sea before any public officials arrived on scene.

And of course, there was the time the familiar, well-preserved, prehistoric reptilian surfaced in that commercial fishing boat's net, turning folklore to tangibility as it brought with it new conversations of the Long Island Sound Serpent. Terrified at the discovery,

fishing ceased for several months, driving up seafood costs the following summer. Matthew Lavigne would attest to that.

The gate to Laurel Hill Drive loomed before him. Curtis unlocked it. The sun, still ascending, reflected brightly down the strip.
The fresh growth of green fern grass on either side suppressed the
decomposing leaves of seasons past. Maturing leaves flourished with
every maple branch from the top of the street down to the edge
of the basin, mostly concealing the habitation. Trumpet-faced daf-
fodils and baby blue scilla bloomed on the outskirts of each yard,
and brambles of rambling white roses brightened the façades of the
estates. Airborne insects, bees, and butterflies hovered low, mutually
contributing to the cycle of life in the season of rebirth.

The neighborhood looked abundant, thoroughly active with its
inhabitants. The felines outstretched the secured terrain, many migrating in groups, occupied in nature, while others kept to themselves in their own space. Some laid out in sunspots taking in the
warm light, and some slept curled up under parasols of burgeoning
thicket. Responsive snouts raised up high, taking in the cool, crisp
air while trotting sprightly from yard to yard. He spotted a few
habitually chewing strands of Dutch clover, and a few more rolling
around wood sorrel and marking up celestial blue brome.

They dust bathed in grassless patches; they kicked back dirt under
hind legs; they chased and hunted one another with swatting paws
and spirited hissing. Hundreds of them lived across yards, in trees,
on the street, moving from house to open house.

Inside number four, a mother birthed a litter of five on a torn,
king-size pillow top mattress in the sunlit corner of the master
bedroom. She lay, cleaning her young, while a clowder gathered
outside the open door, waiting to greet the new family. Similarly,

he imagined, the same transpired in number six days earlier, and in another, before that.

The sunlight shimmered off the Yantic River, straight up Laurel Hill, the emanation illuminating the faded gray asphalt, ranch rooftops, and front lawns. The King stepped forth from a front door, out onto the concrete landing into the light. Its lustrous white coat shone full, protruding down, clumps of thread slightly veiling its front legs. The mane, pristine and bulbous, extended from the shoulders over its torso; a silvery streak ran lengthwise down the back of its head. With a venerable yet inherently wise disposition, the animal sat overlooking its vast kingdom. An aura of light glimmered from its silky fur while the wind gently blew through it.

Ironically, the shelter inside Sandy's Garden Center happened to be called Forgotten Felines, which, now, Curtis found to be amusing. Neither the confined residents of the local shelters nor the inhabitants of Laurel Hill were *forgotten* by any means, but merely misplaced in time. And the existence of time was eternally lost on these creatures—they simply persevered.

A tuxedo kitten emerged from the brush a few yards from Curtis, startled, as it turned to the giant figure standing before it. Gaping up with wide, cerulean eyes, it froze a moment, then slowly backed away before turning and scampering down toward the others. Curtis smiled and then began to step backward, taking in those last moments before exiting the gate. He firmly reattached the lock, tossing the key into the efflorescent mystique.

Then Curtis woke.

REVIEWS

Now that you have finished the book, (and I hope you enjoyed it!) I would love it if you could take a moment to share your thoughts by leaving a great review on Amazon. Reviews are critical to an author's success and even a few lines (or no lines at all, just stars) help propel the book into Amazon's tough marketing algorithms.

AFTERWORD

It wasn't *all* a dream...

In case you were pulling your hair out, wondering. Yes... I've gotten this question quite a lot since publishing *Street*, and I felt it was finally best to address it rather than leave it to interpretation seeing how it was leaving readers (and especially reviewers) flabbergasted. But just to clarify: the last chapter was the dream. If you recall Curtis's conversation with his therapist, he was about to reveal the one "nice dream" he'd have every once in a while before he was cut off by the therapist's next patient's arrival. The cats of Laurel Hill.

It was 2006 when I conceived the idea for The Street Between the Pines, formally titled: Eminent Domain Project. It was completely unexpected, but for someone as unfocused—for lack of a better word—who'd been labeled a daydreamer, a disrupter, even a troublemaker (mostly by elementary and middle school faculty in the early 90s, and much to the point where they would hold group meetings with my parents urging them to send me off to private school), I've always had this innate ability to conjure up the fantastical in just about everything. My imagination ran rampant. Mostly I'd just fantasize myself into hero roles in 80s blockbuster action movies. Not abnormal, right? As an adolescent in the 90s, there wasn't a whole helluva lot going on outside of Super Ninten-do, VHS movies, backyard sports, and causing riffraff at the local cineplex and indoor mall.

I was twelve (I think) when I started "writing," which at the time meant short, made-up stories on lined paper involving myself and all of my friends and classmates—what they were about, I couldn't tell ya. What I do remember is I would include my favorite scenes from random movies, putting myself and my friends into the supporting roles—an amalgamation of nonsense. But to me, an insecure kid with very few friends, they made sense. I would bind these story pages together with staples, finishing with textured wallpaper as the paperback "cover," which I found sheets and sheets of in our shed (looking back, our house wasn't wallpapered, so your guess is as good as mine). I must've written thirty or forty of these "master-pieces," which comprised my personal little library. And I must've read them hundreds of times over the years before eventually moving on to try my creative hand at comic book drawing and illustration projects throughout high school, then eventually pursuing a graphic design degree. Then life happened. The internet happened. Social media happened. And for whatever reason, the motivation returned with the reality that, writing (or anything creative for that matter) and becoming "published" or simply, earning an income for my passion, *wasn't* an impossibility.

Fast-forward to 2006, when the young man in me entered Shel-ley's Garden Center in Branford, Connecticut in a bleak and des-perate search for an all-black cat (sound familiar?). After calling half the shelters in the state and using a pet finder website, I finally came across a cat located at this garden center. A garden center, you ask? Yes, and I don't quite recall why it also sheltered a handful of cats. Either way, like the anxious person I am, fearing he'd be gone before I made the twenty-minute drive, I rushed out to Shelley's and purchased my new friend, which I had been told was a "kitten" before arriving. Turns out, Wesley was a little older; nonetheless, I fell in love. Then the paranoia in me struck, and I asked the woman who ran the store where they got the cat, worried I was going to get scratched or bitten and die of rabies (yeah, I know, I never said I was a rational human being). She said it came from the eminent domain—whatever the fuck *that* was supposed to mean. After all, I was a twenty-seven-year-old bartender. She explained there was a neighborhood in a nearby county left abandoned after a pharmaceutical company went bankrupt shortly after annexing it. And in the nine years this land lay to waste, it had become inhabited once again—this time by stray felines.

That brief conversation got the creative juices flowing—as conversations such as these always do—and the first idea that popped into my absurd imagination was a giant, escaped creature attacking a family in their flooded basement. This vision—among others—sat with me for another ten years until I wrote the first draft of Eminent Domain Project in 2016. And the rest, as they say, is history.

Hope you enjoyed your visit to the street between the pines.

ABOUT THE AUTHOR

J.J. Alo is a commercial actor, model, and author. Prior to becoming a full-time writer, he was a graphic designer, bartender, and library media specialist.

With a macabre fascination, J.J. has spent years weaving award-winning horror screenplays and novels. His anthology series, teeming with deeply etched, complex characters and mesmerizing antiheroes, has become a sinister staple in horror literature, which ensnares readers and refuses to let go.

J.J. lives and works out of his Connecticut Shoreline home with six insane cats and spends his time visiting coffee shops, movie theaters, and concert venues. He is a lifelong pop culture nerd, Comic Con & cosplay fanatic, avid gym enthusiast, and subpar snowboarder (he tries!). And he'll never say no to a perfectly shaken dirty martini. Never.

Subscribe to my horror newsletter and stay informed!
Subscribers will be entered for signed paperback giveaways!
www.jjalo.com

MISERY PLAZA

An Excerpt from the New Novel

PROLOGUE

The pilot lurched forward in a violent, arcing spasm as the sharp object stabbed through its vulnerable chest. It had shed its protective gear prior to takeoff, and now, strapped under a shoulder harness, the Antiquarian found itself pinned to its seat. Its arms, fixed inside the cylindrical steering mechanism on either side of the helm, flexed and flared as it gaped down at the foreign weapon, then up at its surroundings.

Dark blood sprayed the control panel, leaving a streak across the crystalline navigation screen hanging from the ceiling of the cockpit. The spinning digits displayed beneath the splatter indicated that the craft had reached almost three hundred thousand feet. Close to departure. But the ship lurched forward, and the numbers on screen plummeted, the sheer thrust of the pilot's body sending the craft into a downward tailspin.

A creature encased in shiny silver material somersaulted over the helm with a sharp, clattering thud, rolling down the cockpit floor and sprawling across the wide, U-shaped windshield. The pilot blinked at its captive—the creature assumingly responsible for its assault. The WL-9768 native feebly struggled to his feet, gripping the near vertical floor for support, but fell backward as the cockpit rocked back and forth. The ship trembled in a merciless pirouette over the cerulean void of WL-9768's terrestrial sphere, hitting every blustery bump of the rough night sky as they accelerated into a turbulent nosedive.

Warm blood oozed over a curved pincher on the left side of the pilot's quivering mandible. The savory taste of seeping discharge promised that the hapless end neared.

Mission: incomplete.

The pilot braced itself, chest burning with each jostling twist and turn. It needed to land the ship safely, or at least as safely as it could, given the circumstances. With heavy arms, it pulled up and back on the steering mechanism, trying to slow and even the craft. Agony. The glowing landmass behind the oozing splatter rapidly increased, soaring closer and closer at a rough angle. The planet's surface lay just past fifty thousand feet now, and a break on the map indicating a body of water loomed too close for comfort.

The captive, gaining partial footing, slowly crawled the steep incline toward the helm, shakily making his way toward his captor. The pilot pulled its attention from the map, watching the creature from behind its ocular guards. The captive's malevolent stare burned through the visor of his shiny, sinister helmet.

The pilot shuddered. Now at ten thousand feet, it needed to land and proceed with activating the distress signal located under the control panel. But darkness threatened to overtake it, the blood still oozing steadily from its fading form.

Arms tired.

Steering heavy.

The creeping captive neared, gripping the empty seat in front of the helm for balance. The pilot's eyes held his hidden gaze, all three of its stomachs churning. Unable to reduce enough speed to land safely and avoid further savagery to its ship, it reluctantly opted for the last option.

The craft plunged into the water, slamming nose first into the side of the soft terrain. The impact wrenched the sharp object into the Antiquarian's flesh with a vengeance so searing, its vision swam. Something shiny thudded against the ceiling, then clattered back to the cockpit floor. Its captive. He lay unresponsive, possibly dead. Even with armor, the human specimen remained weak to heavy blows.

The pilot drew in quick, hollow breaths, unable to see clearly, waiting for the pain to subside enough for it to begin its work once again. Through the windshield, the craft sunk under the blurry, dark current. Forcing its weak arms to slide from the mechanism and unstrap the harness, the pilot slowly leaned forward, inch by trembling inch, the weapon's edge tearing up its internal organs. Its grisly mandible opened to squeal, though no sound came out.

Consciousness dwindling, the Antiquarian reached for the panel.

— ◆ —

My father was a good man. A decent man, despite what you may have heard about him through folklore or maybe read about him in your history books. That's not to say he wasn't an inherently flawed individual, as many of us can sometimes be described. I mean heck—back in those days, who wasn't? I would defy you to prove me otherwise. Now, don't get me wrong, he was no Saint. Poles apart from. I know this. A mere product of his egregious environment. And I'm certainly not going to stand here and begin to justify any of the things he did or those I happened to be privy to. Some of which still stays with me to this very day. Things I couldn't explain at that time. Things beyond what you good folk would rightfully call rational comprehension. *Now, I truly don't mean to harp on such things, but I would be completely remiss not to mention the impression he left on my brother and me. Especially me. There are some folks who can tell you their earliest memories being three, maybe four years old; even some as far back as a year—year and a half, if you can believe it. I am not one of those folks. Maybe it's something they refer to as repressed memory, but all I can tell you is that I don't remember much before I was nine years old. I can recall my mother's burial. I remember the Big Flood. I remember the first time I saw Joseph Griffin, my father, a broken soul, cry. I will never forget the second time.*

That's when we moved to Missouri Plaza.

— • —

CHAPTER 1

Sullivan walked behind Eugene McCormac, about three feet back, with the filed down barrel of a sawed-off scattergun, waist height, pointing at his lower back. Every few minutes he'd slow his pace a bit, enough to allow some slack between himself and his captive. Just in case McCormac decided to make a daring dash as they entered the heavily wooded area. Firing such a gun at close range meant spending the rest of the day picking Lord-knows-what from your clothing, all kinds of awful, and Sullivan knew better than most that a good clean change didn't come easy. And blood? Those pearly whites—the one of only two pairs he owned—well, they'd be as good as horse shit.

Through the slits of tall, narrow trees, Sullivan caught a glimpse of the sun sinking down behind the silhouetted Pikes Peak range. Rays of golden light exploded from behind the jagged mountains, a partially hidden projection illuminating the distant northwest skyline before the fresh spring growth completely obstructed his view.

They had walked quite a distance through the tranquil grove in silence, save for the irritating clink of McCormac's crooked boot spurs with every bowlegged step. Shrill calls from birds of prey circling high above the treetops punctuated the quiet, along with small woodland creatures rustling through the brush as they passed. Katydids, just beginning their evening song, resonated through the shaded proliferation. Their trilling slowly grew, encompassing the pair the further they walked into the timberland.

McCormac's fingers—which had been behind his head, inter-laced—separated, and his hands began to lower.

"Keep'em up," Sullivan ordered, his voice rolling out low, deep, and slightly broken. He hadn't spoken since riding up on McCormac an hour earlier.

McCormac stopped. "I gotta itch."

The mosquitos, which trickled out only moments before, now flew out of the woodwork in droves. McCormac waved a hand around his head, paused, then began to turn around.

"Epp... eyes forward," Sullivan commanded with a slow wave of the gun. "Keep moving."

"What you planning on doing with me once we get to where we goin?" McCormac's hands rested at shoulder level, head tilted just enough for Sullivan to see the white of his right eye below the frayed brim of a black Stetson.

Sullivan had no idea. Well, some idea. He knew exactly what he wanted to do, what he should do. Whether that was going to happen, he just had to wait and see. He didn't like the situation this *chance encounter* with an old acquaintance had now put him in. Everything was fine. Everything was going fine—fine as he supposed things could go, all things considered.

The men trudged on. By this time, the sun had completely van-ished behind the Front Range as the navy skies of civil twilight bled down from the upper atmosphere, nonchalantly blotting out the remains of the day. Sullivan hadn't brought a lantern, and if he progressed further, as he now realized, making his return could prove difficult. He was armed—heavily armed at that—but just the same, nobody wants to stumble upon the business end of a grizzly bear in the dark. At least it wouldn't be his first time. He shook his head, not wanting to dwell on memories best left for another day.

"Stop," Sullivan uttered, following a moment later with "turn around."

It was as good of a place as any.

"When did you know?" McCormac said.

"Does it matter?"

"Just surprised is all. Been here a few weeks now. Neither one of us lookin like the men we once was."

"How did you find me?"

"I-I didn't. Just dumb luck, I s'pose. It's a big country. We was bound to cross paths again at some point or another."

"Apparently not that big. I guess we were *destined* to do this dance, is what you're sayin?"

"Huh?"

"I'm supposed to believe it was coincidence you stumbled upon Bennett's Mine?" Sullivan, gun in hand, slowly backed McCormac against a tree.

The other man held his arms out, hands crossed as if to keep Sullivan at a distance.

Sullivan peeled back both hammers of the sawed-off.

2

"I-I swear I was just passin through," McCormac pleaded. "That's all! I-I-I was never gonna say nuthin to nobody. Honest! I was plannin on leaving in a day or two, anyway, you-you know? I did what I came to do—now off to the next town, same-ol,' same-ol,' know what I mean?"

Sullivan stared down at him from under a weathered brown hat, motionless, eyes barely visible. Vacuous. The man's empty gaze bore into McCormac, and his heart stuttered. He'd never forgotten that look, despite the twenty years that passed since he'd seen it.

"Besides, what would I stand to gain by sayin somthin? Ruh-ruh-right?" McCormac stammered, his filthy hands—still held out—beginning to quiver before his eyes. Whether his trembling stemmed from the chill in May evening air, or just fear poisoning his bloodstream, he couldn't say.

"You stand to gain everything," Sullivan said, sliding a leather sack down from the heavily worn shoulder of his long brown overcoat.

The bag hit the ground with such force, McCormac wondered—mostly feared—what it might hold.

Without another word, Sullivan pushed his coat aside, sliding his sawed-off into a handmade leather thigh sheath. A waist pistol sat holstered just above it. McCormac recognized its checkered walnut grip; its twin doubtless rested on Sullivan's opposite hip. His own Colt protruded from behind the buckle of Sullivan's gun belt, tucked away to the side of his groin.

Sullivan squatted and reached into the satchel, pulling out a length of twine. "Arms behind the tree."

The katydids' music, pervading the woodlands, amplified. McCormac could barely hear his heart, suddenly hammering against his sternum, while Sullivan disappeared behind the old Cottonwood, binding his wrists to the trunk. The rigid bark and taut rope dug into his skin, and something warm hit his thigh and dripped down his quivering shins. He'd pissed himself.

The stench of ammonia filled the air as Sullivan reappeared from behind the tree. A short smirk brushed his bushy, silver cheek, revealing that he smelled McCormac's fear, too. But any trace of a smile vanished as he reached for his ragged black gun belt, hung low on his narrow hips. Pulling McCormac's own silver Colt from behind the holster, he raised it a foot from the man's face, aiming for his forehead.

"Christ Almighty," McCormac squeaked out. His chest heaved with labored breath, the warm fog of his gasps visible before him in the chilly air.

"I used to think there were only two men in this world, Mac—or whatever it is you call yourself these days," Sullivan said. "The hard truth of it all is there's only one. I'm convinced of that now. I truly am." Sullivan sucked in a breath and exhaled deeply, shaking his head. "It's plain as the Denver day—is—long. And at the end of it, we're all just chasing the same thing, whether we care to realize that. Or not."

"Tuh-tuh-two-two men?"

"One that walks away. And one that doesn't."

Sullivan took a step back, twigs snapping under the Cuban heel of his black Wellingtons. "Now, who else you tell? You be straight with me; I'll make this nice and quick."

McCormac didn't need to consider the alternative. The Colorado woods at night, defenseless, tied to a tree could prove to be a fate worse than death. And it it wasn't the elements—even in May—it was whatever *thing* lurked in the dark.

"Oh-oh-okay, okay, okay... I-I sent cuh-correspondence buh-back home. Tha's it! Said I-I thought I might'a seen't ya, but wasn't sure, ya-ya see."

3

Sullivan's heart sank in his chest. That had not been what he'd expected to hear. Not so quickly, anyway. He'd figured McCormac would lie through gapped teeth, and he'd spend the night smacking him around to free himself of doubt—and even then, he didn't believe this fool would really have the audacity to cross him.

To whom didn't make much difference. Sullivan knew the game, having heard more than enough tales around campfires. A thief or otherwise unsavory character would locate the whereabouts of an accomplice—usually the outcast of an old gang, long removed—and reach out to a friend or extended family member. The contact would tip off the local marshal, then cash in on the reward money and split the proceeds with the snitch. *Not a bad hustle.*

Sigh...

Now, all he could wonder was how much time he had.

The occurrence of this ever-fleeting unit—the measure of a man's existence—had always seemed to elude Sullivan. To be honest, the man had just never paid it any mind. Not until the passing of his wife. He was no stranger to death, having seen many lives taken. Having taken many a life himself. But when Elizabeth met her untimely demise two years earlier, he felt it. The Clock. It was as if his hourglass had turned, beginning his true countdown.

Sullivan had no illusion he wasn't a mortal man—and oh, he was certain he'd crossed paths with the man in the black tattered cloak. Brushed shoulders, even. He liked to think the pale rider trotted past in fear, its hooded head turning to glance back each time he passed by—but by now, he'd eluded death so many times, he *had* to wonder. Was he?

"I—I'm ready," McCormac said.

And Sullivan could tell that he was. McCormac squeezed his eyes shut still, bracing as if about to be struck by a hand. His upper lip curled, revealing a sliver of checkered teeth—what was still intact, stained brown. With the creeping night unfolding around him in its ritual consummation, he waited in silence, ready to pay for his sins in eternity once he got to where they both knew he was headed.

Sullivan, struggling to see the barrel's end through the darkness, took an additional step back for safe measure. Pulling the hammer, he took aim—best he could. His index finger grazed the polished steel trigger, feeling for the perfect position to pull, but eventually found himself, instead, slowly caressing it.

The enchanting tune of the katydids waned, fading into the melodic whirr of a chill breeze shifting down between the trees. Through the surrounding brush, the Cottonwood's fledgling leaves rustled. The woodlands spoke. And with the mellifluent sounds came intermittent, tiny flashes of amber light, which seemed to delicately drift about, encompassing the men. Just a handful, at first, but as Sullivan glanced around, myriad flashes trailed curiously, a cluster sparkling as far as his aging eyes could see. The stellar forest erupted with light, the wind gently dispersing its itinerate constellation.

A twinkling glow from inside the gun's barrel struck Sullivan as odd. He pulled the weapon backward, turning it upon himself, and waited for the flash. The luminous filament of a tiny firefly flickered as it crept out of the tip, hovering in front of his face for a moment before extinguishing its curious effulgence.

The deliberation ended.

Sullivan gently placed the hammer down. He emptied the six-cylinder chamber onto the cold earth and, by the barrel, tossed the pistol into the wooded void.

4

McCormac opened his eyes. Sullivan was gone.

"He-hey, Where'd you go!? Duh-don't you leave me out here you som'bitch! You leave me out here, I'm'a good as dead!" McCormac, instinctually, tried to pull away knowing it was futile, the twine tearing into his wrists causing them to bleed. "You get back here and finish the job, you no good yella coward! I swear to Christ, if I—"

Shrill howling in the distance shut him right up. He recognized the noise, what he knew to be coyotes calling. A signaling of one to another—the response to spotting a potential food source. He wasn't terribly concerned with coyotes, but what would follow—bear, cat—passing in the night...

Blood ran down his fingers.

5

In the distance, Sullivan heard a name being screamed. One he didn't immediately recognize, but one he once knew, decades ago, to be his. With the fireflies dissipating, he reached the edge of the woods, tied McCormac's horse to his own, and rode toward home.

The pale-yellow half-moon still made its ascent, illuminating his pathway—the only source of light for what seemed like miles through the woods and prairie. Not that he minded. Had he encountered some stranger in passing, someone asking for directions, food, or water, he'd have to explain why he was riding in the dark with an extra horse tied to his saddle. He could stumble into someone looking to rob him and steal his horses, or *worse yet*—and this made Sullivan's blood pressure spike—someone hoping to recognize him. Of course, as Sullivan knew from his recent outing, there were far worse things caught doing in the middle of the night.

Fortunately, he had planned for such contingencies well in advance, and he knew exactly where he was. Bennett's Silver Mine lay up ahead about a mile or so. And as an employee of that mine—a manager, mind you—he had an obligation to transport workhorses that needed to be put down, taking them to the massive stable flanking the mine. There was usually one or two every six months, and McCormac's certainly looked the part.

Sullivan gave the mare another appraising glance. *This girl is as tired as an old Bughouse whore. Shiiit. Probably stolen, too.*

Yet another thing for him to worry about. He shook his head and gave his horse a gentle nudge. Provided he remained on his own trail and stayed on the fringes of town, he would be fine.

Everything was fine.

Or everything *had* been fine until McCormac showed up in Bennett's Silver Mine not three weeks ago. At first, Sullivan thought he was just another drifter passing through, looking to make a quick buck. Such men were the primary challenge in the mining industry, particularly in Denver. Labor couldn't come cheaper. It also couldn't come more unreliable. Drifters tore through Bennett's like the cyclonic storm that buried Denver in snow not four weeks ago: materializing out of nowhere and capable of causing indiscriminate, cataclysmic destruction. They'd show up ragged, emaciated, and spitting a fake name, usually one Sullivan had heard so many times that he knew right away they were full of shit.

Not all drifters were a cause for worry, however. Many of these men kept their brows low, worked five to ten days, made some quick green, and went on their way. A few were even incredible finds—the kind that almost made Sullivan want to offer a higher wage, just to keep them on hand. Freddie Montgomery was such a man. Even used his real name, too. Lasted about a month before an Arizona marshal showed up to drag him back to Yuma, where, according to rumor, he had had escaped the "inescapable" new Territorial Prison. But, for the short time Sullivan had him, Freddie was a real workhorse. A *Sun Dog,* as people called them—a bright spot, like the brilliant halo surrounding the sun on a gorgeous blue-bird day, high above a glistening blanket of unmarred snow. The kind you might be fortunate to catch if you ride over yonder through the Rockies on a crisp February afternoon. Incredibly unique. Radiant. Few and far between.

McCormac, though, was neither cyclone nor Sun Dog. The man kept his head down, and the challenge of discerning *who's who* in a company of over thirty men—mostly drifters—left Sullivan focused on the more apparent troublemakers. But the day before last, on the transport wagon back to town from the secluded caverns where they worked, he had noticed McCormac in his peripherals, sitting across and four men down. Staring at him.

McCormac was quiet. Vigilant. Disconcerting. The sly fox—a predator in the night, stalking the shadows, its eye on the henhouse. Awaiting the opportunity. Sullivan knew it *all* too well. He could smell his own, and his keen eye generally spotted such a man a hundred yards out. The fact he didn't this time disquieted him. Perhaps he was just getting old.

As he neared home, he estimated he had four, maybe five days at the most to *make the decision*. The seasoned math told him it would take at least two days for the letter to reach Wichita, its most likely destination. After that, the marshal could either send a telegraph straight to Denver, alerting the authorities or send his own squad, which would take another two to three days. Sullivan figured for the latter; he knew different territories didn't much like the ubiquitous politics and the greasing of hands involved in using local authorities. *Everyone's got their dirty hand out.* They preferred to do things quietly. Covertly. He could only imagine the price on his head.

The whirlwind is coming...

His spontaneous decision to leave McCormac tied to a tree, without a bullet in his forehead, also had him worried. Was he getting lazy? Or just sloppy? He suspected neither. More than a decade had passed since he'd taken a life, long before the arrival of his firstborn—hell, even before he got hitched. At least since his last visit to the infamous Bughouse. His eyes narrowed, lost in thought as he tightened his red paisley hanky to his throat and popped the worn coat collar. Fifteen years. He wondered if Madam Kitty still ran things there.

Christ. Where does the time go?

Sure, he's had to flash the blue steel many a time, mostly in an intimidation capacity... but since Elizabeth had first entered his life, he had never been *this* close to pulling the trigger.

He was still the fastest motherfucker on the draw, though. If nothing else, of this, he was certain.

He smirked.

Ain't no flies on me.

www.ingramcontent.com/pod-product-compliance
Lightning Source LLC
Chambersburg PA
CBHW021442310726
48971CB00005B/1466